CRITICS PRAISE FARRAH ROCHON'S
DELIVER ME!

"Quirky humor and a charming hero make Rochon's debut novel attractive reading. Colorful characters create a down-home appeal that will make readers feel the warm welcome typically indicative of the South. Cute dialogue enhances the story and helps to move the plot along. Set against the backdrop of New Orleans, post-Hurricane Katrina, this novel captures the true essence of a town struggling to get back on its feet."

—*Romantic Times BOOKreviews*

"This is a wonderful story with rich characters and tons of local history. It will definitely leave you wanting more of the hot Doctor Holmes and his equally hot brothers, who, by the way, deserve their own stories."

—Coffee Time Romance

"I look forward to more from this author. I sincerely hope we get stories for both of Eli's brothers and his niece as well; I just loved them."

—Romance Reviews Today

"Elementary my dear readers, as Farrah Rochon captures the city inside her fabulous contemporary medical romance with hopefully more Holmesian sibling tales to follow."

—Harriet Klausner, Romance in Color

THE CALL OF DESIRE

"It's not just about that, Sienna."

The huskiness in Toby's voice caused the hairs on the back of her neck to rise. She slowly lifted her head, and the heated look in his eyes made her stomach pull tight. "I don't want anything to happen to you," he said.

Her hands stilled, the phone hanging from her fingers by the tiny wrist cord. "You, ah, you don't?" she managed to choke.

Toby rose from the chair and came around her desk. He stooped down, resting on his haunches next to her chair. He slid the phone from her fingers.

"In fact," Toby continued in that hushed voice that caused tiny tingles to drizzle down her spine, "the thought of anything happening to you scares the hell out of me. I don't know what I would do without you, Sienna." His eyes never wavered as he leaned forward and brushed her mouth with his lips.

Other *Leisure* books by Farrah Rochon:

DELIVER ME

Release Me

FARRAH ROCHON

LEISURE BOOKS NEW YORK CITY

For Tamara, my first reader and the
best big sister in the world.
I love you.

A LEISURE BOOK®

June 2008

Published by

Dorchester Publishing Co., Inc.
200 Madison Avenue
New York, NY 10016

ISBN 10: 0-8439-6058-2
ISBN 13: 978-0-8439-6058-7

Visit us on the web at www.dorchesterpub.com.

ACKNOWLEDGMENTS

First, thanks be to God for answering every time I call, without fail. I know I call on you a lot. Please keep the line open.

To my mom and dad, thanks for the love, support, and even gas money when things get rough. I know how lucky I am to have you both.

Thanks to my agent, Evan Marshall; my editor, Monica Harris; and the entire Dorchester staff.

To everyone in my hometown who gave me such support during the release of my debut novel, especially Virgie Johnson and her library staff. Enjoy your retirement, Virgie!

Thanks to my critique partners, Laurie, Margaret, Rosalind, and Shauna for being the smartest women on the planet.

To my Dreadnaughts/Rochonettes, especially the entire Dallas '07 crew. I am so blessed to have you all in my life.

Thanks to Allison Studer. Without that brainstorming session in Atlanta, I'm not sure this book would have been finished. I owe you big.

Lastly, to the best publicist and an even better friend, Tara Settembre, of Buy the Book PR. I will never be able to thank you enough.

I can do all things through Christ who strengthens me.
—*Philippians 4:13*

Release Me

Chapter One

Fake right.

Dribble left.

The ball left his hand headed in a graceful arc toward the net.

Swoosh!

Sinking the game-winning shot in the championship game was the only feeling that could compare to the rush that zipped through Tobias Holmes' veins as the crowd rose to its feet. The cacophony of applause, foot stomping, and catcalls played like a raucous melody in his brain, stoking the excitement already roaring through his body like an uncontrollable forest fire.

Toby joined in the ovation, placing his index and middle fingers in his mouth and releasing a high-pitched whistle.

Aria Jordan, the hidden talent he'd stumbled upon only a few months into his new career as a record producer, received the accolade with humility and grace, as she always did after performing. Toby still was not sure if the innocent, almost timid acceptance of her rising fame was an act or not, but he wanted her to stick with it. It was a nice touch. The crowd seemed to cheer even more every time that bashful blush rose to Aria's cheeks.

Their applause continued, making him as giddy as a kid on Christmas morning. Others on the club scene talked about how tough it was to win over the crowd at the popular night-club, *The Hot Spot*, saying it should be called *The Cold Spot* instead, to reflect the supposedly frigid response the audience bestowed to newcomers. The atmosphere was not cold to-night. The place was on fire.

Toby ushered pass the horde of club-goers making their way to the bar and restrooms during the short intermission.

He intercepted Aria as she descended the short staircase behind the stage.

"You kicked butt up there," he greeted her.

A shy smile broke out on her face. "You really think they liked me?"

"Think? Didn't you hear that a minute ago? They were shouting for more. If I were tonight's headliner I'd be afraid to come out on stage."

"Thank you, Toby." Aria crushed herself to his chest, practically knocking the air from his lungs.

"Whoa," Toby chuckled, bracing himself after nearly losing his balance from the force of her hug. "Come on. I don't want anyone to take my table," he said, unfolding Aria's arms from around his waist.

Ever since his older brother, Eli, had questioned his relationship with Aria, Toby had been cautious of rumors concerning him and his client. He was determined that people see him as a professional, and knew better than to start something with one of the performers he managed. Besides, Aria wasn't really his type.

He was still trying to figure out what exactly was his type. None of the women he'd dated over the past couple years appealed to him enough to consider developing anything serious. Then again, he wasn't looking to start a serious relationship. He needed to focus on his new career.

He guided Aria back to the prime table he'd secured.

"I'll get you a drink," Toby said, after settling her at the table. He headed toward the chrome-lined bar that spanned the entire right side of the club. "Can I get a Bud Light and a strawberry daiquiri?" he asked the bartender.

"Tobias Holmes?"

Toby turned. An older man, almost equal to his own impressive 6' 9" height, stood not even a foot behind him. It was hard to keep much of a distance in the packed club.

"Do I know you?" Toby asked.

"Not yet." The man extended his hand. "Marshall Kellerman."

Where had he heard that name before?

"I represent Over the Edge Productions," the man continued.

Ah, that was it. The television production company.

Production company?

Toby's antennae perked up like a foraging ant's. He clasped the man's outstretched hand. "Hello, Mr. Kellerman. What can I do for you?"

"Actually, I want to talk about what *I* can do for *you*. And call me Marshall."

The bartender delivered his drinks. Toby paid for them and picked both up from the bar. He turned back around and said, "Okay, Marshall, what can you do for me?"

"I hear you represent that amazing talent that just captivated everyone in this club a minute ago."

"I'm her manager." And producer. And songwriter. And the only person she knows in the city.

The smile that drew across Kellerman's face was wide enough to park an Oldsmobile inside of it. That feeling of excited anticipation that used to come over Toby before the start of a basketball game skirted down his spine. It had been a long time since he'd felt the sensation. And, man, did it feel good.

Marshall Kellerman wrapped his arm around Toby's shoulder. "Oh, yes, Mr. Holmes. We definitely need to talk."

Toby returned his smile. "Call me Toby."

"Mom, where are the silk scarves you ordered last week?" Sienna Culpepper asked as she straightened a faux pearl necklace in the glass étagère filled with expensive costume jewelry.

"I'm still waiting on the order."

"Do you want me to call the company? The Southern Christian Women Leadership Convention starts next week. You'll need to stock items that are going to appeal to them," she reminded her mother.

"I know how to run my own store, Sienna," came her mother's reply. "I've been doing it successfully for the past twenty years."

Sienna willed the impending headache to take a backseat. It was far too early in the morning to start popping ibuprofen. "I was only offering to help, Mother."

"Since when have I needed your help?" Sylvia Culpepper asked as she rounded the étagère, a collection of earrings hanging from a mahogany and cream velvet display shelf in hand.

Why did she even bother? Sienna asked herself for the 400,000th time. This sadomasochistic ritual of helping out at her mother's French Quarter antique and high-end gift shop had occupied practically every Saturday morning since she was eight years old, and she had never received as much as a simple thank you. She felt more like a bother than the asset she knew she was to her mother's business, yet Sienna found herself coming back every time. Even negative attention was better than none at all.

Preparing for an argument, Sienna broached the subject she had been thinking about all morning. "Mom, have you given any more thought to the advertising ideas I mentioned?"

Silence.

"Mother, did you hear me?"

"You're standing right next to me. I'm not deaf."

The headache was coming on despite her best intentions to curb it. She sprayed glass cleaner on the inside of the étagère's glass door and wiped it off with a lint-free towel.

"So, have you thought about it?" Sienna asked. "You could do so much more business if you put a little more effort into getting the name out. A few ads on the St. Charles Streetcar Line and you can double the foot traffic in here."

"My business is still open, isn't it? You girls never went hungry. And you? You didn't have to pay a single penny for that fancy education that you're wasting. I've never had to advertise before, and I don't have to do it now, especially not on a gaudy streetcar sign."

"It is not gaudy, it's smart business. Some of the top restaurants in this city advertise that way."

"Do not stand in my establishment and tell me how to run

it, Sienna Elaine! What do you know about any of this anyway?"

"Oh, I've only spent the last six years studying this very thing while getting my fancy education," she argued.

Sienna couldn't help rolling her eyes. Most parents would be overwhelmed with pride if their child attained a graduate degree—with honors, at that—and landed a good job by the age of twenty-eight. Not her mother. It had taken her too long to finish school, even though she'd held a full-time job while attending one of the most prestigious historically black colleges in the country. Being picked out of a pool of over two hundred candidates for the only junior associate position offered with the leading marketing firm in New Orleans was only mediocre in her mother's eyes, as well. Accomplishing her careers goals meant nothing if she was still unmarried and not producing grandchildren her mother could brag about to her friends.

Sienna had resigned herself to knowing that she would never be good enough. No matter how hard she worked, or what she accomplished, her mother would always find her lacking.

And just how long will the pity-party last today?

God knows she could stand here berating herself well into next week if she didn't get a handle on it. Sienna retrieved a pink and white feather duster from the janitorial closet and went over to the shelf that held an array of African sculptures.

"Are you going to the Holmeses' today?" her mother asked after several long, uncomfortable minutes. "Margo invited us to a little get-together they're having for Alex's baby. She graduated from kindergarten."

Little get-together? Sienna knew the Holmes family well enough to know nothing they did was ever little, especially where the only grandchild, Jasmine, was concerned. Sienna expected nothing short of a full-blown carnival, complete with dancing bears and a fire-eating lion tamer.

"I guess I can stop by," she answered her mother.

"Good," Sylvia said. "Somebody needs to represent the family. I don't even know where Ivana is these days, and

Tosha's busy packing up for her move back to Atlanta. Besides, she doesn't need that anyway."

Sienna agreed. Tosha should stay far away from the Holmes family, especially the middle son, Elijah. Seeing your ex-fiancé madly in love with another woman could not be an easy thing to witness. Even though what they had shared had been over for more than fifteen years, Sienna knew her sister, and Tosha had a big heart. It was easily broken. They were definitely alike in that regard.

Let it go. The pity-party ended five minutes ago.

"After I finish up here I'll go home and change, then I can head uptown to the Holmeses'."

"What are you doing tomorrow afternoon?" her mother asked.

"I plan on just relaxing a bit if I can get the work I brought home with me this weekend completed after I get back from Margo's."

Her mother turned, her eyes holding the stare that dared its recipient to refuse whatever she was about to ask. "Millicent Perkins has Sunday tea at her home. I want you to come along."

Sienna paused, the feather duster hovering over a carved father and son statuette. A chill traveled down her spine at the thought of Millicent Perkins and the world she represented. The pomp and circumstance of New Orleans' high society, with its teas and debutant balls, had been a part of her life she'd vowed never to return to for reasons she could never bring herself to voice out loud. Sienna's eyes shut tight as she attempted to bite back the memories that begged to surface, memories she had buried in her subconscious. She clamped down on the bile that threatened to rise at the thought of that horrible night nearly eleven years ago.

"You know," her mother's voice propelled Sienna to the present. "Millicent's youngest daughter, Danielle, is expecting her third baby," her mother said.

"I'm surprised her husband stopped beating her long enough for her to even get pregnant," Sienna muttered under her breath. "Really?" she said loud enough for her mother to hear. "That's three babies in just over three years, isn't it?"

"Um-hmm. I also heard Aldonia Lewis's daughter did such a good job planning her wedding that she decided to start her own wedding consulting business. She isn't anyone's assistant."

"I'm not an assistant, Mother," Sienna ground between clenched teeth. "I'm a junior executive. If you cared enough to pay attention to anything I told you, you'd know there is a difference."

"Well, Aldonia's daughter *owns* her business."

"Ivana's business is very successful, or have you forgotten that you have a daughter with her own business only steps away from this store."

Her mother pierced her with another of her infamous looks, turning her nose high enough in the air to smell the exhaust fumes of the airplane flying overhead.

"You need to get over to the Holmeses'," Sylvia said with cold finality, grabbing the duster from Sienna's hand.

Sienna stepped away from the display, questioning yet again why she put herself through this torture on a regular basis. She never asked, nor expected, monetary compensation, but a little appreciation wouldn't hurt.

She looked over at her mother, who kept her back rigid.

Appreciation? Right. She was not holding her breath.

But she wasn't giving up, either. Her grandmother had always told her family was the most important thing. Her mother and sisters were all the family she had and Sienna still held out hope that she and her mother would eventually have the mother and daughter relationship she had always dreamed of. There had to be something she could do to finally make her mother proud.

She knew one way she could start.

Sienna brought her hand up and kneaded the spot between her eyes; her hand shaking as the implications of what she was about to agree to began to sink in.

Her hand on the faux crystal door handle, she said, "I'll see you tomorrow at Mrs. Perkins's tea."

Chapter Two

Sienna dipped the ladle into the bowl of icy punch and had to fight the urge to pour the liquid over her head. It felt as if the sun had decided to take a break from hanging in the sky and found a place to rest—right on her back. It was only mid-March!

She gulped down half of her punch and refilled the plastic cup before heading back to the picnic table under the pecan tree in Margo Holmes' backyard. Just as she'd expected, the Holmes family had pulled out all the stops to celebrate Jasmine's kindergarten graduation. Sienna had not spotted any dancing bears yet, but the afternoon was still young.

Anyone who didn't know the Holmeses would have thought the little girl had won the Nobel Prize upon seeing the hoopla taking place on this stifling Saturday afternoon. One corner of the backyard held a miniature carousel. A clown had just finished her magic show and was now making balloon animals. Alexander, Jasmine's father, had even arranged for an off-duty NOPD officer to give horseback rides on his mount. It was sheer excess.

"Who wants fried fish?" Elijah Holmes came up to the table carrying a platter piled high with bite-size pieces of catfish and hush puppies. He had a red balloon in the shape of a pirate's hat on his head.

"Did you secretly want to be a pirate instead of a doctor?" Sienna asked him as she snatched a couple of pieces of fish from the platter. Eli was one of the top obstetricians in New Orleans. His new fiancée, Monica Gardner, was already making a name for herself as an emergency room physician.

"As if he could survive on the open seas," Monica said.

Eli stepped up behind Monica, and moved the hair from

behind her neck. "I was hoping we could play pirate tonight. You can be my wench."

She slapped his hand away, although the look she gave him clearly said he could expect his wishes to come true.

Sienna tried to contain her envious sigh. It's not that she didn't want other people to be happily in love. It gave her hope. But she didn't want to see it, either. Anytime she witnessed two lovers engaging in that playful, teasing kind of affection, it made her ache even more for what was missing in her life.

"So, Sienna, how's the new job working out?" Eli asked. He sat the catfish down and straddled the bench next to Monica. Sienna told herself not to pay attention to the way he continued to stroke his fiancée's arm.

"Things are going well," she answered. "They tried to stick me with a lot of the grunt work when I first started, but I didn't go through four years of college and two years of grad school to be anyone's secretary."

"You go, girl," Monica said. "Good for you."

"Of course, the only break-the-bank client I've landed pulled out of the city after Katrina, but I'm not worried," she shrugged, picking off another bite of fish and dousing it with hot sauce from the bottle on the table.

The DJ put on the song for the Electric Slide and all conversation ceased. Sienna, Monica, and Eli stood up and joined in as the entire backyard became a dance floor, with even Alexander Holmes, the eldest and most serious of the Holmes brothers, moving from side to side with a pair of barbeque tongs in his hand.

Sienna had to stop midway through the never-ending song. Another minute more of dancing in this blazing sun and she would go into heat stroke. She fished a bottle of water out of the aluminum bin filled to the brim with ice and an assortment of beer, soda, and water. She turned to the bench she'd vacated just a few minutes before, but stopped at the sight of Toby and his current playmate, Aria Jordan, sitting in her spot.

Sienna had always regarded jealousy as one of those wasteful emotions that drained everything from you, and still left pain. But it was hard to keep a rein on her feelings, especially when faced with Toby's flavor of the month who had apparently turned into his flavor of the year. Sienna wasn't used to seeing him with the same woman for this long.

So she was a teeny bit jealous. So what? Maybe she hadn't given the emotion the respect it warranted. Anything that evoked that amount of passion had to be worth something.

"You are so pitiful," Sienna mumbled under her breath. *It's not like he ever noticed you anyway.*

Okay, so that was a lie. Of course Toby had noticed her, just never as someone he could be attracted to. And with Aria Jordan's baby face, Sienna doubted he'd pay any attention to the ex-tomboy who used to beat him at street basketball.

She and Toby had been best friends for longer than Sienna could remember. For some reason, their families clicked. Maybe it was because there were three Culpepper girls to three Holmes boys.

Sure, there were some tense moments when her older sister, Tosha, and Eli had broken up after dating all through high school, although Sienna had no idea what Eli had been thinking to get involved with Tosha in the first place. She loved her, but Sienna would be the first to admit her sister was a certifiable nutcase. Everyone pinned that label on the middle daughter, Ivana, but that *so* was not the case. Ivana was just a little misunderstood; Tosha was good and crazy.

Sienna and Toby had been inseparable until high school when each was sent to separate schools. They had slowly grown apart over the years. It had started with Toby's infrequent visits home after he had gone off to St. John's University on a basketball scholarship. After the car accident that ended his pro basketball career before it even began, Toby hardly came home at all. They had slipped so far away from each other that he had been in New Orleans over a month before Sienna even heard he had moved back home.

Just as she was about to change direction and head for the other side of the yard where several kids were climbing up the combination slide, jungle gym, and swing set, Toby's eyes caught hers. He motioned her over with his head. Sienna pasted on a smile, and with legs that suddenly felt as if they carried a thousand tons of lead, made her way back to the picnic table.

The benches were packed with people trying to cash in on the shaded relief offered by the pecan tree's wide branches.

"Can you scoot over a bit," she asked Eli.

"Of course, Cee Cee," he answered with the nickname she'd been called since they were kids.

The epitome of a tomboy, as a child Sienna hated playing with dolls, much to her mother's consternation. Every Christmas when she received one she would rip the doll's head off. Then she would sneak over to the Holmes' and steal the new basketball Toby and Eli always got on Christmas morning. Although her mother continued to shove dolls in her face, her father soon got the picture, and bought Sienna her very own NBA regulation Spalding.

"So, what's going on," Sienna addressed Toby. The sun streaming through the tree's branches gleamed off his chocolate-colored skin. "I heard you telling your mother you had some big news."

"Eavesdropping?" Toby asked.

"I wasn't eavesdropping," she answered. "It's not like you've ever been known to whisper."

"Anyway," Toby sighed dramatically. "As I was telling the rest of the table, Marshall Kellerman of Over the Edge Productions wants Aria to be a part of the cast for a new reality TV show they're producing, *A Week in the Life of a Wannabe Star.*"

"A wannabe star? I wouldn't exactly call her a 'wannabe.'" Eli said.

"The show will feature seven rising stars at different stages in their careers. From people just starting out, to those who have developed a small following, like Aria, to people they consider are almost there." As Toby continued with his explanation, his eyes lit up with excitement.

"This show is unlike anything that's ever been done on television. Everything happens in the span of one week. The show opens up on Sunday night with a performance by each contestant in a venue of their choosing, then America chooses which performer they want to see more of by voting online. There will be live cameras rolling simultaneously in the seven different cities, and the more votes a contestant gets, the more airtime they get."

"So the cameras will be switching from one person to another based on Internet votes?" Monica asked.

Toby nodded as he took a sip of his beer. "The American public is in total control."

"Sounds pretty interactive," Eli said.

"It's totally interactive," Toby answered. "There will be a constant live feed for all seven contestants on the show's Web site. And, each night, the show will open with a live clip of what's going on with each contestant. Then, America starts to vote, and as the votes come in, the airtime is awarded to the contestant with the most. That means you all will have to cast lots of votes.

"It's really different from the other reality shows out there," Toby continued. "There's going to be a very small window for editing."

"I'm surprised network TV is going to try to pull off something like this, they must be putting a lot of pressure on you," Sienna added.

"I've saved the best for last," Toby rubbed his hands together. "At the end of the week—that following Tuesday, actually—all contestants will participate in a nationally televised competition in Los Angeles. Whoever wins gets a recording contract."

"How'd this come about, Toby?" Monica asked.

"Kellerman was at the club where Aria performed last night," Toby answered.

"Well, that pretty much says it all. We all know this girl can sing," Monica said.

"Thank you," Aria replied, her light brown skin turning

red from the compliment. "Although it would mean nothing if Toby had not discovered me. I'd still be singing in my uncle's place back in Houston."

Aria gazed worshipfully at Toby. Her Bambi-like eyes and Malibu Barbie–body were enough to turn Sienna's stomach, but witnessing her adoration made her want to throw up her fried fish.

Could she really blame Toby for dating a gorgeous twenty-year-old who practically drooled at his feet? It's not as if Sienna had ever come right out and told him how she felt about him.

But he should have seen it, Sienna reasoned with herself. They had been so close. How could he not have known she'd been in love with him?

"Dang, bro. This sounds like the big time," Eli said, slapping palms with Toby across the table. "When do you start?"

"The actual taping doesn't start for another five weeks. If we choose to do it, that is. I haven't signed on the dotted line yet."

"What are you waiting for?" Eli asked.

"I don't want to rush her into this," Toby answered.

"He doesn't think I'm ready," Aria interjected.

"It's not that. I want to be sure they're not going to exploit you," Toby countered. He addressed the rest of the table. "You all know how these reality shows can be. When I took Aria from Houston, I promised her mother that I would take care of her. She specifically said she did not want Aria to forget about her church upbringing, and I agree with her. She's got the voice, and that should be enough. She shouldn't have to dance across a stage half-naked in order to win over fans. I want to prove that you don't have to ooze sex appeal in order to make it in today's music industry."

"Good luck with that," Eli said as if he thought Toby didn't have a chance in hell at proving his theory. "When was the last time you watched BET or MTV? Sex is all you see these days."

Sienna had to agree with Eli on this one. An amazing

singing voice wasn't required these days, as long as the performer had a knockout body that she was willing to show.

"It's going to be tough," Toby was saying, "but we're up to the challenge. I believe in my client's God-given talent."

"But even if I don't win the competition, the national exposure will still be good for my career," Aria put in.

"Don't." Toby put a finger to Aria's lips. "Don't even talk that way. If we agree to do the show, you *will* win this competition."

The intimate gesture caused a spark of resentment to shoot down Sienna's spine. Seeing Toby's finger against the girl's pouty lips made her want to jerk it away and break the finger in half.

She had tried hard to like Aria Jordan the first time she had met her, but figured she was predestined to hate her simply because of the girl's relationship with Toby. It wasn't fair, but neither was life.

"You're right," Aria said, a soft smile tilting the corners of her mouth. Sienna tried not to roll her eyes. One more gooey-eyed look and she really *was* going to be sick.

"So, do you have to move to Hollywood?" Eli asked.

He shook his head. "We only have to go out to California for the final show. Everything else will happen right here in New Orleans."

"Well, congratulations to you both. This should be really exciting," Monica said. She rose from the table, pulling Eli with her. "Come on, I want to dance."

The couple vacated the picnic table, along with a few others who congratulated Toby and Aria before rising from their seats.

Sienna felt like a big, bulky fifth wheel on a sleek, svelte Porsche. This was one of those times when she needed a significant other, somebody to release her from this uncomfortable situation. Of course, it was just a regular day for Toby. He had never had a clue as to how she felt about him.

"This does sound exciting," Sienna said, hoping the measure of fake enthusiasm she interjected sounded convincing.

It wasn't totally fake. She *was* happy for Toby. After all he'd been through, he deserved a little success.

"It's going to take some work," Toby said. "I *Googled* the names of a couple of the performers Kellerman mentioned last night and they are really on the ball. We've got to get rolling if my girl here is going to become a household name," he said, wrapping his arm around Aria's slim shoulders and giving them a squeeze.

She was not going to let that endearment, or the way Toby held on to the other woman, get to her.

"Well, congratulations," Sienna beamed. "I hope it all works out for the two of you."

"Thanks," Aria smiled.

Sienna was not buying the Miss Goody-Two-Shoes act. Nobody was that nice. Just in case, though, she returned the smile as she rose from the table. She would fix her mother a plate and head out of here. She'd had enough of that special Holmes' bonding for one day.

"Hey, Cee Cee, wait up," Toby said.

Sienna stopped but didn't turn. He came around, standing in front of her.

"How many times do I have to ask you not to call me by that name?"

"I've called you by that name your whole life. Why should I stop now?" he laughed.

"Because I asked you to," Sienna answered. "That reason should suffice."

"Fine, I won't call you Cee Cee anymore, if I can help it."

"Try."

"Can we get on with this? I'm growing older by the minute."

"Smart alec," she muttered. "What do you want?"

"I thought you and I could go out later this week."

Sienna stopped short. She had to take a quick breath. Then another.

"An old college friend just moved down here," Toby continued. "I thought maybe the four of us could hang out."

Sienna's shoulders drooped, along with her misguided hopes that Toby had finally caught a clue. "I don't need you hooking me up on blind dates," she said, edging past him.

He caught her by the arm. "It's not a blind date. The grand opening of Jonathan's new club is this week, and Aria is going to perform. It should be fun. Besides, do you have anything better to do on Friday night?" he chuckled.

"Excuse me! What do you know about my life?" She stuck out her chin. "As a matter of fact, I do have plans on Friday."

Toby's head reared back. "Really?"

Yep, that was genuine surprise on his face. Sienna's teeth started to grit.

"I didn't realize you were seeing anyone," he said.

That's what he got for assuming she'd have nothing better to do than babysit one of his college buddies. Sad thing is she really did *not* have anything better to do.

"I'm surprised Mama didn't mention you were dating. You know how she's in everybody's business."

If she didn't refute his assumption, would it be an outright lie? She had promised to cut back on sinning. Although, in the grand scheme of things, this one lie constituted such an itty-bitty sin. God shouldn't mind.

"It's not anything serious," Sienna lied.

"I just thought you and Jonathan would hit it off. I'd fix him up with Aria," he said, tilting his head toward the table, "but if we sign on for this new show, that's where all her concentration has to be focused."

This time it was Sienna's head that reared back.

Something wasn't right here. Why would Toby want to hook up *his* woman with one of his friends?

"My plans may change," Sienna said, way too curious now. She had to know what was going on between the two of them, but she couldn't agree to the date after saying just a minute ago that she was busy. "Call me later this week."

Toby enveloped her in a bear hug. "Thanks, Cee Cee." Sienna pinched him on the arm. "I mean Sienna. Dang, girl. Why do you always have to go for blood?"

"Because it's the best way to get a person's attention."

She disengaged from his arms, although she would have given up her car and half her wardrobe to remain in his embrace for just a few seconds more.

"I'll give you a call after I've talked to Jonathan. He's getting into town on Tuesday."

"In that case, I may have to call you. I do circuit training on Tuesdays. I'd have you call my cell, but it's been acting up lately. I think the battery is going out."

"I can leave a message with your mom."

"I'm not sure I'll see her before Friday."

"Why wouldn't you see her?" he chuckled. "Her house isn't *that* big?"

"I don't live with my mother."

"You don't?" his brows pulled together.

He really didn't know her at all anymore. Sienna stared at him, a mixture of hurt and agitation streaming through her blood. "God, Toby. At least I know where you live," she muttered, edging past him.

"Wait up," he said, grabbing her arm. "I didn't know you'd moved out of your mom's house. When did this happen?"

She crossed her arms over her chest. "It's been long enough."

"I didn't know," he said again. "Where to?"

"Forget it," she said.

"How can I get in touch with you?"

"I'll call you."

She left him standing in the middle of his mother's backyard.

Toby lifted his end of the stack of two-by-fours and he and Alexander walked them over to the sawhorse. Positioning the wood so that it didn't fall off the horse, Toby used his free hand to grab his water bottle. He gulped the slightly chilled water, sighing as it traveled a cool path down his parched throat.

"Don't you have workers who could have helped with

this?" he asked his older brother. Alex's construction company had just been named one of the top small black-owned
businesses in the New Orleans metro area.

"I would have to pay them," Alex answered. "You work
for free."

Toby snorted. He had him there. Alex knew he could get
both of his brothers to help out without much resistance.
That's what you got when you sacrificed your future to take
care of your younger siblings.

"How much more are you going to add onto this house,
anyway?" Toby asked, dropping the pieces of wood in a pile.
"It's already a monster."

"This is it for a while," Alex replied. "It's costing more
than I thought it would."

"That's because it's twice the size you'd originally planned."

Toby could not remember a time when Alex was not
knocking down a wall or expanding a closet. This time, he was
adding an entire new wing for Jasmine. The Princess Suite.

The fixer-upper Alex had bought dirt cheap in the city's
Carrolton area was a construction junkie's wet dream. The
house had been in total disrepair, but with his hammer, nails,
and knack for turning the abysmal into the amazing, Alex had
done wonders. And he roped his younger brothers into helping with every single project.

"Where's Eli?" Toby asked, "I thought he was on his way?"

Alex shook his head, biting his lower lip as he strained to
lift the thick driftwood he had found along the bank of the
Mississippi River. God knows what he planned to make out
of the knotty wood.

"Ahh," Alex expelled as he dropped the log. "One of Eli's
patients went into early labor. He said he's gonna try to make
it if he can."

"I wish I had thought of going into medicine. He's always
got an excuse to get out of doing real work."

Toby dodged the glove Alex pitched at his head.

"Stop complaining," he said, rounding the sawhorse. "You

need to do some physical labor. You don't have basketball to keep you in shape. If you don't watch it, you might get a potbelly," Alex said, playfully socking Toby in the stomach.

"You sure know how to hurt a brother," Toby said, referring to the crack about not having basketball anymore, more than the punch in the stomach.

Alex had always been a logical, no-nonsense guy who did not believe in making excuses. And he didn't stand for his brothers doing so, either. After the accident that had stolen Toby's chances for a professional basketball career, he had at least expected sympathy from his older brother. He should have known better.

After the months of physical therapy were over and the doctors had declared him healed—or as healed as he was going to get—Alex had given Toby precisely one month to dust himself off and get on with his life. He had told him that life was too short to waste it by dwelling on things he could not change. At the time, Toby had not been receptive to that kind of talk. He'd wanted to sulk, to crawl into himself and curse the world for the injustices that had been brought against him.

He'd set out to alienate everyone who'd tried to help him, from his old teammates to his physical therapist. He'd even raised his voice to Mama, the one time he'd ever done so in his life. The day he'd caused tears to stream down his mother's face was the day Toby knew he'd crossed a dangerous line. His callous disregard for his own mother's feelings had terrified him, but he'd plummeted so far into his personal pool of self-pity, he wasn't sure how to drag himself out.

His self-destructive state of mind had been one of the reasons Toby had stayed away from home for so long. He had not been ready to face the future, had figured he was due at least a few more years of wallowing, but Alex refused any excuses. His brother had promised bodily harm if Toby did not snap out of his depression. Instead of snapping out, Toby had sunk deeper. And stayed away.

Instead of relinquishing his stance, as Toby hoped he would do, Alex had issued an ultimatum: either find something else to do with his life besides moping, or don't come back to New Orleans.

No, Alex was not a hand holder.

Still smarting from Alex's remark, Toby reminded his brother, "I did offer to play ball with you and Eli last Saturday."

"Yeah, but only because you knew we would say no. The one-on-one game between me and Eli is sacred."

"Whatever," Toby said. "I still owe the two of you a butt whipping on the golf course."

"In your pitiful dreams," Alex answered. "Grab that miter box."

Toby snatched it from the toolbox and handed the cutting guide to his brother.

"I only caught bits of what you were saying about the TV show yesterday," Alex continued. "When do they start filming?"

"Not for another five weeks. I haven't officially signed on yet," Toby said, bracing the wood while Alex used the backsaw to cut a perfect 45-degree angle.

"What in the hell are you waiting for?"

Toby looked up at his brother, then quickly looked away. Alex always could read him like a book.

Alex braced the saw against the trunk of the oak tree and grabbed a bottle of water. "What's going on with you, Toby? You're the one who decided to jump into this music thing."

"It's not just some *thing*. This is my career."

"Then start acting like it," Alex said, pitching the water bottle on the ground and crossing his arms over a massive chest whose muscles bore the benefits of years of hard labor. Alex treated him to a piercing glare. "What are you afraid of?"

Making a fool of myself.

Proving I really am *destined to be a failure.*

"I'm not afraid of anything," Toby insisted. "I just want to be confident that I'm making the best choices for my client."

"Getting her on national television? Do you know how many rising stars would kill for this opportunity?"

Toby knew Alex was right. He'd been having this same conversation in his head for the past thirty-six hours. He knew this was the right thing for Aria's career, but what if it didn't work out? What if he found a way to screw this up the way he'd screwed up his basketball career? There were so many *what ifs* his head was on the verge of exploding.

"What if I mess this up?" he asked, unable to stop the question from escaping his mouth.

The edges of Alex's mouth tightened. Toby could feel the irritation radiating from his brother's body. Alex reached into his pocket and retrieved his cell phone. "Call the man. Right now, Toby. Call him up and tell him that Aria is going to do the show. I taught you to go after what you want, not run from it like a scared little girl. Now take the damn phone and call the man."

His brother, Mr. Sensitive.

Toby ignored the phone. "I'm meeting with Kellerman later today."

"On a Sunday?"

Toby shrugged. "There's no such thing as a day off in this business."

Alex's chin jutted forward, challenge gleaming in his eyes. "So, what are you going to tell him when you meet with him?"

"That Aria is going to do the show," Toby said, feeling better now that he'd finally made the decision.

Alex pushed the phone back into his pocket. "I still should kick your ass."

"Didn't I just say we're going to sign on for the show? Leave the ass-kicking for your basketball game with Eli."

"I'm an expert at ass-kicking. There's plenty to go around," Alex said with his version of a smile.

Toby grabbed a bunch of the wooden braces his brother had cut and walked over to where half the frame for Jasmine's new room was already up. "You're not worried about moving Jazzy on the opposite side of the house?" he asked.

"No. I'm moving into the guest bedroom," Alex answered. His eyes rose briefly, his silent warning amazingly loud.

Toby did not need the warning. He knew better than to comment about Alex's decision to move out of the bedroom he'd shared with his wife, Chantal. Or as Toby and Eli thought of her "the lying-cheating-bitch-from-hell." Her death nearly two years ago had not caused him any heartache.

Toby decided to drop the subject.

"Speaking of moving." He held the end of a two-by-four steady as Alex went at the other end with an electric saw. "Where is Cee Cee living these days? I heard she moved out of her mom's house."

"Yeah, she moved into her grandmother's place about six, seven months ago. I'm not sure if it's even been that long," Alex answered.

"She's doing pretty well for herself," Toby said. "New job, new house. You know if she's seeing anyone?"

"How would I know that? And why does it matter to you?" his brother asked, putting the saw down and staring at Toby with that look that had always raised his defenses.

"Don't," Toby warned.

Alex had tried to tell him long ago that he was a fool for not making things more serious with Cee Cee. Toby inwardly cringed at the thought. Sienna was like a sister. Other than the time back in high school when they had experimented with the bottle of Tequila she had found in her mother's closet, Toby had never thought of Sienna in an even remotely sexual way. They had kissed that day. A kiss that had gone way further than he had intended for it to go. But it had been the liquor. At least that was the story he was sticking to.

Still, he could never imagine being with Sienna in that way. It was just too weird.

"So, why did you ask?" Alex questioned.

"Because Jonathan is coming into town tomorrow and I was thinking about hooking them up."

Alex's brow shot up in surprise. "You're playing match-maker now? I thought that was Mama's job?"

"Mama will probably try to find some poor young thing at the church to fix him up with, but I think Jonathan and Sienna would get along. They've got a lot in common."

"So do *you* and Sienna."

"Would you leave that alone?"

Alex raised his hands, palms out. "You're stupid. That's all I'm saying."

"That's all? That sounds like enough."

Alex plunked another two-by-four on the sawhorse and started up the saw again. "I'm just trying to help you out here," he shouted over the buzzing. He released the saw's trigger and waited until the whirl of the tool had faded before continuing. "Sienna is smart, fine, and successful. She's not out in the street every night. She goes to church. And—"

"So why don't you go for her?" Toby threw the words at him, his annoyance building by the millisecond. "Or at least go for *some*body."

"Don't worry about me."

"Somebody should. If you don't get some soon, you're going to forget how to do it."

"I thought it was like riding a bike?" Alex said, settling another plank of wood on the sawhorse.

"You keep telling yourself that," Toby snorted.

A grin broke out across Alex's face.

"What?" Toby asked at his brother's uncharacteristic expression.

"I just bought a new ten-speed so I could go riding with Jazzy to the park. First time I tried to get on it, I fell flat on my behind."

Toby burst out laughing. "Oh man, I don't want to be anywhere around when you finally decide to get busy with a woman."

"That won't happen for a very long time."

"Why not?" Toby frowned.

The corner of Alex's mouth twisted in exasperation. "I've

got a daughter to think about, Toby. How do you think it would make Jazzy feel if I started bringing strange women around so close to her mother's death?"

"Chantal has been dead nearly two years. It's not as if you owe that bitch any special mourning period."

"That's the mother of my child you're talking about," Alex warned, his voice cold and hard.

"You can keep her memory sacred for Jasmine's sake, but don't ask me to show her any kind of respect. You may be able to forgive what she did to you, but I won't."

Anger spiked in his blood. If he could bring her back from the dead, Toby would do so just so he could have the chance to kill her with his bare hands. He would *never* forgive Chantal for the pain she'd caused his brother.

"I didn't say I forgave her," Alex murmured. "But I understand."

"You what!" Toby exploded.

"Let's drop this, all right?"

"We're not dropping anything. What do you mean you understand? She died with her lover in the same car with her, and you *understand*?"

"Toby!" The blood vessel on Alex's forehead bulged to twice its normal size. "Drop it," he ground out.

"Fine," Toby said, dropping the two-by-four, as well. "I need to get out of here, anyway."

"You're bailing on me?"

"Hey." Eli came from around the corner of the house, surprising them both. "Oh, hell. What did I just step into?" he asked as he looked from Toby to Alex.

"Nothing. I was just leaving. I have a meeting with the producer of the show."

"Go handle your business," Eli said.

"Maybe while I'm gone you can get someone to come and examine your brother's head."

Alex shot Toby a look that should have sent him running.

Eli turned to Alex. "What's he talking about?"

"Nothing," Alex answered. He picked up the hammer, and

Toby could tell by the look in his eye that his brother wanted to clobber him over the head with it.

"I'm out of here," Toby said. Walking away, he felt a small measure of satisfaction as he heard Eli and Alex arguing.

Chapter Three

Sienna stared up at the stately mansion, with its austere balustrade and towering two-story Grecian columns. A fountain, surrounded by a vivid display of tea roses, wisteria and rhododendrons, gurgled petulantly just beyond the gate. The house mocked her. Standing proudly amongst the other grand structures in the city's Garden District, home to some of New Orleans's wealthiest inhabitants, the mansion was an unforgiving representation of a life she thought she had left behind.

"Sienna," her mother called from where she stood just inside the partially opened wrought-iron gate. "Are you going to stand on the sidewalk the entire afternoon, or are you coming in?"

Was standing on the sidewalk the entire afternoon an option? There wasn't a question which Sienna would pick if given the choice. Millicent Perkins's home stood as a stark reminder of the painful past Sienna had no desire to revisit. Just the thought of the memories being inside that house would conjure sent a cold shudder down her spine.

"Sienna!" Her mother shot her an aggravated look. "I swear, if your sister were not moving, I would have asked Tosha to join me. Lord knows she'd make a better impression."

That's because Tosha lived for this pretentious crap even more than her mother did. Sienna swallowed back her retort. It wasn't worth it.

"I need to get my wrap out of the car," she said instead. She went back over to the car and retrieved her lace wrap.

How ridiculous that she had to get more dressed up for Sunday tea than she was for church this morning.

She followed her mother through the gate, the sound of it closing causing her heart to constrict. The clinking of a prison cell shutting behind her could not have elicited more distress. Sienna swallowed past the emotions clogging her throat as she made her way up the short, stone-laid walk.

"Good afternoon, ladies." The Perkinses' housekeeper greeted them at the door. She was dressed in the black and white maid uniform of years past. "Tea is being served in the courtyard today."

The housekeeper guided them through the richly dressed parlor. Gilded mirrors adorned the silk-covered walls. The dark-colored, paisley pattern was drab enough to sour anyone's mood. An antique, Louis XIV settee, covered in similarly depressing fabric, sat under one of the mirrors.

Everything about the house exuded Old Establishment. It was a lifestyle her mother had never had, and no matter how many teas, bridge parties, or debutante balls she attended, Sylvia Culpepper would never quite fit in. After all these years, many of the women in her mother's circle still looked down on her. Instead of admitting defeat, Sylvia just tried harder.

Sienna could never grasp the logic behind her mother's fierce determination to be accepted by these women. Sylvia allowed the rules of the Camilla Social Club to dictate nearly every aspect of her life. Every time she witnessed her mother compromise her own beliefs for fear that it would be frowned upon by the Camillas, Sienna lost another smidge of respect for her.

And this time, Sienna found herself caught up in the fray. Today's tea was just the beginning of a season of stuffy, pretentious social gatherings her mother would guilt her into attending.

Sienna stifled the expletive that was on the verge of escaping her mouth. Her mother would probably fall in a dead faint if she embarrassed her by uttering a dirty word in her friends' presence.

It was something to think about.

A respectable crowd was already gathered in the courtyard, some sitting at small round tables, while others gathered around the cherub fountain in the center.

"Sylvia, darling."

Sienna made every effort to hide her grimace as Millicent Perkins broke away from the group at the fountain, walking toward them with arms opened. Millicent greeted her mother with two near-kisses on the cheek. She was followed by several of her mother's friends, people Sienna had not seen in years.

Millicent turned her way. "Where have you been hiding, Sienna?"

As far as possible from people like you. "Not hiding, just extremely busy," Sienna answered.

"Tamika will be so excited to see you. She should be here shortly. She, Ahmad, and the kids are having their pictures taken in the gardens at City Park. Today was the only day the photographer could fit them in. But," Millicent delicately hunched her shoulders, "you have to make sacrifices if you want the best."

Sienna wasn't sure she could stomach an entire afternoon of her mother's so-called friends debating whose children had the better jobs, houses, and families. That would lead to an entire night of Sylvia lamenting that her daughters were lacking in every aspect of their lives.

"So, Sienna," Millicent sidled up next to her, taking Sienna's arm and intertwining it with hers, "do you have any kids yet?"

Sienna noticed her mother's face tighten as the woman asked a question she most certainly already knew the answer to.

"No, no kids. Not married."

"Oh, you girls need to make a grandmother out of Sylvia. It isn't fair that the rest of us have to wear that badge of age and she doesn't."

"All in due time," her mother said. Then, quickly changing the subject, she said, "So, Millicent, did you have the chance to visit Tosha's store while you were in Atlanta a few months ago? You know she's moving back there. She and her business partner are opening a second location."

Of course her mother would steer the conversation to the only daughter she deemed a success. Sienna tried not to grit her teeth. Why did her mother even bother to bring her here if she wasn't good enough to flaunt in front of her friends? Tosha should be the one going through this hell.

Then again, it wouldn't be such hell for Tosha. Her older sister fit right into New Orleans's African-American high society sect. But being in this element again dredged up memories Sienna had tried to bury since the night of her debutante ball.

God, she did *not* want to think about that night. But how could she not when she was being bombarded with so many triggers?

Some sixth sense had warned her not to go to Karena Johnson's after-party the night they had made their debut into society. She had ignored her intuition, and instead Sienna had lied to her mother, telling her she was going to spend the night at Ivana's dorm at Xavier University. She'd taken the city bus at night, something her parents never allowed.

Going to Karena's party had not been the worst; it was drinking the punch she'd known was spiked that had been Sienna's downfall. The alcohol had loosened her inhibitions and muddied her brain. She would have never gone out in the alley next to Karena's apartment building with Curtis Henderson if she had been in her right frame of mind.

Just the thought of his name sent a violent chill racing across her skin. She had not allowed that name to surface in her conscious in years. But that's what being back in this world did to her. It made her remember everything from this part of her past. Especially the dark parts.

"Sienna!" Her mother's near shout pulled Sienna back to the present.

"I'm sorry, what were you saying?" she asked her mother, whose neck had puffed to an unnatural size above the clenching collar of her silk blouse.

"Millicent was asking about your job. She said her niece is thinking about going into pharmaceutical sales, and I told her you do something along those lines."

"I'm in marketing," Sienna answered.

"Well, it's selling in a way, isn't it?"

"Mother, they are two totally different things."

"That's all right, Sylvia," Millicent said, turning to another guest.

"Sienna, could you at least try not to embarrass me?" her mother hissed.

"How am I supposed to speak about pharmaceutical sales? I haven't even tried to advertise drugs, let alone sell them."

Her mother just rolled her eyes and turned to the crowd that was gathering at the fountain. A few minutes later, tea was announced. Everyone took seats at various places around the courtyard. Sienna found an unoccupied bench close to a set of French doors. The maid who had let them in passed around puffed pastries and crustless sandwiches shaped like triangles. Sienna heaped as much as possible on the small saucer. She was starving.

She passed on the tea, accepting a glass of lemonade instead.

"Sienna." Her head began to throb at her mother's call. Sienna rose from the bench, folding a napkin over her half-eaten food and placing the plate on the bench.

"Yes, Mother?" Sienna asked as she came upon her mother's table.

"Come over here and say hello to Mrs. Henderson. You remember Edwina, don't you? Her daughter, Tricia, made her debut the same year you did."

And her son, Curtis, had nearly raped her.

Sienna's breath caught in her throat as images of that night came ragging to the forefront of her mind. The rough brick grating against her back, the smell of alcohol on his breath, the thick humidity nearly choking her, along with the fear. So much fear.

She tried to catch her breath, but couldn't. She felt faint; the walls started to close in.

"I—I need to go," she said.

Sienna turned in a semicircle, searching for the door that would lead her out of this cauldron of memories she had never intended to remember again. Ignoring her mother's voice, Sienna grabbed her purse from where she'd laid it next to the bench and took off through the French doors.

"What about a Hawaiian theme?" Monica asked.

Toby looked over at his future sister-in-law. She took a loud bite out of her apple as she lounged in the overstuffed armchair in Eli's spacious den. Eli sat on the floor next to her, his eyes rolling back in his head in pleasure as Monica massaged his scalp with her free hand.

"You're not getting my ass in a grass skirt," Eli drawled.

Walking passed him on the way to the sofa, Alex knocked his brother on the side of the head. "Don't use that kind of language. Jasmine's in the kitchen."

"In that case, we'd better stop talking about this all together," Eli said. "If Jazzy overhears us, Mama's surprise party won't be a surprise much longer."

"You're right about that," Alex admitted with a grin. "My little crumb snatcher is not good at keeping secrets."

"Which is how Mama found out about your speeding ticket the other day," Eli laughed. "I heard she chewed you out."

Alex did an exaggerated shiver. "I'm a grown man. How that woman still manages to scare me, I'll never know."

"She scares all of you," Monica laughed. "I think it's cute."

"It's embarrassing is what it is," Eli said.

"Let's put the party talk on the side for now," Monica suggested. "I want to hear from Mr. Silent over there." She looked to Toby. "What's up with you tonight, Toby? You've hardly said anything, and I counted at least three times you could have teased your older brothers."

"Nothing," Toby shrugged. "Just thinking."

"Ah, that's it, his brain is tired. We all know how taxing thinking is on you."

Toby pitched a throw pillow at Eli's head.

"What's happening with the show?" Monica asked. "Have you signed on the dotted line yet?"

"Last night," he answered with a nod.

Toby stretched his arms across the top of the sofa and lolled his head from side to side, working out the kinks in his neck. He had been on edge these last few days, but now that his plans were beginning to take shape, he was starting to think about just how much doing this show could mean to his career. Even though he still missed it like crazy, this was his chance to prove he was good at something other than dribbling a basketball.

"So, what now?" Alex asked. "Do we have to start opening doors for you and rolling out the red carpet?"

"Bull sh—" Eli stopped at the look Alex sent him. "Bull crap," he amended. "Don't think anybody is going to kiss your butt just because you'll be on TV."

"Who said anything about kissing my butt?" Toby defended. "And Aria's the one who's going to be in front of the camera, not me."

"As long as you don't expect special treatment," Eli said.

"Toby, don't pay any mind to your brothers," Monica said. Rising from the armchair, she came over to sit next to him on the sofa. "Now, tell me about the show."

"I pretty much gave you all the gist of it the other day, but Kellerman laid out more details in our meeting yesterday. He actually liked the fact that Aria is focused more on her music than on her sex appeal. He said she could fill the Miss Goody-Two-Shoes role. All these reality shows have the same theme, whether it's centered on music, or modeling, or any of the other fifty thousand things they make into a TV show these days. There's the Jock, the Bad Boy, the Geek, the Loner, the Loudmouth, the Whiny Brat, the Sex Kitten, and the Sweet, Innocent One—Aria. Kellerman also likes that she fits the young, urban female spot they'd been hoping to fill."

"This is perfect," Monica beamed, nearly as excited as Aria was when Toby had talked to her earlier today. "Aria doesn't have to compromise her morals, and she still gets mega exposure."

"That's my main goal. I'm using this show as a vehicle to what I really want to achieve here, long-term success for my client. I want to focus on broadening her fan base, which is why she's going to sing at my friend Jonathan's new club, The Hard Court. That'll reach the 28 to 45 demographic."

"Listen to you," Eli said. "Talking like you have a clue about this stuff."

Toby flipped his brother the finger. "You don't have to worry about Jazzy hearing that," he said to Alex.

"Would you let him finish," Monica chastised Eli. "Continue, Toby."

"The next step is to meet with the woman from the marketing firm."

"Marketing firm?" Eli asked.

"Now that I've signed on, I want to make sure I do it right. This show is too important to mess up by spreading myself too thin, and after meeting with Kellerman Sunday morning, I decided to hire a marketing firm to help with PR. I need to concentrate on getting the music right; I can't be distracted by the promo."

"Is hiring an outside firm allowed in the rules?"

Toby nodded.

"Does the show pay for it?" Alex asked.

"No, but I've got a little saved." Way more than his brothers knew about. "It's worth the expense. We need to cover a broad area, and sticking flyers on car windshields is not going to cut it."

"Did you talk to Sienna?" Alex asked. Toby shook his head. "But that's her field. Sienna should have been the first person you talked to."

"I need a professional to handle this, Alex."

"The girl has a friggin' master's degree. That's more than you have."

His brother was of the "help out a friend, even at your own expense" school of thinking. Promoting Aria as a cast member of this show was too important to put in Sienna's hand just to throw a little business her way. He needed proven skill for this, which is why he'd parted with a hefty chunk from his checking account for this marketing firm. It would be worth it when there was an Aria Jordan song downloaded onto every MP3 player in America.

Toby pushed himself up from the sofa. "I need to get going. Let me know what theme you guys pick for Mama's party."

"Grandma's having a party?" a squeaky voice asked from behind him. Toby's eyes slid shut as Jasmine walked into the center of the living room.

"Oh, great," Eli muttered.

"Sorry," Toby mouthed. "I'll see you guys later."

"What about Grandma's party?" he heard his niece ask as he headed for the door.

Chapter Four

Sienna quickly skimmed the electronic newsletter that came via email from the American Marketing Society. Finding a few articles of interest, she saved it to her hard drive, promising she would read it and all the others she'd stashed when she had more time. *If* she ever had more time. She was only two days into the workweek and was already craving Friday.

She grabbed the work jackets from her desk and plopped them in her lap. Sienna thumbed through the stack, searching for the insertion orders for the *Tailored Affairs Event Planners* job that would wrap today. She felt no small amount of pride for all the work she'd put into this job, even though as the junior branding strategist on the account she probably wouldn't get so much as a "job well done."

She'd foolishly believed things would be easier when she finished school. Sienna shook her head and grunted. Now that she was officially an "adult," Sienna wasn't so sure she wanted to be one.

The freedom that came with living on her own was a notch in the plus column. She relished being able to come and go as she pleased, to eat mashed potatoes and corn-on-the-cob for breakfast, or lounge around naked on a Sunday afternoon watching TV in her living room.

But with that freedom came responsibilities. And responsibilities were a pain in the behind.

Grandma Elise's decision to leave Sienna her house had been a blessing—and she was extremely grateful—but taking care of an old house required money. Lots of money. And until she started landing more lucrative accounts, many of the improvement projects she'd planned to tackle around the house would have to wait.

Maybe if she were "successful" like the daughters of her mother's uppity cronies at the tea on Sunday, she wouldn't have to worry about keeping a roof over her head. Or, better yet, if she found a husband, he could take care of her and she wouldn't have to work at all. She could spend the rest of her life popping out ugly little babies and showing them around to a bunch of mindless women who smiled in her face one minute then talked behind her back the next.

No, thank you.

Sienna absolutely despised everything about society life. There was nothing more important to those women than getting your picture in the paper at a high-flying social gathering, or even better, having someone of import attend your affair. Millicent Perkins had scored major points having the wife of a well-known councilman at her tea. Sienna would have been more impressed if she'd invited a couple of disadvantaged girls from one of the city's lower income areas. Of course, the women in her mother's cluster of friends stayed as far away from those areas as possible, even though many of them were products of the very same neighborhoods they now shunned. The hypocrisy was enough to turn Sienna's stomach.

She thought of what had happened at the tea, the way she'd fled. Her mother had called over a dozen times, but Sienna could not begin to think how to explain her actions.

"Hey, did you hear?"

Sienna looked up to find Scooter Simon leaning in the doorway to her office. Scooter held the prestigious position of being last year's recruit. He was cute in a five-dollar haircut, J.C. Penney suit-wearing sort of way, but he was as tenacious as they come, and had no qualms about stepping over people to make the biggest impression.

Sienna could hide her irritation at being disturbed, but why bother? It wouldn't make a bit of difference to Scooter anyway.

"Hear what?" she finally addressed him. She was not in the mood for gossip this morning.

"Jamie had a heart attack last night."

"What!" Sienna bolted out of her chair.

"That's what I heard." Scooter nodded. "One minute she's helping her kid with his math homework, the next, she's on the floor."

Scooter had such a flare for the dramatic. Although, the thought of a thirty-five-year-old marathon runner, who lived on health shakes and bean sprouts, having a heart attack *was* a bit dramatic.

"Is she all right?" Sienna asked, sinking back into her chair.

"She's not dead yet."

"Scooter!"

"Sorry," he shrugged. "That's all I know. Let me see what else I can find out."

Sienna stared unseeingly at her computer screen. Jamie Kurshon was the fourth person under the age of fifty to suffer a health-related problem since she'd started at Mulholland, Davis, and French. A senior associate had suffered a heart attack. One of the marketing reps had a stroke, and then another had a nervous breakdown. Was this in store for her?

No. She would not let the stress of this job affect her to the point of jeopardizing her health. Sienna knew it was a tough business. It could be downright cutthroat, especially when the junior associates were vying for the same accounts. But she could handle it. She'd faced much, much more, and had lived through it.

Sienna staved off the unpleasant thoughts. There were some things she refused to let herself think about anymore. Yet she knew she should prepare herself to deal with them now that her mother had brought her back into the world that had harbored such a devastating time in her life.

Pushing her chair away from the desk, Sienna rose. Allen Mulholland, the senior partner, came through her opened door. Sienna sat back down.

"Thank God you're here." He stopped just short of walking into her desk.

"Good morning, Allen," Sienna greeted. "Of course, I'm here. I get in at seven."

Allen gave a pass over his receding hairline and sighed. "It's been a rough morning."

"I heard about Jamie. How is she?"

"She's out of surgery. I'm going over to the hospital in about an hour."

"Tell her I'm thinking about her."

"Of course, of course." Allen stuck his hands in his pockets. "Look, Sienna. We're in a bind."

"How so?" *And why was he coming to her?* Sienna held no delusions about where she fit into the company infrastructure. She was a tiny tadpole in an ocean of marketing sharks.

"Todd, Michael, and Sherrell are out sick. And with Jamie out for God's knows how long—not that I don't understand about health concerns, because believe me, I do—but there is still a business to run."

"I understand, Allen. Being concerned about our clients' welfare doesn't make you insensitive."

He took a deep breath, pulled his hand out of his pocket and dragged it down his face. "I know this is a tough business. I've been in it for nearly twenty years, and I wouldn't be surprised if I fell dead any minute now." He dropped his head and pinched the bridge of his nose.

"Don't worry, I'd call 911," Sienna joked in an attempt to lighten the mood. It worked. Allen looked up and gave her a wan smile.

"So, what exactly has us in this bind?" she asked.

"Jamie has several accounts in various stages that will have to be shuffled around. She'd just accepted another one yesterday afternoon. I was hoping you could take it."

Sienna called on every single bit of restraint she possessed to keep a smile from breaking across her face. Grinning like a buffoon would not be appropriate in light of her co-worker's current condition.

"Jamie speaks so highly of you," Allen continued. "You were the first person I thought of this morning."

"Really?" Sienna asked, the smile lifting a corner of her mouth despite her best efforts to curb it.

"The client is scheduled to be here in just a few minutes. I'm sorry it's such short notice, but after everything that's happened this morning—"

"Don't even think about. All I'll need is a quick glance at the file. The first meeting usually is just going over the preliminaries."

"Usually, yes. But not with this one. This client is on an accelerated timetable. Actually, this should be a fun project." He handed her the file folder he had carried with him into her office. "The client is involved with some kind of reality TV show."

The bottom dropped out of Sienna's stomach.

"Jamie and I talked about it on the phone last night, about an hour before she had her heart attack, if you can believe it. From what she explained, it sounds like another one of those shows where contestants can land a recording contract. Like that *American Idol*."

Oh, God. Sienna suppressed a groan.

Looking slightly sheepish, Allen admitted, "I won't lie. I never miss those shows."

"Me, either," she stuttered after a hard swallow. Sienna's mind went blank as she tried to comprehend what her brain was just beginning to digest. She would be in charge of Aria Jordan's account? It was up to her to make Toby's current plaything a household name?

"This has the potential of being the most significant stepping-stone into the entertainment world this company has ever had," Allen said. "They're calling New Orleans 'Hollywood South,' you know. The explosion of motion pictures being filmed in the area has created an enormous amount of publicity for the city."

Sienna nodded. She couldn't speak if she tried.

"The bulk of our clients are in oil and gas, but as South Louisiana turns more toward the entertainment industry, we need to cash in on every opportunity we can. I think this new reality show is going to be a big hit. Jamie was very excited."

"I must say," Sienna started, thankful for the rebirth of her voice. "I'm honored that you would even consider me as a candidate for such an important project."

"I trust Jamie's judgment."

Sienna felt of twinge of what could only be described as validation. And it felt darn good. After years of having her mother look down on her life choices, hearing her boss's praise was a definite boost to her ego.

"Allen." It was the receptionist, Candi. "Jamie's new clients just arrived."

Her stomach did that nosedive thing again. She wished she had packed Pepto-Bismol. Of course, she could not have known she would have to face Toby and Miss Perfect this morning.

"Sienna will be handling the Holmes/Jordan account," Allen announced. "Thanks again for stepping up like this. It goes a long way in showing your commitment to excellence and to MDF, Inc."

"I'm honored to have this opportunity," Sienna answered with a weak smile as her mind stifled a cringe at hearing the Holmes/Jordan name combination. How long before she saw those two names together in the society pages under the weddings and engagements section?

Sienna wouldn't believe that unless she saw it with her own eyes. Tobias Holmes was not the marrying type.

She went over to her desk and flipped through the file Allen had handed her. More than ever, she needed to make sure she put on a professional face. She certainly didn't want Aria Jordan thinking she didn't know how to do her job. It would be hard to pull off with only a few minutes notice, though.

Sienna sighed. Preparation was not the only reason she was stalling—and stalling she most definitely was doing.

She and Toby had not parted on the best of terms Saturday. She was still insulted that he didn't even know she'd moved out on her own. That meant he hadn't even tried to keep up with what had been going on in her life these past few years.

At least she'd had the decency to inquire about him when she saw either his brothers or Margo. That was, after all, what friends did. It was as if he didn't care about her even as a friend.

After their father died, money had been hard to come by for the Holmeses. As much as Toby tried to show otherwise, Sienna knew he scuffled just to find the money to buy basketball sneakers. Even with Alex dropping out of college so he could get a job and support his mother and younger brothers, there was very little money left after all the household bills were paid.

When Toby went to St. John's on scholarship, he did not have the funds to fly home for visits very often. Yet, the few times he was able to make it, he spent most of his time with his family, leaving very little time for her. After his accident, his trips back home became nonexistent. She never got a phone call or even an e-mail. Nothing.

It takes two people to make a friendship work, and Toby just was not cutting it as a friend.

According to the message her mother left on Sienna's answering machine, he had called Sylvia's house Saturday night, but that was it. Either her mother had not given him her current number, or Toby had decided not to bother with making more of an effort to get in touch with her. Whatever the case, the entire episode had left Sienna with one undeniable certainty. She and Toby were not as close as they used to be, and she doubted they would ever find that companionship again.

Sienna attempted to ignore the pang of sorrow that settled in her chest, but it was no use. The loss of a friendship hurt, especially one as strong as she and Toby once shared. Especially when she'd always hoped it would grow into something more.

"Sienna," Candi's voice came through the phone's intercom. "Mr. Holmes and Ms. Jordan are waiting for you in conference room three."

Sienna pressed the answer button. "Thanks, Candi. I'm on my way."

Taking a fortifying breath, she headed for the conference room.

Toby's heart constricted. This was the type of news he would give anything not to hear.

Devising a killer marketing campaign was paramount to Aria's success. She had the voice. He had the vision. All they needed was the marketing savvy of a firm like MDF, Inc. He knew his limits; understood when he was in over his head. And trying to function as Aria's producer, manager, songwriter, promoter, and advertising guru was more than he could handle—especially with so much at stake.

Of all the times for Jamie Kurshon to have a heart attack!

That was a bit insensitive, Toby mentally chided, but their time was short. He did not need a major setback like this so early in the game.

"Although Ms. Kurshon will not be available, her replacement is the most competent associate to join us in the last few years." The slightly graying man who'd introduced himself as Allen Mulholland continued. "If you cannot have Jamie, Sienna Culpepper is the next best thing."

Who did he say?

"Here she is."

He'd heard right. Toby was torn between laughter and shock as Sienna walked into the conference room. What were the odds?

"Good morning, Mr. Holmes. Miss Jordan." She extended her hand.

"Morning, Ms. Culpepper." Toby returned her handshake, a grin pulling at his lips.

"Sienna, I didn't know you worked here," Aria said.

"You know each other?" Mulholland asked.

"Yes, we do," Sienna answered. "Mr. Holmes and I grew up together, Allen. I only met Ms. Jordan a few months ago."

"Well, isn't this something?"

"It sure is," Toby agreed. Funny how Sienna had left him on Saturday, then avoided him the rest of the weekend, and now she was the one who would be handling his account.

"I'll leave you three. I know you're anxious to get started." With that, Mulholland left the conference room.

"I'm sorry, but I really need to use the restroom before we get started," Aria said. Sienna pointed her down the hall, then took a seat at the cherrywood conference room table.

"This is a surprise," Toby said, since apparently she wasn't going to say anything. He'd spent most of his free time since Saturday trying to determine just what the hell had pissed her off. He still couldn't figure it out.

"For me, as well," she answered. Her voice was as cold as a freezer. What was up with her?

"The big guy seems to think you know what you're doing."

"I *do* know what I'm doing," she shot back.

Toby held up his hand in mock surrender, "Cee Cee, I was just joking."

"Don't call me that."

"What's the matter with you?" Toby frowned.

"This is my place of business," she hissed through clenched teeth. "I do not answer to Cee Cee."

"Sorry about that," Aria said, coming back into the room.

Sienna shut her eyes for a second and expelled a breath. She opened her eyes and with an overly bright smile, said, "Why don't we get started?" She flattened the file folder open on the table.

Toby decided to put a hold on his questions about her attitude. It was time to get to work.

"We have a lot to do here and very little time in which to do it," Sienna continued. "What I suggest is that we come out with all guns blazing. A full-fledged media blitz."

"Just remember we're doing this on a minimal budget," Toby interjected. "The show isn't paying for this, so the capital we use will be from my personal funds."

"That's what sponsors are for," Sienna answered.

"What sponsors?" Aria asked.

"The ones we will find. Did the show specify any rules about how to raise money for your campaign?" she asked, searching through the notes in the file folder.

"No," Toby answered. "All they said is that they are not responsible for any expenses incurred for any promotion outside of what they're already providing for the show. They didn't give us any restrictions on raising money."

"Excellent. We'll get corporate sponsors. You're gorgeous," Sienna told Aria. "Local companies will clamor to get your face associated with their product."

"I'd never thought about that," Toby said. Which is why he was more than willing to pay for MDF, Inc.'s services. He knew his limits. He did not have a mind for marketing, although he planned to learn everything he could while he had the chance. It looked like he could learn a thing or two from Sienna. The girl was on her game.

Toby leaned back in his chair and studied her as she laid out an entire plan. Gone were the cornrows and baseball cap. They had been replaced by a shoulder-length hairstyle that was cut to frame her oval-shaped face. She'd traded in her basketball shorts and high-top sneakers for a business suit that hugged her waist and heels that added a good three inches to her already impressive height. Back in high school, Sienna had never worn makeup, but now her full lips were tinged with a light peach color. She looked . . . good. Different, but good.

"First thing we need to do is get a press kit together. I'll need a bio, whatever press clips you have—there must be a few write-ups from your performances in Houston, right?"

"One or two," Toby said. "It's not much. Just a few words from the local entertainment writer for a small independent music magazine."

"She's got credentials; that's all we're looking for. We'll also need press photos. I know this is going to cost up front, but it will be worth it in the end. Don't worry, Toby, I know what I'm doing."

Whatever doubts he'd had when Sienna had first walked into the room were sufficiently put to rest. She thought of things he had never considered.

"One of the most inexpensive and effective ways to promote you is by word of mouth, which means we have to get as many people out to your performances as we can. But, before we get into any of that, there's something I need you to do, Aria."

Aria's head shot up. "What?" she asked, her voice trembling slightly.

Aria had more talent than anyone he had seen in a long time, but she was easily intimidated. If she was to be the star Toby had in mind, she had to learn how to have a presence away from the stage.

"I need to know why you want this." Sienna said.

"To win on the show?"

"No. To sing," Sienna clarified. "I need to know what your goals are. What is it about music that draws you?"

"I don't know," Aria said. Toby could tell she was overwhelmed.

"Yes, you do," Sienna told her before Toby could intervene.

She sent him a look that clearly said she was going to handle this. Toby sat back and watched.

"Is there anything else you can imagine yourself doing for the rest of your life?" Sienna asked, rising from her seat and walking over to the chair next to Aria. She sat, and taking Aria's hand between her own, she said, "What is it about singing, about music, that drives you like nothing else can?"

"It's the—"

"No." Sienna shook her head. "Don't tell me. This is for you to know, and only you. What I do want to know is where are you most comfortable singing? Is it at the huge clubs with a thousand people around you?"

"I've never played to an audience that big," Aria answered.

"You will," Sienna warned her. "Are you really ready to handle that?"

"I am," Aria said with a firm nod. "I'm okay once I get out on stage. It's just the waiting that kills me. And talking in public. I hate talking in public."

Sienna gave her a sympathetic smile. "You know, there are more people who fear public speaking than death? Unfortunately, it comes with the territory. Luckily, for you, we can work on it. I think we should start out with a few radio interviews. That way, it's only one or two people in the studio. Then we can work our way up to spots on local news channels. Reality shows are so popular these days. They're going to jump at the chance to have you in their studios."

They had been here, for what? Ten minutes? And already, Sienna had weeks worth of promotion laid out.

"How many concert dates do you think we can book between now and the start of taping?" She pulled up a calendar on the computer, which flashed on the large projector screen that took up the entire left wall.

"Not sure," Toby answered. "With the big name headliners at Jazz Fest and the French Quarter Festival this year, it may be hard to get tourists to attend a concert for an unknown artist."

"But it's the local clientele that we want to win over,"

Sienna reasoned. "Locals tend to stay away from the high tourist areas anyway. Native New Orleanians will be looking for ways to unwind that are set apart from the gimmicky atmosphere most businesses use to lure in tourists."

Yeah, she was good.

Toby was almost giddy, his anticipation of the weeks to come making him more and more excited. Slowly, an encouraging realization occurred to him. With Sienna directing their marketing strategy, Aria's chances had just soared.

Sienna tapped on the computer keyboard, but an error message popped up stating the file she was attempting to open was already in use. She cursed.

"I'm sorry," Sienna said, sending an apologetic glance, which was funny since Toby was the one who'd taught her many of the most choice swear words in the first place.

"I forgot to log out of the calendar on my computer. Let me run to my office to see what my schedule looks like this week," Sienna said. "I want a few days to go over this, then we can meet again to set this course into action."

She rose from the table and was out of the conference room before Toby could stop her.

Leaving Aria, Toby got up and headed in the direction Sienna had taken. He passed three offices before coming upon the door, which held a silver plate etched with her name. He gave two quick knocks, then pushed the partially opened door a little wider.

"Nice cubbyhole," he said, giving her small office the once-over. Even though it was a little bigger than a broom closet, Sienna had added her own style. Two potted plants sat in opposite corners, with another, smaller one on her desk. A square geometric-patterned rug took up most of the area in front of her desk.

The wall behind her sported an array of framed and matted postcards, probably from the collection she'd maintained since the third grade project back at Sophie B. Wright Elementary. Sienna had become obsessed with collecting a postcard from every country in the world.

Toby motioned toward the postcards with his head. "How many countries you got left?" he asked.

She glanced behind her at the display. "I stopped collecting," she said. "The internet has made the world much smaller. Why wait weeks for a postcard to arrive from Russia when you can get an e-mail instantly?"

He nodded his agreement. "I guess framed e-mails just don't hold the same appeal."

"No, they don't."

The awkward silence that stretched between them was as foreign as it was uncomfortable. He could not remember a time when he and Sienna could not find something to say to each other. Even when they were fighting, she still talked to him. It usually came in the form of shouting, with a blunt object being pitched at his head, but there was communication. Always.

He didn't know what to make of this stagnant air between them. When they were younger, Sienna had been his salvation when things got rough; the person he could turn to when he was ready to find a machine gun and open fire on the world. He could not fathom a time in his life when his Cee Cee wouldn't be there for him.

Toby knew he was mostly to blame for the gulf between them. During those first few months after the accident, he had shut everybody out. The thought of seeing pity on their faces had been more than he could bear at the time. But in the back of his mind, Toby knew Sienna would always be there for him.

Now, he wasn't so sure.

"Did you need anything in particular?" Sienna asked.

There. That hint of coldness in her voice. He knew he was not imagining it.

"Toby," she said, clearly losing patience. "Why are you standing there like a statue?"

"No reason," he said. "I wanted to check out your office. I had no idea you worked at Mulholland, Davis, and French when I picked them to run Aria's campaign."

"Funny, I knew about your job at Price Waterhouse, the nightclub in Houston, and now as a record producer."

There was no mistaking the acid in her voice. It would not be more apparent if she had the words "Ticked Off" stamped on her forehead in bright red letters.

He knew he should have done a better job at keeping in touch. After all Sienna had done for him, he'd owed her at least that. But she had been the hardest to face. Of all the people in his life, Toby felt that Sienna was the one he'd let down the most by not seeing his promising professional basketball career to fruition.

But that wasn't an excuse, and it's not like he could tell that to Sienna anyway. Bottom line, he should have kept tabs on her, if only to show his interest in what was happening in her life.

Since she stared at him, fully expecting an answer, Toby decided to tell her at least a partial truth.

"To be honest, I didn't have much to do with anything back here in New Orleans. Other than my weekly call to Mama on Sundays, and coming home a couple of Christmases ago . . . I just—" he shrugged.

"Yes, I know," she answered resignedly.

It's a good thing they would be working together on this project. He'd have ample time to get back in his best friend's good graces. That is, if she even considered herself his best friend anymore. From the vibes radiating off her right now, Toby doubted it.

"I was thinking," he continued, sensing an overwhelming urge to change the conversation's direction. "Since you're now in charge of marketing Aria to the general public, I think you need to see your new client in action."

"You're right; if I'm going to create a marketing scheme around her music, I need to see her perform."

A smile widened across Toby's face.

Little Cee Cee definitely took her job seriously. It wasn't a surprise. There was not a single thing Sienna started that she didn't put her entire heart into, no matter the difficulty. Toby had found himself in awe of all she used to take upon her shoulders: working in her mom's store, babysitting, playing ball, maintaining a 4.0 GPA throughout high school, *and* always being there for him.

"When is her next performance?" Sienna asked. "I'm going to need a copy of that schedule as soon as possible, by the way."

Toby's smile became just a bit wider. "Busy Friday night?"

Sienna rolled her eyes, the makings of a smile tipping up her lips. "You are determined to make me admit I don't have plans for Friday, aren't you?"

"Not at all. I never doubted you had plans, but if you do, I think you need to cancel them. This is, after all, your job."

"I hate you," she laughed.

Toby chuckled. Saying she hated him was Sienna's weird way of showing affection. Just hearing it again chipped away a small piece of the boulder that had been weighing on his heart. Cee Cee had always been able to shoo away any gray cloud hanging over him with one of her quick comebacks.

"What time is the performance?" she asked.

"It's at eleven at this new club on Esplanade. It's called The Hard Court."

"The Hard Court?"

"Remember that buddy of mine that just moved down here?"

She sent him her mean eyes. "I really, *really* hate you, Toby."

"I know," he laughed. "Look, Jonathan's cool. He was my freshman buddy at St. John's. He's been a successful corporate attorney for the past five years in Charleston, but just came into a load of money from some property settlement from his dead grandmother. He's been looking for a change, so he decided to move his practice to New Orleans. He just passed the Louisiana Bar, so he's launching both his club and new law practice this week."

"Hmm . . . sounds like me," Sienna said.

"How so?" Toby asked.

"Well, not the load of money part, but I did get my grandmother's house after she died."

"Yeah, Alex mentioned that. How long have you been there?"

"For the past seven months. Granny Elise told her estate manager that I had to finish my master's degree before he could even tell me about the house."

"Inheriting a house? That's great, Cee Cee. Paying rent is a pain in the butt."

"I guess you're right," she sighed. "Of course, I'd rather have my grandma."

"Yeah, Granny Elise was something else. Dang, but that woman could make some good biscuits," Toby reminisced. He wondered if Granny Elise had left the recipe anywhere.

"Well, you surely won't find any of those biscuits baking in her oven now. If it were not for Stouffer's and Pizza Hut, I'd probably starve."

"That kitchen was made for cooking," Toby tsked.

"You can strap on your apron anytime," she laughed.

"Sienna," a lanky guy with red hair and tortoiseshell glasses poked his head in the doorway. "Jamie's out of surgery. I overheard Allen say he was coming to see you in a few minutes."

"Thanks, Scooter," Sienna answered. "Okay, Toby, I'll be there Friday night." She opened the top desk drawer and retrieved a pad of yellow Post-it notes. "Write the directions to the club and a phone number where I can reach you. We'll need to set up another meeting ASAP."

Allen Mulholland showed up at the door, just as the redhead had predicted.

"I'll meet you in your office, Allen," Sienna told him. "I'll see you Friday night," she called over her shoulder as she left Toby standing in the middle of her tiny office.

Chapter Five

Jonathan Campbell stood in the middle of the open space and turned in a slow circle, taking it all in. Indina Holmes, his best friend, Toby's, interior designer cousin, had done an outstanding job. He could not have dreamed up a better layout for The Hard Court.

When his twin sister, Jacqueline, had called a few minutes ago, Jonathan had tried to describe the club's appearance. The best he was able to come up with was a sophisticated basketball court. Indina had taken the thoughts from Jonathan's mind and brought them to life within the walls of the club. She had stayed true to the sports themed décor that he had requested, but added a touch of elegance that catapulted The Hard Court above the average nightclub.

The hardwood floors were shiny enough to blind his eyes. The light fixtures on the wall—what Indina had called sconces—were designed to look like basketball hoops, with a basketball halfway through it. A warm, mellow orange radiated from the soft bulb behind the iron-meshed basketball, lighting the path down the stairs from the restaurant on the second floor.

Jonathan had been very particular about what he wanted to create with this new venture. New Orleans was a city known for its ability to have a good time, and Jonathan wanted to cash in on the resurgence after Hurricane Katrina. The city was going to be better than ever.

The idea to open up a nightclub with a basketball theme seemed natural. Basketball was his first love, and had been more loyal to him than any of the women he'd ever been involved with. But he had cautioned Indina that this was to be a nightclub, not a sports bar. There would be no betting on games, or fighting over whose team was better, or any of the other foolishness that went on in regular bars.

His would be the type of establishment that called to the city's more cultured sector. His goal was to attract a clientele who would appreciate the sophistication that went into this place, yet knew how to let loose and have a good time. Jonathan wanted The Hard Court to be a place where the middle income African-American adult could unwind after a hard day's work. And by the looks of things, that's exactly what he'd gotten.

"Man, this is tight."

Jonathan turned and smiled.

Toby stood at the edge of the dance floor, its boundaries delineated by a white stripe made to resemble the boundaries of a basketball court. Jonathan made his way to him and hooked his arm around Toby's neck, enveloping him in a hug.

"You here to stay?" Toby asked.

"I finished tying up all the loose ends back in Charleston yesterday. I'm officially a New Orleanian."

"You're an implant. One day in town does not make you a New Orleanian."

"Whatever." Jonathan punched him on the shoulder. "So, what's up, man?"

Toby shook his head. "My news doesn't compare to opening a new nightclub and law practice in the same week. People are going to start calling you the black Donald Trump."

Chuckling, Jonathan hooked his arm around Toby's shoulder. "Come over to the bar and let me buy you a drink while you tell me about this show. You know how behind I am on what's happening on television."

The two sat at the bar, and it was almost an hour later before Toby finished filling him in on everything that had developed over the last few days.

"This is huge," Jonathan said.

"It can be," Toby answered, excitement lighting up his eyes.

If he ever got the chance to meet Marshall Kellerman, Jonathan knew he'd have to fight the urge to hug the man. He was just that grateful that someone had alleviated a little of his friend's pain. He hadn't seen Toby this happy since before the accident.

"I guess I'm lucky Aria's even available to perform at my little club's opening night."

"Little?" Pausing to take a drink, Toby threw him a sardonic look over the rim of his glass. "If this is little, I'm going on a date with Beyoncé tonight."

"Well, we both know there's no chance of that."

"You never know, man. It could happen. Technically."

"I could become a monk. Technically." Jonathan raised his eyebrows, waiting for Toby's counter.

"All right, all right. No Beyoncé for me," Toby said. "Really, man. This place is hot. You're going to light this city on fire."

"That's the plan."

"How is the new office space turning out?" Toby asked. He waved off another drink when the bartender came to refill his glass.

"It should be up and ready by the end of the week. I'm headed over there right now. The building contractor has been having a problem with some vagrant who claims she has dibs on the place."

"You'd better get that under control. It sounds like the kind of headache you can do without. I'll be back tomorrow to make sure everything's set up for the performance."

"You don't have to check up on me, man. Just be on time Friday, and I'll handle the rest."

Toby grabbed his fist and brought him in for a hug. "This is going to be hot, man. I can feel it. I'll catch you Friday. Oh, and make sure you look good for your grand opening. I've got somebody I want you to meet."

"Don't do it, Toby," Jonathan called to his retreating form, but his former teammate was already making his way toward the club's smoke-glass doors.

If there's one thing he didn't need, it was Toby playing matchmaker. Jonathan did not need a woman interrupting his life right now. He had enough on his plate with the club opening at the end of the week, and his law practice's first client coming in next Monday. Speaking of which, he had better head over to the new office suite he'd leased to see about the situation with the nutcase that had been causing the contractor all of these problems.

Jonathan suppressed a groan.

It was too much to ask that things would go off without a hitch. He'd prepared himself for glitches—pipes bursting, construction running overtime—but an uncooperative vagrant could lead to more than he'd bargained for. If the nutcase became too vocal, the courts might get involved. And as an officer of said court, he knew better than most that it was best to avoid that type of interference at all cost.

Jonathan left instructions with the bartender to call his cell if anything came up while he was away, and headed out of The Hard Court.

Sliding onto the cool leather seat of his Mercedes SK5, he started up the car, smiling at the soothing hum of the engine. He loved this car. Power and style, wrapped into a sleek, black package. Exactly what he aspired to attain when he dressed in the morning.

Jonathan pulled away from the curb and maneuvered through the narrow streets of the French Quarter, centuries-old brick and wrought-iron structures observable on either side of the street. He'd been ecstatic when his real estate agent had found office space only a few minutes from the site of The Hard Court. The old two-story wooden structure on the edges of the city's most famous neighborhood was on the small side but suited his purposes to a tee. It was the perfect location and layout, and he sure as hell was not going to allow some whack job to cause him any more problems.

Jonathan pulled his car in behind the plumber's pickup truck that took up most of the alley he planned to use as a parking lot. That reminded him; he needed to put in another call to the guy in charge of that project.

He heard voices coming from the newly renovated parlor room that would serve as his lobby. Jonathan walked up the steps to the wraparound porch. Its planks were still bare after being stripped of a hundred years of paint. It would be beautiful with the rich mahogany stain he'd decided on.

He opened the front door to find the contractor in a heated discussion with a rather tall woman whose back was turned to him.

"You're here. Good!" the contractor yelled, throwing his hands in the air. "Now you can deal with her. Fighting off psychopaths is not in my job description."

The woman turned.

Jonathan took a step back.

She wasn't exactly what he envisioned when he thought of a vagrant. The word, by definition, evoked images of a dirty, homeless nobody. From the looks of her, this woman was not homeless. She looked more like one of the palm readers that lined the pedestrian walkway around Jackson Square. She wore a long flowing skirt and loose blouse that had a tie at her slim neck. A purple paisley scarf that dramatically clashed with the bright orange and hot pink colors of her clothing was tied around her head and in a knot over her right ear, its ends brushing her shoulder.

A little eccentric maybe, but definitely not a vagrant. Fascinating, if he were to be honest. She was no more than a few inches shorter than he was, and at six-feet, seven inches, his height was nothing to sneeze at.

Fascinating and formidable.

"Is there a problem?" Jonathan asked. He directed his question to the building contractor who continued to grumble in the corner of the huge room. The plumber was thumping his palm with a pipe wrench. He had yet to open his mouth.

"Yes, there is definitely a problem," the woman answered. "I'm guessing you're the new tenant."

"I am," Jonathan said. "How can I help you?"

"You can tell these men to pack up their tools and get out of this building."

"I beg your pardon?" Jonathan choked. It took a quick mind to catch him off guard, and she had certainly done that.

Definitely fascinating.

"You are messing with history. This building is a landmark."

"I think you're mistaken, Miss . . . ? I'm sorry, but I missed your name."

"My name is irrelevant. The important thing here is that this building holds too much significance for me to allow you to continue gutting it like a fish. I won't stand for another ounce of desecration."

Jonathan's throat had become so dry he could hardly swallow. What was it about her that had him so enthralled?

"Ma'am, I'm sorry, but no one told me about any historical significance when I signed the lease. I consulted the landlord before performing any renovations, and he didn't have a problem with it. In fact, he was thrilled that the place would get a makeover."

"The landlord doesn't care about this building's history. That doesn't lessen its importance."

"If it were all that important, it would be listed in the state's landmark registry, and the city would have prevented renovations before I ever started. I believe you have the wrong building."

She pointed at him with two long, elegant fingers. "This is not over. I will not let you destroy this place." Before he could respond, she rushed past him, leaving a faint, floral scent in her wake.

Jonathan, along with the contractor and plumber, walked out onto the porch and watched as she marched defiantly across the street, then down the sidewalk.

"Fascinating," Jonathan let out on a whispered breath.

Sienna deposited a pack of gummy bears on Candi's desk. "A little something to brighten your day," she greeted her boss's assistant with a smile.

"How did you know my day needed brightening?" Candi asked.

"Uh oh, what happened?" Sienna asked, noticing that the usually composed Candi seemed a bit rushed.

"Oh nothing, just that my boss has turned into Godzilla," Candi answered.

"Not what I wanted to hear, seeing as I have a meeting with him in," Sienna checked her watch, "less than five minutes."

"Make that right now." Sienna turned at Allen's voice. He stood just outside his door. "Candi, get James Beck on the phone, and if a Michael Roberts calls make sure you put him through immediately." He turned to Sienna. "My office, if you please, Sienna."

Candi mouthed *good luck*, and sent her a sympathetic wave.

Sienna entered Allen's spacious office and sat in one of the two leather chairs facing the richly polished desk. Allen took the seat behind the walnut-colored executive workstation and brought his hands up, crossing them over his desk.

"I'm not going to beat around the bush, because frankly, I just don't have the time. I'm going to have to pull you from the Holmes/Jordan account."

Sienna's breath caught in her throat. She had not known what to expect when Allen had requested this meeting, but she certainly hadn't expected to have the rug pulled out from under her. She'd been put in charge of the account less than twenty-four hours ago, how could she have messed up this soon?

"I don't understand, Allen. Just yesterday you were saying how great a fit I am for this account."

"Circumstances have changed." He sighed deeply and set the chrome pendulum on his desk to swinging. The methodical tapping matched the trepidation skirting down her spine. Allen Mulholland was stalling.

He sat back in his chair and held her stare. "Cardinal Studios, the parent company of Over the Edge Productions, has learned of Mr. Holmes' decision to go with MDF, Inc., to handle promotional duties for the reality show. The president of Cardinal Studios called this morning with what could turn out to be the most lucrative deal MDF has ever been offered. They have eight feature films and made-for-TV movies slated for production next year in South Louisiana, and they are looking for a marketing firm to handle the account. I touched on this yesterday. With this new state tax credit, this area is about to explode as it pertains to the motion picture business."

"This is good news, but I still don't understand what it has to do with my account." She already thought of it as *her* account. She'd stayed up half the night trying to devise different angles for marketing Aria.

"Cardinal is looking at how well we handle the Holmes/Jordan account as a benchmark."

So that was it. Allen didn't have as much confidence in her as he'd claimed.

"I know this is disappointing, Sienna, but you have to understand—"

"No, Allen." She was not losing this account. Though, she might lose her job if she spoke to her boss in that tone again. Sienna tapered her voice. "I can do this." He shook his head, but before he could voice another negative thought against her, Sienna stopped him. "I'll guarantee it," she said. "I guarantee Cardinal Studio's satisfaction with the way this account is handled."

"And if they are not one hundred percent satisfied?" Allen asked.

Sienna sent him a leveled gaze. "If Cardinal Studios does not offer their marketing dollars to MDF based on my handling of Aria Jordan's account, then I will tender my resignation," Sienna said.

Allen picked up a pen and began to tap out a rhythm on his desk. "Sienna, do you remember how many people were up for your position?" he asked.

"Two hundred fourteen," she answered.

He raised a brow, a small smile forming at the corner of his mouth. "Most of those people are still looking for a job; many of them will not find one. And not one of them will find one as lucrative as yours."

"I know that, Allen. But I also know that I can do this job."

"You're that confident?"

She nodded.

He lifted his hands in surrender. "Fine. I was planning to put another account on hold so I could take over the Holmes/Jordan account personally, but I'll give you a chance."

Sienna breathed a short-lived sigh of relief.

"But take this as your sole warning," Allen pointed the ink pen at her. "I will be watching. I want to be kept abreast of every aspect of this account."

"Of course," Sienna answered.

"Mr. Mulholland," Candi's voice came through the phone intercom. "James Beck is on line five."

"I'll see myself out," Sienna said. She rose from the chair on legs that could barely support her, and somehow made her way out of the office and onto the elevator.

When she returned to her office, Sienna closed the door and slumped against it, clamping her hand to her chest.

What had she just done?

She closed her eyes and took a couple of deep, calming breaths.

How many times over the last several months had she prayed for the chance to prove her worth? One shot. That's all she needed. Well, she had the mother of all shots now.

Just this morning, no one could have predicted how important Aria Jordan's account would become to the future of MDF, Inc. When Sienna had been asked to take over the account for Jamie, she had been elated simply because she was finally entrusted with her own account again instead of playing assistant to one of the senior executives.

The senior partners had been afraid to give her another chance after the multimillion dollar account she'd landed within her first month on the job had fallen through. It had not been her fault. The company had decided to leave the Gulf South because of its penchant for hurricanes, only to move to the West Coast's even more unpredictable earthquakes. When would people understand that you could not outrun Mother Nature, no matter where you tried to escape to?

But last year's snag was a thing of the past. Within the span of a few hours everything about her career had changed. Drastically.

As she sat at her desk contemplating the responsibility on her shoulders, Sienna feared she was in danger of losing it once again. The biggest account the company could ever hope for was riding on how well she performed, and she'd offered up her job as collateral!

"Lord, help me," Sienna murmured.

Gathering the articles she'd printed from the Internet on the demographics of the New Orleans radio listening area, Sienna grabbed her purse and locked up her office. She had a long night of non-recreational reading ahead of her. She also had to find a killer dress for Friday night.

Toby may have used the fact that since Aria was now her client, she needed to see her in action, but Sienna was not born yesterday. He was going to try to hook her up with his old college friend.

The idiot. Why was she hung up on him? He was so blind; he could not see what was right in front of his face.

Or, maybe he did see it. And trying to set her up with Jonathan was his way of letting her know that she could forget about anything between them.

Sienna brushed that thought off with a wave of her hand. Toby had always been clueless about how she felt about him. Probably always would be.

Sienna suspected that Toby still saw her as that shy, skinny, freakishly-tall-for-her-age girl who used to play ball with him on their elementary school's old basketball court. He had yet to recognize the grown woman she had become. She should just get over him and find someone who would appreciate her as an attractive, successful, self-sufficient woman.

The thought alone scared her to death.

Sienna swallowed past the lump that inevitably lodged in her throat whenever her mind decided to dredge up memories she would pay any price to keep buried. For most of her adult life, Sienna had speculated about why she was so hung up on Toby. She supposed she already knew the answer.

Toby was safe. As long as she continued to pine for what would never be, she didn't have to confront the reality she was too afraid to face.

After that incident with Curtis Henderson, Sienna wasn't sure she could ever have a normal relationship with a man. It was a depressing thought, but one she was beginning to accept. The couple of guys she'd dated in college hardly counted, and the one blind date she'd had last year had been a disaster. Intimacy, on almost any level, scared her to death.

Sienna pushed those awful thoughts from her mind. She had enough on her brain with this new account. She did not need the added stress of her demons coming back to haunt her.

She reached her car and slid behind the wheel, throwing her purse on the passenger seat. As she did so, her father's favorite warning rang in her ears. Warren Culpepper had warned the women in his life about not inviting trouble, and in his book, a purse lying so visible to the public was equivalent to having a "Steal Me" sign strapped across the front of it. Sienna was in no mood to play the victim. She stashed the purse under the front seat.

She drove the quick ten minutes to the wood frame house her grandmother had left her in the lower Faurbourg Marigny. In recent years, the small suburb just down the river from the French Quarter had become a hub of trendy restaurants and live music spots, but somehow maintained a close-knit sense of community. Sienna had always loved this neighborhood, with its collection of old, Creole-style cottages butted up against each other. She had spent more time here than at her own home when she was growing up.

Her close relationship with her grandmother had always been a sore spot between Sienna and her mother. Sylvia had been ashamed of her upbringing, and a mother she labeled as being too "common" and uncouth. Sienna had been in awe of her Granny Elise. To Sienna, she had performed miracles with her meager means, providing food for the hungry, and sewing clothing for the neighborhood's less fortunate. She was the type of woman most people would be proud to have in their lives.

Of course, her mother was not most people. She'd encouraged Sienna to sell the house, claiming she wanted to finally get the atrocity out of the family. It had given Sienna an absurd amount of pleasure to move into the old house despite her mother's wishes.

Sienna smiled to herself as she thought about the termites she'd discovered hiding in the walls of the living room soon after she'd moved in. She'd cursed the pests to hell after receiving the $1,500 estimate from the exterminator. If not for the termites, Sienna would never have put most of Granny Elise's most precious possessions in storage, and they would be lost forever.

Even though water from the breeched levees caused by Hurricane Katrina did not threaten the house, the Category 5 winds had blown away most of her roof. Sienna had been one of the very lucky ones in this city, her grandmother having added extra hurricane insurance when she still owned the house. Nearly all of the repairs had been covered. And the termites had been blown away, too.

Sienna walked through the side door that led to the kitchen, setting her purse and car keys on the counter. She kicked her shoes off in the small alcove between the refrigerator and stove. She looked in the refrigerator for something to drink and came out with a nearly empty pitcher.

Opening the floor to ceiling pantry, Sienna searched for the powdered iced tea mix while mentally going through the list of takeout places she had already ordered from this week. She wasn't in the mood for Mexican, and had eaten Chinese the night before. Pizza would do, but it didn't have the appeal it usually did.

For some unknown reason, she felt like eating . . . *real food*. She wanted red beans and rice, or maybe baked chicken and mashed potatoes. Cautiously, she turned her gaze toward the cabinet that held the pots and pans. The last time she had even opened it was a few weeks ago when she had contemplated grits one morning, only to visit the drive-through at McDonald's for an Egg McMuffin.

It was a shame, indeed. This kitchen had birthed more delectable meals than most people ate in their entire lifetime. Her grandmother had taught her more than her fair share of recipes, and if she put her mind to it, Sienna knew she could probably whip something up.

Sienna's lips thinned with annoyance as she conjured the image of Toby standing in her office, licking his lips. He was the one who had her feeling guilty about not carrying on the tradition of her grandmother's cooking.

Maybe she could . . .

Nah. Cooking would require time and effort, two things she could not devote to food tonight. She had something bigger on her plate. She had to find a way to make Aria Jordan a star.

Closing the pantry door, Sienna headed for the phone. Pizza Hut was on speed dial.

Chapter Six

"So, man, are you ready for tonight?"

Standing at the mirror in the bathroom of Jonathan's St. Charles Avenue condominium, Toby finished buttoning the last of the buttons on his shirt, then went to work on the two at his wrists.

"Shouldn't I be asking you that question?"

"I'm cool as ice. I know everything is going to be perfect," Jonathan said as he moved away from the door and into the bathroom. He picked up the bottle of moisturizer and squirted a dime-size amount into his palm, rubbed his hands together and then smoothed them over his close cut hair.

"This bathroom isn't big enough for the both of us," Toby said. "And, not trying to jinx you or anything, but how do you know everything is going to go off without a hitch?"

"I prayed for it," Jonathan said. "Works every time."

"I can't argue with that. I need to remember that I have that option."

"That's the only option that matters."

"I know. I know. Have you been hanging around with my mom, or something?"

"She's a smart woman."

"A smart woman who can also cook. She wants you to come over for dinner tomorrow night."

"I'm there." Jonathan glanced at his watch. "It's almost that time. I need to get down to the club."

Toby held out his hand, and when Jonathan grabbed it, he pulled his friend close and patted him on the back.

"It's going to be good," he said.

"I feel it," Jonathan said, reciprocating the embrace. "And don't worry about Aria. She's about to blow up. I'm just lucky she's using my place as her starting ground."

Once Jonathan left, Toby turned back to the mirror. Gripping the sides of the bathroom counter, he stared hard at his reflection. Sometimes he was unsure he even knew the person staring back at him. The life he now lived was so drastically different from what he had envisioned.

How had he ended up here? What made him think he could succeed in the music industry? He didn't know a damn thing about music. Yet, here he was. About to launch a star.

Was it just a lucky break?

Did it even matter?

Luck or not, all that should matter is that with the right marketing strategy and enough exposure, Aria Jordan could be the next big thing. He was due. He'd had enough of the unlucky ones.

Unlucky breaks. He knew about those, didn't he?

Toby nearly laughed out loud. It was either that or put his fist through the mirror. He didn't care what anybody said, he was still bitter. He missed playing basketball. He missed the rush he got when he ran out onto the court at the start of the game, high-fiving his teammates. He ached to experience, just one more time, the crowd's excitement when he slam-dunked the ball over an opponent's head. He used to live for that stuff. Now, every time Toby thought about the accident his resentment was reinforced.

But he was not thinking about the accident. Not tonight.

Tonight was the start of a new beginning. He was strong. Resilient. Tonight, the lemons in his life would finally start to make some sweet tasting lemonade. And he was ready to drink it up.

Nervous excitement caused a shiver to race down Toby's back. He could barely grip the razor.

In less than a week, circumstances had radically changed. Lord knows he had not prayed as much as he should have, but somebody must have been looking out for him all the same. It was too perfect to be coincidence. Having Marshall Keller-man spot Aria right before the opening of Jonathan's club was an act of God. Her performance tonight was mutually beneficial to both of them. Jonathan's advertising was certain to bring in a huge crowd, and Aria's performance, which Toby had no doubt would be stellar, would bring subsequent business to The Hard Court. It was perfect.

And with Sienna's brilliance behind it all . . .

Sienna had impressed the heck out of him. He should not be surprised. Sienna excelled at whatever she put her mind to. It had always been that way. But it was still funny to see little Cee Cee play the grown-up professional.

And, damn, but she had grown.

Toby thought back to Jasmine's graduation picnic, and the feeling that had gripped his chest when he first spotted Si-enna in that airy sundress. She still had the body of an athlete, with defined muscles in her arms and her calves, but her body had become more delicate. Delicate looked really, *really* good on her.

Remembering the scrawny girl with cornrows and a bas-ketball permanently tucked in the crook of her arm, Toby could have never imagined she would turn into the woman she had become. Even on those few occasions when he'd seen her during one of his rare trips home, Toby couldn't remembering her being this fine. Or, maybe he just hadn't paid attention.

He passed a final glance in the mirror then exited the bathroom and picked up the freshly pressed linen jacket that matched his bone-colored slacks. The dark brown silk shirt and patterned tie were the perfect complement to the ensemble.

Because The Hard Court was centrally located on the edges of the French Quarters, where Dauphine Street met Esplanade Avenue, it took him only fifteen minutes to get to the club. At just after 9:00 p.m., there was not a full house yet, but it was well known that the party didn't get started in New Orleans until nearly midnight. Considering that, the crowd was a respectable size.

He was hoping for the club's success almost as much as he was pulling for his own. Jonathan had helped him through some of the toughest times of his life; days when he had thought about giving up. Days when he had desperately missed the best friend he had left back home in New Orleans. In a way, Jonathan had taken Sienna's place as confidant. Yet, there were still some things he would not disclose to Jonathan that he would not have had a problem sharing with Sienna.

Not anymore, though. These days, there was an indescribable tension that stretched between him and Sienna like a valley between mountain peaks. It was strange to not have the companionship they once shared. Maybe now that they were working together things would get back to normal.

But tonight was about The Hard Court. Jonathan was like a brother, and like his blood brothers, Toby wanted to see him succeed.

Since Aria was not scheduled to perform until 10:00 p.m., Toby decided to stroll around the club and play spy. Hopefully he could glean some insights from club-goers that Jonathan could use when making future adjustments. He went over to the bar, and was not there more than a minute before someone clamped an arm across his shoulder. He looked back, finding Jonathan.

"Looking good," Toby said by way of greeting.

"I wasn't expecting this many people so early in the evening. The kitchen has been hopping."

Toby had fully agreed with Jonathan's decision to turn the club's second floor into a trendy bistro. During his clubbing days, he had spent many an hour driving around, trying to find something to eat after a night of club hopping. The Hard Court's patrons had to go no farther than the glass enclosed elevator or the curving staircase when they were ready to leave the party atmosphere in exchange for light conversation and a decent meal. The bistro's menu ranged from tasty appetizers, like Buffalo wings and cheese-slathered potato skins, to succulent pasta dishes.

"I could use a little something myself," Toby said, rubbing his stomach. "I've been so nervous about tonight's performance that I haven't eaten anything all day."

"I'm way ahead of you. I've got a table secured upstairs."

Toby turned to follow Jonathan, then stopped as he spotted Sienna striding in from the front entrance. At least he *thought* it was Sienna.

"Good God," he heard Jonathan say.

His thoughts exactly.

What she wore gave the phrase "Little Black Dress" brand new meaning. The dress was damn near nonexistent. As she came closer, Toby noticed the straps holding up the bodice were even thinner than spaghetti. The fact that she had mile long legs was undisputable, but in a dress that barely reached mid-thigh, those legs looked as tall as the Empire State Building.

Unwillingly, he acknowledged the accelerated beat of his pulse. Feeling like an incestuous fiend, he tried to block out the thoughts that had jumped to the forefront of his mind at the sight of Sienna.

Where in the hell had she even gotten a dress like that?

The skimpiest thing Toby had ever seen her wear was a one-piece bathing suit that had a fluffy skirt covering the bottom.

Sienna came to stand before him and Jonathan.

"Well, I'm here."

"You most certainly are," Jonathan said. Stretching out his hand, he continued, "I'm Jonathan Campbell, proprietor. And you are?"

Sienna looked from Jonathan to Toby, smiling. "I'm Sienna Culpepper."

Jonathan's jaw dropped. "*You're* Sienna?" He turned his incredulous stare on Toby. "This is not what I call a tomboy."

Sienna cut her eyes in Toby's direction. He shrugged. "Well, you were a tomboy back when we were in school."

"She's not anymore," Jonathan commented. "Would you care for something to eat? Toby and I were just going up to get something from the restaurant."

Sienna placed her hand in the crook of Jonathan's proffered arm. "I'm starved. I worked late today and only had time to grab a stale energy bar that's been sitting in my desk drawer for months."

"Then, by all means, you must try the sautéed shrimps over angel hair pasta."

Sienna closed her eyes and let out a seductive purr. "That sounds wonderful."

Toby's heart skipped three beats at her sensuous-sounding moan. He was torn between taking off his jacket and covering up her half naked body, and finding a dark corner and relieving her of what was left of that dress.

Whoa! Where the hell had that come from?

To even think of taking off Sienna's clothes was . . . well . . . unthinkable. It was more than unthinkable; it was downright sick.

Toby caught the subtle expression on Jonathan's face, and a cold knot formed in his stomach. He knew all too well what the gleam in his ex-teammate's eyes meant. How many times had they gone scoping for women after games? Toby had participated in enough of that locker room talk to know that he did not want Sienna's name associated with it.

And to think he had actually thought about hooking her up with Jonathan? Chalk it up to temporary insanity. But he was in his right frame of mind now. He would lay things out for Jonathan as soon as he could get him alone.

Sienna led the way up the wide, winding staircase, with Jonathan following and Toby bringing up the rear. At the top of the staircase, Jonathan took the lead, guiding them to a small round table in the corner. It was lit by one of the basketball wall lights.

"The décor is absolutely amazing," Sienna said.

"Thank Toby," Jonathan said.

"Toby?" Sienna turned to him. "Since when do you decorate?"

"I gave him Indina's number," Toby clarified.

Nodding, Sienna laughed. "That sounds more like it. She sure outdid herself this time. As much as I love basketball, I could have never imagined it could be used in such a tasteful theme."

"I'm happy with how it worked out," Jonathan said, nodding as his eyes roamed over the bistro.

"It looks like everyone is enjoying it." Sienna followed his gaze around the top floor. "I'm not sure if it is the novelty of this being a new club, or what, but to have this kind of crowd an hour before the opening performance is pretty amazing."

"Speaking of that performance, did you have a chance to drop in on Aria?" Jonathan directed his question to Toby.

He shook his head, taking a sip of his drink. "Not yet. She gets nervous if I hang around her too much before a show. I'll stick my head in a few minutes before she goes on just to give her a little encouragement."

"I heard her rehearsing earlier today," Jonathan said. "With the jokes they have signing record deals today, I don't know why this girl has not been discovered yet."

"Excuse me," Toby said. "She *has* been discovered. We're just taking the scenic route to stardom."

The waitress, cloaked in a sequin basketball jersey dress, took their order.

As they sipped on drinks while their food order was being prepared, Jonathan laid the charm on Sienna as thick as peanut butter on sliced bread. And, worst, she seemed to be falling for it hook, line, and sinker.

Why should he care? Sienna was a big girl. She could take care of herself. What was wrong with two of his best friends hooking up?

It no longer seemed like the brilliant idea Toby had once thought.

"So, Jonathan, of all the business ventures you could have chosen, what made you choose a nightclub?" Sienna asked.

Jonathan tilted his shoulder in a nonchalant shrug. "I had been on the club scene for a while, and had grown tired of it. I figured there were a lot of people out there like me, so I thought, why not open the kind of place I'd like to go to after a hard day at the office."

"That makes sense."

"What made you go into marketing?" he returned.

"I've always been good at making the mundane seem magnificent and putting a positive spin on anything, no matter how disastrous."

Jonathan shot out a bark of laughter. "You should have become an image consultant. You could have made a killing in D.C."

"Is that where you're from?"

Jonathan nodded.

Toby didn't trust the smile that tipped up the corner of his ex-teammate's mouth. The two of them had practiced that smile together. Toby knew exactly what it did to women.

A Brian McKnight ballad cruised out of the speakers tucked unassumingly against the bistro's tall ceiling.

"Oh, I haven't heard this song in years," Sienna purred.

There she was with the purring again. Didn't she know what those little seductive sounds did to a man?

"Do you want to dance?" Jonathan asked.

"In the restaurant? We can't do that."

"Remember, you're talking to the owner, baby." Jonathan kicked the smile up a notch.

"Our dinner will be here in a minute," Toby reminded them, his voice terse.

"We're not going to Africa," Jonathan said. "Just right over there." He gestured to a miniscule area between the only set of empty tables in the restaurant. It guaranteed a very snug dance.

"Watch my purse, Toby," Sienna said as she placed her hand in Jonathan's and allowed him to pull her from her chair.

Toby watched in frustrated silence as Jonathan placed his hand on the small of Sienna's back. As low cut as the dress was, Jonathan had no choice but to touch skin. All Toby could think about was how soft it must feel.

Where were these thoughts coming from? Sienna was like a sister. Of course, she wasn't his *real* sister, and Toby was enough of a man to acknowledge a beautiful woman when he saw one. And tonight, in that dress, Sienna wasn't just beautiful, she was amazing.

He glanced around the restaurant, searching for someone who even compared. A half dozen fine women sat two tables down. A couple of them were pretty cute. One was damn cute.

Toby caught her eye. She smiled.

Now, that's what he was talking about.

It had been way too long since he had made any type of connection with a woman. That's probably why his mind had been focused on Sienna. She was about the only female, other than his mother and Aria, that he had been in contact with in the last couple of months. He needed to find himself some additional options.

And the first option of the night was sending some pretty serious signals with the look she shot his way.

Toby nodded toward another small area that had been created between two tables that had just been vacated. The woman smiled. She whispered something in the ear of the friend on her left, who looked over at Toby.

Toby grinned. She could be next.

Opportunity numero uno rose from the table and saun-tered toward him like sex for sale. The night's outlook got a whole lot brighter.

Toby stood and matched her seductive smile. "Hello. I'm Tobias." He reached out his hand.

"Amneris." She placed her hand in his, and Toby brought it up and offered it a gentle kiss.

"A beautiful name for a beautiful woman. Would you care to dance?" he asked, just as the ballad ended. Thankfully, the DJ was in his corner, slipping on another slow tune.

Toby settled his hands at the curves of her waist, and irra-tionally hoped Sienna and Jonathan were both catching an eyeful. He cautioned a quick glance their way.

The two were rocking from side to side, lost in conversation.

"So, Tobias, are you from around here?" the woman in his arms asked. What was her name again?

"Born and raised," Toby answered. "Although I've moved around a little bit over the past few years."

"What do you do, if you don't mind my asking?"

Toby looked down and realized she really was hot. If he had any sense, he'd get his mind off those other two and con-centrate on the sure thing pressing her body more firmly against his.

"I manage recording artists," he answered. "I also do a little producing and songwriting."

"Yeah, right," she said with a look that said she didn't believe a word of that. "Is that the answer you give every woman you pick up?"

Toby laughed. "It's the truth. One of my artists is per-forming tonight." He glanced at his watch. "In just about a half hour, actually." Toby noted the waitress bringing three steaming plates of pasta to their table.

"Are you talking about Aria Jordan?"

He nodded.

"That girl can sing. I was too excited when I heard she would be here tonight."

"Let her know it when she walks out on stage."

"I most definitely will. So, you're really a record producer. That must be exciting." She pressed a little closer.

Jonathan and Sienna headed for the table.

Stop thinking about them.

The song ended and his dance partner reluctantly pulled away, dragging her hands down his arms in a slow caress. "I should probably get back to my table. We're celebrating my sister's birthday tonight."

"Tell her I said happy birthday," Toby smiled.

"I will. And . . . " She slipped her fingers into the low cut bodice of her skin tight dress and came out with a small, folded paper. She certainly was prepared, wasn't she? "If you're looking for something to do later, why don't you hit me on my cell?"

Baby girl was definitely a sure thing. But, for reasons he would probably debate for the rest of his natural born life, Toby was more turned off than anything. What was up with that? When had he ever turned down guaranteed sex?

Toby gestured toward his table where Sienna and Jonathan had already started on their food. "I haven't eaten since yesterday, and if I don't get to it now, I probably won't have time to eat anything until after Aria's performance."

"That's fine. Just. Call me." She stood on the tips of her toes and kissed his cheek. "I will blow your mind," she whispered in his ear.

Have mercy.

It had been a long time since he'd had his mind, or anything else, blown. Toby sent her a smile and headed in the opposite direction to his table.

"Welcome back," Sienna said as he approached.

"I was about to send for a bucket of ice from the bar. That was some hot and heavy dancing," Jonathan said.

Yeah, he could say the same about the two of them. Thankfully, Sienna had not pushed all up on Jonathan while they danced. Toby knew he would have lost it.

"She did get kind of close, didn't she," Toby said, taking a bite of his pasta before he was even seated.

"You had better watch yourself, Toby. I doubt Aria would

be too happy hearing about you snuggled up with some random chick."

Here she was again, mentioning Aria, as if she were his girlfriend or something.

The lightbulb went on.

Damn, he could be stupid sometimes. Hadn't Eli thought the same thing? Maybe it was because it was the furthest thing from the truth that it didn't even cross Toby's mind that people would automatically assume he and Aria had something going on. It's not as if he intentionally flirted with her. Sure, they kid around a bit—those days in the studio could get long—but Toby had never intimated to Aria that she was anything more than his client.

Before he could correct Sienna's erroneous assessment of the relationship between him and Aria, Toby heard, "Mr. Holmes?" It was the waitress in the sparkly jersey dress. "Ms. Jordan is asking for you."

"Hmm." Sienna murmured, a knowing smile creasing her eyes. "You see, she's psychic. You are in for it."

"It's not like that," he said as he rose from the table.

"You need me?" Jonathan asked.

"No. Finish your dinner."

Unsure what could have Aria calling for him when she usually didn't want to see him before a performance, Toby practically raced to the back of the club where Jonathan's office was located. He rapped on the door.

"Aria?"

"Come in." Toby heard the slight tremor in her voice. He found Aria perched upon Jonathan's desk, her fisted hands rubbing against her thighs.

"What's wrong?" Coming to her side, he put his arm around her shoulder and gave her a squeeze.

"I'm just a little nervous."

"Why? You've played to bigger crowds than this."

"I know, but tonight's different. This is my first performance since being picked up by the show. The cameras aren't even out there yet, and I'm still nervous."

"Even if they're not there tonight, you will eventually have to perform in front of the cameras, Aria. And in front of much larger audiences." Toby stepped in front of her. He grasped her shoulders and stared into her eyes. "Tell me one thing. Is this what you really want?"

Aria nodded.

Toby shook his head. "No. You tell me. Do you want this?"

"Yes."

"Do you want everything that goes with it? Do you think you can handle the press? The fans?"

"I think so. Maybe."

He shook his head again. "There are no maybes. Either you can do it or you can't. We'll drop out of the show if you're not ready."

Toby hoped she was, because he sure as hell was ready. Turning down this opportunity would be the absolute hardest thing he would ever do.

"I'm ready," Aria said.

"Are you sure?"

"Yes. I can do this. I promise I won't let you down."

"Don't do it for me. This is all about you."

"But it *is* about us," she said. A sense of dread shot down Toby's spine at the way she said *us*. Maybe Sienna was not the only one getting mixed signals. "Besides," Aria continued. "This is your friend's big night, too. When I get up on that stage, I won't be thinking of just me."

There was a knock at the door.

"Hey." Jonathan stuck his head in. "Everything all right in here?"

"We're good," Toby answered.

"Okay, then. It's about that time."

Toby focused his gaze on Aria. "Forget about everybody else. Just do what you do best."

She nodded. "Okay."

He turned back to Jonathan. "All right, man. We're ready."

Chapter Seven

Sienna dug into the pitch-black earth with the shovel, working around in a circle until she was able to lift the shrub out of the ground. She picked it up at the base and placed the roots in the soil she'd prepared in a huge terra cotta pot. Packing the dirt over the tiny roots, Sienna closed her eyes and relished in the sensation of the cool earth sliding between her fingers.

It had been a hellish week. Hellish, but exciting. The pressure of having her own account had kept her awake at night, devising innovative strategies to make Aria Jordan a household name. She had come up with a couple of ideas that she hoped would broaden Aria's appeal to a wider range of audiences, but she still had not found that one thing that would really make her shine.

Last night's performance at The Hard Court had verified that the girl had the talent. Her spots at local clubs were a great way to grow a following, but they were working on an accelerated timetable. Sienna needed to find something that would catch the attention of more than just a few hundred people.

One thing. If only she could find that *one* thing.

Her job was one problem, but it wasn't the only stress maker in her life. Seeing Aria and Toby together added its own dimension of distress. As much as Sienna hated the thought of the two of them together, she was offended by the way Toby treated Aria. As a manager and producer he was everything the girl could want, but as a boyfriend?

If being his girlfriend entailed Toby practically ignoring her and showing no type of affection whatsoever in public, Sienna was better off by herself.

Aria's feelings could not be more obvious if she wore a T-shirt with *I "heart" Toby* across her chest, but Toby hardly ever returned the smiles she sent his way. Sienna hoped he paid her a little more attention in private. Then again, she didn't want to think about the two of them in private.

Sienna packed the last bit of soil around the shrub's base and turned to her rose bushes. She slid the pruning shears from the protective sleeve and knelt in the grass. Hers was one of the few front lawns in the Faurbourg Marigny. One of the neighborhood's unique features was that most of the homes butted right up to the sidewalk.

A honking horn interrupted Sienna's peace. Toby's midnight blue Acura pulled up the short driveway next to her car.

"What are you doing out here?" he yelled from the open driver's side window.

"Dyeing my hair," Sienna sarcastically replied, shielding her eyes from the sun.

"I've been calling your cell phone all morning."

She motioned toward the house. "It's on the charger. This battery is going out, so I'm having to charge it up every day."

"Buy a new battery. There are some parts of this city you do not want to be caught in without your cell phone."

"I know. I'm going to trade the phone in when I get a chance. Now, what was so pressing that you had to drive halfway across the city at," she looked at her watch, "nine in the morning."

"I had a revelation," Toby answered as he strolled up to her.

"Care to elaborate?" Sienna asked. She rose, dusting dirt from her hands.

"How do you feel about attending the Greater New Foundation Full Gospel Baptist Church tomorrow? Damn, that's a mouthful."

Sienna slapped him on the arm. "You do not say 'church' and 'damn' in the same breath."

"You just did."

Sienna made a *get on with it* gesture with her hand. "What about the church?"

"Their eleven o'clock service is televised throughout the entire Gulf South. As far as Pensacola."

Sienna knew where this was headed. And she was *so* there.

"Please tell me Aria grew up singing gospel."

"Since she was six years old."

Yes. This was a market they had not even considered.

"How do we get her on the program?"

"The great Margo Holmes to the rescue." Toby's face lit up with a smile. "One of the ladies in some pottery class Mama just started attends the church. She was bragging about Aria and the show—"

"Of course," Sienna interjected.

"Of course," Toby agreed. "And the woman suggested Aria sing at their eleven o'clock service."

"Where's the church?"

"Out in Slidell. Can you make it?"

Sienna nodded. She was astounded that she had not thought about the gospel arena, as popular as the music was these days. She could only imagine Aria Jordan's soulful voice belting out a gospel spiritual. After her performance last night, Sienna had to give the girl her due. She was better than half the singers out there today.

And, since he was the one who had discovered her, it was only fair to give Toby his due, also.

"She really is amazing, Toby," Sienna said with sincerity.

"I know. Mama comes through for me even when I'm not expecting her to."

"No, I mean Aria. This is going to work out for you. Even if it's not with this show."

His smiled broadened. "So, you enjoyed the performance last night, huh?"

"Of course. The entire club was in an uproar. She's going to be a big draw for Jonathan."

Toby nodded. "He made me guarantee her performances over the next few weeks."

"That's excellent. It's the best way to establish a following—one that's outside of the teenage demographic. I think we've got a pretty good handle on that age group."

"And this church thing is going to tap into another segment of the population."

"One we never even contemplated," Sienna agreed, unable to contain a matching smile.

"Yeah, I may have to buy Mama a new Sunday hat for coming up with this idea."

"You know, it might not be a bad idea if we could get her in on a brainstorming session. I'll bet if we get your mom and brothers and maybe even Jonathan together, we can think of a bunch of untapped audiences. We've got to think outside the box with this, Toby. We don't have time to sit around and wait for inspiration to strike."

"Good thinking."

"Naturally," Sienna teased. "You're paying good money for me to come up with these brilliant ideas."

"I was thinking about that. Since you're the one handling Aria's account, maybe I could fire MDF, Inc., and you can just continue on as a friend," Toby winked.

"Not on your life," Sienna laughed. "C'mon, help me with this wheelbarrow."

Carrying the shovel, she led him around the side of the house where she had filled half the bed of her grandmother's rusty wheelbarrow with a coffee ground and table scrap compost.

"Since when do you do yard work?" Toby asked. He went around and gripped the handles of the wheelbarrow.

"Since I got a yard of my own," Sienna quipped. "Bring it around the front for me. I need to get some fertilizer from the shed."

Heading to the back of her property, Sienna went to the small aluminum building she'd purchased at Home Depot to replace the wooden shed that had been blown to pieces by Hurricane Katrina. She retrieved the bag of fertilizer and a trowel from the wall-mounted tool shelf.

When Sienna returned to the front of the house, she found Toby already scooping the compost mixture and situating it around the edge of the flower bed.

"Since when do *you* do yard work?" she asked.

"Since five minutes ago," he answered. He looked around

at her composition of shrubs and perennials. "This is really nice, Cee Cee. Granny Elise would be happy with what you've done."

She let her eyes roam over the landscaping she'd put so much time and energy into making her own. "I think so, too. Granny always wanted a rose garden, but she never got around to it. This is sort of like a tribute. Makes me feel closer to her, you know."

Toby nodded and they both stared at each other. Silence stretched between them like a long winding road. Sienna's level of discomfort grew with each millisecond of excruciating quiet.

Finally, Toby broke the connection. Rising from where he knelt in the dirt, he dusted his hands off and planted them on his hips. "Sienna, when did this happen?"

"What?" But she knew what. It was painfully obvious.

"I never imagined a time in my life when I would feel awkward around you. I've been trying to pretend everything is okay, but it's not."

"I know," she shrugged. "But what can we do about it? Friendships grow apart all the time."

"I know that, but us?"

Another shrug. "I guess if you don't work at it, even the closest relationships are going to fade. I admit I never thought it could happen to us, either. I was closer to you than I was to my own sisters. But—" Sienna added water to the soil. She mixed in a handful of fertilizer and tamped it down around the base of the flowers.

"At least you're home," she said after several somber moments. And for the first time since his return, Sienna made certain the depth of her feelings were evident in her eyes, if only he was willing to see them.

"I've missed you, Toby," she said, nearly aching with the breadth of emotions rioting through her. Would he finally understand just what it is she felt for him?

"I missed you, too," Toby answered. "I haven't had anyone to give me a hard time for no reason at all. You're the only friend who can do that." His playful punch on the arm was like a fist to the gut.

Sienna pasted on a smile. It took effort to keep her disappointment hidden. "That's my specialty, right?"

"Maybe we can work on being the friends we used to be, huh?"

"I'd love that more than anything," Sienna answered.

At least she knew she could lie with a straight face.

Sienna jumped as her cellular phone rang. Waving at Candi as the assistant drove out of MDF's employee parking garage, Sienna pulled the phone out of her purse and checked the tiny screen to see who was calling. It was a number she didn't recognize.

She pressed the button with the little green phone receiver on it and put the phone to her ear.

"This is Sienna," she answered.

"Hey, I'm glad I caught you."

"Toby? Where are you calling from?"

"Jonathan's club. Look, can you stop at Mama's tonight? I've been making some phone calls and scored two more spots for Aria for this week. I've got a couple of ideas that I want to run by you before I send anything out to the radio stations."

"Can't we handle this over the phone? I'm supposed to have dinner with Ivana in an hour."

"You're the one who suggested just this morning that we brainstorm outside of the office. Bring your sister over, too. Mama won't mind. She's making dinner for Jonathan. You know how Mama is when it comes to food. There'll be enough to feed the entire neighborhood."

She certainly could use some of Margo Holmes's cooking. It would be a hundred times better than anything she ordered in a restaurant. And it was free.

"Okay, I'll be there. But I'm warning you, Toby, I don't want you pushing Jonathan and me together as soon as I get to the house, alright?"

"Maybe you should take your own advice."

"What's that supposed to mean?" Sienna asked.

"Nothing," Toby answered.

She knew she had not imagined the sharpness in his voice, but decided not to inquire further. "Is seven-thirty okay? I need to drop by Ivana's and pick her up."

"Cool. See you in a little while."

Sienna finally made it to her car. Locking her purse in the trunk—sans the cellular phone she kept in her hand—she got in and took off for Ivana's, hoping her sister still remembered their dinner date. It was a crapshoot where Ivana was concerned. Her older sister had no problem blowing her off if there was some worthy cause that needed her help.

Sienna didn't mind. It was what made Ivana special. Her sister would give her last dime, the food from her mouth, and the clothes on her back—all at the same time—if it meant someone less fortunate would not have to suffer. That's why Sienna took it personally when people called her sister a witch doctor or a wacko, or any of the other horrible names that were used to describe Ivana. Some even by their own mother.

Sienna's hands tightened involuntarily on the steering wheel.

She pulled up to the shotgun house in the Treme neighborhood that Ivana shared with her best friend from college, Lelo, who was out front watering one of the huge ferns on the porch.

"Hey, girl," Lelo called.

"Hi there. Is my sister home, or did she ditch me?" Sienna answered, making her way up the concrete walkway.

"She's here," Lelo said. "So, how is the job, Miss Big Time Marketing Executive?"

"It's pretty good. I was just given my very own account."

"Congratulations, sweetie," Lelo said, sitting the plastic watering can on the porch ledge and enveloping Sienna in a hug. "You're going to own that company sooner than you know."

"I like the way you think," Sienna laughed.

"You made it," Ivana called from inside the house. Even

with the meshed screened door partially obscuring her view, Sienna could still make out the wild colors her sister wore. Ivana had her own style, and she was not ashamed to show it no matter what others thought about her.

"Give me a minute," Ivana said. "I need to get something from my room."

Sienna opened the screened door and entered the house. The strong scent of patchouli smacked her in the face. Ivana and Lelo were best friends, but their individual tastes clashed unmercifully, creating a house with some of the most mismatched décor Sienna had ever seen.

Ivana's penchant for bold colors and patterns rioted against Lelo's frilly lace and soft pastels. At first sight, it was hard for the brain to comprehend just what was so off about it. If she stayed for very long, she developed a headache.

Sienna walked to the back of the house toward Ivana's room. She found her sister at the mirror, looping a strand of faux pearls over her head. She wore her gorgeous mass of hair in its natural and most beautiful state tonight, free flowing over her shoulders and down her back. They both had a tall, slim build, but Sienna had always envied her sister's elegance. While she'd always considered herself tall and lanky, Ivana was willowy and graceful.

"You look awesome," Sienna told her. "Although, it's a bit much for a drive-through window." She laughed when Ivana's middle finger shot up, flipping her off. "I can't believe you did that."

"That's what you get for thinking of taking me to a drive-through for dinner," Ivana answered.

"Doesn't matter. There's been a change of plans." Sienna walked over to the bed and fell facedown into the soft, well-worn comforter. She kicked one shoe off and left the other dangling from her big toe. She turned her head to Ivana. "We've been invited to dinner at Margo Holmes's house."

"Really?" Ivana gave her a raised eyebrow stare through the mirror. "What did little Jasmine do, lose a tooth?"

Sienna grinned. "No. It's a long story, but to give you the short version, I'm heading an account for this singer Toby discovered. There are some things we need to go over that couldn't wait until Monday."

"You're dumping me on our traditional dinner night for business?"

"Call it payback for all the times *you've* bailed on *me*."

Ivana nodded. "I deserve it. And if your payback involves Margo's cooking, you can pay me back any time."

Sienna picked up the catalog she'd spotted on the night stand. Thumbing through the pages and grimacing at the clothing that was too outdated for a woman Ivana's age, she asked, "What's happening with that house in the Quarter you're trying to save?"

"Don't ask."

"What happened?" Sienna tossed the catalog back on the night stand. "The last time I talked to you, you said the contractor was ready to give in."

"The contractor was at his breaking point, but the new tenant will not be so easy to manipulate."

"You met him?"

"Unfortunately."

"Just keep at it," Sienna encouraged. "I have total faith in the tenacity of Ivana 'The Pitbull' Culpepper."

Ivana laughed. "I don't think I've earned the nickname 'Pitbull' yet."

"Oh, yeah? I'll bet that contractor would beg to differ."

Ivana smiled at her through the mirror. She picked up an old-fashioned perfume diffuser and misted herself.

"I'm ready," Ivana announced. She turned, and sashayed back and forth, her long turquoise skirt bellowing, while the oversized sleeves of her gauzy white blouse mimicked a downed fighter signaling surrender.

Sienna speared her with a curious glance. "Are you trying to land a man?"

Ivana's hazel-colored eyes shot daggers. "Shut up."

Sienna burst out laughing. "Come on. One of Toby's college

friends is in town. Hopefully, Margo made some gumbo to welcome him to the city."

"If only we could be so lucky."

Ivana groaned as the hem of her skirt caught in the car door. That's why she didn't own a car; they clashed with her usual attire. She'd ruined many a skirt by getting it caught in a car door. She'd even lost one that way. *That* had been embarrassing.

The rich aroma of home cooking filtered out of Margo Holmes's open kitchen window, greeting them in the front yard.

"Girl, come on," Sienna said. "I smell jambalaya."

Ivana followed her along the graveled walkway toward the back door, but even the delicious smelling food was not enough enticement to put an extra pep in her step. She loved the Holmeses as if they were her own family, but just like her own family, they thought she was weird. Of course, Margo had never said anything to her face, but Ivana knew better than to think she didn't get whispered about when she left a room.

She was the fruitcake. Sylvia Culpepper's lost cause.

If it were not for Sienna and her unwavering support, Ivana would have probably cut off all ties to her family long ago. They just didn't understand her. Nobody understood her, except for her sisters in the struggle to save New Orleans's misguided souls.

She was a voodoo priestess, and proud of it. She fought for what she believed in, and did everything within her power to preserve the increasingly dissipating history of the *real* voodoo of this city.

But it still hurt when people misjudged her.

Ivana followed Sienna through the screened door and pass the dozens of plants overtaking the back porch. A beautiful sign with *Margo's Jungle* hand-carved into the wood hung over the door that led to the kitchen.

"Come on in." She heard Margo say from within the house. Closing the door behind her, Ivana took a deep breath and put on her confident, talk-about-me-all-you-want-I'm-still-my-own-woman face. As much as their cautious looks and whispered comments hurt, she refused to hide her true self.

"Ivana, honey. It's been so long since I've seen you." Margo was alone in the kitchen, but male voices could be heard coming from one of the front rooms of the house. "You look wonderful. I love that color on you," Margo said, holding out Ivana's long skirt.

"Thank you," Ivana said, bending down to give the extremely petite woman a hug. "It's great to see you. Thanks for inviting us."

"You know my kitchen is always open," Margo said with a wave of her hand. "The two of you arrived just in time. Tobias and Jonathan have been waiting in the living room like a couple of starving dogs. If you all could help me bring this to the dining table"—she handed a bowl of steaming, aromatic jambalaya to Sienna and gestured with her head for Ivana to grab the large bowl of green salad—"we can start dinner."

The dining table was set with mismatched plates, silverware, and plastic go-cups like the ones thrown from the parade floats at Mardi Gras.

"I apologize for the place settings. Jasmine was here with Alex earlier and she begged to set the table. And you know I was not letting that little girl touch my good dishes."

"At least she wants to help," Sienna said.

"Help, my foot. Miss Thang had the nerve to demand five dollars after she was done."

Ivana laughed, but inside, she could not control the small prick of pain that pierced her chest at the thought of Margo's beautiful granddaughter. She longed for a child of her own.

"Tobias? Jonathan?" Margo called from the door of the dining room. "Dinner is ready." She came back to the table. "Take a seat, girls. They should be out in just a minute."

Before Ivana had a chance to sit, Toby Holmes came through the door that led to the living room.

"Hey there, Mrs. Trump," Toby said, greeting her as he had since Donald Trump was married to his ex-wife, Ivana.

She had forgotten how tall he was. Ivana told him so as they embraced. "Somebody should have told you to stop growing, Toby."

"I'm the same size I was the last time you saw me."

"I don't think so. Any man that dwarfs me is too tall for his own good."

"Where's Jonathan?" Margo asked.

"Washing up. He should be out in a minute."

"What about Aria?" Sienna asked from the seat she'd taken at the table. Ivana rounded the table and sat beside her.

"Aria's not coming, is she, Mama?" Toby sent raised eyebrows Margo's way, who shrugged and said, "Not if you didn't invite her."

"I didn't think Aria needed to be here for this discussion. She's still trying to recover from her performance at The Hard Court."

"But she did so well," Sienna said. "I couldn't tell she was nervous."

"She gets like that sometimes, but once she's on stage, she's good to go."

"She was definitely impressive," Sienna admitted.

"How did the club turn out? Did Indina do a good job?" Margo asked.

"It's first class, all the way. But that's to be expected with Jonathan. He never does anything half-ass. Sorry, Mama," Toby said.

Ivana smiled at Toby's apology. The Holmes boys did not use questionable language in front of their mother. It was refreshing to see that type of respect still in place.

Toby shook his head. "After last night's success, I don't know how I'm going to handle that boy. Jonathan's head is big enough as it is."

Ivana discreetly rubbed the side of her own head. It was still throbbing as a result of the confrontation from a few days ago with a bigheaded attorney who was destroying one of the first homes that was ever used as a haven for the city's sick.

She needed to devise another tactic. She'd beaten the contractor nearly to his breaking point. He'd been ready to crack; she knew it. But Ivana's instincts told her the building's new lessee would not be as easy to intimidate.

Her blood boiled just at the thought of his superciliousness.

She dropped her napkin on the floor and blamed him for that too. Her nerves had been on edge ever since she'd left his office. Ivana bent to retrieve the napkin, silently cursing her new foe.

Arrogant, overconfident . . .

"Here he comes," she heard Toby say, "Ivana, I want you to meet my buddy and teammate from St. John's—"

Bigheaded, egotistical . . .

"Jonathan Campbell."

Ivana raised her head and her heart stopped.

Lord Almighty, there he was. Her foe. Her arrogant, overconfident, bigheaded, egotistical foe. Her handsome-as-all-get-out foe.

Ivana could tell he recognized her instantly. The corner of his mouth lifted in a grin that sent a shot of something tingly straight to the pit of her stomach. He came around the table and captured Sienna's hand, placing a perfect kiss upon the back of it, all the while still staring at her with those keen brown eyes.

"How are you doing, Sienna?" he asked.

"Wonderful," Sienna answered. "Congratulations on last night."

"Thank you," he answered, then he turned to Ivana, and the grin escalated to a full wattage smile. The rush of nervous energy she'd experienced when she first met him came over her once again.

"And here is the second of the infamous Culpepper girls, Ivana Coleman," Toby introduced.

She inwardly cringed at hearing her married name. "I went back to Culpepper," Ivana corrected him.

Jonathan walked around the back of her chair and Ivana's heart rate multiplied. She needed a sip of water, but feared her hands would shake the liquid right out of the cup. Instead, Ivana put her elbows on the table and rested her chin on her folded hands, thwarting any plans he may have had of repeating the greeting he used on Sienna. She did not want this man's lips anywhere on her. *Really, she didn't*, Ivana told herself.

"Hello, Ivana."

Electric sparks raced down her back at the sound of his deep voice softly calling her name. He held out an extremely large palm the color of a rich caramel latte.

Ivana tipped her head to the side but kept her hands planted firmly under her chin. "Welcome to New Orleans," she said. She refused to lie and say she was happy to meet him because she most certainly was not.

His eyes sparkled with knowing amusement and she was sorry she even deigned to look at him at all.

"Thank you," he answered and walked around to the seat next to Toby. He didn't sit directly across from her, but with the small size of the Holmeses' table, he very well could have been in her lap for all the distance between them. Margo's cooking didn't seem all that appetizing anymore. Ivana would have given just about anything to leave.

"We didn't get a chance to talk much last night," Sienna said, placing her napkin in her lap and reaching for the spicy smelling dish. "How are you enjoying the city so far?"

"It's getting more and more interesting every day," Jonathan answered, still looking at Ivana. She shifted uncomfortably under his gaze.

"This isn't your first time here, is it?"

He finally turned his attention fully to Sienna. "I've been down a couple of times before, but not since Toby and I were in school."

"I was in Atlanta at the time," Sienna said.

He nodded, taking a sip from his plastic cup filled to the brim with iced tea. "Spellman. I remember Toby talking about how you passed on all those athletic scholarships and picked the academic one instead."

As they feasted on jambalaya, the conversation turned to both of Jonathan Campbell's new endeavors. Ivana's estimation of him dwindled with each syllable spoken. The man encompassed everything she loathed. By what she surmised from tonight's conversation, he was a power-hungry lawyer whose only concern was finding ways to fill his coffers.

Not only was he the attorney who was single-handedly ruining that beautiful house in the Quarter; he was also the proprietor of the monstrosity of a nightclub recently constructed on Esplanade Avenue. As if this city needed another place to provide liquor and loud music.

"So, what do you do, Ivana?"

Ivana jerked her head up, looking around the suddenly eerily quiet table. The question had come from Jonathan, who sat with that slip of a smile edging up the corner of his mouth.

"Ivana is a . . . umm . . . priestess," Toby provided.

"A priestess?"

"I'm a voodoo priestess," she clarified, raising her chin so high in the air she nearly caught a nosebleed. She would not let this slick-skinned lawyer make her feel ashamed of what she was. She'd faced enough ridicule from her ex-husband, Michael, and her own mother. She certainly would not flinch under the censure of this man whom she barely knew.

But there was no censure in his surprised gaze. His right brow quirked, he simply nodded. "Extremely interesting. I guess I should steer clear from you, then. I wouldn't want you to put a hex on me."

Ignorant fool. If she could cast hexes, she'd turn him into the jackass he was, complete with floppy ears and gigantic teeth.

Ivana settled for sending him a stare that said quite clearly "don't mess with me." She would leave him to his ill-informed ideas. He would have no interest in learning what the *real* voodoo of New Orleans stood for anyway. And it's not like she had never heard remarks such as his before. Ivana had dealt with them from the moment she joined the Cause. If she took the time out to actually explain the culture to everyone she met, she'd never get any work done.

The original voodoo did not operate the way history tended to portray; calling on evil spirits to wreak havoc on society. The *real* voodoo was a benevolent society who took care of the sick by utilizing the power of spirituality that was found inside all human beings. She and her sister priestesses simply had a better way of harnessing that power.

Unfortunately, people chose to believe lies and half-truths when it came to understanding her kind, and Ivana no longer had the energy to change their minds. She surely was not going to waste her breath on people like Jonathan Campbell, who obviously had no desire to resuscitate the city's less fortunate. Instead, he was more interested in destroying history for personal gain.

Ivana glanced at the old, but delicately cared for, grandfather clock in the corner. They hadn't been here a half hour. Toby and Sienna still had to talk business.

It was going to be a very long night.

Jonathan leaned back in the chair and mulled over the possible reasons behind his uncharacteristic reaction to the woman sitting across the table.

What was it about her that fascinated him so? Without a doubt, she was unlike any woman he'd ever encountered. She was different. A challenge.

Even though he never reached the NBA like Toby and a couple of his other teammates at St. John's, Jonathan never had to put forth much effort when it came to the fairer sex. As soon as most women discovered he was both single and a lawyer, they kicked their game into full gear. Neither his career nor his marital status seemed to matter to Ivana, and that intrigued the heck out of him.

Hell, maybe she *had* cast some sort of spell on him. Probably happened back at his office. That's why he couldn't think of anything but her.

Her scent had lingered in the lobby long after she had left on Thursday. After a while, Jonathan had grabbed his notes and legal tablet and set up shop at the parlor's coffee table. He'd wanted to enjoy her essence for as long as possible.

And now she sat less than three feet away, with nothing but a pine table and a pecan pie separating them. That and the chip the size of Gibraltar she held on her shoulder. Jonathan had watched her throughout the night. He couldn't help it. It was as if she held magnets in those astute brown eyes.

She had conversed with Margo while Toby and Sienna brought him in on the discussion of various alternatives to help promote Aria. But Jonathan found it hard to concentrate on much of anything, save for the woman sitting across the table.

She had tried not to look at him. In fact, she looked everywhere else—her food, Toby, the ceiling. But when her eyes happened to wander back his way, there was no mistaking her disgust. That was the one thing he did not want to elicit in this woman. And not because he was afraid she would fashion a little doll after him and prick it with needles. If Jonathan had his way, he would give Ivana Culpepper something much more exciting to do with her time than calling on spirits and trying to stop people from renovating old buildings.

Margo rose from the table. "Sorry to leave, but I promised Etta Louis I would help put together care packages the church is sending for the troops in the Middle East. I'll be right across the street," she said.

"Wait, Mama," Toby said, pushing his chair back. "I'll walk you over there."

Margo's hands flew to her hips. "Tobias Anthony Holmes, I am a grown woman. I am capable of crossing the street by myself, thank you very much."

"Do you all need any help putting together the care packages?" Ivana asked.

Jonathan could not contain his smile as Ivana latched onto an excuse to get out of Dodge. She had looked on the verge of bolting all evening. He'd guessed the only reason she remained is because she'd come over with Sienna.

"No thanks, honey," Margo answered. "The deaconess board is going to be there. But I can use help with the dishes," Margo said, looking pointedly at Toby.

Toby put his hands up. "Sienna and I have to work."

"I'll do the dishes," Ivana offered. "It'll give me something to do while I wait for Sienna."

Jonathan had to stop himself from rolling up his sleeves at the table. He had never been more excited about busting suds.

"Thanks for dinner," Sienna called out to Margo.

"As I said earlier, my kitchen is always open to you girls. I'll leave a container of jambalaya for your mother."

"I'll make sure she gets it," Sienna said.

The table's four remaining occupants rose and started clearing the dishes.

"I've got that," Ivana said, reaching across the table for Toby's plate. "You two need to finish your work."

So they could leave as soon as possible, Jonathan could practically hear her say. She wanted out of here.

She was not getting off that easy.

But before he could even turn toward the kitchen, Toby said, "J., why don't you join us? You can help brainstorm."

Jonathan stifled the curse he nearly let loose. He didn't want to brainstorm. He didn't want to do anything that did not involve a certain woman who claimed to be into voodoo.

But he didn't want to broadcast his intentions just yet. At least not to anyone other than Ivana. So instead of saying *hell no*, which is what he was thinking, Jonathan said, "Sure."

They went into the living room. Toby and Sienna sat on the long sofa, while he took a seat in the lounge chair that sat at a right angle, but as soon as his butt hit the chair, Jonathan was ready to get up again. He wanted to be in that kitchen. His mind was focused solely on getting Ivana alone.

After a full five minutes of not comprehending a single thing that had been discussed, Jonathan lied, saying he had an important call to make, and hopped out of the chair as if it were on fire. He passed through the dining room and stopped in the kitchen doorway. Leaning his shoulder against the door frame, he studied her. She was beautiful. Long, flowing hair, creamy, caramel-colored skin, and a slim, statuesque body that inspired all sorts of illicit thoughts.

"So, are you going to pretend you don't know who I am?"

Her hands stilled. Her back became as rigid as a surfboard. Jonathan contemplated all the things he could do to the smooth column of her neck.

"I *don't* know you," Ivana finally said. She dunked another dish in the water and continued scrubbing.

"You can't make me believe you don't remember me."

"Spending five minutes in the presence of someone does not constitute *knowing* them. I did not consider you an actual person the other day." She turned slightly and looked at him over her slim shoulder. "Just a heartless monster with poor decorating taste."

Jonathan flattened his palm against his chest as if covering a knife wound. He pushed away from the doorjamb and walked over to the double sink, grabbing a dish towel hanging from the oven's chrome handle on the way. He helped himself to a bowl and began wiping away the excess moisture.

"I've got this taken care of," she said.

"I want to help," Jonathan replied.

She turned her attention back to the sink full of sudsy water. She had left on the bracelet she wore around her left wrist. The overhead light radiated sparks on it every time her hands came out of the water. After a few minutes of a surprisingly comfortable silence, Jonathan realized they could go on like this for the rest of the night. But that's not what he wanted. For reasons still unknown even to himself, Jonathan was determined to learn more about her.

She fascinated him.

Jonathan watched as she opened the bottom cabinet and retrieved a small plastic container. She transferred the leftover rice and put the empty rice pot in the sink. Apparently, she wasn't in a talkative mood.

He reached for a spoon and gently caressed it with the towel, biding his time.

Wait. Forget that!

Time was a precious commodity that was likely running out. Toby and Sienna could not have much more that could be handled over a coffee table discussion. And Jonathan knew as soon as they were finished, Ivana would demand she and Sienna leave.

If he was going to start up a conversation with her, he'd have to do it now. "So, are you really a voodoo priestess?"

"Yes," she answered. Her eyes remained focused on something outside the window over the sink.

"How did that come about?" Whether Ivana knew it or not, this wasn't just small talk on his part. He really was interested. He knew very little about the occult, other than what came out of Hollywood. Actually, the thought of all that stuff scared the hell out of him, but if the typical voodoo queen was like Ivana Culpepper, Jonathan was willing to grow a little backbone where this creepy stuff was concerned.

Ivana ignored his question. For as much lip as she had given him back at his office, she surely was quiet tonight.

"How long have you been practicing voodoo?" he tried. At least he geared their one-way conversation toward her interests. Wasn't the biggest complaint of most women that men only talked about themselves? What more did she want?

Probably for him to walk in front of a bus.

Too bad. His grandmama taught him long ago to look both ways before crossing the street.

He tried again. "Was this your childhood dream, or did you just happen upon it?" Okay. He'll admit that was a stupid one, but he was running out of questions. But—*look at that*—it got her attention.

Ivana finally turned to him. "You don't take hints well, do you?"

Jonathan smiled. "Not really."

"Try."

"Are you still upset about what happened back at my office?"

"What is your problem? Didn't you hear what they said in there?" she pointed to the dining room. "I'm a voodoo priestess. I rip the heads off chickens with my teeth and crush glass with my bare hands." Sarcasm oozed out of her mouth. Her eyes teemed with it.

"And what is that supposed to mean to me?" Jonathan asked.

"It means you should be running out the house, trying to get as far away from me as you can," she answered. The sarcasm in her eyes had been replaced by something else. Was it sadness? Whatever it was, he didn't like it. He much preferred the fire he'd seen in her eyes just a minute ago.

Jonathan reached into the water and grasped one of her hands. He slowly pulled it out and ran his fingers along the slick, warm flesh. The slight wrinkles from being immersed in water could not detract from the smoothness of her skin.

"You must be really good at that glass crushing thing." He turned her hand over and studied her palm, tracing his thumb over it. "I can't find a single sign of damage."

She looked up from where he held her hand, and damn if those big brown eyes didn't snatch the breath right from his lungs. Her eyes widened. Her lips parted. The air around them crackled and sizzled.

"Ivana, are you just about done?"

Jonathan's eyelids slid shut at Sienna's interruption. Ivana jerked her hand away.

"I'm done," she called, wiping her hands on the dish towel he had left on the counter.

"You sure you don't need me to write the directions to my apartment?" Toby was asking Sienna as they walked into the kitchen.

"I've lived here my entire life," she laughed. "I think I can find my way around Carrolton."

"Okay. Let me just fix a plate to go and I'll meet you there. All I have to do is print Aria's schedule off my hard drive," Toby said.

Sienna walked over to Jonathan and held out her hand.

"Good luck with your next grand opening. Hopefully, I won't have to see you in that capacity."

"I doubt you can steer clear of me. I practice contract law, remember. I'm sure our paths will cross."

"Well, I'll just make sure you're on my side."

"For now, why don't you make plans to be back at the club this Tuesday. I'm going to try establishing a Ladies Night."

Still holding her hand, Jonathan bent over and placed a friendly peck on Sienna's cheek. He turned to Ivana, but the look she gave him said very clearly he had best keep his hands and lips to himself.

Not for long, the voice in his head sang.

"Will I see you on Tuesday, Ivana?" he asked.

"I do not patronize establishments such as yours," she answered.

The silence that followed her coldly delivered edict was suffocating as everyone stood in the kitchen staring uncomfortably at one another. With that one statement she had undeniably made her feelings known. Jonathan picked up the gauntlet like a fierce warrior. If that was how she wanted to play this, so be it.

A wide grin spread across his face.

Let the games begin.

Chapter Eight

"Did you have to be so rude?"

Sienna backed out of the driveway and headed up Amelia Street.

"Was I rude?"

Sienna rolled her eyes at Ivana's laconically spoken words, and wondered just how much of the grief her sister experienced was self-inflicted.

"Why don't you try giving people the benefit of the doubt

before automatically assuming they are going to treat you differently because of your beliefs? Some of them may surprise you."

"It's easier this way." Sienna could barely hear Ivana's whispered reply. "Besides, why should I bother?"

She loved her sister and wanted to reassure her, but Sienna did not have time to worry about Ivana's insecurities tonight. She had enough of her own issues. And even though trying to find the best avenue to pursue in order to make Aria Jordan the next big thing should have top billing, it was not Sienna's number one concern. The problem causing the most conflict was figuring out how she would work so closely with Toby without going crazy.

This should have been so easy. At one point in her life, there was not a single person she was more comfortable with than Toby. Yet tonight she had been on the verge of coming out of her skin. What pissed her off even more was that Toby could not have been less affected. He was, just as he'd said, strictly professional. It was time for her to be the same where Toby was concerned.

Maybe she should make a play for Jonathan. Mr. Campbell was definitely pleasing to the eye. And he was a go-getter, like her. But there was no spark between them whatsoever. Sienna had had a fun time hanging out with him last night, but she could not foresee anything other than friendship between them.

If Sienna had sensed correctly, Jonathan seemed more than a little interested in Ivana. Several times over dinner she had looked over to find him staring at her sister under the hood of his dark eyes.

Sienna glanced at her sister.

Ivana had never showed much interest in men after her jerk of an ex-husband, Michael, had broken her heart. She'd dated once in a while, but nothing serious. For all the talk about the Culpepper girls' beauty, they sure didn't get around much.

Sienna pulled up to the walkway in front of Ivana's house.

"Do you want to come in for a bit?" her sister asked.

"No, I need to get to Toby's. We're going to go over Aria's schedule with a fine-tooth comb and try to find as many spots for her to perform as we can." Sienna dropped her head against the steering wheel. "It's going to take a miracle to pull this off."

Ivana covered the hand Sienna still had on the steering wheel, and gave it a reassuring squeeze. "You can do this, Cee Cee. Don't let anyone tell you differently. You are a smart, strong black woman. With enough perseverance and faith, you can do anything."

Sienna raised her head and smiled. She leaned over and gave her sister a kiss on her cheek. "Thank you, honey. You always know the right thing to say."

"Just fulfilling my big sister duty."

Ivana reached to open the door, but Sienna stopped her. "Vonnie?" She had not called her sister that in forever.

"What is it?" Ivana asked.

"Do you really think I'm ready for this?"

"Without a doubt. You have nothing to be afraid of, Sienna. Go out there and do what you do. Show Sylvia that her baby girl is good for more than stacking the shelves of that high-priced shop."

Sienna smiled. "And dribbling a basketball."

She patted Sienna on the hand. "You go and get to work. I'll see you next week."

"Love you."

She waited until Ivana entered her house, then took off for Toby's apartment. Sienna spotted his Acura as soon as she pulled into the lot surrounding his apartment complex. She parked two spaces down and got out of the car. Toby was waiting for her at the entrance to the building.

"Come on up. I'm on the second floor," he said.

Sienna followed him up to the third apartment on the right. He opened the door, reached in and flipped on a light. Then he stood back, letting her walk in ahead of him.

"Give me a minute to fire up the computer and print down the schedule," he said, heading down the short hallway and disappearing into a room.

Sienna put her purse down on a small table next to the door and looked around. The apartment wasn't all that big, but she supposed it was enough for one person. It made her appreciate having an entire house to herself. She had more space than she could ever need.

The furniture was sparse, but new; not even the slightest dent marred the cherry red sofa cushions. Count on Toby to have a bright red sofa. It worked well with the muted gold and soft earth tones throughout the rest of the open living and dining room.

The coffee and end tables looked as if they were made of polished stone.

"That can't be real," Sienna muttered to herself.

She walked over to the closest table and ran her hand across the top. Cold. Smooth. She tried pushing the base with her foot. Yep. That was stone. She had never seen anything like it. They were beautiful pieces.

Foraying deeper into the apartment, she walked to the huge flat screen television that hung on the wall opposite the sofa. It had to be at least forty-two inches wide. What was it with men and tech toys?

The television was flanked by two display shelves that ran from floor to ceiling. The one on the right was packed with hardback books. Toby had always been a closet nerd; afraid to admit he liked reading for pleasure. Apparently, he no longer cared if anyone knew of his love of crime novels.

Sienna moved to the other shelf that housed a DVD collection that had to number over a thousand. She smiled at the rows of kung-fu movies, remembering how they used to "play" Bruce Lee.

Tomboy. That's what Jonathan said Toby had called her.

Her eyes moved toward the top shelves and stopped short.

"Oh, no he doesn't."

She plucked a slim case from the shelf. *The Candy Strippers of Horny Hill Hospital.* Sienna's eyes bucked as they roamed the other titles. A quarter of the top shelf was devoted to porn.

"What are you doing?"

Sienna jumped at Toby's question, guilty at being caught just looking at the cases for this smut.

Wait a minute. *He* should be the one to feel guilty.

Sienna waved the *Horny Hill* DVD under his nose. "I cannot believe you have this crap in your home, Tobias Anthony Holmes."

"Oh, Lord. And I thought Mama and Jasmine were the only two I had to worry about finding these. Give me that, *Margo*."

He reached for the DVD, but Sienna switched it to her other hand. "Why do you even watch this?"

He shrugged, an incredulous look on his face. "Why does anyone?"

"My point exactly."

"What? It's just a movie."

"With people having sex."

"Actually, there's not much sex in this one. It's just a bunch of girls dressed as nurses who strip for elderly patients."

Sienna twisted her nose in repulsion. "You are disgusting." She pointed at the girl on the DVD cover who looked like she had enough silicon in her breasts to fill the Grand Canyon. "Do you realize this girl will be someone's grandmother one day? How would you feel if you found an old videocassette of your grandmother in a porn movie?"

Toby stared at her for a full five seconds. Finally, he said, "Thank you."

"For what?"

"Ruining porn for me. I'll never be able to watch another skin flick without fearing that my grandmother will show up on the screen." Sienna smiled triumphantly as he snatched the slim jewel case from her hands. "Now, can you get your nose out of my DVDs before you find fault with something else."

"Well, those Jean Claude Van Damme movies do have a lot of gratuitous violence."

"This from a girl who had pictures of Van Damme and Steven Seagal plastered over her notebook back in junior high."

"I do have a thing for men who can kick butt," Sienna said with a rueful smile. "So, you have the schedule?" she asked, motioning to the document he held.

Toby waved the sheet and cocked his head toward the sofa. "I'll give you the rundown."

"We need to get her in front of as many people as possible before the show starts taping; not only for the exposure, but she needs to be more comfortable in front of crowds."

As they poured over the list of open dates and compared them to what Toby already had lined up, Sienna mentally tried to recall as many of the clubs she knew that held open mike nights. Not being much of a club-goer, she was woefully lacking in suggestions.

"I could give you a list of the clubs in Houston off the top of my head," Toby said. "But I haven't been back in New Orleans long enough to have a good feel for the club scene."

Rising from the sofa, Sienna stretched. "Well, let's do what everyone does when they need to know something. Where's the Internet connection?"

"The computer is in my bedroom," he answered.

Toby led her to the back of the apartment, through the door he had entered earlier when he had first gone to print down the schedule. After the collection of porno movies in the living room, Sienna was afraid of what she would find in Toby's bedroom. Her stomach gave a slight drop and a tingle traveled down her spine at the thought of being in his bedroom at all.

It was stupid. She'd spent hours in the room Toby and Eli shared as children. But that had been years ago. And the feelings she'd had for an eight-year-old Toby were completely different from those she held for the twenty-eight-year-old.

He took the seat in front of the chrome and glass computer desk, motioning for Sienna to sit on the edge of the king-size bed that took up most of the room.

"Try Digital City dot com," Sienna suggested. "There should be a list of all the clubs in the city, searchable by music type."

Toby tapped on the keyboard and Sienna moved in closer as the page slowly loaded.

"You need to step into the new millennium and get a high-speed connection. Dial-up went out about five years ago."

"I'm not on here all that much," Toby replied.

"That's right, you get all your porn from DVDs, not the Internet," Sienna snorted.

"Is that where you get yours?"

Sienna's voice froze in her throat.

Toby laughed out loud. "You should see the look on your face. You look as if I accused you of murder." He shook his head. "You've probably never seen a porno flick before, have you?"

No, she had not. And for some reason, it made her feel naïve and unworldly. Since when was it considered not cool to refrain from watching two complete strangers going at it in front of a camera?

"You should watch one," Toby said. "You can learn a lot."

Was he out of his mind? "There is not a single thing one of those movies can teach me," Sienna spat.

"Really?" Toby's brows rose. "You know everything there is to know about that particular subject?"

This conversation had plummeted to the eighth level of hell in less than a minute. This was *not* something she planned to discuss with Toby.

"It's none of your business what I know about . . . *that*."

"I'll bet the guy you were going to go out with last week would appreciate it if you borrowed a few from my collection."

"Could we please get back to what I came here to talk about? My love life"—or lack thereof, Sienna thought—"is not open for discussion. Save the sex talk for when Aria's here."

Toby's expression instantly turned serious. "There is nothing going on between me and Aria."

"What?" Sienna asked.

"You mentioned that last night and I didn't get a chance to

correct you. Aria and I have nothing other than a professional relationship."

"She's not—"

Toby shook his head. "You're not the first person to make the wrong assumption. I'm her manager and producer, that's all."

Oh, my God.

Sienna's heart started to beat triple time at the implication of Toby's statement. He was unattached?

"So, who are you seeing?" she asked, unwilling to believe Toby was actually available. He had never been without a girlfriend draped over his arm.

"Nobody." His face was devoid of emotion. He had no idea his simple declaration had just turned her world upside down. "I don't have the time," Toby continued. "Maybe once this show is over and things calm down, but not right now. It wouldn't be fair."

"Fair to whom?" Sienna asked. It was the least probing question she could think of at the moment. There was so much flowing around in her mind. *How long had it been since his last serious relationship? What type of woman was he looking for? Was he looking for just a good time, or was he really ready to open his heart and genuinely commit?*

"I guess to both of us, but more so for the woman," Toby answered her question, and Sienna had to think a minute about what she had asked. "It wouldn't be right to start something up with someone when I know my time will be limited. How do you do it?" he asked.

"Do what?"

"Make a relationship work when you're always so busy with your career?"

Yeah, like she had that to worry about. Of course, Toby still believed she had this imaginary boyfriend. Unsure that is was the smartest thing to do, Sienna decided to come clean.

"I'm not in an actual relationship, Toby."

He was quiet for a moment, then nodded and said, "After

the flirting you and Jonathan did last night I figured you were not all that serious about the guy."

"I was not flirting," Sienna said. Okay, so maybe she had flirted a little, but her idea of flirting was tame compared to most women. "And there is no guy. I made that up."

At that, Toby turned fully to look at her from where he sat in front of the computer and chuckled. "Why?"

"Because you automatically assumed that I didn't have anything to do on a Friday night, and I didn't want to admit you were right."

He shook his head. "Cee Cee, I don't know what to say about you."

"Say that I'm good at what I do. That's all that matters," she said, trying to bring things back to a safe level. She needed time to mull over the revelations that had just been brought to light.

Toby was unattached.

"You are extremely good at what you do," Toby said. "And, since you are so good at your job, why don't you take over the task of finding some clubs while I fix us something to drink. I've got lemonade, beer, and chocolate milk."

"Lemonade," Sienna answered.

"Here," he said, rising from the rolling chair in front of the computer. He slid open a drawer and extracted a steno pad and ink pen. "Why don't you jot down the numbers of some of the R&B and jazz clubs from here to Baton Rouge? I'm going to start calling first thing tomorrow morning."

"You do realize this will cost extra, right?"

Toby pulled at her hair as he headed for the door. "Add it to my tab."

Toby grabbed two glasses from the cabinet over his microwave and filled them with ice, and had to force himself not to slam the freezer door shut.

He should have guessed that Sienna had gotten the wrong impression about his and Aria's relationship. Everyone did.

It was frustrating as hell to constantly have to defend his

professionalism. Not that there was anything wrong with Aria. If they played their cards right, she would soon be on the minds of every teenage boy in the country. But Aria didn't do a thing for him, and Toby did not want to score a reputation of messing around with the clients he managed. That was not the way professionals operated.

Toby found it interesting that Sienna was not dating anyone. Even more interesting was the knowledge that she had made up an imaginary boyfriend. Why would she do that?

Well, she had given him a reason. She didn't want him to know that she had nothing to do on a Friday night. But why should it matter to her what he knew of her dating situation?

Toby could admit he *had* been thinking about that very thing. Her love life had been on his mind a little too much lately, especially after last night. He could not get the image of Sienna in that clingy dress out of his mind. It was her legs. Why had he never noticed how long her legs were?

There were a lot of things he had not noticed about Sienna when they were back in high school that he undeniably noticed now. Like her hair, and the way it fell just past her delicate shoulders. And her smile; the way it naturally appeared just when he needed a bit of reassurance.

Sienna had always had a lot going for her in the looks department. How many times had he been seconds away from decking one of his teammates for making some lewd comment after Cee Cee had come to congratulate him after a game? At the time, it felt as if he were protecting his little sister. But she didn't fit the little sister mold anymore. For the first time, Toby was beginning to notice what his friends had probably seen all along.

Sienna was fine as hell.

God, that sounded strange. But Toby could no more deny his thoughts than he could deny that she was sitting in his bedroom right now.

Something pulled tight in his stomach, and a deep, throbbing pain that was sure to cause him to think too damn much about all of this later on, gripped an area south. An area that had *never* reacted to Sienna's presence before.

Well, except for that long ago liquor cabinet incident. But he'd been a sixteen-year-old horny teenager back then. He would get that particular reaction from the breeze when a city bus passed by.

So what was his excuse now?

Oh, yeah. Sienna was in his bedroom. On his bed.

Toby shook his head in frustrated confusion. Was he seriously having these thoughts about Sienna? She was his friend. His *best* friend. A person did not imagine their best friend naked and on their bed.

But now that his mind had brought it up, the image was there in big, bold, Times Square-at-night living color.

"Oh, hell," Toby muttered to the kitchen, as if the empty room could offer answers to the dozens of questions floating around his mind. He didn't have time for this. He needed to concentrate on getting Aria as much exposure as possible.

He went to the freezer and took out a package of microwavable pizza snacks. Maybe the time it took to cook them would be sufficient enough for him to get his body under control.

Toby placed the two glasses of ice cold lemonade and the plate of pizza snacks on the only tray he owned, and tried not to think about what it would be like to have the tray laden with breakfast, and a lusciously satisfied Sienna waiting in his bed to receive it.

"You have got to stop this," he warned himself.

He made his way down the short hallway balancing the tray in one hand as he reached for the doorknob. The door opened and Sienna stepped forward, bringing their bodies in brief contact.

"Oh," she screeched, jumping back as if he had burned her. "I'm sorry."

The current of electricity that spiked through his body nearly knocked Toby to his knees, tray and all. He had a hard time swallowing past the lump of instant desire holding him paralyzed.

"Excuse me," Sienna said. Her eyes met and held his for a brief moment and what he saw there was enough to make Toby question everything he had ever known. Too quickly, she looked away.

"Bathroom," Sienna said, her voice hoarse. "Where is it?"

"Over there," Toby answered, nodding toward the door just to the right of his bedroom.

She shot to the door, and Toby heard the distinct click of the lock. He stood in the open doorway for several interminable moments, trying to get a handle on what had just transpired. He may not be the brightest bulb in the lightbulb factory, but he knew *something* had happened.

There was a look in her eyes. It was that look he could never really place a name on, but that every guy who'd ever been lucky enough to actually receive it knew all too well. Awareness? Interest? *Some*thing.

One thing it definitely was *not* was the look of someone who wanted to be considered "just a friend."

This was some heavy stuff. Way too much for him to try to make sense of tonight. Maybe he should wait to see how she reacted. If Sienna didn't mention it, neither would he. At least not tonight.

He was probably reading way more into this than necessary. No doubt this was just the lingering effect of seeing her all dolled up last night. She had taken him by surprise in that sexy little dress and subtly made-up face. Add to it that it had been so long since he'd had a woman, and what did he expect? Of course he would have an unprecedented, and certainly unexpected, reaction to being pushed up against Sienna. He could have bumped into any woman—save for his own mother—and his body would have reacted the same way.

Toby expelled an audible sigh of relief. He was not losing his mind. His body was just hyperaware of everything female. And just like he had told himself last night, the only thing that would bring him back to a semblance of his normal, anxiety-free existence would be to find himself a woman. Fast.

Sienna opened the bathroom door and stopped short. She stared at him.

Why wouldn't she stare with him still standing in the doorway holding onto that tray like a freaking idiot?

"Waiting for me?" she asked.

"No. I was just—"

What could he say? That he was contemplating getting a woman—*any woman*—to help relieve his mind and body so that he could stop picturing her naked? Yeah, that would go over about as well as a Hummer over quicksand.

"Did you find some clubs?" Toby asked, moving into the bedroom, and avoiding the unanswerable question.

Sienna followed. She didn't seem all that disturbed by their moment. Probably because he was the only one who thought of it as a *moment*.

He needed to snap the hell out of this and get back to work. He did not have time for these bouts of ridiculousness that were suddenly taking far too much of his brainpower.

"I have a few," Sienna said when she sat at the computer desk. She picked up a glass of lemonade from the tray he'd sat on the dresser and took a long drink. She picked up the steno pad and tossed it next to him on the bed, then reached for a pizza snack. "Have you heard of any of these?"

Toby scanned the list. "A few. Doesn't *The Amazon* cater to a . . . umm . . . different crowd?" As far as he knew, the club played strictly rock and roll, and for a much older crowd than what they were targeting.

"Oops," Sienna chuckled. "I guess that's why it's better to have firsthand knowledge than to trust what you get from the Internet."

"I may be wrong," Toby quickly retracted. "All it would take is a call."

"I was thinking we could try to put together the most feasible schedule with what we have here, then modify it as we go along."

He nodded in agreement. "Sounds like a plan."

Sienna reached over for another pizza snack and the V-collared blouse she wore gaped a little, providing way more of a view than Toby's overheated body could handle at the moment.

"All right, then," Sienna smiled. "I hope you're ready for a long night."

Toby stifled another groan, thinking the night could not end soon enough.

Chapter Nine

Ivana plucked three boxes of bandages from the shelf and scanned the collage of colorful packages before her in search of antibiotic ointment. There were only a few more items she needed to restock the first aid kits at the battered women's shelter, then she could head to the book section to pick out the titles some of the women had requested, and a few for herself.

A worker with a bright blue smock passed and Ivana stopped her. "Excuse me, is there any Bactine?"

"There's none out here?" the woman asked, scanning the shelf. "Let me look in the back," the worker offered, smiling. It must be in the contract workers signed before being hired. Everybody who worked here smiled constantly. Ivana liked it. The world needed more smilers.

"Isn't this an unexpected surprise?" came a voice just to the left of her.

Oh, please, no.

She turned her eyes from the antacids.

Oh, darn, yes.

Jonathan Campbell. Looking like a delicious caramel delicacy one could find in only the most elite confectionary shops.

So it was too much to ask never to see him again, right, God?

And wasn't it just her luck that she would run into him in

the middle of a drug store, with a shopping cart filled to the brim with every embarrassing product one could purchase? No, wait. There was no need for hemorrhoid cream this month. Scratch one thing off the embarrassing items list. Still, she would pay a hundred bucks for the industrial-size box of tampons to magically disappear from her cart.

"Hello," Ivana said coolly. Maybe if she was polite, she could make a quick escape. Forget the antibiotic ointment.

She tried to move past him. He stopped her.

Positioning his own shopping cart, which at first glance did not have anything equally as embarrassing as hers, horizontally across the aisle, Jonathan turned his dazzlingly white, stop-her-heart-from-beating-for-a-full-three-seconds smile on her.

"It's kind of late to be out shopping," he said, his eyes roaming over her impending purchases. Ivana wished she could shrink to the size of an insect and crawl under the squeaky wheel of the shopping cart.

"I'm shopping for a friend," she said, and his smile immediately widened.

And just why was she making fake excuses? If she wanted to buy enough tampons to supply a dormitory at an all girls' school, it was her business.

"That doesn't explain why you're out so late," he said.

"Excuse me, but my father died years ago. There is not another man I have to be accountable to."

He continued smiling. Lord, but he had an amazing smile.

"What do you have against me, Ivana? Besides the whole thing with the building, which, by the way, is not listed as a historical landmark. I looked into it."

"Just because the 'powers that be' do not appreciate the historical significance of that structure doesn't mean there is none."

"What if I told you I would move my practice somewhere else?"

For a minute, Ivana was rendered speechless. "I would be

very grateful," she answered. "Are you considering doing that?"

He hitched a shoulder. Nonchalantly, he said, "No. I just wanted to know if it would change your opinion of me."

Ivana narrowed her eyes, shooting him a look that was meant to elicit alarm. It didn't seem to work. The stock clerk returned, bearing a cardboard box filled with at least a dozen antiseptic spray bottles.

"Is this what you're looking for?" the girl asked.

Ivana took the entire box from her hands and placed it on top of the tampons. "Yes, thank you," she answered. She turned to Jonathan. "Could you please get out of my way? I would like to finish my shopping so I can get home."

"What would change your opinion of me?" He continued the conversation as if she had not spoken.

"Why does my opinion of you even matter?" Ivana asked.

"Why do you think?" he retorted, as if the answer were obvious. Of course, it *was* obvious to her. She wasn't totally clueless where men were concerned. It had just been so very long since she'd had more than a ten-minute conversation with one. As soon as most men learned of her affiliation with the voodoo, they ran off. She had expected the same from Jonathan. That he had not lived up to those expectations baffled her.

Ivana lifted her hands and let them slap down on her hips, making an exaggerated show of her mounting frustration. Although she was honest enough to admit a bulk of the frustration was self-directed. She should *not* be so attracted to this man.

Then again, she was a woman. Any woman in her right mind would be drawn in by his chocolate brown eyes. And, contrary to popular opinion, she was very much in her right mind. For now, at least. Every minute she spent around him chipped away at her sanity.

"Hello?" Jonathan was waving his hands. "Do you always space out like that?"

Good God, Ivana. And you wonder why people think you're crazy?

She tried to summon a good comeback so he wouldn't realize her spacing out had been the result of fantasizing about his deliciously good looks.

"You know what they say about an idle mind?" He winked and her heart jumped into her throat.

Good Lord!

Forget a good comeback. She needed to be out of here.

"I have shopping to do," she said. Ivana wrestled to turn her shopping cart around in the narrow aisle. She hastily made her way out of the first aid area, and was severely tempted to abort the entire shopping excursion altogether. Right now, all she could think of was putting as much distance between herself and Jonathan Campbell as soon as possible.

The man was dangerous. That smile! That wink! They had her contemplating things she had not thought about in far too long. Like what it would feel like to have a man smile at her across a candlelit table, or grace her with a sexy wink right before closing in on a slow, sensual kiss.

Ivana chanced a look back to find Jonathan standing at the head of the aisle she had so hurriedly vacated, staring at her.

She had never run from anything in her life, but today, she was running. And all she could think was, thank goodness she got out with her sanity intact.

Toby opened the car door and reached in to help his mother out of the front passenger seat.

"Looks like they have a full house," he said.

Gazing around the parking lot, Toby doubted a playoff match-up between the Hornets and Lakers could draw more of a crowd. He supposed it was only fitting the Lord would rate higher than a basketball game. At one time in his life, Toby believed the opposite.

He'd once thought his accident was somehow correlated to his twisted beliefs that basketball was above everything, even

God. The thought had occurred to him often over the years since he'd nearly died. But Mama had taught him that God was a forgiving God, who did not hand down revengeful punishment. It was more comforting to believe in Mama's version.

Toby guided his mother up the landscaped walk that led from the parking lot to the church.

"Good morning," Sienna greeted them at the first set of massive doors. She was dressed in another of those airy sundresses, her face framed by bouncy curls. It was a new look. Toby liked it on her.

"Good morning, honey," Margo said, giving her a kiss on the cheek.

"Morning, Cee Cee," Toby said. He'd been a little on edge after last night. He continued to wonder if Sienna had felt the zing that had passed between them. It didn't appear as though she had, but how could she not? It had been too powerful to be felt just on his end.

Toby looked up, finally bringing his attention to the monstrous structure before him. "Damn, this is a big church!"

He received a slap on each arm, one from his mother, the other from Sienna. "Don't say damn," they said in unison.

"The service is about to start," his mother said. "I've wanted to hear this minister preach. I hear he's really good."

"Is he long-winded?" Toby asked, knowing the inquiry would warrant another slap from Mama. She didn't disappoint.

"You had better pay attention," she warned, as if he were still six years old. "And no falling asleep either. You did that last week."

So maybe he sometimes behaved like a six-year-old. He opened the door and stood back as both women entered. Glancing over the stadium-style seating, Toby searched for somewhere with a good view of the choir section.

"Toby will not be falling asleep this morning," Sienna interjected with a whisper, "not with Aria singing."

"I'm just hoping she doesn't mess up. When she rehearsed earlier this morning, she had a hard time hitting one of the notes in the solo she's performing." He motioned to a couple of seats with his head. "I think I may be pushing her a little too hard. Her voice needs to rest for a couple of days."

"That's not a bad idea," Sienna said. "You want to make sure she's at her peak performance level when they start taping."

"Well, don't worry about her this morning," his mother whispered as they made their way to the empty seats halfway down the aisle. "God is controlling this. He's going to be with her."

Apparently, God was all over the place.

Toby would be the first to admit that over the last few years, he'd been more of a warm body to fill the pew than an active participant in church services, but it didn't take long to get back in the spirit. The Holy Ghost had touched everybody this morning. The entire congregation was on their feet, and when Aria began singing "Amazing Grace," hands flew in the air in praise.

Sienna tapped him on the shoulder. Toby leaned over, and she had to practically put her mouth on his ear to be heard above the shouts and hand-clapping.

"I think we've got this section of the population covered," she said.

The moist warmth of her breath caused a reaction that was a bit inappropriate for him to have in church. Fingers of sensual awareness cascaded down his spine. He thought back to last night and how hard it had been to concentrate on anything but the way her silk blouse played across the ride of her breasts.

Do *not* think about her breasts in church.

He could think about her legs, and how he had been dying to run his hands over them. Last night, after they'd finished their drinks, she had kicked off her shoes and sat with her back against the headboard, stretching her legs out on his bed. They'd looked so inviting under those sheer stockings. It had taken everything he had not to reach out and test her legs out for himself. Toby chanced a glance down and noticed she wore another pair of those stockings. Did she even realize what that shimmering fabric did to her legs?

Instead of soaking in the preacher's message, Toby spent the remainder of the service trying unsuccessfully to keep his eyes averted from Sienna's body.

After the service, Aria met them as they were walking out of the church. Sienna greeted her before Toby had the chance.

"You were unbelievable," she said. "You were born to sing gospel."

Aria blushed. "I grew up in the church. It's something I'll never lose."

"Amen, honey," his mother added. "You two are coming over to the house, aren't you? I've had a roast baking at two hundred degrees for about five hours now. It's probably tender enough to cut with a spoon."

"That sounds delicious, Margo, but I've got so much work to do," Sienna said.

"Not on a Sunday," his mother said.

Sienna nodded apologetically, "I'm afraid so."

"Not when I baked a coconut cake for dessert," Margo tried.

Sienna hesitated, looked over at Toby and said, "We can go over potential sponsors at your mom's, right?"

"I don't see why not," he answered with a grin. "You coming to dinner?" he asked Aria.

She shook her head. "I'm meeting my best friend, Shelby, in a few minutes. She's driving from Houston to Jacksonville, Florida, and since New Orleans is on the route, we decided to get together for a few hours this afternoon."

"That sounds like fun," Sienna commented. She pointed to Toby and Margo. "I'll meet ya'll at the house."

By the time they arrived at his mother's, Alex's truck was already parked at the curb. Toby pulled into the driveway with Sienna coming in behind him. Alex was taking a casserole dish out of the oven when they walked into the kitchen.

"Uh oh, don't tell me you cooked," Toby said.

"And what would be so bad about that?"

Toby laughed at Alex's offended tone.

"Don't let him get to you, baby," Mama said, patting Alex on the back.

"Thank you." Alex bent to give her a kiss. "And thanks for leaving the casserole in the freezer," he finished with a grin. "How did everything go this morning?"

"Wonderfully," Sienna answered, receiving a kiss on the cheek from Alex. "You should have joined us."

"I was ordered to attend services at Morning Star Baptist. Mama needed a spy. And before you ask"—Alex turned his attention to Margo—"no, Ella King's daughter did not show up with her new boyfriend."

"I sent you to church to be touched by the Holy Spirit, not spy," Mama defended. "And she was supposed to show up with her new *girlfriend*," she said in a hushed voice.

"Well, she didn't have a girlfriend, either," Alex said.

"Too bad you missed Aria," Sienna interjected. "She was phenomenal."

"I have no doubt about that. But from what I hear, Aria isn't the only one who's been doing some phenomenal work these days. According to Toby, it sounds like you're approaching Superwoman status," Alex said.

Sienna eyes shot to Toby. "You said that?"

Actually, he hadn't told Alex much of anything about the work Sienna was doing for the show. No doubt his brother was up to his meddling again, but instead of intervening, Toby remained quiet. He wanted to gauge Sienna's reaction. Instead of answering her question, Toby just sat back at the kitchen table as Alex continued dropping not-so-subtle hints that Toby and Sienna should think about expanding their relationship outside of the show.

Sienna's expression remained amused, but Toby sensed the discomfort radiating from her as she picked over a slice of coconut cake. Her uneasiness created a similar reaction in Toby. He was a little wounded by her lukewarm response to Alex's suggestion that she and Toby finally seek a more romantic involvement.

"I have to go to the worksite," Alex said, rising from the table. "Jasmine's in the living room watching the Disney Channel. Can you make sure she changes out of her church dress? She'd sleep in that thing if I let her."

"I'll handle it," Mama answered.

Alex filled a plastic container with eggplant and shrimp casserole and grabbed a can of soda out of the refrigerator. "See y'all later," he said, bending over to give both Mama and Sienna parting kisses.

He reached his hand out to him and Toby grabbed it, pulling his brother in close. "Don't think I don't know what you were doing," Toby whispered in Alex's ear.

When Alex stepped back from the hug, his eyes held a teasing gleam. "I'm just trying to help you out."

"I can do without your kind of help," Toby answered, walking his brother to the door. When he turned back to the kitchen, Sienna was rising from the table.

"I need to head out, too," she said. "Things really start hopping this week, so I want to get my house cleaned today so I don't have to worry about it."

"Smart thinking, honey," Mama said.

Sienna pressed a kiss to her cheek. "The cake was delicious. If I hadn't missed my workout the past two mornings I would take a piece with me."

"As if you need to work out," Mama answered. "Well, let me see if I can tear my granddaughter away from the television long enough to pry that dress off her," Mama said and headed for the living room.

"Everything set for this week?" Toby asked when they were alone.

"I've got meetings with six potential sponsors over the next four days, and I plan to put on my game face."

"Sounds like you have everything you need. I don't know anyone who can resist that face," he said, brushing away a wayward curl from her jaw.

Toby knew he was treading in dangerous waters even before the words left his mouth, but an overwhelming compulsion to test this delicate situation forced him to say them anyway. He saw the flash of bewilderment in her eyes as she lifted her purse from where she'd hung it on the chair.

"Uh . . . well, I need to be going," she said again.

"Good luck," Toby offered. "Call my cell if you need anything."

She stared back at him, her hand resting on the jamb of the partially opened screen door. A powerful sense of awareness permeated the air between them.

"I will," she finally answered.

For long moments after she'd left, Toby stood in the middle of his mother's kitchen, wondering just what he was going to do about Sienna.

Chapter Ten

Sienna plopped behind the wheel of her car and heaved an exhausted sigh. This had to rate as one of the longest days of her life, but she was three for three in landing spots at the city's premier clubs, which made the ache in her neck and the developing blister on her left heel well worth the trouble.

Thank goodness she had a knack for persuading people to see things her way. Sienna was infinitely proud that she'd been able to land a performance at Caesar's Ghost. The final club on today's agenda had been the toughest sale, but crucial if they were going to make any kind of headway in crossing over to the young Caucasian market. It took some fancy talking to convince the club's management that the college-aged patrons Caesar's Ghost catered to would accept an R&B singer, but Sienna had done it.

Now, it was up to Toby and Aria to come up with an

arrangement of songs that would live up to the promises she'd just made to the club owners.

Sienna parked across the street from the nondescript brick-front building, unsure if Toby had given her the correct address Saturday night.

Saturday night.

She'd told herself she would not think about that again today, but for the past five days she'd had a hard time thinking of anything else. Ever since Toby returned to New Orleans, Sienna had tried to convince herself that these lingering feelings meant nothing. He was a high school crush, nothing more. Well, except she'd wanted him in college, too. And in grad school. And last week.

Being in such close proximity to Toby had her brain more scrambled than eggs on a breakfast buffet. Several years of separation and instead of letting up, the feelings were even stronger, and they definitely did not equate to a high school crush anymore. Her thoughts about Toby these days were very much those of a grown, sexually conscious woman.

But what about his feelings?

Sienna would be the first to admit that in the reading men department, she was probably a two on a scale of one to one hundred, but even she knew desire when it was staring her right in the face. For a few moments last Saturday night, Toby's eyes had held desire.

Sienna got out of the car and made her way across the street. She looked down at the yellow Post-it note in her hand and back up at the numbers etched into the small window on the door. This was the place.

When she'd called yesterday to relay the news about the newest sponsor to sign on, Toby had suggested she drop in on Aria's session at the recording studio. Sienna had expected something a little more glamorous than this plain, single story structure. The lobby was as unassuming as the outside of the building, with a tweed-covered love seat that was probably older than she was, and a potted plant in dire need of water and Miracle Gro. Sienna walked down the short hallway and entered the open door of a darkened studio. Toby and two men she didn't recognize sat at a large counter that was completely covered with what seemed to be every type of electronic equipment known to man. All three sported large headphones over their ears.

Aria stood behind a plate-glass window, wearing her own pair of headphones and singing sweetly into a microphone that was suspended from the ceiling. Sienna had to admit Aria Jordan had one of the most amazing voices she'd ever heard.

She vowed to make more of an effort of accepting Aria. But regardless of her attempts at civility, Sienna just could not refrain from those twinges of envy that pulled at her. Aria was such a girly girl. And she was, well, not.

"Hey, Cee Cee," Toby called, removing his headphones. Sienna didn't bother reminding him that she did not want him using that nickname. "It's about time you made it."

"What do you mean, it's about time? Do you know all the ripping and running I've done today?"

"Take a chill pill, girl. I was only playing with you." Toby got up from his seat at the console. "Give me a minute and then we can talk about what you were able to line up." He went into the room with Aria and Sienna watched as the two discussed whatever artists and their producers discuss while working on an album.

It was interesting seeing Toby in his new career. Since the first time he saw Michael Jordan as a North Carolina Tarheel, Toby had vowed he would play college and professional basketball. Believing her best friend could capture the moon in the palm of his hand if he tried hard enough, Sienna had never doubted Toby would not see his dreams through to fruition.

No one had expected a driver asleep at the wheel of a SUV would crush Toby's aspirations so soundly.

The day Eli had told her of Toby's accident was a crystal clear memory. Sienna had come home for a weekend visit during her junior year in college. Eli had caught her at her mother's just as she was leaving out for the eight-hour drive back to Atlanta. He broke the news about the accident, and told her that he, his mother, and Alex were heading for the airport so they could get to Toby in the hospital.

Even now, Sienna could feel that tightness in her chest, the overwhelming sense of nausea and fear when Eli had said, "they're not sure he's going to make it."

She'd wanted to curse whoever *they* were. The faceless *they* who'd dared to discount the courage and fight that raced through every single drop of Toby's blood. Days after the accident, she'd flown up to Washington, D.C., to be at Toby's side. As she'd held his hand while he lay in a coma, Sienna had had no doubt he would make it. Not only that, she knew he would one day play professional basketball.

But that never happened. No NBA team was willing to bank on a player who was one hard foul away from being crippled for life.

He was forced to give up on one dream, but true to his nature, Toby just found another. It made Sienna even more determined to make this project with Aria a success. Well, that and the fact that her own career was on the line. She had some pretty big dreams of her own, and not a moment passed that Sienna was not aware of what this account meant for her future. This was the stuff legends were made of.

Toby came out of the room and went over to the console. "Savion, why don't we try *Only Today*?" he asked the guy sitting behind the big desk with about a thousand levers and buttons.

Toby turned to Sienna. "Let's get some coffee."

Sienna followed him out of the recording studio to a coffeehouse on the corner of the next block. She ordered a mocha with extra whipped cream—it had been a long day—and a chocolate chip scone. It had been a *really* long day.

She took a seat at the counter that ran the length of the floor to ceiling windows and looked out at the people moving effortlessly about their business.

New Orleans was an easygoing town. It was a blessing to

see the city gradually returning to its former glory after the devastation Hurricane Katrina had inflicted. Things were slowly turning around. And, true to its name, the Big Easy inspired even the most dedicated Type A personality to just chill out. Sienna needed to take that advice.

"Tell me you were able to get Caesar's Ghost," Toby said, taking the stool next to her.

"Two weeks from tonight."

"Yes." Toby slapped the counter and pumped his fist in the air. "You are the bomb, Cee Cee. Would it be wrong to say that I'm happy Jamie Kurshon had that heart attack?"

"Yes, it would," Sienna answered, sipping from the hot coffee. Thank goodness this place was air-conditioned. Only the most addicted caffeine fiends drank coffee in the middle of a 90-degree scorcher.

"I know," he admitted. "I just never thought I'd feel lucky that you ended up with this account."

"Sounds like you doubted I could do a good job," Sienna replied. To her surprise he didn't deny it.

"Actually, I did."

The level of hurt his statement catapulted her to was painful enough to strike a physical ache in Sienna's chest.

"Wait. Let me clarify that." Toby took a sip from his iced tea, then put the cup on the counter. "It's not that I doubted your professionalism or your intelligence. But I knew you were just starting out, Cee Cee. This show means everything to my career."

"Mine, too," she managed to choke out past the mixture of hurt and anger. "If you were not sure about my handling the account, why didn't you say anything when Allen first suggested it?"

"To be honest, I was so surprised when you walked into that room, I didn't know what to think." He shrugged. "Maybe my not saying anything was God's way of looking out for me. At least that's what Mama would say."

No one ever accused Margo Holmes of being a fool. Although her son could be a complete jackass.

"Still in all," Toby continued, "I'm proud of you, as con-descending as that sounds."

"Very condescending," Sienna returned. "I know how im-portant this is to you, Toby. Just like I know how important every account is to every single client I've ever worked with at MDF."

"I didn't mean to—"

"If my boss had enough faith to recommend me for this account, then you should have had enough faith in me, too. And not just because I've always had your back."

"I never said I didn't have faith in you."

"That's exactly what you said." Sienna realized her voice had risen high enough to cause the heads of several coffee-house patrons to turn, but darn it, she had a right to be upset.

She was the one who'd stuck around with Toby for hours while he practiced free throws and raised his percentage from forty-two to seventy during his sophomore year of high school. She was the one who had tutored him in literature, dissecting *Beowulf* and *The Iliad*, and all those other epic stories she had not been assigned but had read anyway be-cause she *knew* if she helped Toby, he would walk through his barriers and come out victorious.

She'd been there for him because that's what best friends did for each other. Yet, when it was *his* turn to be there for *her*, he'd doubted her.

"Would you stop blowing things out of proportion and let me finish?" Toby pleaded. "You never change, you know that?"

"What is that supposed to mean?" If she were not holding her coffee cup, both fists would be firmly planted on her hips. Sienna settled for one.

"You always make a bigger deal out of everything than you should."

"When have I ever?"

Cutting her off, he counted instances on his fingers. "The St. Aug/Warren Easton basketball game. Mardi Gras, 1994. Your junior prom."

"I did not make a big deal out of the prom."

"You didn't talk to me for a month."

Incredulity made her voice spike. "You sent a pity date to pick me up!"

His eyes widened, an affronted frown creasing his forehead. "I was trying to help."

"I never asked for your help," Sienna argued. "I had a date."

"Who bailed on you. I may have talked to Jamal Sanders about going out with you, but if you want to know the truth, I didn't have to do all that much talking. He was more than happy to go. But did I get a thank you? No. I got a black eye and had to wear sunglasses like I was trying to impersonate Ray Charles."

"And the entire neighborhood took it as some new fashion statement. Everyone under the age of fifteen started wearing sunglasses at all times of the day and night."

"That's not the point." Toby took the cup of coffee from her hand, grabbed her other hand from where it was still propped against her hip, and clasped both between his palms. "All I was trying to say is that even though I had a sliver—a teeny, tiny, insignificant sliver—of doubt, it took very little time to see that you are on top of your game. I cannot imagine anyone pounding the pavement the way you have. Talking to club owners, booking spots? You've risen above my expectations, Cee Cee. Sienna," he amended. "I couldn't have asked for a better marketing exec."

So maybe her reaction to his comment had been a little unreasonable. And maybe if she had given him a chance to finish his statement, half the people in the coffeehouse wouldn't be looking over the edges of their paperbacks or outright staring at them like they were today's live entertainment.

Sienna tried to think back. Did she only fly off the handle with Toby?

Nope. There were several incidents with her mother she could recall. Then there was that horrid display a couple of Easters ago when she thought Tosha was criticizing her Sunday dress, only to discover that her sister wanted to borrow it instead. She *did* blow things out of proportion. Yet another character flaw she needed to work on.

Trying to figure out how best not to choke on her words, Sienna took a sip of coffee and said, "I'm sorry."

Toby's head reared back, genuine disbelief washed across his face. *"What?"*

"Don't make me say it again," she grounded out through clinched teeth.

"I'm about to mark the date. In all the years I've known you, I don't think I've ever heard those two words come out of your mouth."

"You are really pushing it," Sienna warned.

"I know, I know. I'm sorry. See, it's not hard for me to say." She rolled her eyes.

"Finished already?" Toby said.

It took Sienna a few seconds to realize he was talking to someone behind her. She turned to find the guy from the recording studio walking up to where they were sitting. Aria was in line for coffee.

"We needed a break," the guy said. His hair was done in long, thick dreadlocks bound by a ponytail holder at the base of his head.

"Hey, you two haven't met. Sienna," Toby turned to her. "This is Savion. He's the engineer who's been helping arrange Aria's album."

Extending her hand, Sienna said, "Pleasure to meet you."

"My man here says you're gonna put Aria on the map."

Sienna shrugged. "That's my job."

"Sounds like one big happy family. Aria's got the vocals. Toby does the writing. I provide the beats. And you bring it to the masses."

"Yeah, well, it's costing me a couple of hundred to rent out the studio for this session, so the two of you had better head back. We'll be there in a minute."

"Alright, man. She's hitting the notes. You need to come and check it out."

"In a minute," Toby said.

Sienna waited for Savion to leave, then she tapped Toby on the forearm. "So, when did you start writing music?"

"I don't know," he answered. "A few years ago."

The past few weeks was the first she'd heard of it. Sienna swallowed the hurt evoked by the knowledge that he'd kept such an important part of himself from her.

She asked, "Where does it come from?"

"What do you mean?"

Sienna glowered at his obtuseness. "People don't just write music to write it, Toby. It has to come from somewhere." She watched a mother pushing a covered stroller just outside the coffee shop window, then looked back at Toby. In a soft voice, she asked, "Was it because of the accident? Was it your way of coping?"

"Don't start trying to psychoanalyze me," he said, and began to rise, but Sienna stopped him again with a hand on his arm.

"We've never really talked about it, Toby."

He settled back on the stool. With a shrug he said, "Why should we?"

"Because it's an important part of your life," Sienna pointed out. "At one time we used to talk about stuff like this."

"It's a part of my life that's over. I don't want to relive it, and I sure as hell don't feel like talking about it in the middle of a damn coffee shop."

She held her hands out. "Then when and where?"

"Never and nowhere."

"Fine," Sienna relented. "Then just answer my first question."

"Which was?"

"Your music, where does it come from?"

Toby rolled his eyes and let out an exasperated sigh. "I truly don't have an answer for you. I was sitting in traffic one day, and lyrics just came to me. I found a funky napkin I'd used to blow my nose with earlier that morning and started writing them down. The end."

Sienna narrowed her eyes, shooting him a look to convey that the conversation was not over. It had always bothered her that Toby had never opened up to her after his accident. In reality, it was the beginning of the end of the friendship they once had. But now that he was back home, and their friendship was slowly making its way back to what it used to be, Sienna was determined to ask all the questions she'd longed to ask years ago.

She needed to know his feelings, to know how he'd picked himself up and gotten his life back on track. The one thing he loved above all had been snatched out of his grasp, yet he had survived. Sienna needed a lesson or two on how to overcome her own demons.

"Are you finished with that?" he asked, motioning to her coffee cup with his head. "I need to wrap things up at the studio and get Aria ready for tomorrow night's performance. She's probably on the verge of a nervous breakdown."

"We really have to work on her stage fright. These spots at The Hard Court are nothing compared to what she'll have to face once those cameras start rolling."

"I know. I've been trying to figure out a way to deal with this," Toby said. He opened the door and stepped to the side to allow Sienna to exit first. They headed back toward the recording studio. "She's fine once she gets on stage, but she makes herself sick the couple of hours before the performance. If she doesn't kick this fear soon, she's going to ruin her chance."

"She can get over it if we work hard enough. Barbra Streisand suffered from stage fright for years without it having much of an effect on her career. And let's face it; Aria is beautiful with an amazing voice. She's going to land a recording contract soon."

"But it would be better all around if she got over this. I've got to think of something."

"Let's just get her through tomorrow night's performance and her first radio interview."

"I should write a script. I know she's going to get all choked up."

"She's going to be fine, Toby," Sienna assured. "They're going to ask her about her music. She doesn't have a problem talking about that anymore."

"Not since you had her to actually sit and think about it. That was brilliant, Sienna. I don't know why I didn't think of it."

"You did just say the idea required brilliance, right? I think that answers your question."

Toby snorted, giving her a playful shove with his shoulder.

They came upon her car. Sienna unlocked the driver's side door and sat behind the wheel. "I need to stop in at my mother's store tomorrow, so I'll just meet you at The Hard Court, okay?"

"Be there for eight."

"But Aria doesn't go on until ten."

"I know. I'm treating you to dinner," Toby answered. He closed her door and slapped on the hood of the car before heading back into the studio.

There was a little butterfly action floating around in her stomach, but Sienna decided to ignore it. She wouldn't read any more into this dinner invitation than she should. In Toby's eyes, their relationship was strictly professional. And she'd do well to remember that.

"Rack 'em."

Toby fitted the wooden triangle over the freshly polished pool balls, using his forearm to stop the seven and nine ball Jonathan sent careening across the table, and adding them to the triangle with the others.

"Eli asked to order him a beer," Alex said by way of greeting. His eldest brother still sported his dust-ridden Holmes Construction t-shirt and faded jeans. "He's running late, but he said he should be here in a few minutes."

Alex joined Toby and Jonathan at the pool table in the VIP room of The Hard Court. It had been a few weeks since the three brothers had hung out, and this was the first chance they'd had to add Jonathan to the mix since he'd moved to New Orleans. Toby had suggested a game of pool so they could catch up. He needed a stress-free atmosphere, and kicking back with a beer would help him unwind before Aria's performance tonight . . . and his dinner with Sienna.

Toby suppressed a groan. What in the hell had he been thinking? The words had just popped out of his mouth. A part of him had wanted to take them back, but an even bigger part of him would not allow it. Things were slowly getting better between the two of them. He and Sienna were not the friends they used to be—not by a long shot. But she was definitely warming up to him.

And he was sure as hell warming up to her.

The inkling that it was wrong to think about Sienna in an even remotely sexual way was still there, but it was starting to fade as each hour passed. Seeing her on top of her game, wheeling and dealing with everyone, from the sponsors to club owners, was just . . . well . . . sexy. Powerful women turned him on.

Was he really thinking of Sienna as a turn-on? If anyone had told him ten years ago that he'd be jonesing for skinny little Cee Cee, Toby would have laughed himself sick. He wasn't laughing now.

Toby could do little more than shake his head in frustration and embarrassment. He wasn't sure if he should act on these feelings that were getting stronger by the minute. Then again, he *did* invite her to dinner tonight. That was a pretty big step toward acting on it.

Toby twisted the pool cue, clutching his fingers around the smooth wood. An unsettling realization gnawed at his brain, forcing him to accept the real reason he struggled with his blossoming feelings for Sienna.

In his heart, Toby knew he would hurt her in the end. It was his trademark. Every relationship he'd ever had ended in heartache for the woman who'd had the misfortune of getting involved with him.

Once he set his sights on a target, whether it was playing in the NBA or building a record label, it took over every aspect of his life. Given the choice between attaining his goal, and putting forth the effort to foster a meaningful relationship, Toby always chose to follow his own aspirations, with little regard for the pain his selfishness inflicted.

He couldn't do that to Sienna. She deserved more than he could give her.

"Oh, man, this place is tight." Eli's proclamation knocked Toby out of his musings. "I've been hearing the buzz, but I thought people were exaggerating," Eli continued as he walked through the entrance to the VIP room. The windows were designed to see out into the club from the room, but they did not reciprocate to those on the dance floor.

"It's about time you checked out my club," Jonathan said, greeting Eli with a handshake and hug.

"I've been meaning to make it out here."

"*You* haven't been here?" Alex asked. "Mr. Party All Night?"

Eli shook his head. "Between work and this tai chi class Monica has me taking in the evenings."

"What are you doing taking tai chi?" Toby asked. "See what happens when you give a woman control."

A catlike grin turned up the corners of Eli's mouth. "For what I get in return, it's a small price to pay."

Alex heaved an overly dramatic sigh, rolling his eyes. "Is there a reason every conversation has to turn to sex when we get together?"

"What else is there to talk about?" Eli grabbed a handful of cashews from a bowl on the chrome and onyx bar and popped a few in his mouth. "The Hornets don't have a chance to make the playoffs this year, so basketball season is over, in my opinion. That only leaves sex."

"He's got a point," Jonathan interjected. A waitress came in with a tray of drinks. Jonathan took the tray from her hands and placed it on the bar, then fished a twenty out of his pocket and handed it to her.

Alex offered him a ten, but Jonathan waved him away. "You get the next round," he said.

"Anyway," Alex continued, turning his attention back to Eli. "I'm not in the mood for sex stories today."

"Me neither," Jonathan said. "They're not as much fun when you can't contribute to the conversation."

"Don't tell me you haven't had any luck with all the women swarming around this place?"

"Forgive him," Alex said, taking a swig of his pineapple juice. "Eli thinks it's unhealthy for a man to go without sex for more than a week."

"It's a medical fact," Eli countered. "Going too long without getting some causes blindness. Remember, I'm a doctor. I know about this stuff," he finished with a grin.

Toby laughed as Alex shot an irritated look at their brother.

"Seriously," Eli continued. "It's sad as hell that Toby is the only one who can relate."

Toby rested his chin on the hand he had draped over the pool cue. He raised his brows sardonically as he looked at his brother.

"You're not getting any, either?" Eli shook his head. "I'll do tai chi for the rest of my life if I have to, as long as I'm not in the same boat as you three. This is pathetic."

"Sure is," Jonathan said. "Just give me a chance to settle into running the club and law practice. It won't take long to get back into the swing of things."

"Why do y'all make it seem as if being celibate is the end of the world?" Alex asked, walking to the other side of the table and breaking the set. The balls scattered across the table; the four and five both landing in the far right pocket.

"You're just saying that because you haven't had any in so long," Toby told him.

"Catholic priests go without."

"You're comparing yourself to a priest?" Eli asked, an incredulous look creasing his forehead.

"Stop being an ass," Alex shot back.

"I don't know how you've done it for so long," Toby said. "I'm about ready to crawl out of my skin."

"It is pretty decent of you not to make a play for Aria," Eli said, taking his turn. "Makes me believe you really are serious about this music thing."

Toby raised his chin long enough to flip his brother off. Eli made as if he was going to knock Toby in the head with his cue stick as he headed for the tray that held their drinks.

"I still think it's time for Toby and Sienna to finally get together," Alex said.

Jonathan straightened abruptly from his position over the pool table where he was just about to take his shot. "You and Sienna got something going on?"

Toby's first instinct was to deny, but he thought better of it. He was curious as to just how interested Jonathan was about Sienna. Toby regretted ever introducing the two of them. The thought of a woman coming between him and Jonathan was stupid, and the fact that the woman might be Sienna seemed preposterous. But if Jonathan had plans concerning her, Toby wanted to nip them in the bud.

"You know, hooking up with Sienna isn't a bad idea," Eli commented. Sitting with his elbows against the bar, he popped another cashew in his mouth and followed it with a swig of beer. "Sienna is about the only sane Culpepper girl."

"You're saying Ivana's insane?" Jonathan asked.

"She's into that voodoo." Eli shivered. "That stuff creeps me out."

"Yeah, but that doesn't mean she's crazy."

His old teammate's vehemence gave Toby pause. Since when had Jonathan become Ivana's defender? He'd only met her a few days ago, and had not mentioned her since.

"Ivana isn't as bad as people make her out to be," Alex said. "Now, Tosha? *That* girl is crazy."

"I *would* pick the biggest fruitcake of the bunch," Eli shook his head. "Too bad Sienna wasn't a few years older."

"I've been trying to tell *somebody* that Sienna has everything going for her, but the fool over here is too stupid to see it."

"What does it matter to you whether I'm seeing anybody

or not? It's none of your damn business, Alex." Toby realized he should have kept his trap shut before the words finished coming out of his mouth. If anybody had a right to rib him about not having a girlfriend, it was Alex, since he mercilessly chided his older brother about his lack of a sex life.

"Why does it matter to me?" Alex replied.

"Ooh, ooh." Eli called from the bar, raising his hand like a second-grader wanting to impress his teacher. "Can I answer that one?"

"You can stay the hell out of this," Toby shot at him. "The reason why I'm alone is completely different from Alex's reason."

"And you know this how, exactly?" his older brother asked.

"You told me yourself. You're not seeing anyone because you're trying to punish yourself for Chantal cheating on you."

"What the hell is he talking about?" Eli jumped from the barstool, all joking erased from his expression.

"Nothing," Alex answered, staring at Toby with a keen, knowing look in his eyes that always sent the hairs on the back of Toby's neck standing at attention. "He's just trying to take the spotlight off himself by bringing up something he knows nothing about."

Eli rounded the pool table and came to stand next to their older brother. Jonathan joined them, leaving Toby alone at the head of the table, like he was facing down a jury.

"I don't have time for a relationship. I spend half my time in the studio with Aria and the other half trying to come up with a marketing strategy."

"With Sienna," Alex added.

"Yes, with Sienna," Toby conceded. "Just because I'm working with her doesn't mean I automatically have to start up a relationship with her. Eli works with dozens of women; you don't see him sleeping with all of them."

"Only the unmarried ones. That was before Monica,

of course," he grinned. "Now all I have to do is a little relaxing tai chi. Actually I recommended it. It loosens you up."

Toby rolled his eyes. "Can we just get off this subject?"

"Now you see how I've felt these past few years."

Toby actually felt a bit of remorse for all the times he'd poked fun at Alex's choice to live like a monk. Before, he'd thought his brother was crazy to go so long without making love to a woman, especially when so many of them threw themselves at him—literally and figuratively.

Toby had been propositioned a time or two these past few weeks. But unlike in the past, he had not taken any of the women up on their very blatant offers. What was different this time?

Damn. He knew. He was having dinner with the *difference* in just a few hours.

Taking a pull on his beer, he set the bottle on the edge of the pool table, lined up the cue stick, and sent the nine ball into the far right corner pocket.

"What do you think about highlights?"

Sienna looked up from her novel and glanced over at Aria. Sitting back in the pedicure chair, she pulled at one of the bouncy curls framing her oval face. That she possessed the drop-dead features of a rising starlet was undeniable. Sienna had no doubt her flawless, honey-colored skin, pouty lips, and exotic, almond-shaped eyes would give Aria an edge in the appearance-obsessed entertainment business.

"I'm not sure you need highlights," Sienna answered.

Aria sighed and placed the mirror on the table next to her. "Well, I need to do something. Nothing I try seems to be working."

"Working with what?"

"Getting Toby's attention," Aria answered.

Oh, Lord. Sienna slipped in a bookmark to hold her place and sat the paperback in her lap. They were somewhat secluded in the spacious salon, the pedicure chairs separated from the rest of the area by a three foot high glass wall and an array of potted tropical plants.

"I've been trying in every way imaginable," Aria continued. "Sometimes I get the feeling something's about to happen, but at other times he treats me like I'm a kid sister or something."

"Uh," Sienna reached over for her water bottle, not sure how to handle this.

"I should just catch him alone and strip out of my clothes," Aria said. "Maybe then he'll get the picture."

Sienna put the water bottle back on the end table, grateful she had not taken a drink. She would have spewed water all over the poor girl diligently exfoliating the sole of her foot.

"Has Toby given you any indication that he'd be receptive to you . . . ah, stripping for him?" Sienna asked.

"Not in so many words, but why wouldn't he want it? He doesn't have a girlfriend. At this point I'm willing to settle for a one-night stand if he'll have me."

Oh, Lord.

"Okay, Aria. We are, um, we're friends, right?"

Aria looked at her warily. Granted, she had not been as friendly as she could have been, but Sienna gave herself credit for not being a total bitch this past week.

"I think you need to make sure Toby sees you the same way you see him."

"I know he doesn't," Aria said. "He wants things to stay professional between us."

"Don't you think that's for the best?"

"But it's not what I want. The only reason I signed with Toby is because I wanted to hook up with him."

"I *know* he doesn't know that," Sienna returned, shocked at Aria's revelation.

Aria shook her head. "I never really thought my singing career would go anywhere, and I knew Toby had never worked in the music business so I figured I'd just go along with it, and then when the music thing fell through we'd just, you know, be together."

Sienna could hardly believe what she was hearing.

"Aria, you've been lying to him."

"No, I haven't," Aria argued. "Once I realized he was serious then I sort of got serious about it, too. And now that this show's come up, I think there's a real shot that I can make it."

"You'd better do more than think there's a shot. You'd better work harder than you've ever worked before to make sure you make it to the top, because that's Toby's sole priority.

"I've known Toby all my life, and I have never seen him put so much of his heart and soul into anything, even basketball. If you are not one hundred percent serious about this, then you'd better tell me right now," Sienna warned.

"I am," Aria insisted. "Really, I'm totally into this now. But I want Toby, too."

Sienna was tempted to come right out and tell her that she couldn't have him. But it wasn't her place. This was between Toby and his client. She wasn't sure if Toby had given Aria an indication that there could be something more between them, but if he had he'd better straighten the girl out right now. There was too much at stake—her job, for one thing— to have it all wiped out over some misbegotten puppy dog infatuation.

"You're not going to tell Toby, are you?" Aria asked.

"Are you still planning on cornering him and stripping down to your birthday suit?"

"No," Aria laughed, but Sienna could almost see the wheels turning in the girl's head. She would try in some way to get Toby where she wanted him. For someone who was so adamant about keeping things on a professional level with his client, Toby had not done a good job of making his feelings known to Aria.

What if Toby had been giving Aria a false sense of hope with the intention of getting her to bend to his will? Sienna knew more than most that when Toby was hell-bent on doing something he went to extraordinary lengths to accomplish his goal.

"Our feet are done," Aria said, bright and bubbly. "Time to work on the hair."

Sienna rubbed the side of her head in an attempt to ease the pounding behind her eyes. Her afternoon of relaxation wasn't all that relaxing anymore.

Chapter Eleven

The foot traffic in the French Quarter was in full force, with tourists dipping in and out of the assortment of restaurants and shops lining Decatur Street. The festival season was just beginning, with Jazz Fest only two weeks away. The crowd would be doubled by the time that came around.

Toby pulled open the door to Sylvia's Treasures and was greeted by an overly strong floral scent he suspected was coming from the candle burning on a little round table to the right of the door.

"Well, well. Hello, Tobias." Sylvia Culpepper called from behind the glass top counter. She didn't bother to rise from her perch upon a stool behind the cash register. No surprise. He had been on Sylvia's bad side ever since he broke her treasured decorative plate with a picture of the White House. Good thing she never found out about the Tequila incident. If she still held a grudge after all these years over a plate, she would damn him to hell for getting her fifteen-year-old daughter wasted and feeling her up in her closet.

"Hi, Mrs. Culpepper." Toby leaned over the counter to plant a barely there kiss on her cheek. "How are you?"

"I'm fine. It's been a long time since I've seen you. I thought you'd forgotten about New Orleans."

"I could never forget my home."

"I guess Margo's excited to have all three of her boys back at home. I was hoping to get a chance to talk to her at church on Sunday, but she wasn't there."

"We went to a church in Slidell."

"She must have attended their Bible study this week, too."

"No, she went to Bible study at her church."

"I have known Margo Holmes long enough to remember what she looks like, and she was not at Bible study," Sylvia said, annoyance in her voice.

"I'm sorry," Toby answered. "It's just that Alex dropped her off and I picked her up at the church hall."

"Well, I don't know whose Bible study she went to, but it wasn't Morning Star Baptist."

"What are you doing here?" Toby turned at the sound of Sienna's voice.

Lord, have mercy.

The dress she wore put the little black one she'd worn to The Hard Court's opening night to shame. It was deep blue, low cut, and skintight. A lump of emotion lodged in Toby's throat, making it hard to speak.

"I thought we were meeting at the club at eight o'clock?" Sienna asked, making her way from the back of the store to the front counter.

"Sienna Elaine, where are you going dressed like that?" Sylvia asked.

"I told you, Mother. Aria Jordan, the singer Toby discovered, is singing at Toby's friend's club."

"You'd better hope they don't turn you around wearing a dress like that."

Damn, she looked good. Toby wished he could get to her closet to see what other sexy treasures she had stored in there.

Ignoring her mother, Sienna asked, "Are you ready?"

"If you are," Toby said, ecstatic that his voice decided to come out and play. "I know I'm a little early, but I figured we could walk from here since it's not all that far."

"Actually, I was going to walk anyway, but I thought I'd just meet you there. Mother, Toby and I have a meeting with the producers of the show, so I won't be able to come by this Saturday to help with inventory," Sienna said.

"I'll manage," Sylvia drawled.

Sienna rolled her eyes, then stood on her tiptoes and leaned over the counter to place a kiss on her mother's cheek. Toby tried hard not to stare at the way the dress stretched over her behind, but apparently there was a lack of communication between his eyes and his brain. Her butt was just begging to be held. It reminded Toby of his basketball days, and how perfectly the round ball used to fit in his palms. It had been a long time since he'd gripped a basketball. It had been a long time since he'd held a woman, too.

But he didn't want just *any* woman.

Sienna turned. "Let me run to the restroom, and then we can go."

As he watched her walk toward the restroom at the back of the store, Toby struggled with the thoughts that had plagued him constantly lately. For the past few days, any time his mind even ventured around thoughts of sex, only one woman showed up in his dreams.

Sienna.

It was driving him crazy. He shouldn't have these thoughts about her. Toby still doubted he could provide everything Sienna deserved in a man. She needed someone who would put her ahead of his own needs, who'd put her first.

Sienna wasn't his idea of prospective girlfriend material anyway. She was a jock. Well, she *used* to be a jock. In that dress, she was the furthest thing from a jock Toby had ever seen. But still, he could not seriously try to start something up with Sienna. There was too much history there.

Although, if he were honest, which he usually was—at least with himself—Toby could admit that things were drastically different between him and Sienna. They were not the friends they used to be, and no matter how much they attempted to rediscover that camaraderie, it just was not the same.

Could there be something more serious between them? How would he even broach the subject with her? He couldn't just say, "Hey, Cee Cee, I've been picturing you naked. You want to get together and see how things work out?"

She would kick his ass.

Toby took a deep breath, and tried to rein in the chaotic thoughts twisting through his mind. This was way too much for him to handle right now.

"Okay, I'm ready," Sienna said, coming out of the restroom. She preceded him out the door and they headed left down Royal Street, past a high-end furniture store displaying antiques emblazoned with a fleur de lis.

"My goodness, even at eight o'clock in the evening, it still feels like the middle of the day," Sienna said.

"Yeah, it took some getting used to. After being gone for so long, I had to recondition my body to function in this heat and humidity."

"I guess that would be a plus to living up north, although you did have all that cold and snow to deal with. I'm not sure how well I'd do in the snow. The few times it's ever snowed down here, the entire city shut down."

Toby took her by the elbow as they dodged a huge break in the sidewalk at the corner of Royal and Governor Nicholls Streets.

"The first day it snowed when I was at St. John's, I missed all my classes. When I found out the professors had marked me absent, I told them where I'm from everything goes into hibernation when it snows."

Sienna threw her head back and let out a peal of laughter, the illumination from the Old World–style street lamp casting a warm glow over her coffee-colored skin. Toby stared at the column of her throat, imagining his tongue running along the slope under her jaw.

"Do you miss it?" she asked.

"What? The snow?" He asked, trying to pull his thoughts away from her delectable looking neck.

"No, living up north. When you never came home, I figured you must really like it up there."

"It was all right," he shrugged. "I fell into the flow of things pretty easily."

"Too easily," she remarked quietly, glancing down at the sidewalk. "It made you forget everything and everyone back here."

Toby flinched at her accusation. "I didn't forget, Cee Cee."

"Could have fooled me," she mumbled, picking up her step.

"Sienna, wait a minute." He placed a restraining hand on her arm and waited until she looked up at him before saying, "You know I didn't forget about you."

"Am I really supposed to believe that, Toby? I hardly ever saw you once you left for school."

"You were in Atlanta!" he said, his chest constricting at the hurt evident in her eyes.

"I wasn't in Atlanta all the time. I came home on holidays."

"It was too expensive to travel during holidays," he defended. "I had to come home during the offseason, when airfare was more reasonable."

"I know things were rough, but a phone call every now and then would not have broken the bank, Toby."

"You could have called, too, you know," Toby charged, his defenses spurred by her insinuation that this gap between them was his fault. "Hell, you could have come up to New York if you wanted to,"

"I was afraid," she said, her voice small.

"Of what?"

"I was afraid I would cramp your style," she said with a hesitant shrug, uncertainty naked in her apprehensive eyes. "I figured you were the big man on campus who wouldn't want your skinny, tomboy friend from back home messing with your reputation."

Regret expanded in his chest. "You know I would never have said that."

"No, I didn't know," she said with a choked, desperate laugh. Sienna shook her head, her eyes, when she looked back at him, were filled with the same regret Toby felt. "It had been so long since I'd talked to you, I wasn't sure what you would say or think. You changed while you were out there, Toby." Her expressive eyes darkened even more with remorse. "You were not the same person. You're still not."

"And you are?" he said, gesturing up and down the length of her. "The Sienna Culpepper who played point guard at

St. Mary's Academy wouldn't have even known where to buy a dress like this. The shoes. The makeup. You're not the same Cee Cee I left back in New Orleans."

Sienna gaped at him. "You're comparing a dress and a little makeup to the changes you've undergone?"

"That is more than *just* a dress."

Sienna's eyes narrowed, and Toby told himself to look away. He wasn't sure he was ready for her to see the desire he knew was in his eyes. He was still trying to figure this out for himself. But he couldn't help it. And he couldn't look away. Instead, his fingers rose to her face and trailed lightly across her smooth jaw.

"Neither of us are the people we were when we left for college," he said, his gaze falling to her full lips.

"No, we're not." Her words came out on a husky breath.

"We used to be best friends."

"We still could be," she said.

Acute desire blossomed in his chest. "Or—"

"Or?"

"We . . . can—" Confusion stalled his words. Were they ready for this next step? Was he? How would this affect their already tenuous relationship? How would it affect his career?

Toby gave his head an imperceptible shake, flinging off the residual desire thrumming through his brain. He and Sienna still had to work together. Starting something up with her could be a distraction, and he couldn't allow anything to get in the way of the success of the show.

"It's getting late," he said, taking her by the arm. "We need to keep walking if we're going to have dinner before Aria performs."

"Umm, okay," Sienna answered, clearly shaken.

They continued their way down Governor Nicholls Street without another word spoken between them.

Sienna walked through the door Toby held open for her. The tension radiating between them had been building throughout their walk over to The Hard Court, and she was at the breaking point.

This entire thing was getting far too complicated. It was less intimidating when she thought Toby and Aria were a couple. Now that she knew he was unattached, it took away her excuses. If she was having this same conversation with Ivana, instead of with herself, how would she answer her sister if she asked for the reasons she chose to not seriously pursue Toby?

There was no answer. At least not one she could share with Ivana or with anyone else. After all this time, how could she reveal the nightmare that had shattered her world?

Not a single soul knew about the night she had been pinned against that building; how the despicable hands of that monster had ripped her dress. How he'd forced her legs apart and rammed his fingers into her body. The remembered stench of alcohol on his breath hit her like a violent fist. Her stomach twisted, bile rising in her throat.

Sienna shut her eyes tight against the memories. Humiliation shuddered throughout her body. How could she have allowed it? Why didn't she fight?

A disturbing knot of anxiety balled in her stomach. Sienna pulled her bottom lip between her teeth to stop them from trembling. She had to get control of herself. This was neither the time nor the place to allow her emotions to overwhelm her.

She had nearly convinced herself that she was over the assault. She'd tried. Lord knows she'd done everything she could to get on with her life. But vamping up her wardrobe with daring dresses and trying to use the flirting techniques she read about in magazines did little to instill in Sienna the confidence she witnessed in her friends. At the end of the day, her attempts at exploring her sexuality were futile. She clammed up whenever a guy showed interest.

"Cee Cee, you okay?" Toby asked.

Startled, Sienna's eyes widened. How had she allowed herself to be pulled in by those memories again?

She gazed up at Toby and a shower of relief washed over her. Toby was the one person Sienna knew would never hurt her—at least not physically. His inability to see her as anything but a friend sent a familiar pang of longing rushing through Sienna's veins. But over the years, Sienna had come to recognize that the ache carried with it a hint of comfort. As long as she pined for a relationship with Toby, something that would probably never come to fruition, she didn't have to face the fears of intimacy that had been born the night of her debutante ball.

"Sienna?" Toby squeezed her upper arm.

"I'm—" the word came out hoarse. She cleared her throat, tried again. "I'm fine. A glass of water wouldn't hurt, though."

"Let's go to the bar before we head upstairs," Toby suggested.

They walked past the lobby and onto the main floor of the club. There was a crowd gathering at the far right end, toward the bar. Sienna spotted Jonathan breaking away from the pack.

"There's Jonathan," she said to Toby, pointing.

"Hey, man." The two shared their usual greeting, clasping palms and embracing in a half hug. "What's going on over there?" Toby asked.

Sienna could feel the discomfort shooting off Jonathan as he shifted his stance. "We've got ourselves a celebrity in the club tonight," he answered, nervously running a hand over his head and shoving the other in his pocket.

"Who?" Toby asked.

"Isaac Payton."

The transformation was instant. Toby's expression went from laid-back to utterly hostile in less than a second. He glared at Jonathan. "Of all the players in the NBA, that's who you invite to your club?" Toby asked accusingly.

"I didn't invite him," Jonathan argued. "He showed up about an hour ago, but I'm not sending him away. Do you see the amount of people here? And it's not even nine o'clock yet."

Toby's jaw clenched, his eyes deadly.

Sienna wasn't sure of exactly what was going on. Toby's anger was evident in the hand balled at his side and the scowl he shot Jonathan's way.

"You know, Toby, I'm not all that hungry. Maybe we can get out of here until Aria's performance," Sienna suggested in an attempt to diffuse his anger. She knew Toby and NBA superstar Isaac Payton had played together at St. John's, but that's about all she knew. Well, and that the other man pulled in about twelve million a year just in endorsements. By the look on Toby's face, there was some bad blood between those two.

"Even if you leave, I'm not promising that Payton will be gone by the time Aria gets on stage," Jonathan said to Sienna. He turned his attention to Toby. "Look, man. All that stuff happened years ago. You need to put it behind you and use this jackass's fame to your advantage. Think of all the exposure Aria will get tonight."

Jonathan was right, Sienna decided. Whatever problem Toby had with Isaac Payton was not worth losing the chance to expose Aria to tonight's massive crowd. This was business. Personal issues had no part in it.

Maybe she should think about that the next time she started thinking about Toby in a less than professional way.

"We're here to have dinner," Toby said, taking Sienna by the hand. "Let the bastard stay right where he is. You're right; he'll be helping me out without even knowing it."

"That's the way to look at it, brother," Jonathan said, throwing his arm over Toby's shoulder. Together, the three of them walked upstairs. Jonathan sat them at the same out of the way table where they'd dined the first time they came to dinner.

The waitress arrived within minutes, and Sienna waited until they'd placed their drink order before folding her hands on the table and leaning over to say, "Okay, spill it."

"Spill what?"

"I just knew you were going to say that," she said, shaking her head.

"Say what?"

"That. Whenever you want to avoid a subject you answer all my questions with questions until I get irritated and drop it. Well, I'm not dropping it this time."

"You didn't ask a question. You made a demand."

"Stop skirting around the issue, Toby. What's up with you and Isaac Payton?"

"Not a damn thing."

"Fine," Sienna said, they'd get back to this soon enough. Sienna had something more pressing she wanted to discuss. Although she'd promised Aria that she wouldn't say anything to Toby, Sienna thought he had a right to know. "There's something else we need to talk about."

He sent her a guarded look.

"Aria and I had a real heart-to-heart at the salon today," Sienna continued. "There's just something about a hairdresser's chair that gets a person talking."

"And?" he asked, reaching for his glass of water.

"And, she's in love with you," Sienna said with a casual wave of her hand.

Toby put the glass down without taking a sip. "She is *not* in love with me," he insisted.

The waitress came over to take their order, but Toby sent her away.

"We've been over this already, Sienna. There is nothing going on between me and Aria."

"Are you really that blind, Toby? The girl worships the ground you walk on."

His eyes slid shut. He slouched back in the chair, a pained expression on his face. "Did you at least set her straight?"

"That's not my responsibility. You're the one who's been giving her mixed signals."

He sat up straight. "The hell I have."

Sienna made a production of looking at her watch. "Maybe we should get the waitress to take our order."

"We've got time. Now, why would you say I've been giving Aria mixed signals? I've been nothing but professional with her."

"Are you kidding?" Sienna asked with an incredulous snort. "The two of you are always together. Most managers don't bring their clients to every family function. Maybe that's what gave her the impression that she was more than just a 'client.'" Sienna made air quotes on the last word.

The waitress returned, and Sienna ordered them both garden salads topped with fried crawfish tails. "All I'm saying is that you need to talk to her to find out exactly what she is expecting from this client/manager relationship," she continued.

Toby swore. "How could I have even prepared myself for something like this? You don't have to worry about your teammates getting mixed signals when you play basketball."

"Speaking of which, why don't you answer my first question?" He pinned her with another stare. Sienna was getting really tired of those. "Come on, Toby. What's with the hostility toward Payton?"

"I told you it's nothing."

"Oh, that's why you looked as if you were ready to rip Jonathan's head from his shoulders when you thought he'd invited him here?"

"Payton is an ass, okay?"

"Hell-*o-o-o*. I watch ESPN. I know that already. Exactly what is *your* particular beef with him? The two of you started at St. John's together, but I don't remember ever hearing about any kind of animosity on the team. Was something happening behind the scenes?"

He sighed and leaned back in his chair, looking like he was posing for the dictionary example of the word "irritated." Sienna didn't care. To her surprise, it looked as if Toby would concede before she had to get nasty.

Toby ran his hand down his face and relinquished his slouched pose. Setting his elbows on the table, he leaned forward and spoke in a hushed, but no less harsh, tone.

"Payton and I used to be tight back at St. John's. His childhood nearly mirrored mine; two older brothers, and a single mother raising them. Except his dad is still alive somewhere, as far as I know. But, basically, it was the same situation. I don't know, I guess that's why we clicked."

Toby removed the wet paper napkin from under his glass and started tearing it into jumbled, soggy pieces. The waitress brought their salads, but Toby ignored his.

"Anyway, this agent out of Seattle was scouting around the campus and tried to get both me and Isaac to enter the draft early. We both agreed, but at the last minute, Isaac pulled out. He'd made a deal with another agent behind my back, who told him if he stayed in school his senior year he would go in the first round."

"Which he did," Sienna said. She remembered the draft that year.

"He went sixth, to Philly." Toby picked up one of the wet strips of paper and rolled it between his fingers. "This other agent had inside information on the health of some of the players. He knew the next year's draft class would be weaker, so Isaac had a better chance of moving up in the draft if he waited. Isaac stayed in school, worked hard, and managed to become a first team All-American his senior year, so he got a two-point-five million dollar signing bonus."

Sienna winced. She clearly remembered when Toby was drafted. He'd been taken toward the end of the second round, and his signing bonus was nowhere near $2,500,000.

"The worst of it is, I didn't want to come out early," he said, shoving the wet scraps away. "The only reason I even agreed to speak with the agent is because Isaac wanted to. Can you believe I let him talk me into doing something like that?"

No, she couldn't. Toby had a mind of his own, and rarely, even as a young boy, did he let anyone influence him. Even his brothers had a hard time getting through once Toby set his mind to do something.

"Why didn't you pull out once you realized Isaac had backtracked?"

He shot her a quick, uneasy look. "You remember that Benz I was driving the night of the accident?"

Sienna narrowed her eyes. "You did not."

"The car. The watch." He rolled up the cuff of his sleeve. "And cash. More than I'd ever seen."

"You accepted money from an agent while you were still playing college ball?"

He nodded.

Sienna tried to close her mouth, but couldn't. She could not believe Toby had sold out.

"I still have about five hundred grand saved." He shrugged like it was no big deal.

"Did your brothers know about this?" Sienna asked.

"Hell no! Can you imagine that ass kicking?"

Sienna shuddered, wondering how Toby could have gotten so seduced by money.

"I've been planning to send Mama and her sister on that twenty-one-day cruise to Russia they've wanted to go on for as long as I can remember, but I know Mama would question where the money came from. None of the jobs I've had can account for that kind of cash, and the modest amount I made in my nonexistent basketball career is tied up in investments. Mama's already told me not to think about touching it."

Margo Holmes was probably the one person who could influence him.

"So, you accepted a car and cash from the agent in exchange for coming into the draft early?" Sienna clarified.

"Yeah. Probably the biggest mistake of my life. No, definitely *the* biggest mistake. If I'd stayed my butt in school, I wouldn't have been on the highway that night."

Sienna's chest tightened. "Toby," she whispered.

He tried to hide his pain behind a smile, but Sienna could see right through it. She didn't know what to say, so she just stretched her hand out across the table, praying he'd take it.

He did.

His smile was more genuine this time, with a little relief tipping up the edges. Sienna wasn't sure she should press anymore, but she had tried for so long to get Toby to talk about his accident. Maybe if he did, it wouldn't hurt so much.

"You ever thought that maybe the accident was a part of a bigger plan?" she asked softly.

His head kicked back as if she'd slapped him, his gaze slicing into her. "You think it was divine intervention that an SUV came flying over the median, crashed into me head-on, and nearly ripped my spine apart?"

She shuddered again. "Okay, you don't have to be so graphic."

"But it *was* graphic. Very graphic," he said, his voice edged with steel, his knuckles white where he gripped the table.

"I'm sorry," Sienna said.

"No, I'm sorry." Toby ran a hand down his face. "I'm just so tired of hearing that the accident was meant to happen. I guess that's everyone's way of trying to help me accept it, but it's hard." He looked up at her, his eyes laced with pain. "I nearly died, Sienna. I was in the hospital for months."

"I remember," she said softly. She had actually been there a few days after his accident, when he was still in a coma, even though she never told him that she had flown up to D.C. The image of Toby with those dozens of wires and machines hooked up to him would remain with her for the rest of her life.

"You know what the worst part is? There's nobody to blame. It's not like I was hit by a drunk driver who shouldn't have been on the road in the first place. Gina Carson was just like my mother, a single parent trying to provide for her children. Remember all those years Mama fought with the insurance company after my dad died? Mama worked two jobs, too. She probably fell asleep behind the wheel more than once. Mama was just lucky enough she never crashed the car into something or somebody."

Toby lifted his shoulders in a helpless shrug.

"How can I fault the woman who hit me for trying to make a better life for her kids when my own mother did the same for me?"

"I'm sorry," Sienna said because she didn't know what else to say. She'd wanted him to open up, but had not counted on the complete despair clouding Toby's face.

"Maybe it *was* part of a bigger plan," he said. "It was probably my penance for taking the car and money."

"Toby—"

He waved her off. "I'm joking. At least I've learned to do that again. You know, you should be happy I never came around after the accident. I was a mean S.O.B. Nobody wanted to be around me."

Sienna could not share his humor. It was a façade. He was still hurting. It was written all over his face, seeping out of every pore of his body.

Unsure of what his reaction might be to what she was going to say, she took a deep breath before speaking. "You may not want to hear this, but yes, I do believe the accident was meant to happen," she said. His head snapped back again and he blinked a few times, but Sienna forged ahead. "You are an unbelievable manager and a gifted songwriter, Toby. You are going to make Aria Jordan's and countless other aspiring singers' dreams come true. Basketball was not in the cards for you—as much as you may love it and miss it. I truly believe *this* is what you were meant to do."

He stared at her, not saying anything.

"Toby," Sienna said when he continued to just stare.

"Thank you," he finally said. Sienna's heart leapt at the true sincerity in his eyes. "When I first told Eli and Alex about my plan to go into music, they had no problem telling me how ridiculous it was for me to attempt to be a manager. That's why I tried to keep the songwriting private. You're the first person to tell me I'm good at what I do, Sienna."

"No, I'm not," she said.

His eyes bored into hers and he squeezed her hand. "The first that matters."

Sienna's stomach trembled at the seriousness in his voice.

They ate the remainder of their meal in relative silence, which was fine after the heavy discussion that had just taken place. When they finished, Toby rose from the table and came around to help her out of her seat.

"You ready to face the backstabber?" she asked him.

"Might as well," he said. "As Jonathan pointed out, Payton brought along an entourage the size of a small town. This can only be good for Aria and the show. Let's go and get this over with."

As they made their way down the wide staircase, Toby mentally pictured all the things he wished he could do to Isaac Payton. First being slamming his fist into the man's face. But as he approached The Hard Court's main floor, Toby decided to be the bigger man and leave the pettiness aside. He was over his former teammate's treachery.

Well, he wasn't entirely over it, but it didn't burn as much as it used to.

He had more important things to think about than the butcher knife Isaac had planted squarely between his shoulder blades all those years ago. He had a new career. A brand new life. And according to Sienna, he was good at what he did.

God, it felt good to hear that. After years of floundering from one interest to another, something about music had finally clicked. He had worked his butt off trying to develop the right image. Convincing his family that this was what he wanted to do with his life was a monumental task; convincing himself that it was right proved harder than anything else. But Sienna believed in him. And, for some reason, that made all the difference in the world.

As they arrived at the bottom of the stairs, bitterness clogged in Toby's throat as he noticed Isaac Payton's entourage taking up nearly a third of the floor. The jerk probably paid them to hang on to his every word.

Toby didn't have the time or the energy to devote to resenting his ex-teammate. Tonight was Aria's last performance before the cameras arrived for *A Week in the Life of a Wannabe Star*. He had to focus on every nuance of her performance in order to pick out the things they needed to work on.

"Why don't we stand back here," Sienna said. "It's the perfect view of the stage. We can really study Aria from this vantage point."

It was like she'd read his mind.

That was scary. For a multitude of reasons. If Sienna had even an inkling of some of the images that had been floating through his mind today, she would skewer him.

Before Toby could examine that thought further, Jonathan took to the stage as the emcee. He acknowledged Payton, because first and foremost, Jonathan was a businessman, and having Isaac Payton in his club was good for business. If anyone had missed the fact that the pro basketball star was in the house, Jonathan would make sure they knew.

He introduced Aria, and Toby could only smile at the acclaim that resounded around the club.

He and Sienna stood in the back and watched as Aria performed. Her vocals were on target, as always, but he sensed skittishness lurking under the false confidence Toby could see right through.

"She's still too stiff," Sienna said, again reading his mind. She had to stop doing that.

"She is," Toby agreed. "How else am I supposed to loosen her up? That's what these practice runs at The Hard Court were supposed to do."

Sienna shook her head. "I'm not sure, but we have to do something before those cameras start rolling. They are going to add extra stress as it is."

Toby knew what she said was true; he just didn't know what to do about it. Thankfully, the crowd at The Hard Court either didn't notice Aria's tendency for stage fright, or they didn't care. When she finished her third and final song of the night on a loud and clear high note, the place went into an uproar.

If making it in the music business were only about singing, Aria would be a shoo-in. But in today's music world, it took a lot more than a powerful voice to win over the masses. Performers had to portray a certain persona. They had to have a certain style. Charisma. They still had a long way to go where Aria was concerned.

She acknowledged the applause with her usual shy grace,

but in a move that surprised the heck out of Toby, Aria pointed straight back, saying, "I'd like to give a shout out to my manager, Tobias Holmes."

Most of the heads in the club turned to him, and the crowd continued to roar.

Toby accepted pats on the back from the people surrounding him, but he knew by making his presence known, Aria had just made him a prime target for Isaac Payton. He had hoped to go the night without having to face his former teammate. Toby had no doubt that Payton knew he was bitter about how things had gone down between them when he left St. John's, and he could tell the guy took pleasure in rubbing his success in Toby's face.

It looked like his reprieve would be even shorter than he'd hoped. Payton's entourage had parted, and the man was making his way toward the back of the club where he and Sienna were standing. Toby spotted Jonathan in the crowd about fifty feet away, but all Jonathan could offer was a helpless hunch of his shoulders.

Toby braced himself for his first exchange with his former friend in over four years.

"Tobias Holmes."

"Payton." Toby nodded, unable to keep the stoicism out of his voice. How in the hell was he supposed to greet the man who'd stabbed him so soundly in the back? With a hug?

"Did I hear that correctly?" Payton asked. "You're the one who manages that lovely creature?"

"Aria is one of the artists under Tobias Holmes Management."

Payton's eyebrows rose. "You have your own management firm? I guess it takes more than a broken spine to keep you down."

Anger rippled down Toby's back at the jab.

"And who is this?" Isaac asked, turning his attention to Sienna.

She stuck out her hand. "Sienna Culpepper. I'm Toby's marketing director."

Okay, so that was a pretty good stretch of the truth. Handling Aria's account definitely didn't make Sienna the marketing director for the entire agency, but since he managed only two other acts, which he hadn't really concentrated on much since this entire thing with Aria began anyway, Toby decided to roll with it.

Isaac took Sienna's hand and brought it to his lips. "You know, I'm about to fire my publicist. Are you looking to move up in the world?"

Sienna pulled her hand free and gave a halfhearted laugh. "I think I'll pass. I'm more than happy in my current position."

Isaac cocked one brow. "That's only because you don't know how much greener the grass is on the other side."

"Having that much trouble finding people to work for you that you have to sink to poaching, Isaac?" Toby asked.

Payton shook his head. "I'm just giving the woman options."

"She doesn't need options," Toby said, thrusting his body between them. He was so close to punching the hell out of Payton he could almost feel his fist hitting the side of the man's head.

"Toby." Sienna caught his shoulder. "Here's Aria. I think this would be a good time to go over some of the things we discussed."

Aria sidled up next to him. She was obviously starstruck by the night's honored guest.

"Oh, my goodness," Aria said, gushing like the barely postteen that she was. "I cannot believe I'm standing next to Isaac Payton. I thought I would die when I heard you were in the audience tonight."

"I heard about this brand new singing sensation performing at my former college teammate's new club, so I had to check it out. Of course, I didn't realize I'd get to see *another* former teammate of mine," he jeered. "Toby and I go way back," Payton finished with a wink of an eye and flash of his bleached teeth.

"I didn't know that," Aria said, looking at Toby as if he was somehow more important because he *knew* the great Isaac Payton.

"I've got tons of stories about my old friend," Isaac answered her. "Why don't we all go back over to my table and catch up. Drinks are on me."

"I don't think so," Toby said. The smirk on Isaac's face pissed him off. "I've got more important things to do."

"Oh, c'mon, Toby," Aria pleaded. "Please."

He rolled his eyes, but relented.

A prisoner on his way to the electric chair probably had more of a bounce in his step than Toby did, but he still managed to make it to the side of the club Isaac and his entourage had commandeered.

Sienna and Aria sat next to each other at the round table, and instead of taking the available seat next to the woman who was openly worshipping him; Isaac chose to sit next to Sienna.

The hairs on the back of Toby's neck stood at attention.

There was no way his ex-teammate would give up the opportunity to be idolized by an adoring fan in exchange for a cold shoulder. Unless he was looking for a challenge.

As Isaac went on about the glamorous life of an NBA superstar, Aria looked on the verge of melting into a pool of mush. Sienna, on the other hand, wasn't in any danger of being blown away by Isaac's hot air. With every word he said, Toby could see Sienna's face stiffening to the point that he figured he'd have to throw her in a sauna to loosen her skin. And, Isaac, being the idiot of the decade, as usual, didn't seem to take the hint.

"So," Isaac turned toward Sienna. "Tell me about what you've done to help out Toby. Being creative isn't his strong point. At least, it never was on the basketball court."

Toby gritted his teeth and counted to five in an attempt to control his temper.

"Hmm . . . the team that drafted him didn't seem to think so," Sienna countered smoothly, folding her hands on the table. "I've played ball with Toby more times than I can count, and although I hate to admit it, I was fooled quite a few times by some of his trick moves."

"Wait!" Issac said. "Are you the one Toby used to call Cee Cee? You're *that* Sienna?"

"I am," Sienna answered in an even colder voice.

"Oh, man. Toby used to talk about you all the time. He forgot to mention you were fine as hell."

"Toby knows I do not appreciate being discussed in that way," Sienna answered, smoothly.

Thank God Sienna had such a good head on her shoulders. The girl was reading the situation like a book, and not falling for a thing Isaac said. But that wasn't enough to stop Payton. Refusing to storm out of the club, thus giving Payton the satisfaction of knowing his jibes still ate at him, Toby sat there for the next hour, drowning in pure humiliation, as the man he once called a friend did his very best to make him feel like nothing.

Chapter Twelve

"You're concentrating pretty hard there," Sienna said as she scooted onto a high back barstool and balanced her pool cue next to her.

"I want to make sure I cover all of my angles," Toby answered.

He picked up his beer bottle and strolled to the other side of the table, his feet sticking to the grimy, slightly uneven floorboards. A thin haze of cigarette smoke hovered just above their heads like a threadbare blanket, the wall of colorful neon beer signs bathing them with an ethereal, vivid hue.

The thwack of dented balls clashing upon the occupied pool tables competed with the bluesy music flowing from a boom box, circa 1983, sitting on the far edge of the bar.

Toby took a slow pull on his longneck, letting out a satisfied sigh at the rush of the icy liquid trickling down his throat. But the cold beer did nothing to cool him down. Toby was still steaming over what had gone down at the club earlier.

Isaac Payton had personified arrogance as a cocky freshman back at St. John's, but now that he was a credible star in the NBA, his head had swelled to gargantuan proportions. Toby was surprised he could fit it inside that silver Maserati he took off in after leaving the club.

Toby had spent the last few years trying to ignore the hype surrounding his former teammate's career, but it was impossible. The man had everything Toby had ever wanted—fame, endorsements, contracts, a great career. Isaac Payton was living *his* life.

Toby could still remember lying in the hospital bed and watching Isaac go in the first round of the NBA draft. The stinging metallic taste of bitterness still lingered on his tongue. Seeing his former teammate tonight had dug up memories Toby had hoped to keep buried deep. Witnessing Isaac's success and seeing the throng of people crowding at his feet tonight had nearly torn the small shred of confidence he had regained. No matter how popular Aria became on the local music scene, Toby had a long way to go before he could ever hope to experience the success Isaac enjoyed.

Toby took another long gulp of his beer in an attempt to wash away the depressing thoughts.

"Are you going to take your shot, or what?" Sienna asked.

His mouth curved into a grin at her teasing impatience.

After all these years, Sienna was still doing her best to ease his pain when she knew he was hurting. He hadn't had to say anything; she'd seemed to know what seeing Isaac had done to him tonight. When he'd tried to go home after leaving the club, Sienna wouldn't let him. She'd practically dragged him to this all night pool hall/rib joint, claming she was hungry and needed to unwind.

For the past two hours they had managed to get slamming drunk, but when Sienna foolishly suggested they play for money—ten dollars a ball—Toby got serious. He was up two hundred dollars.

Toby bent low over the table, and set his sights on the eight ball.

"Black-eyed Susan in the right corner pocket."

The cool wood slid between his fingers a couple of times before he jutted the stick forward, propelling the cue ball across the worn green velvet and connecting with his target. The eight ball clicked against the others already in the pocket.

"You should just sign over your paycheck," Toby teased.

He guessed the look she sent him was supposed to be a glare, but it wasn't convincing.

Earlier, Toby had been surprised by her skills. She explained that she had gotten into pool while attending Spellman, when her sorority had played in a competition against one of the Morehouse fraternities. But those skills had rapidly deteriorated when she switched from drinking beer to apple martinis. She probably didn't realize she was too drunk to do anything more than keep herself upright.

Her pool skills had not been the only thing affected by the alcohol she had consumed tonight. Sienna's inhibitions had loosened considerably. Toby was convinced some of the things she had said tonight were straight out of a porno flick. The more inebriated she became, the bolder she had become.

Like now.

She sat on the edge of the pool table while he took his next shot, her unbearably short dress inching even higher. Toby's eyes were drawn to her smooth, delicately muscled thighs as she crossed her fabulous legs. They glistened as if they had been sprinkled with pixie dust by a fairy hell-bent on driving him crazy.

She leaned over, thrusting her chest out a little, and whispering in his ear, "Make sure you get it in the right hole."

Toby nearly missed the cue ball, but his shot still managed to go in.

Sienna cursed as she scooted off the pool table.

Now that he'd won most of her money, she was angry, which Toby vastly preferred. Maybe now she would lay off with the suggestive comments that had him ready to crawl out of his skin.

"Move," she said, edging past him, and nearly falling over her feet.

"Whoa, there." Toby caught her, clenching her curvy waist in his hands.

The spark of electricity that shot through him was enough to light up all of New Orleans. He had to clench his teeth against the urge to pull Sienna's body even closer to his. He wanted to feel those curves flush against him, to move his hands from her waist to her backside and pull her close.

Calm down, boy. He silently chastised the part of his body that was getting way more excited than it should. Toby moved his hands from Sienna's waist to her shoulders. She looped her arm around his neck, trying to gain purchase.

"Maybe you . . . uhh . . . should sit for a while," he suggested, his hands burning as they fitted against her slightly warmed skin.

Sienna raised her gaze to his, searching his face. Her breath was warm and sweet with the scent of her apple-flavored drink.

"I'm good right here," she whispered.

Toby took a breath.

Then another.

He could have used a third, but then Sienna pressed her chest against his and he lost all ability to breathe. Toby searched her gaze, finding frank honesty in her bright stare. It would be so easy to make those little fantasies that had been running through his mind hard reality. A couple of inches, and his mouth would be on hers. He could almost taste it, was dying to taste it. Would give anything to taste it. Just this once.

Instead, Toby gently pushed her away.

"Hold on there, Cee Cee. I think you've had a little too much to drink."

"A couple of beers? That's not enough to get me drunk." Her slightly slurred words belied her statement.

"Maybe not," Toby answered, "But those martinis did a fine job. I think we should call it a night."

A sexy, catlike smile curled the corners of her mouth, and Toby knew he was in trouble. But before she could utter another word, Sienna's eyes widened and she doubled over, throwing up her dinner and about a liter of alcohol all over the floor.

Sienna chanced lifting an eyelid and thought better of it. She had been debating whether or not to wake up for the past half hour. Just the thought of letting in the tiniest hint of light made her head spin and her stomach lurch.

Why did people drink? Ever?

She felt as if her entire body was going to stage a revolt any minute now, with the spot just beyond her eyes leading the cavalry, and her throbbing temples acting as seconds in command.

Sienna groaned, wincing at the effort it took just to turn over on the bed. She couldn't lie here all day, as much as she wanted to do just that. There was too much to do, the first thing being figuring out how she had gotten into her bed in the first place.

She vaguely remembered going to Ray's Rib Shack after leaving The Hard Court with Toby. She was the one who had suggested pool. But why?

Oh yeah, because that jerk Isaac Payton had clowned Toby and she'd wanted to give him an outlet to release his frustration. She'd been afraid of what he would do if he had gone home and spent the entire night thinking about Payton.

So why had *she* gotten sloppy drunk?

Right. Because Toby had looked so good last night that she couldn't stand to be near him and not touch him, so she'd used martinis as a way to relieve *her* frustration.

Big. Dumb. Stupid. Mistake.

When had alcohol ever done her any good? The last time

she drank more than she should have, she'd nearly been raped. It was a lesson she had never forgotten, until last night.

Maybe it was because she knew, no matter what, she could trust Toby to never treat her the way that monster, Curtis Henderson, had. But that still didn't give her license to let her guard down the way she had last night. Mixing Toby and alcohol created an entirely different danger.

God, she hoped she didn't do anything embarrassing last night. Just the possibility of some of the thoughts she'd been having about Toby actually coming out of her mouth had Sienna ready to bury her head under the covers and not surface for a year.

Her phone rang, nearly scaring her heart out of her chest. Sienna reached over and groaned as her head brought the concept of pounding to an entirely new level.

"Hello," she croaked.

"I'm surprised you're awake," came a voice tinged with amusement. Her stomach bottomed out at the sound of his low murmur.

"Barely," Sienna answered. "Did you put me in bed last night?" How embarrassing that she even had to ask that.

"You were in no condition to make it to bed on your own. I gave you a chance, but you didn't make it past your kitchen floor. I couldn't leave you there."

"Oh, God. I should have stopped after the first martini."

"You should have stopped after the second beer. You should have never started on the martinis. You know you can't hold your liquor," he teased.

Sienna nodded her head, as if he could see her agreement through the phone.

"Do you think you'll be okay for the meeting with the producers today?" he asked.

"That's today?" How could she have forgotten about that?

"In about two hours," Toby reminded her.

Sienna stifled another groan. "All I need is a shower and a gallon of coffee," she answered.

"Breakfast probably wouldn't hurt, either. I can bring you some of the grits and eggs Mama cooked this morning."

"Oh, shut up, please. I don't want to be within ten feet of food."

"You sure?" Sienna could hear the laughter in his voice. "The eggs were over easy. You know how good it is when the yoke runs over the grits."

She hung up the phone.

Sienna forced herself to get out of bed and into the shower. They were meeting with the producers of *A Week in the Life of a Wannabe Star* and the crew that would be shooting Aria's portion of the show would be arriving to start scouting the area and do preliminary taping for the pretaped segments that would air between the live broadcasts. This was the time for her to be her most impressive, and here she was with a hangover.

Sienna dressed and headed toward the aroma of the fresh chicory coffee she'd started brewing before taking her shower. She'd need a Big Gulp–sized cup if she had a chance in hell of making it through today.

She was never, ever drinking again. Ever.

Ivana pulled the wire rope hanging overhead, indicating to the streetcar driver that she would be getting off at the next stop.

It had been the kind of morning that put her usual positive outlook on life to the test. First, her incense supplier had not been able to fulfill this week's order, which meant she now had unhappy customers. Then, as she had been setting up the few supplies she did have available, a leg gave way on her table, sending everything tumbling into the street. Ivana had taken it as a sign and packed up for the day.

She made good money with her booth in the French Market that ran along the river at the base of the French Quarter, but most of her business came from locals who expected her to supply their incense needs in a timely manner. When her supplier was late, she looked bad. She could not afford to tick off her regulars.

Of course, if she listened to her mother and found herself a "real" job, she wouldn't have to worry about suppliers with flat tires or angry customers. And it's not as if it would be hard to find that real job. With a Master's degree in International Finance there were more than enough opportunities, especially living in one of the busiest port cities in the United States.

But how could she ever be happy dressed in a suit and carrying a leather briefcase again?

Corporate America was not in her future, despite her mother's disapproval. Ivana had lived that life for years, and the only thing she got in return was an ulcer.

She had reached a turning point when she'd checked herself into a hospital for exhaustion. Michael, her ex-husband, had criticized her, calling her weak, but Ivana knew it was her body's way of telling her she could no longer live in that world. It had been divine intervention when the night nurse had approached her, claiming that something about Ivana had called to her. She'd talked to her about the work of the city's voodoo, and Ivana knew she'd found her calling.

She was needed right where she was, fighting for the Cause. The number of people caring for this city's poor and destitute was far too little as it was. She had to carry on the work of the original voodoo of New Orleans before the religion died out completely.

"I'm starting to believe you're following me."

Ivana froze at the sound of the rich baritone. The voice sent a chill down her back despite the sun set high in the sky.

Had this man planted a GPS on her?

She turned, and at first sight of him, had to beg her heart to continue beating at a normal rhythm. "Let me set your mind at ease, Mr. Campbell. I am not following you." Ivana hoped she'd managed to pull off the apathetic expression she was striving for.

"Then it must be fate," Jonathan said. He was dressed in a

suit that was tailored especially for his incredibly built body. It probably costs more than Ivana made in an entire year selling incense. How could anyone be so wasteful when there were so many needy people in this city?

"I don't think it's fate. More like a string of bad luck," Ivana retorted.

"Ouch." Jonathan put his hand over his chest, as if covering a wound. "I see the attitude doesn't take the weekend off."

"I do not have an attitude."

"You mean this is normal?"

Ivana plunked a hand on her hip. "Don't you have anything better to do than harass me in the middle of the street?"

His smile widened. "At the moment? No."

Ivana seared him with a disgusted look.

"Actually, I do have something better to do than harass you in the street." He looked up Canal Street toward the river, and checked his watched, switching his briefcase to his right hand.

Who carried a briefcase on a Saturday morning?

"I was wondering if I could harass you over coffee," Jonathan continued.

Ivana nearly swallowed her tongue. "Coffee?"

His shoulder shrugged under the fine cut of his suit coat. "Coffee, tea, Jack Daniels. Whatever you'd like."

Having coffee with him—that was almost a date!

"You don't have to look like I just asked you to jump into the Mississippi River," Jonathan said. "What's wrong with grabbing a cup of coffee? I'm still new to the city. I was hoping maybe you could give me some insights."

"I can do that right here."

"True. But it would be a lot more enjoyable at a table with a drink and maybe a nice lunch."

So now it was lunch?

"Come on, Ivana." He captured her elbow, his intense stare full of purpose.

Ivana jerked her arm away. She turned to leave, but

Jonathan caught her arm again and held firm. He wasn't hurting her, but Ivana knew if she tried to jerk her arm away again he'd just squeeze harder.

"What's your problem?" he asked. "Do you really find the prospect of spending just an hour with me that detestable?"

Ivana could not allow herself to be affected by the disappointment she thought she heard in his voice. Having a man like Jonathan Campbell in her life presented problems Ivana was afraid to contemplate. Everything about him reminded her of the person she used to be: ambitious, career-driven, concerned only with getting ahead. She could not allow herself to fall back into that way of thinking again.

"I . . . I can't do this." She pulled free from him and headed up Canal Street. Ivana wasn't even sure of where she was going anymore. She just knew she needed to get away from Jonathan Campbell and the indescribable feelings his nearness evoked.

Chapter Thirteen

The producers were impressed.

Toby breathed a sigh of relief he hadn't realized he had been holding. The bigwigs from *A Week in the Life of a Wannabe Star* had arrived in town and had gone straight to work. There wasn't any time for entertaining, not when there was money to be made.

"Aria is in the third slot. Her segment opens with a ninety second intro which will be taped between Friday and Saturday," the New Orleans segment producer, David Reynolds, explained. "We want a shot of her in the studio, and something that spotlights New Orleans. Maybe we can get a shot of her walking down Bourbon Street, or show her riding on the St. Charles streetcar line."

"Will she be speaking to the camera at all?" Toby asked.

"No. It'll be a voiceover of her explaining her love of music, how long she's dreamed of an opportunity like this, etc., etc. That'll be recorded Friday morning, as well. She'll need to work on what she wants to say this week."

Toby silently said a prayer of thanks. Because of Sienna, Aria had already written her thoughts.

David Reynolds continued. "Following her intro, we break live to The Hard Court, and Aria gives her four and a half minute performance. From that moment, we have two cameramen who will follow Miss Jordan around twenty-four seven, but a larger crew will be staged at her performances and the other preplanned events."

Marshall Kellerman, the scout who'd first approached him about the show, had explained this part from the very beginning, but Toby nodded anyway. They were prepared for this. He had performances set up at six of the hottest clubs in the city, and had taken a little out of his savings to buy some extra time in the studio. He'd even rented a luxury executive apartment on St. Charles Avenue. One week cost more than twice the amount of his normal rent, but it was worth it. He needed to portray the look of a high-rolling producer.

"So, are you ready for this, Miss Jordan?" the producer asked Aria.

She smiled, and the hairs on the back of Toby's neck stood on end. It was her nervous smile.

Sienna had set up a special session with someone from a local chapter of Toastmasters to give Aria a crash course in reducing her camera shyness. It didn't bode well that she was already nervous and the cameras had not even started to roll yet.

"She's ready," Toby answered for her. "She's just going to be herself."

"That's right." Sienna walked through the door. "It's like the camera won't even be there, right, Aria?"

Toby breathed another relieved sigh.

After last night, he wasn't sure Sienna would be up to the meeting this morning. She'd been completely wasted. He should have stopped her when he realized she was getting tipsy, but something had prevented him from making the effort. The more she drank the sexier she had become. And he liked it.

Leaving Sienna alone in bed last night had been one of the hardest things he'd ever had to do. The ferocity of his desire had been a shock, but only initially. These feelings had been building over the past few weeks, and Toby had already decided to stop trying to deny what had become a certain truth—he had it bad for Sienna.

Who would have ever imagined that? Alex, maybe. His brother had spent enough time telling Toby he should look at Sienna as more than just a friend.

Toby's brain told him he should just wrap up any wayward thoughts he had about Sienna and throw them away. This was not the time to get involved with *any* woman.

Yet, would it really be that strange to be with Sienna? Friends became lovers all the time. According to all those love gurus on *Oprah*, that was the best way to start a relationship. He and Sienna probably knew more about each other than most married couples did.

Except in one area.

Toby clenched his teeth. He did not need to think about Sienna in bed with him, especially while sitting in a meeting with a group of television producers who could make or break his future.

"Toby?"

He blinked, completely oblivious to the conversation.

"I was just telling Mr. Reynolds about why we chose The Hard Court as the venue where Aria will kick off her *Week in the Life* segment."

"Uh, yes." He had to get his head together. Fast. "Aria has developed a solid following at The Hard Court. The owner recently reported that he's yielded his highest gross on the nights Aria performed. It's also one of the trendiest new night clubs in New Orleans."

"We have a full media blitz planned that will capitalize on the markets that have brought Aria the most success while exposing her talents to a variety of other sectors of the listening public," Sienna asserted. "Starting this week, Aria will begin making the rounds at several local radio stations. We've landed spots on a couple of the morning television shows, as well."

Sienna went on, laying out Aria's entire schedule for the next two weeks along with the list of sponsors she had managed to garner. She'd even had color handouts made. She was poised, professional and on top of everything—and that was *with* a hangover.

"Best of all," Sienna continued, "Aria will close out *A Week in the Life of a Wannabe Star* with a performance on the R&B stage at Jazz Fest."

Toby's head jerked up in surprise.

Reynolds was duly impressed. "I had a guy working on our end trying to land a spot. How were you able to do that?"

Toby wanted to see the magic hat she'd managed to pull that rabbit out of, too. The New Orleans Jazz and Heritage Festival was held over two weekends and was one of the biggest musical celebrations in the world. Every genre of music was on display, with some of the biggest names in the industry sharing their talent. And Sienna had managed to get Aria a spot on stage with them?

"This is fantastic," David Reynolds said. "We're expecting Aria Jordan to finish in the top three."

Try the top one, Toby thought to himself. There was no way Aria was not winning this competition. He wouldn't settle for anything less.

He looked over at Sienna. She sent him a wink that she probably thought was conspiratory, but all Toby could think of was how sexy it was.

If he was going to get anything worthwhile done, he needed to focus on the show and regulate these thoughts of her to a dark corner of his mind. Toby took a breath, and tried clenching and unclenching his hands to relieve the incredible mass of sexual frustration suffocating him. He couldn't think of anything but having Sienna's thighs wrapped around his head.

Reynolds and the other two producers rose from their seats. Toby followed, sticking out his hand and shaking with all of them.

"Good luck next week."

"Thanks," Toby answered. "Be prepared to be blown away."

"I look forward to it," Reynolds answered.

Sienna turned as soon as the three men exited the studio. "I thought I was the only one allowed to have a hangover this morning," she said. "Why did you space out like that?"

"I didn't space out," Toby defended.

Sienna gathered the leftover handouts from the table. "Have you finalized everything with Jonathan? We have all the spaces for the cameras blocked off, right?"

They were going to do their own run through for next Monday night so that Aria could be coached on which spots on The Hard Court's stage worked to her advantage.

Toby crossed his arms over his chest. "Explain to me about Jazz Fest. How did you pull that off?"

An entrancing smile brightened her face. "I remembered hearing that one of my sorority sisters was on the committee for Jazz Fest, so I gave Tianna a call. There was a message from her when I checked my voice mail this morning letting me know there was a slot open on the R&B stage for Aria."

"Yes," Toby said, squeezing her shoulders. It was something he had done hundreds of times before, but now there was a measure of awareness that sent a brush of heat across his skin. Just the slightest touch made his hands burn with wanting. He ached to skim his fingers over her body.

Oh, God, if Sienna knew what was going through his mind right now, she would slug him.

But, then again, maybe she wouldn't.

The thought gave him pause. What would happen if he made his feelings known? After her actions last night, Toby wasn't so sure her reaction would be all that discouraging.

How had they come to this? He would have never imagined in a million years that he would have these types of feelings for Sienna. And to think that she would actually reciprocate . . .

"Toby," Sienna squeezed his forearms. "What's up with you today? Are you thinking about the show?"

"Of course," he answered. It wasn't an outright lie. He had been thinking about the show. He just had not been thinking about it that very instant. Toby wasn't sure he was ready to tell her exactly what had been on his mind. He still needed to figure it all out for himself before he brought Sienna into the mix.

"It's going to go fine, Toby. And if it doesn't, that's what editors are for. Remember, even though they're touting the show as live,"—she made quotation marks with her fingers—"there is a twenty-second delay. The producers are not going to allow anything to air that will negatively affect their ratings."

"I guess you're right."

"Concentrate on the exposure, and what this will mean for her career. Good or bad, Aria Jordan is going to be in the homes of millions of Americans. When you think about it, sometimes the bad get more attention than the good. Look at *American Idol*. William Hung carved a place in American television history singing that Ricky Martin song."

"I never thought about it that way. Maybe I should tell Aria to tank during one of the performances," he said with a wink.

"Don't you dare," Sienna warned. "I think she'd rather have long-term success than fifteen minutes of humiliating fame. She has the voice. As long as we work on her stage fright, there is no way Aria is going to lose this competition."

"It's money in the bank," he said.

"Yeah, maybe after she blows up the charts, you can finally start touching your illegal money."

Toby looked over his shoulder and put a finger up to his lips. "I told you never to mention that," he said in a hushed tone.

"Come on," Sienna laughed. "We need to get to The Hard

Court. I want to make sure everything is in place for the practice run. This is going to be another long week of preparation. I hope you're ready."

"It's a little too late to question it now," Toby answered. "Ready or not, the show is on."

Jonathan sat at his desk, tapping the end of the Mont Blanc pen against his lips. He needed to get through this brief before tomorrow, but for the life of him he just could not concentrate.

Ivana Culpepper was beginning to take up more of his thoughts than she had right to. If he believed in such a thing, Jonathan would have thought some mystic power had brought them together after all their run-ins over the past few days.

He'd had to sit back and think about if he'd heard someone talk about where she would be prior to those times he'd bumped into her. It wouldn't surprise him if his subconscious had sought her out. There was no way he could have known where she would be.

Fate? Coincidence? God?

Something had brought them together. Now he needed to figure out a way to make her see him as more than some slick-tongued lawyer who would serve the world better living at the bottom of the ocean than practicing law in her city.

"What's up, man?"

Jonathan raised his head. "Hey," he said as Toby entered the office. Jonathan rose from his desk and met him halfway. They slapped palms, and Toby brought him in for a hug.

"Haven't seen much of you this past week," Jonathan commented. "This show has you hopping."

"I've got a feeling it'll be nothing compared to the coming week. I'm nervous as hell," his buddy admitted.

Toby settled in one of the leather chairs in the seating area to the right of his desk, while Jonathan returned to his seat behind the desk.

"I forget that you have another business to tend to." Toby's eyes roamed around the office. "I didn't know where to find you when you weren't at the club."

"Why didn't you call my cell phone?"

"I did. It said you weren't available."

Jonathan slipped the Blackberry from its holder, and stared at the blank screen. "I forgot to charge it last night. So, are you all ready?"

"We're set. The club looks great. Aria's warming up at the studio right now and Sienna's on the phone with more press people. You should make serious bank tonight."

"That is what it's all about, right."

"Oh, yeah. I've got my eyes set on one of those babies you drive."

"Which you could have if you weren't scared of your mama," Jonathan joked. He still could not believe Toby had never touched the money he'd scored all those years ago. He rarely took the opportunity to rib his friend about it. He knew the money, and what it represented, had been a sore spot for Toby.

"Give me about a year," Toby answered. "You up for lunch?"

Jonathan shook his head and motioned to the brief on his desk. "I've got too much work to do. Why don't you go with Sienna?" Jonathan suggested.

Toby stared him down, his eyes slant.

"Don't even try it," Jonathan said before Toby could summon a denial. "If you don't want to acknowledge how you feel about her, you need to pay more attention to how you look at her when you think no one else is looking."

Toby dropped his head to his chest. "Is it that obvious?"

"It was last Friday night. Especially when Payton tried hitting on her. I thought I would have to hold you back."

"I guess it's too much to ask that no one else noticed, huh?"

"I think Sienna is about the only one who didn't," Jonathan laughed.

"Man, I don't understand it. Sienna and I were best friends for as long as I can remember. I never thought about her in that way before. Now, it's all I can think about. And after we left the club last Friday—"

Jonathan sat up straight. "What happened after you left the club?"

"Sienna and I went to an all night pool hall. She didn't want me going home alone after all that crap with Payton."

"And?"

"And she got pretty wasted." Toby's brow quirked, along with one side of his mouth, in a rueful grin. "She said some things she probably wouldn't have said if she'd been sober."

"Like what?" Jonathan motioned with his hand. "Come on, man, you gotta spell it out for me."

"Let's just say if I were to suggest starting something up with her, I'm not all that certain I'd get a direct 'no.'"

Jonathan leveled his friend with a measured gaze, "So what are you gonna do about it?"

Toby shrugged. "I don't know if I should do anything, at least not right now. Tonight is the start of the most important week in my career. I need to concentrate on making sure everything goes smoothly."

"What do you have to worry about? Isn't the whole point of this week to show people what really goes on in the life of a rising star? Why don't you just let whatever happens happen?"

"That may be what the others are doing, but I'm making the most of Aria's time in front of the camera," Toby answered. "Even though it may be a little more exciting than the average American's life, a week of watching Aria go in the studio and record for seven hours a day is not going to hold anybody's interest. We've set up an entire schedule of the type of stuff people imagine when they think about music stars."

"Such as?"

"The televised portion takes place at the different music venues we have set up every night, including the two at The Hard Court. But during the day people will be watching Aria over a webcast on the show's Web site. So, to make sure things remain interesting, Sienna has set up a ton of different events. Aria will be helping out voice teachers at an area high school one day, doing a concert at a retirement home another day, then on Sunday, before closing out the show at Jazz Fest, she's filling in for the youth choir director at my mom's church."

Jonathan laughed. "And that's supposed to be a typical week in Aria Jordan's life? Is she trying to win a music competition, or are you petitioning her for sainthood? I'm surprised you didn't try to work in a couple of days of her volunteering in war-torn Iraq."

"It would have taken an entire day just to fly her there," Toby answered, not missing a beat.

"You're full of it, man."

"We're just embellishing a little."

"Embellishing sounds so much better than lying," Jonathan chuckled.

"I just want to make sure America remembers her when it's time to vote for who they want to see."

"Yeah, it'll be nice if they remember The Hard Court when they vacation in New Orleans, too."

"That's why we need to make sure it's perfect tonight." Toby rose from his chair. "I need to head out. Aria has her first live radio interview early this afternoon, and I requested that the cameras be there so she could get used to having them in her face the rest of the week."

"Tell her I said good luck. I'll see you tonight."

"Later."

Jonathan glanced at the legal brief spread out over his desk, then pushed his chair back and headed for the closet where he kept a pair of tennis and sweats. If he was going to get any work done, he first needed to clear his head. Nothing else had worked, maybe a few hours at the gym would.

Sienna stood at the rear of the radio station's studio with Toby at her side, amazed at how well Aria was doing in her interview. The crew from Hollywood had arrived at the studio before they had, and the cameras had begun rolling immediately. But Aria had been surprisingly calm. As the host of the local morning show fed her questions, Aria answered them with an ease Sienna had never witnessed in her before.

They had gone through possible questions last night, and Aria had confessed that she had been doing mock interviews in the mirror. Her preparation had done wonders. Sienna found herself experiencing feelings of pride. How weird was that?

"She's doing great," Sienna whispered to Toby. She could feel the tension radiating off him.

"It's almost over," he answered. "I'm just ready for it to be over."

Sienna squeezed his hand. "Get it together. You're more nervous than she is."

She heard him pull in a deep breath and let it out slowly.

"And there you have it," the morning show DJ said. "The next big star to come out of the South, Aria Jordan."

"Thank God," Toby said as Aria pulled off her headphones, shook the host's hand and practically skipped over to where they stood. The cameras followed.

Aria first gave Toby a hug, then threw her arms around Sienna, surprising the heck out of her.

"Thank you so much, Sienna."

"You're welcome," Sienna said, patting Aria on the back before releasing her.

"If you had not forced me to do that bio, I probably would have stuttered my way through that entire interview. It really made me think about why I'm doing this, and it's made such a difference."

"You were awesome," Sienna said, and she meant it. Over the past few weeks, Aria had begun to grow on her. She had this infectious exuberance that was just about the most charming thing Sienna had ever seen. It was one of the reasons Sienna was confident that Aria would win over the heart of every American within three feet of a television screen.

Of course, she had also become a lot more open-minded toward her once she found out Aria and Toby were not attached. She had been envious, and had not given the girl much of a chance. Sienna was happy she had taken the blinders off long enough to get to know Aria better.

"Time to go back to the studio," Toby said. "We're recording a new one today, and then it's The Hard Court tonight," he said with a tinge of fake enthusiasm in his voice.

The reality of being on camera had affected them all; although what was being recorded this afternoon would not be broadcast on the web cast. The producers had warned that the initial reaction to being on camera could not be avoided, no matter how much they attempted to do so. They also claimed they would soon forget the cameras were rolling, but Sienna wasn't sure she could. She didn't know how the people on those reality shows did it. Having your every move recorded was about as uncomfortable as . . . well . . . having your every move recorded.

"I'll meet you at The Hard Court tonight," she told Toby. "I'm going back to the office and then I'm meeting Tianna for lunch to discuss the particulars on Jazz Fest."

Sienna left the radio station, and was heading back to her office when her cell phone rang.

"This is Sienna."

"Cee Cee, are you terribly busy?"

"Ivana?"

"We need to talk," her sister said.

"Ivana, what's wrong?" Sienna's chest tightened. Tosha was the overly sensitive sister, not Ivana.

"I just really need to talk to someone. Can you get away for a bit?"

Sienna looked at the digital clock on the dashboard. She still wanted to go over Aria's schedule with a fine-tooth comb, but she could do that after lunch.

"I'll make time," Sienna told her sister. "Where are you?"

"I'm still at home, but on my way to the French Market."

"I'll come and pick you up. We can have coffee."

Sienna made a U-turn and headed for her sister's house. Ivana was waiting at the curb when she pulled up. She put her small folding table and the Pullman that carried her incense on the backseat. Sienna wished her sister would get a car. She didn't know how Ivana hauled all that stuff on the bus every day.

"Okay, what's up?" she asked when Ivana took a seat.

"Coffee first, then we talk."

Sienna rolled her eyes. At least it wasn't life threatening.

Sienna turned down Ursulines Avenue then onto Decatur. She said a prayer of thanks when she found a parking spot around Jackson Brewery. They got out and headed for Café du Monde. Sienna ordered two café au laits and a single order of beignets for her and Ivana to share.

When they were seated, she said, "Okay, spill it."

Ivana ran her fingers through her hair, her hands trembling. Sienna's chest did that tightening thing again.

"Ivana, what's wrong? You're scaring me."

Her sister took a sip from her mug and blurted, "I want to have sex."

Sienna stared at her, stunned. Speechless, in fact. As sisters they talked about a lot of things, but sex wasn't one of them. Probably because there was so little sex in either of their lives.

"Uh . . . okay," Sienna said.

"Oh, God," Ivana folded her arms on the table and put her head down. "I can't believe I just said that."

"Me either," Sienna answered. "But, now that you have—"

"It's Toby's friend."

"Jonathan?"

"Yes," Ivana muttered. "It's driving me crazy. I keep running into him. I think he's following me."

"Do you think he wants to, uh, have sex with you?" Sienna lowered her voice as a couple sat a few tables away from them.

"I don't know," Ivana moaned. "He's only asked me to have coffee. And, well, lunch, too."

Sienna's eyebrows rose. "You had lunch with him?"

"No," Ivana nearly shouted. "No," she restated, lower this

time. "He asked me to tell him about the city over coffee or lunch, but I said no and ran. I literally ran away from him. It was so humiliating."

"And you ran because you want to have sex with him?"

"Shhh," her sister chastised. Sienna could have reminded her that she was the one who first blurted out the words.

"It has been so long since I felt this way," Ivana admitted. "Not since Michael."

Sienna winced at the mention of her sister's ex-husband. Michael had not been good for Ivana; almost as bad as their mother.

"So, are you going to—have sex with him?"

"No!" Ivana gasped.

"Why not?"

Ivana sputtered, but no words came out of her mouth.

"Okay, Vonnie, here's the deal," Sienna said, covering her sister's hands that where still folded on the table. "I could tell since that dinner at Margo's that Jonathan is interested in you. If you're interested in him too, why not go for it?"

"Sienna! You're supposed to be talking some sense into me, not encouraging me to rip this man's clothes off the next time I see him!"

"I didn't say anything about ripping his clothes off, but since the fantasy has apparently been on your mind, maybe you should. I doubt he'd mind." Sienna grinned.

"You are no help at all."

Sienna held her hands out. "What did you expect me to tell you?"

"That I'm crazy for even thinking of Jonathan Campbell in this way."

"I'd think you were crazy if you *didn't* think about him in this way. Jonathan is gorgeous. He has the sweetest personality. He's successful."

"He's a lawyer! A lawyer, for God's sake! And he owns a nightclub. I want to have sex with a nightclub-owning lawyer."

"He's a very successful lawyer, and his nightclub is becoming one of the premier spots in the city. You should come there tonight."

"Me in a nightclub?"

"What's wrong with that?"

"Other than the fact that it is against everything I stand for?"

"You are not against people hanging out and having a good time. Jonathan's club is very classy. You may even enjoy yourself. Just try not to tear his clothes off as soon as you see him." Sienna laughed when Ivana shot her a dirty look.

This was a side to her sister she had not seen in a very long time. Flustered, unsure of herself. It was good for her. Ivana took things too seriously. She spent so much of her time and energy on the "Cause" that Sienna was afraid her sister sometimes forgot that she had her own life to live.

"So, am I going to see you tonight?" Sienna asked.

Ivana chewed her bottom lip. "I'll have to think about it."

"Please come, Vonnie. You'll have a good time, I promise. And I need the moral support. This is Aria Jordan's first performance in front of the cameras. I'm going to be a nervous wreck."

"It's not like you'll be singing."

"Thank God," they both said and laughed.

"Still, Ivana, I think it would be good for you."

Ivana continued her nervous, bottom lip chewing. "Okay," she said after a few moments. "I'll meet you there."

"No, I'll pick you up," Sienna said. She wanted to make sure her sister got there. She would not be surprised one bit if Ivana stood her up. "I'll be at your place around eight o'clock."

"Fine. I'll be ready. What should I wear?"

"You don't own jeans or tennis shoes, so you don't have to worry about the dress code. Just wear whatever you're comfortable in."

Ivana's face took on a pained expression. "Are you sure this is a good idea?"

"Yes," Sienna reiterated. "You need to let your hair down

every once and a while." She grinned. "I think Jonathan prefers your hair down."

Sienna laughed as she received another of her sister's mean looks. She rose from the table, placed a kiss on Ivana's cheek, and headed for her car.

Chapter Fourteen

Toby sat on the leather sofa in Jonathan's office at The Hard Court, then hopped back up and began to pace again.

"Would you sit down? You're driving me crazy," Eli said as he continued to flip through the rich wood and glass CD display case in the corner behind Jonathan's desk. "You think Jonathan would mind if I borrowed this Sade CD? I used to roll with 'Sweetest Taboo.'"

"Can you stop thinking about yourself for a minute? This is the most important night of my life, and you're worrying about a CD."

"How is this the most important night of *your* life? Aria is the one who's going to be up on stage. Besides," Eli shrugged, "what's so different about this performance than the one she had last week?"

Toby pointed toward the door. "Have you noticed all those cameras set up out there? This is real."

"Did you not know all those cameras would be set up out there when you decided to do this show?" Eli asked. "This is what you signed up for. Don't start backing down now."

"I'm not backing down. It's just . . . real. This is really happening, Eli."

"Yes, it is," his brother said. "And you're damn lucky it is. This is a once in a lifetime opportunity, so don't blow it by getting cold feet."

"I won't," Toby said, trying to reaffirm things in his own mind as much as he wanted to reassure Eli. He had been a nervous wreck ever since those cameramen flipped the switch on their equipment and his client's life became a part of television history. There was just so much that could go wrong. That's what Eli and everybody else had a hard time understanding.

"What if she messes up on stage?" Toby asked, pacing the length of the massive office.

"Then they'll switch to another contestant. You told me yourself that they're going to pick the stuff that makes good TV."

"And Aria choking on stage would make good TV," Toby pointed out. "Why do you think that funniest home video show is still on after all these years? People love to see other people make fools out of themselves."

Eli lowered the CD he'd been looking over. "Where is all this coming from?" he asked Toby. "You were confident as hell when you were giving Aria her little pep talk. Weren't you listening to what you said?"

"I just said that so Aria wouldn't be nervous."

"Like I said, take your own advice. You've got this covered, man."

Toby took a deep breath and tried to tell himself that Eli was right, but how could he be calm when there was so much riding on tonight? This performance would dictate how well the entire week went. If Aria clammed up tonight, her confidence would be shot to hell.

"Okay, I've got to calm down," Toby decided.

"That's what I've been trying to tell you," Eli said. "Just forget the cameras, okay? Why don't we go out to the bar? You need something to help you relax, and since you haven't been getting any sex, alcohol will have to do."

Great. Like he needed to be reminded of his pitiful excuse for a sex life.

He had been in a state of frustrated semi-arousal ever since that night at the pool hall with Sienna. He'd been dreaming about that night, remembering the way she'd licked her lips when she bent her sweet butt over and attempted a shot. Toby had nearly lost it in the middle of the pool hall.

He needed to find relief. And now he couldn't even get off with a damn porno flick because of her. Cee Cee was making his life crazy.

"You coming or what?" Eli asked.

Toby winced. Not the best choice of words his brother could have used.

"Okay, but I'm not drinking anything. I can't risk losing control."

Toby followed him out of Jonathan's office. They walked down the small corridor and onto the main floor of the club.

It was surreal. Tonight's performance was the first full-fledged staged production. It had been hard enough having the two cameramen and a boom operator following them around earlier today, but tonight went way beyond what Toby had expected. There was a first camera assistant, second camera assistant, lighting technician, key grip, hair stylist, makeup artist, and a bunch of other people that Toby had no idea what purpose they served.

The location manager, whose job was to scope out the filming area and find the best camera angles, had been at The Hard Court since early this morning, from what Jonathan had told him. They had set up camera and lighting equipment at five different stations around the club in order to catch Aria at every possible angle on stage and get the best shots of the audience. According to the producers, they would do this for every one of her performances.

Toby made the decision to take his own advice and just put the cameras out of his mind. They were a part of the scenery, like the bar stool, or the stage.

"Toby," Aria called out and started walking toward him. "Look who's here!"

Damn.

Valerie Jordan, Aria's mother, who was more of a Bible-thumper than his own mother, was following Aria. When

Toby had first approached her about signing Aria to his label, she'd given him a three hour lecture on how she would not have her baby singing the devil's music. Toby silently prayed Valerie wouldn't give the cameras some kind of drama for the show. This had the potential to turn into the kind of stuff shows like this ate up.

He found a smile from somewhere in his repertoire. "Mrs. Jordan, I'm happy you could make it. You should have told us you were coming out to New Orleans."

"It was a last minute decision," she answered. "One of my church member's daughter's best friends told me she'd seen Aria singing in a nightclub."

Yep, they were about to make the drama clip. Hopefully, one of the other contestants would get in a fist fight during the week, so that whatever transpired in the next few minutes wouldn't seem all that bad.

"As you can see, this isn't your usual nightclub."

"I wouldn't know. This is my first time in a nightclub. Aria had never been in one either, until she met you," Valerie said with a sweet, passive-aggressive smile pasted across her face.

Toby clenched his teeth to keep as much of a smile as possible for the cameras now that they were shoved in his face. *Please don't cause a scene*, he silently prayed.

"Actually, I discovered Aria in your brother's club. It isn't nearly as nice as this establishment."

"Mama," Aria stepped in. "Why don't you have a seat at one of the tables? Or maybe we can go upstairs and get something to eat?"

Her mother looked around, and obviously, unable to find any visible diseases climbing the walls, deigned the place suitable to eat in. "Fine," she said, and Toby saw Aria sigh in relief.

The cameras followed the two up the staircase, leaving Toby to pray that their conversation would be just another boring mother and daughter talking about shoe shopping or whatever mothers and daughters talked about.

"Let me guess, you and Aria's mother are not best friends?" Eli asked.

"She thinks Aria should be a kindergarten teacher, not a singer," Toby answered, his eyes still following Aria and her mother as they made their way up the staircase.

"That voice was not made for singing 'Itsy-Bitsy Spider.'"

"Exactly," Toby agreed. "I'm not too worried about her mother. Aria is old enough to make her own decisions. I knew once I got her to leave Houston I didn't have to worry about her wavering. She wants this. She's not going to let her mother stop her."

Now, he just had to make sure nothing else got in the way.

Jonathan filled the cup with ice cubes and poured on the whiskey, cursing under his breath. It was just his luck that one of his bartenders would call in sick with a stomach virus on the night Ivana Culpepper came to his club.

Jonathan shook his head, unsure if that was really her with Sienna, or if he was hallucinating.

She had forgone her usual bright colors and long, flowing clothes for a slim, sedate sage-colored dress. Her hair was straight instead of its usual bouncy, natural curls. Even without the wild colors, she still had that exotic aura that pulled him in.

Sienna gave him a wave and started toward the bar, with Ivana following.

Damn this. Charles and Brandon would have to handle the drink orders for a few minutes. He moved from behind the bar and greeted the ladies.

"Good evening," he said, kissing Sienna's hand. He turned to Ivana and grabbed her fingers before she could pull away. He pressed a kiss, and nearly shivered at how soft her skin felt on his lips. He knew she would feel like silk.

"How are you doing, Ivana?" Jonathan asked. He would figure out a way to get her to talk to him tonight even if it killed him in the process.

"I'm fine," she answered in her usual manner whenever she spoke to him, strained and disgusted.

"I'm surprised to see you here. Happy, but surprised."

"I came to support Sienna," she said. "This doesn't mean I support your nightclub."

He didn't care if she came with the intention of torching the place to the ground. He just wanted to see her again.

"But she doesn't have anything against your club either, right, Vonnie?" Sienna interjected with a trying-to-keep-the-peace voice.

"Vonnie," Jonathan allowed the nickname to roll across his tongue. "Not sure how I like that. Ivana is so much more exotic."

Her eyes narrowed to thin slits. "Do you think of me as a toy to be played with?"

She did not want him to answer that one. He wanted to spend hours playing with her body. His entire being thrummed at the thought of what he could do with this woman.

Apparently, Sienna saw where his mind was headed, because she quickly took Ivana by the arm and said, "I see Toby and Eli. Let's go, Ivana." As they turned, Sienna looked back and gave him a knowing smile and wink.

He started after them, but Brandon called from behind the bar. There was a line forming.

Jonathan spent the next half hour trying to interpret Sienna's actions while he served up drinks. The crowd at the bar thinned once the DJ started his *Hits from the '90s* dance mix. Jonathan left the bar in search of Sienna. He cornered her as she left the downstairs ladies' restroom.

"What's up, Sienna?" he asked, impeding her progress.

"Oh, Jonathan, hey. Toby was just looking for you."

"I'll talk to him later. Why don't you tell me what that wink was about?"

"What wink?" she asked innocently.

He assessed her with a shrewd stare.

She folded her arms, releasing a resigned sigh. "Alright, alright. What do you want to know?"

"How did Ivana end up in my club tonight? Did you have to drag her here?"

"Sort of."

Jonathan matched her pose. "Straight answers, if you don't mind."

"I asked her to come for moral support."

"But she said she would never set foot in my club."

"Well, I guess her desire to show her support of me is stronger than her feelings of hatred toward you," Sienna laughed.

Jonathan ignored that. He refused to believe Ivana actually hated him. A strong dislike sounded better. He could overcome a strong dislike.

"What was that wink and smile about?" he asked again. "What is it you know, Sienna?"

"Look, if Ivana has anything to say to you, wait for her to say it."

"Has she been talking about me to you?"

"Wait for her." Sienna's voice turned from playful to sincere. She hesitated for a minute, as if she was unsure she should say anything further. Then she said, "If you give her time, she'll come around. Just don't let her push you away, Jonathan. Ivana is a terrific woman. She is one of the smartest people I know, and you'll never find another person with more passion and heart. But she can be stubborn. Don't fall for her tough girl act. Just . . . give her time. In the end, she'll be worth it."

Of that, Jonathan had no doubt.

He would give Ivana time if that's what she needed. But he was going to do everything within his power to break down her defenses.

Sienna took a tiny sip from her Mojito. She'd only ordered the mint-flavored cocktail because Eli bought a round for the table, but she vowed to make this her one and only drink of the night. After the debacle at the pool hall, Sienna was hesitant to come within twenty feet of an alcoholic beverage. Liquor did crazy things to a person. Like forced them to say totally inappropriate things they would never say if they were sober. Now if only she could remember half the things she'd said that night.

Toby had been tight-lipped about it all, but from the way he'd reacted to her this past week, Sienna feared her tongue had gotten looser than it should have.

Thankfully, they had been too busy with preparations for the show to rehash that night.

Things had definitely been put into motion, and in a big way. The cameras had been a constant since this morning, but amazingly, Sienna was starting to get used to them already. When she'd taken on Toby's account, she had not expected to be in front of the cameras all that much, but it was unavoidable. Anytime she interacted with Aria, the cameras were there. Sienna could admit to some reservations now that the time was upon them to actually have things rolling, but Aria's poise had been a welcome surprise earlier at the radio station.

Tonight, however, would be the first real test. The Hard Court looked more like a movie set than a nightclub, with all the spotlights and people with huge headsets walking around.

Sienna said a silent prayer that tonight's performance would go off without a hitch. Though she'd been too busy to actually dwell on it, the importance of this week was never far from her mind. Her entire career was riding on this. If the powers that be at Cardinal Studios were not happy with how things turned out, she would be without a job. What would she do then, go back to helping out her mother five days a week? Just the thought was enough to make Sienna's head start to pound.

"Hey there everybody," Monica Gardner greeted them as she arrived at the booth where she, Eli, and Ivana were seated. Jonathan came walking up right behind her.

Eli made a production of looking at his watch. "Looks like someone forgot how to tell time."

"Hmm, let's see," Monica said as she scooted into the booth. "In the last two hours I had to stabilize two MI's, a boy who would not stop seizing, and deliver a baby since a certain OB was hanging out at a nightclub," she smiled at her fiancé.

"Thanks for picking up my slack, baby," Eli said, covering Monica's mouth with a kiss.

Jonathan opted for the seat on the other side of the booth, which placed him directly across from Ivana. Sienna felt her sister stiffened, though Vonnie did a credible job of keeping her face devoid of any emotion. It was infinitely amusing. Watching the interaction between these two was becoming her new favorite pastime.

"How are things going so far?" Monica asked. "I haven't missed Aria's performance, have I?"

"No, she doesn't go on for another half hour," Jonathan answered. "But watching Toby is just as entertaining if you ask me. I think he's going to have a nervous breakdown any minute now."

"I've been trying to get him to calm down," Sienna said, "But I can understand his plight. I'm ready to have a coronary myself."

"At least you're at the right table," Jonathan said, motioning his head to the two doctors. He reached across the table and snagged an onion ring from the complimentary appetizer tray he'd sent over earlier, his eyes never leaving Ivana.

"This is a little more than I expected," Sienna said. "They did warn us that the performances would have more equipment, but this seems like overkill."

"It's all good. As soon as word gets out that there was a camera crew at my club, the crowds are going to triple."

"Is that all you think about?" Ivana inquired. "How to make another dollar?" At her coldly asked question, the conversation at the table dried up like a creek in the desert.

A devious smile curled up the corners of Jonathan's mouth. "That's not all I think about," he countered in a slow, sensual, send-shivers-down-your-back voice.

Sienna, Monica, and Eli sat in silence as the two volleyed

back and forth, Ivana with inaccurate accusations, and Jonathan with more sexual innuendos than one man had the right to think up on such short notice. Ivana should just admit defeat. The sexual tension radiating between these two was thicker than Granny Elise's gravy.

And apparently, Sienna wasn't the only one who noticed it. Monica leaned over, whispering, "Twenty bucks says they're in bed by the end of the night."

Sienna shook her head. "I know my sister. She'll hold out for at least another week."

Before Monica could reply, Aria was called to the stage and Sienna tuned out every other sound around her.

This was it. Everything they had worked for the past couple of weeks was riding on this first performance. Sienna knew how these things worked. All these reality shows had at least one fall guy. If something went wrong tonight, Aria would probably be pegged as the joke of the show. They could not let that happen. Too much was at stake.

Sienna looked for Toby in the crowd. He stood to the right of the stage, nervousness etched across his face. Her own skin felt as tense as piano strings, but Sienna prayed she did a better job at hiding her anxiety. Just in case Aria sought them out during her performance, at least one of them should portray a picture of confidence.

Sienna scooted from the booth and moved to the dance floor to join the rest of the standing-room-only crowd.

As soon as the first note flowed from Aria's mouth, Sienna's anxiety level took a nosedive. The girl had this covered.

Toby caught her eye from where he stood and gave Sienna thumbs up.

Toby and Aria wanted to kick things off with a bang, so she opened with a high octane dance number that had the crowd hopping. Sienna couldn't help getting caught up in the energy. She swayed her hips to the beat, moving along with the crowd.

The club was electrified. Aria was in her element, with a crowd that had grown to love her and an arrangement of songs that complemented her voice to perfection. Even better, the cameras were soaking it all up, spanning from one corner of the club to the other.

After three up-tempo songs, Aria ended with a spine-tingling rendition of a classic Patti LaBelle favorite. Toby waited for Aria to come down from the stage, gave her a hug, then released her. They went opposite ways, Aria heading for the back while Toby started making his way toward her.

Sienna greeted him with a hug.

"She did an awesome job, Toby."

"I know," he said, guiding her toward the table where the rest of their party sat. "I can't believe how well everything went."

"Well, I can," Jonathan said as they came upon the table. "That girl's been lighting up the crowd with every performance. I'm making the first prediction. This show is already won."

"From your lips to God's ears," Sienna and Toby said in unison. They looked over at each other and the entire table burst out laughing, except for Ivana.

When Sienna went to sit down, Ivana halted her.

"I need to use the powder room. Can you show me where it is?" Ivana asked, grabbing Sienna by the arm and dragging her toward the restroom.

"It looks like you know where you're going just fine," Sienna told her.

A few steps before the restroom's door, Ivana turned to Sienna and pointed an accusatory finger at her chest.

"What did you tell that man?" she demanded.

"And that man would be?"

"Don't pretend as though you don't know what I'm talking about. I saw you talking to him earlier. Did you talk about what we discussed over coffee, Sienna?"

"Of course not," Sienna said, hurt that her sister could think she would betray her that way. "Look, Ivana. Everybody else can see what's going on between you and Jonathan."

"There is nothing going on."

"He's a good guy," Sienna pleaded. "Maybe if you gave it a chance."

Ivana speared her with an incensed stare. "I'm out of here. Don't expect me to come back."

Sienna contemplated stopping her, but then thought better of it. From the look on Ivana's face, any attempt she made would be futile. Instead, Sienna opted for saying a quick prayer that Ivana was not foolish enough to close her eyes to the possibilities that were in front of her.

Sienna stopped short.

Was she doing the same thing with Toby?

She had spent countless moments bemoaning the reasons she and Toby would never be anything more than friends. Yet, when he showed a spark of interest, she'd clammed up. Now that Toby was home, free from romantic entanglements and willing to take a chance, the potential for a real relationship was finally within her grasp. All she had to do was reach out and grab it. She didn't want to end up like Ivana, afraid to take a chance on love.

Sienna took a labored breath as her gaze wandered over to the table where Toby sat with the others. She could only hope she would not be blind to the possibilities that lay ahead.

Chapter Fifteen

Sienna's head rose at the two solid raps on her office's open door. Toby was standing in the doorway.

"What are you doing here?" she asked.

Toby shrugged. "I had some free time."

"There's no such thing as free time this week. I thought Aria was in the studio this morning."

"So did I. But, apparently, the producers thought a mother

and daughter shopping trip would make for better television. So the studio and I are out and Valerie is in. I'm so happy she's going back to Houston today."

"Poor Toby, feeling left out of the party," Sienna cooed.

He gave her an exasperated look as he sat in the chair Sienna had dragged in from the conference room earlier that day. "It's not that," he said. "Her being here goes against the script I have in my mind of how I want this week to play out." He ran his hands down his face, and Sienna noticed the exhaustion evident in his drooping eyelids.

"How much sleep have you gotten this week?" she asked.

"I'll sleep when all this is over. Hey, we'll be in the studio this afternoon before the song giveaway. You'll be there, right."

She nodded, closing the word processing program and pulling up the Internet. "Let me ask you something," Sienna said. She typed in the Web address of her bank; she needed to make sure her check had been direct deposited. "Has Jonathan mentioned Ivana to you?"

Toby started to laugh, which meant Jonathan had obviously said something. "You'd better tell me now."

"He hasn't really said anything."

"So why are you laughing?"

"Because it's funny."

Sienna slapped her hand on the desk. "You think it's funny that Jonathan would be interested in my sister? Do you think Ivana doesn't deserve to have someone in her life just because of her beliefs? I'm tired of everybody calling Ivana a kook. She is *not* crazy. She is *not* a witch. She does *not* call on spirits or do any of the other ridiculous stuff people think she does. Ivana has dedicated her life to taking care of the people everyone else in this city walks right over without seeing. She's a—"

Sienna stopped short as Toby lunged from the chair. He planted his hands on her desk and leaned in, their faces just inches apart.

"And you say you don't blow things out of proportion."

Shaking his head, he returned to the chair. "You know I've always admired your sister, both before and after she started practicing voodoo."

It was true. Ivana and Toby had always had a good relationship.

"Then why did you laugh?"

"I'm laughing because before he moved to New Orleans, Jonathan was determined not to get serious about anybody."

"So, you think he's serious about Ivana?"

He hunched a shoulder. "He hasn't come right out and said anything to me, but from what I can see he sure is interested in her. Is Ivana interested in him?"

Oh, no. She was not giving away any of Vonnie's secrets just so Toby could run back and tell Jonathan. When her sister was ready to admit her feelings toward Jonathan, it would be in her own time.

Sienna shook her head, and sent her electronic bank statement to print on the private ink jet printer. "You know how Ivana is. She's too deep into her work to think about something as paltry as dating. The only reason I asked is because Jonathan had such a strong reaction to her being at the club last night. I was wondering if he was serious about her. I don't want Ivana getting hurt."

"Always taking care of other people," Toby said. "When are you going to start taking care of *you*?"

Sienna looked away from the computer screen and gave him a blank stare. "I do take care of me."

"Why haven't you bought a new battery for that cell phone?"

Sienna opened her mouth and closed it. He had her there.

"Besides the fact that I need to be able to get in touch with you, especially this week, there's also the safety issue, Sienna. You know you should not be riding around this city without a cell phone. What if something happens?"

"I'm going to get one today. I promise."

"I already did that," Toby said, reaching into the right pocket of his slacks and coming out with a slim cartridge.

Sienna was stunned, her heart melting right then and there. Forget flowers. Buying a girl a battery for her dead cell phone showed he cared more than a bunch of stupid roses any day of the week.

"Thank you, Toby. I'll write you a check to cover it."

He waved her off. "Just make sure you keep that thing charged."

"I will." She tried to pry the old battery from the back of the phone, but it wouldn't budge. "Don't worry, if anything comes up with the show, you'll be able to reach me."

"It's not just about that, Sienna." The huskiness in Toby's voice caused the hairs on the back of her neck to rise. She slowly lifted her head, and the heated look in his eyes made her stomach pull tight. "I don't want anything to happen to you," he said.

Her hands stilled, the phone hanging from her fingers by the tiny wrist cord.

"You, ah, you don't?" she managed to choke.

The corner of his mouth quirked, and he shook his head. "No, I don't."

Toby rose from the chair and came around her desk. He stooped down, resting on his haunches next to her chair. He slid the phone from her fingers, his intense stare still holding her captive.

"In fact," Toby continued in that hushed voice that caused tiny tingles to drizzle down her spine, "the thought of anything happening to you scares the hell out of me. I don't know what I would do without you, Sienna."

Sienna tried to take a deep breath, but lost it somewhere in the middle of the act when she realized Toby was closing in. His eyes never wavered as he leaned forward and brushed her mouth with his lips.

"Toby, what are you doing?" she breathed.

He pulled back an inch, his gaze roaming over her face, that smirk still tipping up the corner of his mouth. "If you have to ask, then you really need to check out my porn collection."

Sienna was rendered speechless as Toby closed in again, connecting with her mouth. He gripped the armrest, his big body ensconcing her into the cave of the chair. Sienna relinquished her resistance, closing her eyes and falling in love with his kiss.

It was pure ecstasy wrapped up in a bit of heaven. His tongue pushed through her closed lips, opening her mouth and delving into its depths. He captured her tongue and pulled it inside his mouth, sucking, licking, tasting.

Devouring.

She used to fantasize about how it would feel to have Toby's mouth on hers, but not one of her imaginings could hold a candle to the real thing. His kiss was solid, yet gentle, the cadence setting a pace that sent tiny sparks shooting through her veins.

Then she remembered where they were.

She pulled back. "Toby, we can't do this. Not here."

"Why not?" he breathed against her lips.

"I'm at work," she said, trying to catch her breath.

"And?"

"And it's a conflict of interest." Sienna finally pushed him away. "If anyone walks past that door, I'm off Aria's account." That got his attention. He finally rose and backed away, but he didn't go far.

"You kissed me," she said softly, then repeated in an accusing tone, "You *kissed* me."

There was not even a hint of remorse on his face as he stared at her for a very long, very intense minute. His gaze captured hers, not letting go, even though Sienna wanted nothing more than to close her eyes and relive those few precious moments when his lips had danced with hers.

Finally, Toby asked, "Are you sorry I did?"

Sienna couldn't summon an answer. For so long she'd dreamed that Toby would see her as more than just a friend, but the thought of becoming involved with any man scared her to death.

"I should have kissed you a long time ago," Toby said, running his fingers along her jaw. "But you're right, we can't do this here."

Finding her voice, Sienna tried to make him see reason, "We can't do this at all, Toby."

"Yes, we can." He reached for her again, but she pushed his hand away.

"No, we cannot."

Panic rose in her throat. Sienna could feel her safety shield slipping away. Toby's inaccessibility had been protection against facing the fears of intimacy that had plagued her since the attack all those years ago. To have her trusted excuse abruptly pulled from under her scared her stiff.

"Sienna," he captured her chin in his hand and raised her head. "You know there's something happening between us. It's been building for weeks. Don't try to deny it," he cut her off when she opened her mouth to do just that. "Before you get sloppy drunk again, you need to remember that alcohol loosens both the tongue and inhibitions."

"Oh, God." Sienna knocked his hand away and dropped her head to her desk. "What did I do that night?" came her muffled cry.

She heard Toby chuckle. "It was nothing as bad as you're probably imagining, but you said enough for me to know that you've been thinking about this thing that's been brewing between us."

"What *is* this *thing*, Toby?" she asked, honestly wanting to know what this attraction was doing to him. "Doesn't this seem weird to you?"

"Hell yeah, it's weird. I've been more confused these past few weeks than you'll ever know. Why do you think I've been fighting it all this time?" He took her hand again, bringing it to his lips and placing a gentle kiss on the crest of her fingers. "But I don't want to fight it anymore, Cee Cee. Why don't we just go with the flow and see where it takes us?"

Even though she had been thinking about him this way almost her entire life, Sienna had never allowed herself to believe

Toby would ever love her. If she had, Sienna knew she would have run from him a long time ago.

"What if it takes us nowhere?" Sienna whispered, looking at the hand he'd kissed as if it were foreign from her body.

"In my experience, asking *what if* just sets you up for failure. Stop questioning it, and let's just let it happen."

"Are you sure?"

He nodded, a slow smile tipping up the corner of his mouth.

Sienna didn't know what to think. This was all happening too fast. Toby was her safeguard against relationships. They were never going to have one, and because of that, she never had to fear all the things that came with a normal relationship. Like intimacy.

Sienna put her elbows on her desk and started massaging her temples.

"What's wrong? You look like you're in pain," Toby said.

"I just don't know about this," she whispered.

"Sienna," he said, perching on the edge of her desk and bringing her closer to him. "I'm not saying we have to jump into bed. Nothing really has to change at all. We already see each other every day, and we've gone out to dinner a couple of times like a regular dating couple. It's just that now we can finally acknowledge this pull between us instead of doing a poor job of ignoring it."

"And if it doesn't work out, we're still friends, right?"

He threw his head back and took a deep breath. "Would you get rid of that *if* word?" Lowering his head, Toby captured her hands and brought them to his lips again. "You will always be one of the most important people in my life. Always. Even over these past ten years when I hardly saw you, you were never far from my mind."

"As a friend," Sienna reminded him. "Not in the way you're speaking of now."

"True," Toby agreed, "but that doesn't matter. Friend or more than just a friend, you never have to worry about losing me."

The well of emotion that had formed in her throat prevented Sienna from speaking. Instead, she nodded, praying the tears so close to the edge of her eyes would not spill over.

Toby kissed her hand again. "What do you say to dinner before going to the Caesar's Ghost performance tonight?"

"Well, I've got to eat," she replied in a shaky voice, trying to inject a bit of humor.

"We'll take this slow, okay. There's no pressure. I just want to be able to kiss you when I feel the urge."

"Just try not to feel the urge in front of my boss," Sienna giggled. Those tears were still on the brink of falling, were they due to happiness? Fear? Excitement?

"I promise," Toby said. "I'll see you tonight." Then he was gone.

Sienna stared at the door Toby left partially opened, expecting the guy from Candid Camera to come bursting through any minute. That could not have just been real. Toby had kissed her, like a lover. He wanted to "see where things went between them." He wanted a real relationship.

Sienna sat at her desk, cradling her head in her hands as an old cliché resounded in her mind.

Be careful what you wish for.

Toby completely ignored the activity buzzing around him as he adjusted the tempo on the control panel. He had too much on his mind to worry about the cameras in his face.

He'd kissed Sienna. And it had been good.

Unbelievably good. She'd tasted like candy, sweet and forbidden. This entire thing seemed like it should be illegal, but why should it be? He and Sienna were both adults. They had the right to explore this new attraction. Forget that stuff about not being good enough for her. He would *make* himself good enough for her.

He'd told her the absolute truth; he should have kissed her a long time ago. But he wouldn't waste time lamenting over lost opportunities. His time was better spent figuring out what had Sienna so afraid at the thought of them together.

Her reaction, or lack there of, had him stumped. Sure, the idea of them as an actual couple would take a little getting used to, but considering their history, going from best friends to lovers wasn't all that much of a stretch. Sienna had acted as if he'd asked her to follow him off a cliff.

What about all the stuff she's said when flying high on apple martinis at the pool hall? Was he supposed to believe that was just drunken ramblings?

"How'd that sound to you, Toby?" Savion's voice coming through the headset catapulted him out of his daydreaming.

"Sounds good," Toby answered, although he hadn't really been paying much attention to today's session.

Damn. He needed to get it together. This was not the time for him to lose focus.

"Savion, any word on when the music download codes will be ready?" Toby asked, shutting down the digital sampler and removing the headset.

"Mike said he'd bring them in around four o'clock."

"The school lets out at three-thirty!" Toby said.

"Sorry, man. That's what he said."

Toby groaned. There wasn't much point to going out there without the codes. Sienna had suggested Aria do a promotional song giveaway at some of the biggest high schools in the New Orleans area. Toby had not thought twice about withdrawing a few thousand dollars from his bank account to add the special feature to the Website he'd had built especially for the show. He'd had to pay an obscene amount of money to get the business card–size mailers printed on such short notice, especially since each had its own unique music download code, but it was worth it.

Ivana's roommate, Lelo, had done a slamming job at Aria's photo shoot. Toby had a thousand eight-by-tens of the best shot made, with Aria autographing most of them between practice sessions. He doubted the footage of her signing hundreds of pictures would help with today's Internet votes, but it had to be done.

"I'm hoping I can give the songs away," Aria said, coming

up next to him. "Wouldn't it be embarrassing if people don't even want it even though it's free?"

"Those little cards are going to become collector's items in about a month. Once you go national, you're going to find people selling them on eBay," Toby reassured her. "Stop doubting yourself. If you lack confidence in yourself, it's going to come out in your performance."

"I know," Aria said. "I'm just really nervous about tonight. I'm not used to performing for this kind of crowd."

He was a little edgy about it too, but no way would he let her see it.

"They're people, that's all. You've performed in front of people before."

"Yeah," Aria smiled. "People are my usual crowd. Oh, hey, Sienna."

Toby turned to find Sienna coming through the door burdened by a large box. "This was outside beside the door."

Toby rushed over, relieving her of the package.

"Is it the codes?" Savion asked.

Toby nodded. "Thanks for coming over." He said to Sienna. She didn't try to avoid eye contact, which was a good thing. But she didn't give any indication that she was on board with what they had discussed earlier, which did not bode well.

"How's it going?" she asked Aria, who was autographing more pictures. Sienna picked one up. "These came out really good. We need to do one of those beauty sessions again soon."

Aria nodded. "That was fun."

"And oh, so relaxing," Sienna laughed.

"You should join us next time, Toby," Aria suggested. "They had a lot of men there."

"I'm not the pedicure type," Toby said.

"You don't know what you're missing," Sienna said with a blissful sigh. "There's nothing better than having someone massage your feet."

And so she was not ignoring him. Add that to the good column.

He wanted a definite answer to his suggestion that they start seeing each other, but she gave no indication that she was ready to provide one. That notion became even clearer when Sienna said, "Are we ready to give away some free music downloads?"

"I am," Aria answered.

"Let's do it," Toby said.

He followed Sienna and Aria, with the camera crew bringing up the rear. Toby was relieved the two women were actually becoming friends. He'd gotten the impression that Sienna did not care all that much for Aria in the beginning, but in the last few weeks she'd warmed up to her. That belonged in the good column, too. He wanted his girlfriend and client to get along.

Toby shook his head. This was the first time he'd actually put the *girlfriend* label on Sienna. He was probably being presumptuous, since she still had not given him a clear answer to what he'd suggested. But he was persuasive as hell when it came to getting something he wanted. He would convince her to give the concept of the two of them being together a try. Alex was going to get a kick out of it.

Toby groaned. He was not up for the "I told you so" speech from his older brother. Alex would rub it in until he was hearing the phrase in his sleep.

Mama would be ecstatic.

He needed to stop by tonight. He had been so busy that he'd skipped Sunday dinner and hadn't had a chance to call in a couple of days. But now that he thought about it, Mama hadn't called him either. And he had not had the chance to question her about what Sylvia Culpepper had said when he'd stopped at her store the other night. He wanted to know why Sylvia had not seen her at Bible study.

Toby parked in an abandoned lot behind the school.

"Good, the school hasn't let out yet," he called as Sienna and Aria exited Sienna's car. They headed for the bus stop, getting everything in place only minutes before the school bell rang.

The students swarmed around like bees at a honey pot, snatching up autographed pictures and music download codes like they were hundred dollar bills. And Aria thought she wouldn't be able to give them away. People love free stuff.

"This is great, Toby," Sienna whispered as they stood to the side and watched Aria work the crowd. She was taking the time to personalize the photographs, and autograph the cards that held the download codes. A couple of the kids took pictures of her with their camera phones.

And the *Week in the Life* cameras were catching it all.

"She looks like a seasoned artist," Sienna commented. "And you know what's even better; a lot of the kids already knew who she was. That says a lot, Toby."

"How hard do you think it would be to set up a free concert at the high school?"

"I was just thinking the same thing. I'm going to talk to the principal right now."

"What would I do without you?" he asked.

Moments passed before she answered, "That's something you don't have to worry about." She started for the school, but Toby stopped her, grabbing her shoulder.

"What are you saying, Sienna?"

She hesitated, bit her lip. When she looked up at him, her eyes were uncertain, but still held a bit of resolve. "That I'm willing to give it a try. I have no idea what this is going to look like, but I want to give us a chance."

It took everything he had not to snatch her in his arms and kiss her right in the middle of the street, but professional decorum had to be observed during daylight hours. Tonight, however, would be a different story.

"By the way, you're taking me to Arnaud's for dinner tonight, so bring lots of money," she smiled before heading for the school.

Toby chuckled, shaking his head. He wasn't sure what this new relationship was going to look like either, but as he watched her walk away, he was eager to see where it led.

Once they were done at the school, Toby headed back into

the studio for a few hours then to the ridiculously overpriced penthouse he'd rented for the week to shower and get ready for his first official date with Sienna. He left a half hour early so he could stop in at Mama's.

Toby pulled in behind Monica's light green Honda in his mother's driveway. He walked around back to the porch that led to the kitchen. Monica and Jasmine were at the kitchen table with an orange and gray monstrosity of clay, a bottle of vinegar, and baking soda.

"Let me guess, it's science project time," Toby said by way of greeting.

"Hey Uncle Toby," Jasmine said, then went right back to painting the side of the clay mountain with orange-red paint.

"Hi there," Monica said. She got up from the table, wiping her hands on a dish towel.

"How'd you get roped into building a volcano?" Toby asked, kissing her on the cheek.

"I was off tonight, and Alex had an emergency meeting at the school board office over that contract with the magnet school."

"Where's Mama?"

"She's . . . umm . . . out," Monica answered, moving quickly to the refrigerator

"Out?"

"Can I get you something to drink?" she asked. "There's iced tea."

"No. What do you mean Mama went out? Where did she go?"

"The casino," Jasmine called from the table.

"Jasmine," Monica hissed.

"What is Mama doing at a casino? She doesn't gamble."

"She went to hear a man sing," Jasmine said.

Monica did an exasperated eye roll and rubbed her temples. "Jazz, why don't you get those little toy soldiers your dad bought for the valley?"

"Oh, yeah. Uncle Toby, daddy got me some little toy men,

and barn animals, and little boats, and when my volcano explodes, the hot stuff is going to drown all the people and the animals."

Toby was mildly disturbed by the excitement his niece exuded at the thought of drowning a bunch of toy soldiers in fake lava, but that played second fiddle to the situation with his mother. Something was going on, and he wanted to know what it was.

He waited until Jasmine left the room before turning back to Monica. "Okay, I want to know what you know."

"What makes you assume I know anything?" she asked innocently, gulping from her glass of iced tea.

"Don't play dumb with me, Monica. You know something. Hell, even Jasmine knows more than I do."

"She told you everything I know," Monica said. "Your mother went to hear someone sing at the casino."

"She's not gambling, is she? I don't want Mama getting sucked into that trap."

"I've known her for less than a year, and even I wouldn't question whether she went to a casino to gamble." She hunched her shoulders, returning the pitcher of tea to the fridge. "It's nothing, Toby. One of her friends won tickets to hear a lounge act at the casino, and invited your mom to go along. I practically had to push her out the door."

"Because she probably didn't want to go," Toby deduced.

"No, she wanted to go, but she felt guilty leaving Jasmine after Alex's meeting came up. Your mom needs to get out of the house every once in a while. It's good for her."

Toby's gaze roamed over his future sister-in-law's face, his suspicion building. He knew he was not getting the whole story.

"Do you know why she wasn't at Bible study a couple of weeks ago? Sylvia Culpepper said she didn't see her, even though Alex dropped her at the church and I picked her up."

Monica shook her head. "If your mother was not at Bible study, I'm sure she has a good reason. But, before you question her, *you'd* better have a good excuse for not being at church this past Sunday. Eli heard a mouthful yesterday, and he delivered a set of twins Sunday morning. You'd better have been saving the world."

Good point. "We're still getting together to discuss the plans for Mama's party, right?"

"Barring any emergencies."

"Tell Mama I dropped by, and I'll definitely be in church on Sunday. You and Eli should try to make it. Aria's directing the youth choir."

"I have all the nurses in the ER voting, and we've got the TV set to watch in a few hours."

"We're at that club out in Metairie tonight. Not Aria's usual crowd, but I want her to hook the crossover market."

Monica nodded, then smiled conspiratorially. "And how are things working out with Sienna?"

Toby couldn't help but smile, too. "Sienna's a whiz at marketing."

"That is not what I'm talking about and you know it. You are a fool for not dating Sienna."

"You and Alex have been talking, haven't you?"

"No, but if Alex has told you the same thing, then you're even more of a fool not to listen to him. Sienna is perfect for you, and she's crazy about you."

"You hardly know her. What makes you say that?"

"You only have to see the way she looks at you, Toby. I remember the first time I met her when I came over to your mother's. I saw it then. That girl is crazy about you," Monica reiterated.

Toby playfully pulled her hair. "Well, we're having dinner tonight."

Monica's brows rose. "Really?"

"And *not* in a professional capacity," Toby clarified.

Monica started clapping. "I knew it."

"You'd better not tell Alex. I don't want to hear anything from him."

"I *knew* it. This is so cool. We can have a double wedding."

"Good night, Monica," Toby said, heading for the door. "Tell Mama I'll stop by tomorrow."

"Good luck tonight. With, uh, everything," she laughed.

Toby gave her a backwards wave and left.

Chapter Sixteen

Sienna checked her watch and looked up and down Canal Street, searching for sign of Toby's car. Standing her up was not a good start to this new "thing" between them. She'd been questioning the wisdom of agreeing to pursue an actual relationship with Toby and his tardiness only gave her more time to doubt her decision.

Sienna spotted his Acura coming down Canal Street toward the river. The car made a U-turn, waiting for a streetcar to pass. A car parked alongside the street drove away just as Toby was pulling up to the curb, and he was able to slip right into the spot.

Sienna purposely kept her hand on her hip.

"You're late," she said by way of greeting.

"Good evening to you, too," Toby laughed. "I got caught up at Mama's."

She smiled with relief. "Well, since it's your mother, you're forgiven."

Okay, so things weren't all that different. She would have ribbed Toby for being late even if they were not an "item." Gosh, that sounded so high school.

They headed down Bourbon Street toward the world-famous restaurant at the corner of Bourbon and Bienville.

"I think something's going on with Mama," Toby said. "I haven't been able to catch up with her in a couple of days. Then, the other night when I met you at your mom's store, she said my mom wasn't at Bible study, even though I picked her up from the church."

Sienna's eyebrows rose. "Is she sick?"

"No. In fact, she's out on the town. Monica's at the house babysitting Jasmine because Mama had plans."

"So, what's strange about that?"

"My mother is not the type of person who has *plans*, Sienna," he said.

"Well, maybe it's time she becomes that type of person. Now, stop worrying about your mother." She wrapped her hand around his upper arm and said, "So, are you ready to go broke buying me dinner?"

He covered her hand and laughed. "So that's your plan— to suck me dry?"

They both stopped short.

"Damn, that sounded really bad, didn't it?" Toby said, shaking his head.

Sienna nodded, unsure if she could speak.

"Come on, Cee Cee. Any other time you would have laughed at that."

"Any other time, your double entendre would have been directed toward another woman."

"So I have to analyze every little thing I say before I speak to you? Be real, Sienna." He stepped to the side as a couple exited the front door of the restaurant. "If we are really going to give this a fighting chance, we've got to be comfortable with each other. Things shouldn't change just because we've gone from being friends to being lov—"

"More than friends," Sienna cut him off before the word lovers left his mouth. She had not agreed to taking things anywhere close to the bedroom.

"Fine. More than friends," Toby conceded. "Now can we go into this restaurant and enjoy our very expensive meal?" He glanced at his watch. "We only have a couple of hours before we have to be at Caesar's Ghost, and if I'm going to break the bank here, I at least want to have enough time to savor every bite."

"Okay," Sienna nodded. "I think they're serving Lobster Napoleon."

She giggled as Toby rolled his eyes. "It's a good thing I remembered to bring the Platinum Visa."

Sienna decided to be merciful and order a grilled chicken Caesar salad, in reverence to the venue where Aria would be performing tonight. Halfway through their meal, Toby reminded her that they needed to get to Caesar's Ghost early to go over a few last minute issues with Aria, so they ate quickly so they could get out to the club. When they arrived, the parking lot was full and cars lined the streets.

"Can you believe this?" Toby asked as he pulled up to the massive building that commanded nearly half the block. The line to enter the club was out the door and around the side of the building.

"There must be a few hundred people still waiting to get in," Sienna said.

Toby crept along the street, searching for a parking spot. "I'm not sure Aria's ready for a crowd this size."

"What are you talking about?" Sienna asked. "This is exactly what she needs. You don't give Aria enough credit, Toby. She's more prepared for this than you think. Look how well she did last night at The Hard Court. You, on the other hand, will need to borrow one of my mom's Valium before the night is over if you don't chill out."

"I'll be okay after tonight." He parked illegally about a fourth of a mile from the club. "The way I see it, The Hard Court was a test run. Aria's had that crowd eating out the palm of her hand for the past couple of weeks. Tonight's crowd, however, is an entirely new ballgame."

Sienna took his hand as Toby helped her out of the car. She squeezed it, trying to reassure him. "I know you have a lot riding on this, Toby. It means a lot to your career."

"Yours, too."

Sienna nodded. "Don't worry, I haven't forgotten."

The sheer magnitude of this week sent a shudder of nervous energy through her blood whenever she thought about it—which was at least a dozen times a day. Her career hung in the balance. If they didn't pull this off, she could kiss everything she'd worked so hard for good-bye. Every major marketing firm in the region was looking at MDF, Inc.'s execution of this sought after account. If she screwed this up, Sienna knew she wouldn't be able to find a job anywhere in the city.

The thought sent a familiar rush of panic skittering down Sienna's spine. She did her best to shake it off, but how could she? Allen Mulholland was checking up on her like a parent whose teenager had just received their driver's license. He'd called after learning Aria would be performing at Caesar's Ghost, a club which catered to an alternative pop music crowd. He said he was concerned Sienna was spreading Aria too thin, and suggested she stick to the demographic that had served Aria so well already.

For a moment Sienna had thought the same thing. She'd questioned Aria's appeal outside the R&B market, but after Allen had suggested she back out of the Caesar's Ghost performance, Sienna completely threw out the idea. This was *her* account. It was *her* neck on the chopping block. Allen needed to trust her. She needed to trust herself.

Sienna guided Toby to the back entrance the club owner had showed her when she initially set up Aria's performance. It wasn't a secret entrance, as evident by the group of people crowding the back door, but at least they didn't have to deal with the mob at the front of the club. Sienna called the owner on her cell phone and a minute later he appeared, escorting them into the building.

They walked through a short hallway and entered the club. It was fashioned to resemble an ancient Roman temple. A replica of a classic triumphal arch greeted club-goers who entered through the main entrance. Soaring, ornate pillars hugged the four corners of the club's main floor, reaching to the top of the two-story ceiling. A life-size chariot stood as the centerpiece, proudly displayed atop a towering pedestal in the center of the club, a fully circular bar at its base.

"Dang, this is tight," Toby said, his gaze roaming the massive club.

"I told you," Sienna said. To the club owner she asked, "Can you bring us to the dressing room?"

They went through another door just to the right of the stage. The club owner walked up to the door straight ahead of them, knocked, opened, and made a gesture for Sienna and Toby to enter.

"Hey there," Aria greeted, the ever-present cameramen in tow. She was seated at a well lit vanity, bottle of water in her hand.

"How did things go this afternoon?" Toby asked.

"It was fine. I stopped in at the studio and cleaned up the track Savion has been working on. It sounds really good, if I do say so myself," Aria preened.

One of the cameramen stepped in. "We've got twenty minutes before the show. We're going to take a quick break."

As soon as they left the room, Aria's features softened with relief.

"Are you doing okay with the twenty-four seven attention?" Sienna asked, moving to her side.

"It's still kinda strange. People are constantly staring, but I guess you can't blame them when you have a couple of camera guys following you around."

"Are you sure you're ready for tonight?" Toby asked. "This isn't your usual crowd, but you know we had to do this, right?"

Aria nodded.

Sienna knew this had been on his mind. Thus far, Aria had performed mostly for young, urban professionals, à la The Hard Court's clientele. Caesar's Ghost was located in a suburb of New Orleans, and its usual crowd consisted of college-aged alternative rock and pop listeners. Winning over this crowd could present a challenge, but if they were able to pull it off, it would be a huge mark in the plus column for convincing the producers of Aria's worldwide appeal.

"Don't worry, Toby," Sienna assured him. "The songs we

selected should go over well with this demographic. I told you, all we have to worry about is having enough headshots for her autograph at the end of the night."

Toby smiled. "I didn't realize cheerleader was a part of your job description."

"You didn't see that in the contract?" Sienna quipped.

"It's going to be okay, Toby," Aria said. She stood and wrapped her arms around Toby's waist, giving him a hug. "Thank you for everything. This is more than I could have ever hoped for."

Toby looked over at Sienna, a helpless look on his face. Sienna fixed him with an I-told-you-so stare as Aria continued to hug him.

"Um, okay," Toby said, extricating himself from Aria's hold. "Well, we need to go and find a good spot."

"Okay, I'll see you both after the show," Aria said, then she stood on her tiptoes, and placed a kiss right on Toby's lips. "Thanks again," she said, a hint of sultriness in her voice.

"Uh . . . okay," Toby said. He took Sienna by the hand and led her out of the dressing room.

"I told you," Sienna remarked as soon as they entered the hallway. "That girl has a mega-size crush on you."

"Why do I have to be so damn irresistible?" he said. Sienna pinched him on the arm.

She stopped him before he could open the door they'd come through from the club's main floor. "Seriously, Toby, you need to make sure she has no illusions regarding the two of you."

"I know," he said. "I will."

As soon as they re-entered the club, Sienna spotted Marshall Kellerman standing close to the stage, not ten feet away. "There's Kellerman," she said.

"Where?"

"And there's David Reynolds," Sienna tried to be as discreet as possible as she pointed. "I didn't realize the producers would be attending tonight's performance."

"Oh, great. Let's hope Aria doesn't notice they're here. Act like you don't see them," he said, charging straight past the stage. "If they're with us when Aria seeks us out while she's on stage, she'll get nervous."

But it was too late. Kellerman had spotted them and waved them over. He offered to buy them drinks, which both Toby and Sienna declined. A minute later, Aria took to the stage. The crowd welcomed her with a roaring ovation, probably because they knew she was the reason for all the cameras and their possible shot to get their faces on national television, Sienna thought.

Aria opened with Kelly Clarkson's hit "Walk Away," which started the crowd to dancing. After engaging the crowd with a couple more songs currently topping the Billboard charts, she moved on to cover several rock classics. Sienna was amazed at the way the normally demure Aria commanded the stage, bobbing her head up and down, dragging the microphone stand behind her as she moved from one edge of the stage to the other like a seasoned rocker. When she belted out Janis Joplin's "Take Another Little Piece of My Heart," she managed to hold onto the legendary singer's raspy sultriness while making the song her own.

She went through the musical arrangement with aplomb, as if she'd spent her entire life singing rock and pop music instead of R&B. Sienna was bowled over by Aria's ability to lose herself in the music. Or, maybe she didn't lose herself. Maybe the music was where she *found* herself. This is what Aria was meant to do; the girl was a natural on any stage.

She surprised everybody in the club, including Sienna and Toby, when she belted out "Crazy in Love" by Beyoncé Knowles, and did the booty-bouncing dance the singer had made famous.

The crowd went wild.

The number was not included in the line up, but apparently Aria had made plans with the band beforehand. The smile on Kellerman's face was a mile wide.

"This is what the show is all about," the producer said.

"She's amazing," David Reynolds put in. "How many performers have you seen win over a crowd this quickly?"

Aria ended her performance with a Celine Dion number that left the audience mesmerized. When she exited the stage and started elbowing her way through the crowd, Aria could hardly make it through the adoring horde who all wanted to get close to the night's new star. Toby went to help her out, adding bodyguard to his list of duties to his client.

Kellerman and Reynolds lavished their praise upon her, and Sienna's spirits buoyed with every minute that passed. Aria wouldn't be the only one to reach star status with the success of this show. She couldn't wait to get Allen's reaction when the producers told him how fabulous Aria did with a crowd that was "outside her normal demographic." Maybe this would erase her boss's doubts and, instead, he'd give her the respect she'd deserved.

Toby motioned for Sienna to follow them to the dressing room. Sienna headed toward the back of the club, trying to decide which of the spacious executive offices she would demand at Mulholland, Davis, and French.

Toby stood sentry beside Aria as she autographed at least two hundred photographs outside the back door at Caesar's Ghost. The crowd couldn't get enough of her. The cameramen both looked on the verge of collapse. Toby couldn't blame them; it couldn't be easy to shoulder that equipment for hours.

When the last picture was signed, Toby, along with the cameramen and the club owner, escorted Aria back into the club's dressing room.

"We've got to take fifteen," one of the cameramen said. He dropped his camera and pack, the other cameraman following suit.

The club owner held up a finger. "Give me a minute, you've both earn a drink on the house."

"Nothing alcoholic while we're on the clock," the other cameraman said, earning a glare from the one who'd suggested the break.

The club owner walked up to Toby. "Whenever Ms. Jordan is in need of a venue, you call me," he pointed his stubby thumb to his chest. He looked down at Aria, who'd resumed her seat at the lighted vanity table. Her smile stretched from one side of her face to the other. "You, young lady, have a long career ahead of you. This club has never been as electrified as it was when you took to the stage."

"Thank you," Aria said, still beaming.

"Don't worry about picking up any of this," he motioned to the makeup-stained cotton balls and tissues strewn across the vanity. "Someone'll be in to clean up once you're done."

Toby clasped the man's hand. "Thanks again for having us."

He nodded and left the dressing room, pulling the door closed behind him. As soon as he was gone, Aria bolted from the chair and crashed into Toby's chest, wrapping her arms around his waist.

"Toby, can you believe it!" she gasped. "Tonight was unbelievable."

"Yeah, it was," he said, trying to extract her arms from around him.

Aria stared up at him from where she'd laid her head on his chest. The look in her eyes caused trepidation to race down Toby's back.

Oh, damn.

"Uh . . . Aria."

She kissed him.

For a moment, Toby was rendered speechless, unsure of how he should even try to respond. When he didn't do anything, she must have taken it as his acquiescence and reached up to kiss him again.

Toby reared back. "Whoa . . . Aria, wait a minute."

"What?" she asked, those doelike brown eyes staring straight at him. "What's the matter? Don't you want to—"

"No," Toby pulled her arms from around his waist and took three huge steps back. Damn, this was awkward. "Look, Aria, I'm not sure where you got the impression that I wanted anything more than a professional relationship."

She took a step toward him. "But—"

"But nothing," Toby said with another step back. "I'm your manager and producer. You're my client. That's it."

The pain-filled look she shot him attacked Toby's conscience. He ran a hand down his face and swallowed a groan. He should have addressed this the minute Sienna had told him to. Now, here he was, in the middle of the most important week of his career, breaking the heart of his most important client.

"Aria, I'm sorry," Toby said, taking a tentative step forward. He was about to reach for her hand but decided against it. He needed to set a firm boundary, starting now.

Aria looked up at him, then quickly lowered her eyes to the floor. "I just thought . . . you know. We've been together for nearly a year."

"Working together," Toby said softly. "It's always been about the work. I thought you understood that."

"I did . . . I just. Well, you don't have a girlfriend," she returned accusingly.

Toby hesitated, then said, "Actually, Sienna and I are seeing each other." The minute he said it, Toby wished he could take the words back. Aria blinked. She looked as if she were going to speak, but instead, she nodded, wrapping her arms around herself, her expression going from bewildered to resigned, with a bit of hurt still mixed in.

"Well, okay," she said, with the most fake smile Toby had ever seen. "I guess that's that."

"Aria," Toby reached for her, despite his vow to maintain his distance. But Aria stepped out of the way. "No, I'm okay," she said.

The door to the dressing room pushed open and one of the cameramen came through, clutching a can of soda. If he noticed a change in the room's atmosphere, he didn't acknowledge it.

"I'm gonna turn in early," Aria said, turning to the vanity. "I've got a full day tomorrow."

Toby briefly closed his eyes in relief. She was sticking to

the plan. Before they started the taping, Toby had given her an hour-by-hour itinerary to follow so there would be no surprises. Other than the visit by her mother, they'd been able to stick to the plan.

"Yeah, you should probably head home," Toby said. He walked over to the chair that held her duffle bag, but when he picked up the bag, she stopped him.

"I've got it," she said, the false brightness still in her voice. "You can go."

Toby debated saying more, then figured it was best to quit while he was ahead. For a minute, he thought he saw tears forming in Aria's eyes, and he damn sure didn't want the cameras to catch her crying.

"Okay, then," Toby said, dropping the bag back on the chair. "I'll see you tomorrow." He made his way to the door, but before leaving, turned back and said, "Congratulations again, Aria. You wrote your own ticket to stardom with to-night's performance."

"Thanks," she answered, her voice sullen.

Toby shut the door before those tears he'd glimpsed could fall.

"I could have asked for things to go better, but I don't think it's possible," Toby said as he handed Sienna a glass of wine. He took a seat beside her on the sofa that faced an amazing view of the city.

"Tonight was unbelievable," Sienna replied, sipping her wine. "Almost as unbelievable as this apartment. Just how much is this setting you back?"

"You don't want to know," Toby answered.

Sienna's eyes roamed over her surroundings, overwhelmed by the sheer opulence.

Honey-colored hardwood floors, dotted with plush rugs, spanned the entire penthouse. The kitchen was done with stainless steel appliances and beautiful teal-tinged granite coun-tertops above the sand-colored cabinetry. A narrow bar, with high, backless stools separated the kitchen from the living room.

A rust-colored leather sofa faced a vista of windows that ran from the floor to the top of the eleven foot ceilings. Sienna walked over to the windows and took in the glorious view they afforded. Lights shimmered across the Mississippi River like fireflies as the few commuters still up at this hour made the trek across the Crescent City Connection that linked the city's east and west banks.

"Pretty nice, huh?" Toby came up behind her, wrapping his arm around her waist.

Sienna tipped her head back. "Tell me again why you felt the need to rent this apartment in the first place?"

"I wanted to impress the producers, but I doubt they'll even have the opportunity to see it. That's okay, though. It's practice for when I really do own a place like this."

"Thinking big, huh?"

"Why shouldn't I? After the way my girl put it down tonight, it's only a matter of time."

"Speaking of your girl," Sienna said, disengaging from his hold and marching him back toward the sofa. She waited until they were both seated and she had Toby's undivided attention. "Aria wasn't all that shy about making her feelings known tonight."

"No, she was not," Toby answered with a sigh.

"What are you going to do about her not-so-subtle infatuation?"

"I took care of it."

Her brows rose.

"I talked to her after the show," Toby clarified.

She studied him with guarded uncertainty. "Are you sure that was a good idea?"

"What else would you have had me do?"

Sienna lifted her shoulder. "I'm not sure. It's just that I don't think this was some insignificant thing on Aria's part. She's really into you, Toby. What if your crushing her hopes messes with her mind? That's something you definitely don't want this week."

"She assured me she was okay with it. I let her down easy,

Cee Cee. I told her that I was sorry if I'd led her on in any way, but that I've always wanted only a professional relationship with her."

"So, how did she take it?"

"She'll be okay," Toby reassured her. "She's still flying high after her performance. Honestly, I doubt it matters all that much to her."

"Well, I hope so," Sienna said, settling on the sofa with her back against Toby's chest. "After pining away for someone for so long, having your dreams crushed can be a severe blow."

Toby caressed her arm. "Do you know much about that?"

Sienna thought about the nights she'd lain in bed, fantasizing about making her best friend more than just a friend. Nights when she knew he had been out with other girls. Heck, she'd even helped him pick out clothes for some of those dates.

"A little," she finally answered his question.

"Who was foolish enough to break your heart?" he asked.

Sienna remained silent. She wasn't about to admit to Toby that she had been just as infatuated with him as Aria had been. Probably even more.

He grasped her chin between his fingers and tipped her head up. "Whoever it was, that fool's loss was my gain," Toby said, angling his head and dipping low. His lips touched hers, tentatively at first, brushing slowly back and forth over her mouth. Sienna felt the moist tip of his tongue as he licked at her closed lips with gentle pressure, becoming more insistent with each pass. She reached her hand over and placed it behind his neck, pulling Toby down.

He groaned, twisting her around and gently pushing her onto the sofa, his demanding lips never leaving hers. He guided her down, cradling her head as they both sank into the butter smooth leather.

Sienna's head spun in the sweet, seductive swirl of emotion that had captured her. The sensation of Toby's mouth molding to hers was straight out of long ago dreams. And when she finally opened her lips and accepted his tongue, Sienna was certain she had never encountered anything more powerful.

He consumed her, his tongue bathing the recesses of her mouth with fierce tenderness. Tasting. Exploring. Possessing.

Toby's hand trailed from her hair to run along her cheek with a caress so tender it wrenched a moan from her. His knee rode along her hip before settling between her thighs. Sienna fought the urge to open fully for him, but her body did so involuntarily. It felt all too natural, too right, to relax her legs and create a cradle for his body.

Toby settled his strong thigh between her legs, teasing her with gentle pressure as his mouth's insistent plundering continued to wreak havoc with her senses. Sienna wrapped her arms over his shoulders, drawing him closer, reveling in the sensation of his sculpted muscles against her breasts.

She let herself drift on the wave of desire. So long she had dreamed of joining her mouth to his. Patiently, she had waited for him to see her as a woman instead of the awkward teenager he'd left behind. Now that the time was finally here, Sienna nearly laughed at how unbelievably altered her expectation was to reality. Toby's kiss was ten times sweeter, hotter, and more passionate than anything she had ever dreamed.

He released her mouth, dipping his head low and drawing his tongue along her collarbone. He laved her skin with slow, luxurious swipes of a tongue wicked enough to elicit raw, potent desire from a woman who'd been deprived of such pleasure for far too long. Toby captured her hand and drew her fingers into his mouth, tasting and suckling like he couldn't get enough of her.

Sienna moaned. The warmth of his mouth shot sparks of heated need through her bloodstream. He moved his thigh up and down between her legs, testing it against her core, wringing groans of desire from deep in her throat. Sienna could feel the part of his body she both craved and, in ways, still feared, pulsing against her stomach.

Toby ran his hands under her silk shell, roaming over the crest of cleavage thrusting forward from her lacy bra.

"Damn, you taste good," he whispered, nipping at her lips. Sienna wasn't sure she could take anymore. She wasn't sure if she *should*. It was all moving too fast. If they continued at this pace, Toby would be inside of her in a matter of minutes. The thought made her dizzy with anticipation and fear. She had never allowed a man to get this close to her. After what had happen the night of her debutante ball, she had been too afraid to offer herself as a part of this intimate dance so many women her age took for granted. She wanted it to be with Toby when it finally happened, but Sienna wasn't sure she was ready just yet.

If she didn't put a stop to his kisses soon, she wouldn't have a choice.

"Toby, stop," Sienna whispered.

Either he didn't hear her, or he ignored her, too wrapped up in his pursuit to get the rest of her clothes from barricading his final destination. Toby trailed his tongue across the rise of her shoulder, pushing her shirt up and feathering light kisses along her neck.

"Toby!" Sienna shouted in a near panic. Capturing his wrist before he could undress her any further, she started to squirm on the sofa, trying to wrangle free from him.

Toby's head popped up. "Cee Cee, what's wrong?"

Sienna managed to get one hand between them and pushed against his chest. "This is going a little too fast for me, Toby."

He looked at her, saw she was serious. He instantly sat back, and Sienna nearly cried in relief. The last boy who'd attempted to go this far had not stopped so willingly.

Sienna straightened to a sitting position on the sofa, wrapping her arms around her stomach. Toby grabbed the chenille throw that lay across the arm of the sofa and draped it around her. Sienna shivered despite the warmth the throw provided, her mind reeling from the intense emotions dancing through her body.

Why was she so afraid? She knew Toby better than to think he'd ever do anything to hurt her. She could not allow what Curtis Henderson did all those years ago to rule her life.

"Sienna?" Toby's soft query drew her out of her musing. "Sienna, what's wrong?"

"Nothing," she lied. "I just . . . I'm not ready to go there yet, okay?"

"Hey," he put his hands up. "You only have to say the word. Always. It felt as if you were afraid I wouldn't stop." He captured her chin between his fingers and raised her head. "You know I will never do anything you don't want me to do, right Cee Cee?"

She nodded, the emotion welling up in her throat preventing her from uttering a single sound.

"Okay," Toby said. "When you're ready, we'll only go as far as you say."

Sienna leaned over and placed a soft kiss on his lips. "Thank you."

A slight smile curved one corner of his mouth. "You're welcome. Now," he settled another peck on her mouth. "If you don't mind, there is a cold shower with my name on it."

Gathering the wrap more closely around her, Sienna watched as he moved across the living room on his way to the penthouse's master suite. "Toby," she called out before he reached the glass French doors that led to the hallway.

He turned.

Sienna stared at him for a moment, before making him a quiet, solemn promise.

"Soon."

Chapter Seventeen

Katie LeBlanc of the *Wake-Up with Katie* morning show kept the plastic smile plastered across her face. Toby wished he could rip her head off.

What they'd been promised would be a standard question and answer session about Aria's blossoming career and her participation in a *Week in the Life of a Wannabe Star* had turned into a bludgeoning of probing questions that had caught everyone, especially Aria, totally off guard. The confidence she had built up had plummeted. Katie fired questions at her at lightening speed. But it was all done with a smile, so apparently, it was okay.

"The temptation of drugs and sex is so strong in the hip hop music world. How do you avoid getting caught up in that lifestyle, Miss Jordan? Or, have you taken a walk on the wild side?" Katie asked, all bleached white teeth.

"I . . . ah, I've never done drugs," Aria said. Her eyes were as wide as a deer caught in headlights. A blush turning her caramel cheeks to crimson. "And, well, as for sex . . . um . . . I've only done it a couple of times."

Standing just to the right of the morning show's set, which was made to look like an inviting living room, Toby groaned in frustration and dragged his hands down his face. "This is a freaking disaster."

Sienna stood beside him, biting her fingernails. "I'm trying to find the bright side, Toby, but I really can't with this one. It *is* a freaking disaster."

Toby shot her a glance and chuckled. "Don't you go using that language around your mother. She'll blame me for corrupting you again."

"With good reason," Sienna said, the knowing look on her face intimating that a mere cuss word was not what she was thinking about at the moment. Toby couldn't afford to comment. He'd had a hard enough time pushing thoughts of last night from his mind. If he thought about the way Sienna's silken skin had felt on his tongue, his day would be shot to hell for thinking about anything else.

"We should have demanded to see the questions before the interview," Toby said after a moment.

Sienna shook her head. "I'm not sure it would have made a difference. I think Katie LeBlanc wanted this ambush."

Toby had a feeling Sienna was right, but thankfully, the interview was almost over.

"What we need to do today is work on a way to counter any backlash that may come from this interview," she continued.

"The only thing that may raise a few eyebrows were her views on *American Idol*. I'll construct a more tactful response, indicating that Aria was misunderstood.

"Don't worry, Toby. This is just an extremely small bump in the road. You knew it wouldn't go perfectly."

"You're right. There are always snags. And if we're lucky enough to have this as the only thing that goes wrong, we'll be in good shape."

"Let's hope," Sienna said. "I'm going into the office for a bit, then I'll meet you at this afternoon's radio interview."

He leaned over and placed a soft kiss on her lips.

"Thank you," Toby said. "For everything."

"Why me?"

Ivana stood in the newly renovated lobby of Jonathan Campbell's law office, trying to make sense of the transformation that had taken place, or as the case may be, the lack of the transformation she had been expecting. Instead of being destroyed, the interior of the home had been restored to its eighteenth-century splendor. But that couldn't be. Hadn't he torn down the original woodwork?

"What happened to this place?" Ivana asked before he could answer her previous question. "Didn't you have the contractor strip down these walls?"

"I tore the walls down because they were rotting."

"But where is all the chrome and black crap? The first day I came here there was a sketch of an office on a poster board. Everything was ugly and cold and metal and black leather."

A devilish grin tilted his lips. "That was for my office at the club. Happy to hear you like my style."

"So you had no plans to have that modern décor in this office?"

He shook his head.

"What about the room in the back? I asked you specifically not to touch it."

"And I won't touch it if you have dinner with me."

"And if I don't?"

He shrugged. "My original intentions were to gut it and turn it into a personal gym. The mirror panels to replace the existing walls are already on order."

Ivana could not hide her revulsion. A gym? Could this man do anything more to make her detest him? Apparently he could. Blackmailing her into going out with him was pretty darn detestable.

"Are you so desperate for a date that you're willing to sink to blackmail?"

"Not just any date. Only with a certain woman who pretends it's the hardest thing in the world to simply give me the time of day."

"I don't wear a watch," Ivana said, which made him laugh that deep, rich laugh that sent tremors along her skin. "You still didn't answer my question," she said. "Why me?"

"Why not you?"

"Stop answering my questions with a question and get straight with me. I want to know what game you're playing."

"Is this the way you treat every man who asks you to dinner?"

"I don't get asked to dinner," Ivana told him.

One brow cocked.

She decided to be truthful. "Most men are intimidated by me."

He stepped in closer, boring into her with heated eyes and slowly shaking his head. "It would be a mistake to compare me to other men, Ivana."

Ivana thought she was taking a deep breath, but it was only a fraction of the oxygen she needed to help clear her head.

"Now, do I call in the contractor to continue with the renovations, or sign up for membership at the gym down the street? You make the call."

"You are unbelievable," Ivana said.

He looked at his watch. "Time's passing pretty quickly."

"Wait, you expect me to go to dinner with you now? Tonight?"

"It's nearly seven o'clock. I haven't eaten since nine this morning."

"But tonight? I'm not dressed for dinner."

"You look perfect," he said, then laughed. "Why do you look at me that way whenever I give you a compliment?" With an exaggerated look at his watch he asked, "So, Ivana. What's it gonna be?"

Ivana's gut clenched with anxiety at the thought of accepting Jonathan's invitation, but she knew what she had to do. She'd learned of the room's significance during her research soon after she'd joined the religion. Dinner with Jonathan was a small sacrifice to save the room where the first voodoo healing in New Orleans had taken place.

She gave him a resigned shrug. "Italian or seafood?"

"Sienna, are you ignoring me?"

Her lids briefly slid shut. Sienna opened her eyes and refocused on the road ahead. "Mother, I couldn't ignore you if I tried," she barely gritted the words through her teeth.

"I don't know what's gotten into you lately, but I don't like it. And it had better change, soon. Now let's go over what you're going to say at the introduction ceremony."

"I know who I am, Mother. I do not need to rehearse, and I am not lying."

"It's not lying, it's embellishing. Everybody does it."

It was bad enough she had to spend another hour of her life at yet another high society function. She was not up to dealing with her mother's elitist friends. In fact, until her mother's call in the middle of Aria's radio interview, Sienna had forgotten all about tonight's introduction ceremony.

As if they all didn't know each other, and constantly talk about each other already. This was just another way for the Queen Bees to show off in front of the Wannabes. Her mother so wanted to be a Queen Bee, but her misfit daughters prohibited her from fitting all the criteria, which included having successful children and grandchildren to dote on.

As all powerful as her mother was, even Sylvia Culpepper

could not produce grandchildren out of thin air. However, she had been trying to get Sienna to go along with "embellishing" her successes in order to fit her friends' standards.

She was not going to do it. The feats she had accomplished these past few weeks were big enough to get her name mentioned in every water cooler conversation at every marketing firm in the city. If it was not enough for her mother, than that was too bad.

Sienna pulled into the parking lot of the restaurant, and turned the car off, but before her mother could open the door, she hit the automatic door locks, locking them in.

"Sienna, what are you doing?"

The look her mother pierced her with would have caused her to shirk just a few months ago. But Sienna was sick of cowering. She'd agreed to do this, but it was the last time she would allow her mother to reign over her life. And she was doing it on her terms.

"We need to set some ground rules before we walk into that restaurant."

"Sienna, I don't have time for your nonsense. Now unlock these doors so we can go."

"You'll either sit and listen to me, or we'll spend the entire time in the parking lot. Take your pick."

The gasp that escaped her mother's lips was priceless. "Just who do you think you're talking to in that tone?"

"Are you listening?"

"I am not about to let you talk to me this way, Sienna Elaine."

"You don't have a choice." Sienna twisted in her seat. Her mother needed to see her face when she said what she had to say. "The only reason I am still going along with this is because I don't want you to look like a total fool, but after the ball on Sunday that's it, Mother. I will not let you use me to live out some ridiculous dream you've had."

Her mother opened her mouth to speak, but Sienna cut her off.

"Listen to me. We are going to go in there, and you will

not make anything more of my career than what it is. If you cannot be proud of the fact that I'm a very successful *junior* marketing executive, then find yourself another more acceptable daughter to pass around to your friends."

If it were possible for a person's head to pop right off their shoulders, Sienna was sure her mother's would have by now. She could practically see the steam building under her perfectly coiffed hair.

"Furthermore, I will not tolerate you lying about any romantic relationships, or even worse, trying to push me onto an unmarried son of one of your so-called friends."

"You should be grateful any of my friends would want their sons with you. Most of them think you're gay."

Sienna thought about Toby's hand traveling up her stomach, his mouth pulling on her nipple through her blouse.

"Perfect," Sienna answered. "I'll start my introduction by telling them all that I'm gay."

"Sienna!"

Dang. She wasn't holding onto her chest. Sienna was sure that would have given her mother a heart attack.

"Do you promise not to change me into your version of the ideal daughter when we get in there?"

Oh, yeah. Her mother could cook a head of cabbage with the steam radiating from under her collar.

"Just unlock the door," Sylvia spat.

"Not until you give me your word."

She gave the most imperceptible nod.

Pressing the automatic lock, Sienna shivered from the rush of pleasure that came with just this one small victory. "Okay, let's get this over with."

Chapter Eighteen

Imitating Michael Jackson's moonwalk would have been inappropriate, but that's exactly what Jonathan felt like doing. He should feel guilty for lying about remodeling that back room, but when Ivana had barged into his office demanding the room not be touched, inspiration had struck, and Jonathan refused to feel even a twinge of guilt. He'd started to doubt he'd ever get Ivana to agree to go out with him.

Of course, this was not what he'd had in mind when he suggested dinner. Even though he was still new to the city, Jonathan had questioned Ivana's directions when she'd told him the location of the restaurant where she wanted to have dinner. Toby had given him a crash course in the neighborhoods to avoid, and this one ranked high on the list. As he looked over the scores of faces crowding the rows of tables of the soup kitchen, Jonathan couldn't help but say a prayer for their situation.

"I don't eat no green beans," an old lady, who had on at least three coats even though it was pushing eighty-five degrees outside, yelled at him.

"Sorry, Ms. Mable. He's new," Ivana said as she placed an extra roll on the woman's plate.

Jonathan leaned closer to her. "When I suggested we have dinner, I envisioned sitting at a table while people served us, not the other way around."

"We eat when everyone else has been fed," Ivana said.

"Hurry it up," came a call from somewhere down the line.

"Get back to your green beans," Ivana said. "You're slowing down the line."

"They'll get the damn beans when I give it to them," Jonathan muttered under his breath. "Ungrateful sons of—"

His respect for Ivana grew by leaps and bounds with

every abusive remark one of the vagrants hurled her way. Jonathan had been ready to fight the first person who'd insulted her, but Ivana had stopped him. She'd told him he needed to understand that most of these people were angry at the world because of their current circumstances, and that he shouldn't hold their sour attitudes against them. The way Jonathan saw it, they all should be grateful that people like Ivana and the rest of her friends cared enough to fix them a hot meal.

By the time everyone had eaten their fill, which included seconds and even thirds for some people, there were a few pieces of roast beef and about ten string beans left for both he and Ivana to split. Ever the gentleman, Jonathan gave up his claim to the green beans so Ivana could have them all.

They took a seat at the table one of the other helpers had just cleared.

Now all he had to do was get her to talk about herself, which he had not been able to accomplish the entire time they'd served the homeless their meals.

"So, what's the age difference between you and Sienna?" Jonathan asked, since his earlier question about her business had tanked.

"When did it become appropriate to ask a woman her age?" she countered.

Jonathan held off on gritting his teeth. "Come on, Ivana. You practically ignored me the entire time we were serving. Did you agree to go out with me just to be difficult all night?"

"I agreed to go out with you because you gave me no other choice."

"So you're saying you would never have gone out with me if it were not for wanting to save that back room from becoming my private gym?"

The look she gave him told him that was exactly the case.

Forget this. Why was he bothering with a woman who didn't want anything to do with him? He was getting hit on at least a dozen times a night at the club. All he had to do was crook his finger and he could have a string of women in his bed.

But not a single one of them had intrigued him the way Ivana had. There was something about her that captivated him, so much so that he decided against ending the date early, as he had been about to do just a second ago. Instead, Jonathan employed another tactic, something he knew she couldn't resist.

"Why don't you explain just why this room is so important to you?"

She gave him the suspicious eye before taking a sip of water and asking, "Why?"

Jonathan shrugged, "It must mean a lot if you were willing to stoop to having dinner with me."

She gave him a saccharine smile. "Only fools fall for reverse psychology, Mr. Campbell, and despite what the vast majority of people think, I am no fool."

That. That right there was what had him coming back even though she shot him down at every turn. She had a hint of sass that tended to surface from time to time. It was such a contradiction to the no-nonsense image she usually portrayed. She fascinated him, plain and simple.

He was about to speak when she said, "The building that houses your new law practice is where the first voodoo healing took place in New Orleans." She pushed a few green beans around with her fork. "It's an important part of the religion's history, at least to us practicing it here in New Orleans."

"What made you turn to voodoo?" he asked, because he desperately wanted to know. He knew her religion was important to her, and Jonathan was dying for just a small look through this window to her soul.

"I was raised a Christian," Ivana provided. "Actually, in many ways I still believe in God, but it was the compassion of the voodoo that appealed to me. I'd never witnessed such generosity." She looked up at him, her expression softened. "I was like you, you know. All about my career without a thought about others."

Jonathan swallowed back his reaction to her baseless account of his personality. She'd drawn her own conclusions
about him based on his being an attorney. He would set her
straight soon enough. For the moment, he didn't want to say
anything that would stop her now that he'd finally gotten her
to open up to him.

"I got tired of Corporate America pretty quick," Ivana
continued, still pushing the food around. "One day, one of my
fellow voodoo sisters approached me. She said something
within me called to her, and invited me to join her at a healing. It was life-changing," she said, passion gleaming brightly
in her eyes. "It was the most beautiful thing I've ever seen. I
get chills just thinking about the love that was present in that
room."

She expelled a breath, looked down at her plate. "That's
why I was so against you moving into the building and tearing it apart," she said when she looked back up at him.

Jonathan hitched a shoulder apologetically. "I didn't
know," he said.

"Forget it," she waved him off, but Jonathan didn't want
anything fueling the insensitive jerk persona she'd mentally
created with regards to him.

He reached over and wrapped a hand around her wrist.
God, her skin was soft. He looked into her eyes. "I'm sorry," he
said. "I know I've given you grief over the room. I didn't
know how important it was to you."

She stared at him, a wisp of hair bellowing softly in and
out of her partially opened mouth. Jonathan ached to capture
her full bottom lip between his teeth and suck.

A loud crash came from the kitchen, jerking them both out
of the intense haze of awareness that had wrapped itself
around them.

"Everything's okay," came a call from the kitchen.

Ivana pulled her hand from his hold, using it to tuck the
wayward strand of hair behind her ear. "Well, I'm glad I got
through this dinner. I can rest easy knowing the room is safe."

Disappointment assaulted him. "Is that really the only reason you agreed to have dinner with me?" Jonathan asked, knowing his hurt showed in his face, but unable to do anything about it.

"It's the only option you gave me," she returned.

Jonathan shook his head. "I'm trying really hard here, Ivana, but you're not making it easy." He pushed his plate to the side and folded his hands on top of the table. "Why don't we pretend we've never met? Forget that you don't like me, for whatever reason you choose not to like me."

She held up her hand. "Before you go any further, let me explain just why I don't like you."

Oh, great. He *had* just asked for this, hadn't he?

Ivana used her fingers to tick off the reasons. "Your office. Your club. Your car."

"My car?"

"Yes. Your job."

"Hold up. Back to the car. Why don't you like my car?"

"Because it is the most ostentatious heap of wasted money I've ever seen. The only reason a man would pay that much money for a car is to compensate for his insecurities and low self-esteem."

"You can tell all that just by the car I drive? Who's practicing pop psychology now?"

She ignored him and went on with her *Why I Despise Jonathan* list. "The way you dress."

"Wait, wait, wait. What have my clothes got to do with any of this?"

"Same as the car. Why else would you spend so much money on those suits and silk ties if not to make yourself feel special?"

"Isn't that why anyone does anything for themselves? That's the point of life, to be happy. At least for the majority of the population. And what about you?" Jonathan asked, past the point of being a little miffed. In fact he was well on his way to be damn offended by her observations. "Do you spend your evenings working in a soup kitchen only because you want to help people, or because you want to feel good about yourself?"

"Excuse me!"

"Do you really think you're not getting pleasure from all your altruistic work?"

She sat up straighter, fire in her eyes. "The work I do actually does some good for society. All you do is provide a place for people to get drunk, then defend them in court when they crash their cars into someone."

Tamping down his irritation became the hardest thing in the world. Jonathan took a second to find his center of control before speaking. "You've known of my existence for what, two . . . three weeks? Yet you've already got me all figured out."

She plastered him with one of those superior looks.

Why should he even bother? She'd already made up her mind about him. He should just cut his losses and move the hell on.

But her assumptions were completely wrong, and he refused to just sit back while she continued to think the worst of him.

"What would you say if I told you one of the first things I did when I came to New Orleans was sign up for the Big Brother's program? And," he cut her off when she started to speak, "what if I told you that a percentage of the profit made on Ladies' Night at The Hard Court goes to a battered women's shelter my sister runs back in D.C.? And what if I told you that twenty percent of my law practice's case load is pro bono? You're not the only one who fights for a cause, Ivana."

Some of that hauteur had taken a backseat to surprise. She really did have a low opinion of him. But, apparently, his justification, which he was pissed he had to provide in the first place, still was not enough for her.

After a moment, the aloofness returned and she said, "And I'm supposed to believe that?"

Jonathan hit the table with his fist. "I give up. You're going to believe only what you want to believe, no matter what I say. But let me clue you in to something, Ivana. All work and no play—even if you love the work—makes for an unful-filled life. When you realize there's more to living than fight-ing for 'the Cause,' give me a call."

He pushed away from the table and left her sitting in the middle of the soup kitchen.

Toby walked through the gate of the newly erected chain-link fence that surrounded the playground. The plastic equip-ment was new, its bright reds, yellows, blues, and greens much different than the old metal swings, monkey bars, and merry-go-rounds that were here when he and Sienna were in ele-mentary school.

"Looks like an entirely different place, huh?" Sienna said, reading his thoughts.

"I guess those lawsuits Roberta Taylor's mother filed every time she got a scratch on that old playground equipment had more of an impact than I first thought," Toby replied.

They walked passed a row of seesaws and a giant sandbox with a huge plastic green worm in the center, on their way to the basketball courts at the far end of the playground.

After the day they'd both had, Sienna had suggested they do something to unwind. Aria's radio interview had basically been a continuation of her interview on Katie LeBlanc's tele-vision show earlier that morning. The radio disc jockey had seen the show, and even though Toby had stipulated before they went on the air that there would be no overly personal questions; the host had done just enough to toe the line with-out actually crossing it. Aria had been better prepared to skirt around the answers than she had been earlier this morning, but still, the ripples from the LeBlanc debacle were still being felt.

And it reflected in Aria's performance earlier tonight. She'd been stiff, and the performance lackluster compared to the two previous nights.

Toby was trying not to worry too much. Sienna had dam-age control in hand. But Toby wasn't so sure he was ready for her method of unwinding. He could have come up with something just as physical and a lot more to his liking than playing a game of basketball.

"Finish telling me what happened at the shindig you went to today," he said.

She rolled her eyes. "I don't want to even think about it, let alone talk about it. I'm sure my mother will disown me. She's probably drawing up papers right now to have me permanently kicked out of the Culpepper family."

"Did you really tell them you're gay?"

"No, I just threatened my mother I would. She has a strong heart, because I was sure it would send her into cardiac arrest."

Toby caught her by the arm and pulled her close. "Well, at least *I* know you're not gay." He captured her open lips and quickly sucked her tongue into his mouth.

When he finally let her go, Sienna stared up at him, an awed look on her face. "I can't believe I'm kissing you this way," she whispered, the awe making its way to her voice.

"Does it still seem strange to you?" Toby asked.

She slowly shook her head, as if running the idea through her mind. "Not so much anymore. You?"

"Not so much," he mimicked, unable to help the smile that drew across his lips. "I've got a question. Which do you think Sylvia would rather, that you were gay, or that you're dating me?"

Sienna's crack of laughter echoed across the empty playground. "I'm not sure. Maybe I should just tell her the truth next time."

"You might just get that heart attack out of her after all."

They walked side by side past swing sets, a merry-go-round, and hop scotches painted on the spongy playground floor. "Is the basketball court made of this material?" Toby asked.

"No, it's real asphalt," Sienna said. "It's on the side designated for the junior high students."

Moments later they arrived at the basketball and tennis courts. If he'd had rackets in his trunk, Toby would have suggested they play a little tennis instead.

What in the hell made him agree to play basketball after all this time? He'd tried over the years. He'd even managed to make it to an actual court once when Jonathan had dared him. But because God liked him so much, the sky had opened up with a huge rain shower just as Jonathan had passed the ball.

Toby looked up. This was probably the clearest night New Orleans had seen since he'd been back home. Guess God thought he'd had enough reprieves.

"What's the matter, Toby?" Sienna asked, balancing the basketball on her hip. She was dressed in loose-fitting nylon shorts and a white T-shirt with a hot pink Nike swoosh.

"Nothing," Toby lied, waiting for lightning to strike despite the clear skies.

"You're frowning."

"Am I?"

Sienna placed the ball on the asphalt and closed the distance between them. She took both of his hands in hers and swung them from side to side.

"When I suggested basketball, I had a feeling it had been a while since you'd played. Was I right?"

He swallowed hard, and then admitted, "The Friday before the accident."

The swinging stopped.

For a moment that seemed to last a lifetime, she stood there staring at him as if he were a stranger.

"Why?" she finally asked.

If he knew the answer to that question, he could give meaning to the reason of the universe. Then again, Toby had known all along why he hadn't held a basketball in all these years; he just wasn't ready to say it aloud.

In some ways, he missed basketball more than anything in the world. He ached to return to the court and experience the thrill of the game. Yet other days, the thought of playing again scared the crap out of him.

Answering her question, he shrugged. "I haven't had the desire." It was partially true. Who desired to be scared out of their minds, other than crazy thrill seekers who bungee jumped, or sky dived? He wasn't about to leap head first out of an airplane anytime soon, either.

"Here's the thing," Sienna said, letting go of one of his hands and hooking his arm in the crook of her elbow. "That answer would probably fly with just about anybody, but you need to remember who you're talking to. You not having the desire to play basketball is like my mom not having the desire to criticize me. What's the real reason, Toby?"

Toby tried to stave off the irritation, but he could feel it building. Sienna was not the first person to try to get him to "talk it out." It had not worked with Alex, Eli, Jonathan, or even his mother. It wasn't going to work this time either. He didn't want to ruin their night by stopping her cold, but she wasn't giving him a choice.

She took it out of his hands by laying out the truth.

"You're scared," she said simply.

Denying it would be fruitless, so Toby decided to say nothing at all.

"You have every right to be," Sienna continued. "Basketball represents a dark part of your past."

"When did your marketing degree turn into a Ph.D. in counseling?" He didn't mean for his voice to have that edge, but damn, she was asking more of him than he was willing to give.

"It doesn't take a degree to understand human emotion, Toby."

Don't roll your eyes, he told himself, but they rolled anyway. Pop-psychoanalysis had that affect on him.

"So, do you think if I break past this barrier and actually play a game of basketball my entire life will be one big party?"

"No," Sienna said, frustration making the word clip. "I was thinking if you played a game of basketball you'd remember the game for what it was before college scholarships, sports agents, and skanky cheerleaders shaking their butts in your face."

Despite his annoyance, Toby couldn't help his chuckle.

"When did you start feeling this way about the cheerleaders?" he asked.

"Seventh grade," she answered. "Now back to the point I was trying to make. It's just a game, Toby. I know you inadvertently blame basketball for much of the pain you've experienced since the accident, but you need to remember the good times, too." She stretched her hands out and turned in a slow circle. "This is where we had the most fun of our lives; right on these courts. Well," she looked at the coal black asphalt underneath them, "on the same grounds, at least. They've spruced up the actual court."

A mini tug-of-war played out in his brain as Toby debated whether he was ready to take such a huge step? But why was it such a big deal? What'd he think, that an SUV would come careering through the fence and knock the rest of his vertebrae out of place?

Sienna was right. For most of his life, basketball had been everything to him, and not because of the glitz and glamour that came with an NBA career. He loved the game because it was fun. Period.

Toby reached over, grabbed the ball, and did a Harlem Globetrotter–caliber finger spin. "So, first to ten wins?"

Whatever agony he would experience as a result of playing basketball after all these years would be worth it just for the chance to see the smile that lit up Sienna's face.

"You haven't played in a while," she smiled. "You sure you don't want to stop at five?"

"I think I can hang," Toby replied. "After all, you're a girl. That gives me a slight advantage."

Sienna punched him on the arm. "I would tell you to kiss my behind, but you'd probably take it literally."

"Most definitely," Toby said, leaning over and planting a quick kiss right below her ear. "Come on. Let's see if I've still got it."

"I'll take it easy on you since you're so out of practice."

"Don't bother, baby. When I win, I want to know that I've earned my prize fair and square."

"What prize?" Sienna asked.

He let his eyes roam up and down her body and grinned at her instant blush. "As much as you're willing to give me."

Toby in-bounded the ball to her and Sienna made a quick pass behind her back as she darted to the goal, laying the ball in.

"I see you've kept up your game."

"Not really. The only people I can get to play with are Ivana and Lelo. And they *do* play like girls," she laughed. "You don't have anything to worry about. That was my best move. I just figured I'd come out with all guns blazing and rattle you a bit."

Toby soon discovered Sienna had a lot more moves where that one had come from. The only thing she hadn't managed to do was dunk on his head.

"Okay, play time is over," he said after she got away with an easy lay-up. Back in the day, he could have blocked that shot with his eyes closed.

"You think just because you're ready to get serious that the game's gonna change?" Sienna asked, teasingly holding the ball just out of his reach. She crooked two fingers. "Bring it on, baby."

Toby dove for the ball, stealing it away. He quickly put it through the hoop and followed with another three shots to Sienna's one.

God, this felt good. Watching his perfectly executed jump shot arching to the hoop sent a rush of satisfaction coursing through his blood. It felt natural to palm the ball, to dribble it back and forth between his legs.

"Where's all that talk?" Toby held his hand to his ear. "I don't hear you saying much."

"Shut up," Sienna said after an unsuccessful steal attempt.

Toby's head fell back with a crack of laughter. Damn, he'd missed this. Nothing had ever set his blood to pumping like a physically exerting pick-up game.

And their game was definitely a physical one.

The bump and grind of their bodies as they each jockeyed

for position was as erotic as anything Toby had experienced in the bedroom. Moist skin collided with moist skin. Lush breasts branded his chest. The stimulation from Sienna's sweat-soaked body brushing against his left him hard and aching.

"I guess you don't buy into the notion of sparing your girlfriend's feelings by letting her win, do you?" she asked after Toby sunk another jump shot.

Toby shook his head. "You'd never accept a gimme win."

"Yes, I would." Sienna puffed. "God, it's hot out here." She made a T with her hands. "Timeout. I've got to take off this shirt."

"Whoa, girl." Toby said, halting her as she reached for the bottom of the T-shirt. "Leave the striptease for later."

"I have a shirt on under this. And you can forget a striptease," she finished, then pulled away from him and brought the T-shirt over her head.

Instant salivation started within his mouth. He'd run his hands over that toned stomach just last night, but damn if his imagination had dreamt up anything even close to the soft curves and silken skin displayed before him.

"Don't tell me you've always looked like this under your shirt."

"Like what?" Sienna asked, as if that delicately defined six-pack could be found on the average woman walking down the street.

"I just want to make sure you haven't always been this fine, because if you have, Alex deserves the right to tell me 'I told you so' to my face."

"What are you talking about?"

He shook his head, chuckling at her obtuseness. "For years Alex has been telling me I should hook up with you. It's true," Toby assured her, when she gave him a look of disbelief. "But it's always seemed too strange, you know? I mean, you're you. Cee Cee. At that time, I couldn't imagine the thought of us being together."

Sienna plunked her hands on her hips. "Do you want me to kick your butt?"

"Why are you getting upset with me? I had to practically beg you to start dating. If I'd asked you back then, you would have laughed in my face."

Before he knew what had happened, the basketball crashed into his chest.

"Ow!"

"I wouldn't have laughed in your face, you idiot! I would have asked what had taken you so long!" Sienna choked.

Wait, was she crying?

"Sienna." Toby reached for her, but she pulled away.

"How blind can you be?" she asked. "I've spent most of my life loving you. Do you have any idea how hard it was to listen to you talk about all the girls you got with in high school? Some of the stuff you told me shouldn't even be said in a locker room with just guys around."

"That's the way we talked to each other back then."

"Not we. You! I never had anything to say about boys I slept with back then because I had *never* slept with any boys. But there I was, listening to the one I was in love with talk about skeez after skeez. You probably don't even remember their names."

No. He didn't. But that wasn't important right now. He was way more interested in that other thing she'd said. She had been *in love* with him?

"Cee Cee," he reached out for her again, and this time she allowed him to pull her into his arms. The blow from the basketball had been replaced by a different kind of pain, and it hurt a thousand times worse.

"Why didn't you say anything?" Toby whispered.

"Why did I have to?" her muffled reply came from where she rested her face against his chest. She tilted back a little. "You knew me so well, yet you never saw how I felt about you. Why is that, Toby?"

How was he supposed to answer that? He *did* know her. He knew her better than he knew anyone else in the world, but he had never even suspected Sienna thought about him in an even remotely romantic way. She'd done a fine job of masking her feelings.

Even if he had known, would it have changed anything? Back then he would never have gone for a jock like Sienna. He had preferred the pretty girls who dressed in tummy-baring shirts and skintight jeans. Those were the girls who guaranteed a little action at the end of the night. The Toby of years ago probably would have laughed in Sienna's face if she had suggested anything romantic between the two of them. It's a good thing he'd grown up, because *that* Toby was a fool for not seeing the woman hiding behind the tomboy she used to be.

"I'm sorry, baby." He rubbed his hand up and down her back. "I never wanted to hurt you. You know that don't you, Sienna?"

She rubbed her face against his chest, wiping her nose on his shirt.

"Now I feel stupid for blubbering like an idiot."

"No, I'm the idiot," Toby said.

She raised her head a smidgen. "No argument here."

Toby laughed. "Why don't we call it a tie and go find some dessert? You feel like a little peach cobbler from Mother's Restaurant?"

"With ice cream?"

Toby nodded, still rubbing his hands up and down her back. "Anything you want."

"That's a dangerous offer," Sienna chuckled through another sniff. "I could wipe you out."

"I wouldn't mind," Toby answered. "It would serve me right for being so stupid."

"Not stupid, just blind," Sienna told him.

He raised her chin, staring into brown eyes made luminous by barely shed tears. "Not anymore," Toby reassured her.

Chapter Nineteen

Sienna knew something was wrong the minute she walked through the doors of Mulholland, Davis, and French. The instant silence and heads turning were a dead giveaway. The pained look on Allen Mulholland's face as he waited at her office door started the bells to ringing in her head like she'd won the top prize at a carnival.

"What's going on, Allen?" she asked as she unlocked her office door.

"What's going on?" He did not wait to be invited in. "How do you plan to clean up this mess, Sienna?"

Uh, if she knew what mess he was talking about maybe she could provide him with an intelligent answer. Sienna had a feeling it was something she should have known, and since she had no idea, she kept quiet.

She found out just what had Allen so riled up when he plopped a copy of the *Gulf Coast Reporter* on her desk. Dead center on the front page was a picture of Aria with her skirt hiked up and her legs wrapped around someone who looked extremely familiar.

The headline read: *Rising Star Gets More Practice.*

Sienna read the first line of the story, and her stomach dropped.

Local singing sensation, Aria Jordan, gets a firsthand taste of how it feels to live the highlife as she spends the night partying with NBA Superstar Isaac Payton.

Oh, God. Toby's going to kill him.

"Sienna," Allen said, irritation lacing his voice.

Her cell phone rang.

"One minute," she raised a solitary finger. "Hello," she answered.

"I'm gonna kill him."

Sienna closed her eyes. "Good morning, Toby."

"Did you see the paper? I'm gonna kill that bastard."

"Toby, my boss is in my office. I'll call you as soon as we're done," she said, and hung up.

"I'm sorry, Sienna, but you *are* done," Allen said.

"Wait."

Allen sliced his hand through the air, silencing her. "I gave you a chance, but the damage control it's going to take to clean up this mess is way over your head. I cannot allow you to throw away what can be the biggest account this company has ever seen."

"But—"

"It isn't fair, I know," Allen continued, his tone softening. "You never know what these music industry types are going to do, but that's the nature of the business. You've got to anticipate things like this happening and have a quick way to counteract."

"Then give me the chance to counteract. We don't even know what the fallout is yet."

"Yes, we do. One of the sponsors has already called to pull out. You weren't even here to field the call, and even if you were, apparently you wouldn't have known what to do about it because you had no idea something was amiss until I showed you the paper."

Sienna felt things spiraling out of control so quickly the whirlwind was giving her a headache. She had guaranteed her damn job! She had to figure out a way to save it.

"Allen, you cannot take me off this account. No one knows it as well as I do." He was shaking his head. "Allen!" she screamed.

The look on her boss's face told Sienna she'd gone too far.

"You've had your chance, Sienna," was all he said before he turned and walked out of her office.

Sienna grabbed the pen holder on her desk and sent it flying across the room. She was ready to murder Isaac Payton. And Aria Jordan, for that matter. What had that girl been thinking?

She so deserved a minute to wallow in self-pity, but she didn't have the time. Armed with her Internet-compatible Palm Pilot, Sienna closed up her office and hoped to God the locks wouldn't be changed when she came back later today.

Ivana jerked her hand from the antique gold handle and raked it through her hair. She made another attempt to open the door, clenching her teeth as her palm once again refused to squeeze the handle.

All she wanted to do was defend herself. After the way Jonathan hurled his accusations about her having ulterior motives, she needed to set the record straight. How dare he question why she did the work she performed for the community! He knew nothing about her. He had no idea how many countless days she'd spent tending the sick, helping the poor and disenfranchised. She'd never asked for anything in return, and not because she wanted to play the martyr. She'd worked all these years out of the kindness of her heart.

Of course she felt good about herself after a particularly grueling day at the soup kitchen, or pounding the steps of City Hall to get some poor family's electricity bill wiped clean. Didn't she deserve to feel a little satisfaction for all of her sacrifice? What gave him the right to judge her?

Ivana faltered as she reached for the door handle again, another thought occurring to her.

What if he was right?

Would she be so enthusiastic to help if she did not receive the accolades her fellow sisters in the struggle showered upon her? She prided herself on never turning away a weary soul who was in need of assistance, either spiritual or physical. But didn't she always make sure her fellow voodoo sisters heard about every unfortunate family she helped to save? What did that say about her?

Nothing, that's what!

She had never questioned her motives before. It was only after that hound, Jonathan, had flung his accusations that she had begun to question herself.

He did things to her, scary things. Things that made her question the path she'd chosen in life. She'd spent most of the night thinking about the pleasures of life she was missing out on, like a family and children.

Ivana closed her eyes as the familiar warmth washed over her whenever she pictured holding her own child in her arms. She'd had those dreams once, had always imagined she would have the chance to treat a child the right way, a way that was totally opposite from how her mother had treated her.

When her ex-husband left, he'd crushed her heart and obliterated those dreams. Ivana had found her satisfaction through her work with helping to save the people of this city.

Now, because of Jonathan Campbell, she was questioning just how true her intentions were.

Damn him!

Before she could talk herself out of it, Ivana gripped the door handle and pushed—and fell straight into a set of strong arms.

"Whoa." Jonathan captured her under her arm. Ivana quickly extricated herself from his hold, righting her blouse and smoothing her hair.

"What are you doing here?" Jonathan asked.

She stood straighter. "I have something I need to say to you, and you're going to listen." She jutted her chin forward. "You had no right to throw out those accusations last night. You don't know me. You don't know the sacrifices I've made, or why I make them. To insinuate that I have any motives other than giving my whole heart to my work is going way over the line. You need to—"

Jonathan grabbed her face and crashed his mouth to hers. The moment his strong lips touched her, Ivana went up in flames. His mouth was scorching; intense and full of purpose. A torrent of confusing emotions cascaded through her body. Anger, bafflement, desire. Yes, there was desire. And lust. Lust like she'd never experienced in her life.

After what seemed like a lifetime—yet not nearly long

enough—Jonathan released her lips from his sensual prison and took a step back.

He looked just as blown away by the kiss as Ivana felt, but he was much quicker on the recovery. Straightening himself and tugging at his perfectly knotted tie, he said, "I'm sorry, but that was the only way I could think to shut you up."

As if it were an extension of her body she had no control over, Ivana looked in awe as her hand rose and slapped Jonathan across the face.

He hardly flinched. "Doesn't hurt so much when you're expecting it," he said with a shrug.

Ivana went to slap him again, but he caught her by the wrist.

"However, I don't think that paltry kiss deserves two wallops. You pack quite a punch for such a delicate little thing." With the wrist he still held, he pulled her in close. "I really wish we could continue this, but I need to be in court in a few minutes. I'll meet you at your booth in the French Market tonight. You can knock me around as much as you want."

He placed a hard, quick kiss on her lips and headed for his car.

Ivana had no idea how long she remained on that porch debating whether or not to show up for work today, or just pack everything and leave town. Permanently.

He definitely deserved an Academy Award for *Best Actor in a Messed Up Situation*. It took calling on patience Toby didn't realize he possessed to maintain his composure as Aria sat on the sofa in his apartment. He wanted to throw the freaking cameramen and their equipment over the balcony, but then having an assault charge brought against him would just add to the troubles of the day.

"So, you decided to celebrate last night?" Toby asked Aria.

She nodded, looking like she'd just got caught snatching an Oreo from the cookie jar. She should feel guilty; she'd just robbed them both of the chance of a lifetime by fouling up this show. Once again, his dreams were crushed by no fault of his own.

Toby's fists clenched.

"You realize this is going to look really bad, right? We've built this image of you as a sweet, innocent girl next door, but after last night, that's shot to hell."

"I know, and I'm sorry, Toby. I wasn't thinking about how it would look in front of the cameras."

Toby gave up trying to pretend that everything was okay. He couldn't keep up this sunshine and roses façade, not when he was ready to put his fist through the nearest wall.

"Why don't you guys let me have a few minutes off camera with Aria?" Toby asked the cameraman.

The guy shook his head. "Against the rules."

"Forget the rules!" He shot up from the sofa.

"That's good," the cameraman said, moving around so he could get a better angle. "Let us see more of that anger."

"Why don't I let you see how far I can shove that camera up your ass?"

"That's it. Get mad, man. That's what the American people want to see."

Toby took a deep breath and made an effort to ignore the cameraman. He would not be the token erratic manager.

"Toby, I am so sorry," Aria said with a hiccupping sob.

He sat back down on the sofa and somehow managed to come up with what he hoped was a convincing smile. He would show the cameras exactly what they *didn't* want to see.

He gripped Aria's hand and patted her on the knee. "Hey, you need to get used to the paparazzi getting in your business if you're going to be a real celebrity." Toby noticed the two cameramen exchange disappointed looks, and tasted a small drop of victory. Show that to the American people, you drama-hungry sons of bitches.

"But what if this hurts my chance of winning the show?" Aria asked.

Now she thinks about how her actions would affect the show?

Toby commanded the smile stay on his lips. "Let this be a lesson learned. You'll have to be more careful with what you do in public if you don't want your name splattered across the papers."

"You're not mad?" Aria asked, still fidgeting.

Telling her he wasn't mad wouldn't be an outright lie. Mad didn't begin to describe what he was feeling right now.

Murderous? Yeah, that seemed about right.

"Will you be at the sound check?" Her voice trembled so badly Toby almost felt sorry for her. Almost. If she'd just used a little common sense, they wouldn't be in this mess right now.

He answered with a curt nod.

Aria rose from the couch. "Again, I'm really, really sorry, Toby."

He waved her off. One of the cameramen followed Aria to the penthouse's elevator bank, but the other stayed behind.

"I've never seen someone do such a good job of keeping their cool. Just promise me you'll let us know if you go after Isaac Payton. I could lose my job if I miss getting something like that on camera."

"Your job is to follow around Aria Jordan, not me."

The cameraman gave him a wry look.

"I'm not going after Payton," Toby lied.

"Whatever you say," the cameraman said. He hefted the camera bag over his shoulder and looped wires around his arm as he made his way to the door.

That had been one of the hardest, most frustrating hours of his life. When he'd first saw this morning's paper, he had been ready to strangle Aria. If those cameramen hadn't been around, he probably would have, Toby concluded.

Was it too much to hope that for once he could have a shot at happiness? What the hell had he done to deserve this agony of being so close to attaining his dreams, just to have them snatched away? How much more penance did he have to pay?

Toby heard a buzz and saw his vibrating cell phone dance across the marble countertop in the kitchen.

"Hello?"

"Don't you go doing anything stupid."

"Stay out of this, Alex."

"I mean it, Toby. It's bad enough Aria has this blemish on her name. You'd better not do anything to bring even more negative attention to your camp."

"I'm not letting him get away with this."

"I'll beat the crap out of Payton if you want me to, but you stay away from him."

Toby laughed despite himself. "Fine. I need to figure out how to fix this mess Aria's gotten herself into. After that interview on Katie LeBlanc's show and this stuff with Payton, we sure as hell can't portray her as the Mary Poppins of pop music."

"Between you and Sienna, ya'll will come up with something," Alex said. "I'll holler at you later, man. I've got a meeting with the Downtown Development District."

"Give Jazzy a kiss for me."

Toby disconnected and slipped the phone in his pocket. He walked over to the sliding glass doors, opened them and stepped out onto the balcony. The morning was sweltering, but a slight breeze made its way under his collar. Toby rested his arms across the wrought iron balcony and looked out over the city. It was thriving once again after being brought to its knees by Hurricane Katrina, but other than a few horns blowing, the city was relatively quite for a Thursday morning.

Despite annoyance at his brother's intrusion, Toby was grateful for Alex's call. It gave him the extra moments he'd needed to calm down. Toby didn't know what he had planned to do to Payton, and anything he did would have gotten him in trouble. He was tired of messing up his life because of that asshole. And Toby had no doubt that's exactly why Payton had done this.

His phone rang again. He pulled it out of his pocket and recognized Sienna's number on the caller ID.

"Toby, why didn't you call me as soon as you heard about this?" she barked into the phone.

He knew better than to expect a gentle hello. "I'm sorry. I should have called."

"You think? My boss just chewed my butt off. He's trying to take me off the account."

Toby stood up straight. "He can't do that."

"Yes, he can. He's the managing partner, he can do whatever he wants, and he wants to take me off this account. I told you about the potential deal with Cardinal Studios. My handling of Aria's account has been under close scrutiny, Toby, and having Aria get caught with her legs wrapped around Isaac Payton did not sit well with my boss. It makes everything we've been saying about Aria look like total bull."

"I know. What in the hell made her do this?"

"I know what made her . . . this. You!"

"Me?"

"Yes. If . . . hadn't . . . she would . . . and this . . . happened."

"Wait. Wait. Your phone is breaking up, Sienna. What did you just say?"

"We'll . . . bout . . . later."

"Sienna!"

The phone disconnected. Toby stared at it as if it could explain what had just happened.

How was this *his* fault?

Toby cursed. His plate was full today, but he needed to add one more thing to his list. He had to talk to Sienna's boss. She'd put her job on the line, and he would not allow Isaac Payton to ruin her future, too.

"I couldn't sell you ice water in hell," Sienna muttered as she left the Pan American building on Poydras Street. She'd tried every marketing tool in her power to convince Baker Cosmetics not to pull their sponsorship, but nothing worked. Someone who got caught with their pants around their ankles, so to speak, was not their ideal spokesperson.

Sienna slammed her car door shut, the shock of it reverberating through her arm. "Damn it." She banged the steering wheel, and felt like an idiot when a sharp pain shot up her arm from the impact. All she needed to do was break her hand trying to release her frustration over this debacle.

She was going to lose her job, and all because Aria Jordan had decided to explore her inner sex kitten.

Sienna pulled from the curb and out into traffic. She got caught at a red light and cursed that, too. A city bus passed and Sienna rolled her eyes at the picture plastered against its side; a trumped up model with barely any clothes covering her generously displayed assets. It took her a second before she realized the sign was an advertisement for shaving cream.

Men were such amoebas. You could sell them anything as long as you used a hot woman to advertise it.

You could sell them . . . anything. *Anything!*

A thought formed and, instantly, ideas began sprouting like wildflowers. Her pulse quickened, a smile drawing across her face. Sienna popped open the compartment between the front seats, digging around for the tiny memo tablet she kept in there. She had to get this down.

The pen moving frantically across the page, Sienna jotted key phrases that would jar her memory when she stood at the white board in her home office and fleshed out her ideas. She could barely write legibly for the anticipation coursing through her veins.

God, she loved when everything clicked into place. She knew exactly how she would spin this story.

A horn blew behind her, and Sienna's eyes jerked to the light that had turned green. She pitched the pen and tablet onto the passenger seat and drove.

She knew what she needed to do. It was dicey. It was drastic. But if the male population lived up to their baser nature, it was going to save her job.

Chapter Twenty

He shouldn't be here.

He should get back in his car and drive away. But Toby knew turning back was not an option. He'd waited years for this, and now that he finally had the chance to pay Payton back for his backstabbing, Toby was going to make sure his ex-teammate got it good.

He stomped across the parking lot, his eyes on the gymnasium's double steel doors. Toby wasn't even sure Isaac was in there, but somebody who knew somebody, who knew somebody else, told him Isaac had rented out the gymnasium for a private workout session.

When Toby burst through the doors, two of the guys from Payton's entourage met him, looking like a couple of bouncers at a nightclub. Toby pushed right passed them and marched onto the basketball court.

"Yo, Payton," he called. Stepping up to his former teammate, Toby pulled his arm back and laid into Isaac's face. The other man went spiraling back on the floor. Toby followed him.

But before he could land another punch, the goon squad was there, pulling him off.

"Let him go," Payton said, holding his nose.

Toby wrenched free from the two guys.

"Admit it, man. You've wanted to get a piece of me ever since that stuff went down back in college." Payton pushed himself up from the floor, wobbling only slightly. "Well, here's your chance, Lightning."

Toby's jaw clenched at hearing the nickname he had not been called since his basketball days back at St. John's. Why should he stoop to Payton's level? He was better than this piece of crap.

Because Payton deserved it, that's why!

Toby figured he'd probably spend the night in jail but after everything that had happened this morning, what harm could her manager spending the night in central lock-up do to Aria's reputation?

"Come on, Toby. Show me you're not the little girl you were back in college."

Toby charged Payton, pushing him to the floor again. Payton flipped him over, and Toby found himself on his back. His shoulder blades burned as they hit the hard floor.

"That's all you got?" Payton taunted.

Toby used his leg muscles to raise the lower part of his body off the floor, finding the leverage he needed to turn the tables on Isaac. He pushed him off and managed to land a punch across Payton's jaw. Isaac countered with the same punch, in the same spot just under Toby's eye.

They went back and forth, trading blows, cleaning the floor of the gymnasium with their clothes as they rolled around on the punishing hardwood. Toby didn't know how long the scuffle lasted, but he knew his body would ache for a helluva lot longer.

"You done getting back at me?" Payton huffed, barely able to stand.

"Not nearly done," Toby answered. He cradled his left elbow that stung like hell after he'd inadvertently elbowed the floor instead of Payton's chest. "But I'm not wasting any more of my time on you," he finished.

"You think I'm a waste of time?" Payton covered his chest with his hand. "I'm crushed."

Toby was tempted to lay into him again. He took a step forward, getting in Payton's face. "Stay the hell away from my client."

His former teammate's brow cocked. "That's who this is about?" Payton laughed. "Man, you should have said that from the beginning. You can have Aria. I've got my eye on Sienna. That sweet, sexy thing is—"

Toby's fist connected with Payton's jaw.

* * *

That was a lesson in humility if he'd ever had one.

Toby walked out of MDF, Inc., feeling like he had no control over anything in his life. He despised the sense of helplessness.

Allen Mulholland had not been overcome with goodwill by Toby's impassioned plea to save Sienna's job. The money the company would make from the deal with Cardinal Studios was a thousand times what Toby was paying them. When it all came down to it, Mulholland, Davis, and French probably had more vested in the outcome of *A Week in the Life* than he, Sienna, and Aria combined. And it was all in jeopardy because of Isaac Payton.

Toby tried to devise a means of resolving this situation, but his brain was too muddled to come up with anything that didn't include running a baronet-tipped musket through Payton's stomach. That scuffle hadn't given him nearly as much pleasure as he would have hoped. He wanted to kill that son of a bitch. The most that would do is put him in jail for the rest of his life, though he'd feel a hell of a lot better than he did right now.

Toby cursed. He was doing it again, blaming someone else for his misfortune. He was the manager here; he had to take responsibility for the fiasco. If he had just allowed Aria to be herself instead of going for a particular angle, they wouldn't be in this situation. Getting caught in that compromising position with Payton would have been damaging to her image, but not nearly the A-bomb it had turned out to be.

Why hadn't she just stuck to the plan? The cameras were supposed to follow her as she had a late meal, then it was to her apartment where she'd turn in for the night. What had happened to the plan?

Toby ran a hand down his face.

Katie LeBlanc had had a field day, harping that her show had been the first to give the public a glimpse of Aria Jordan, The Vixen.

Maybe they should have portrayed Aria as a minx from the

very beginning; her late night escapade with Payton would have helped them. But the bad girl persona wasn't her true nature, either.

Toby slammed his car door shut. Before the brilliant idea to go over to MDF and try to save Sienna's job, he'd spent the last few hours riding around the city, trying to figure out how to fix this mess, and he'd come up with jack. He groaned at the thought of putting on a façade for the cameras, but he knew he needed to be in the studios. Aria was closing out *A Week in the Life* with a performance at Jazz Fest this Saturday, by far her biggest performance yet. The music had to be right, and standing outside abusing his car would not help.

Toby stepped into the studio and nodded at Savion. Behind the Plexiglas, Aria's eyes were closed as she belted out the ballad they had been working on for the last few weeks. Despite her huge error in judgment in getting involved with Payton, the girl still had the voice of an angel. If only they could get America to forget about this one little slip and just focus on her voice, they still had a chance.

His cell phone vibrated in his pocket. He pulled it out and silently cursed as he recognized Marshall Kellerman's phone number illuminated on the tiny screen. He'd avoided the producer's last two calls, but there was no point in dodging him anymore. He needed to face the music. Toby slipped out of the studio and walked back outside to get better reception.

"Marshall, how's it going?" Toby said into the phone.

"Finally," came Kellerman's voice. "I've been trying to get in touch with you since this morning. It's been a hell of a day for you and Ms. Jordan."

"You can say that," Toby said. "Look, Marshall. I know this casts a bad light on the show, at least on the role Aria was cast to fulfill—"

"Bad light? Are you nuts, Holmes? This is genius. I know you and Payton both played at St. John's together. Did you set all of this up?"

Toby pulled the phone from his ear and looked at it before

answering Kellerman. "You think I wanted Aria's reputation to get slammed?"

"If you'd planned on turning her into the show's resident bad girl, then yes. Her Internet votes are soaring by the minute. We've been getting confirmation calls from Aria's new sponsors all afternoon, and the boys in charge are loving it."

New sponsors? What in the hell?

"We're willing to look past the fact that you didn't go over your plans with any of the producers, but don't make a habit of it. We can't have things coming out of left field.

"This spin is guaranteed to make *A Week in the Life* the sleeper hit of the spring. And by bringing in a celebrity of Isaac Payton's stature into the mix, we're looking at top ten ratings. I'm happy I'm the one who spotted you, Holmes."

"Um, me, too," Toby answered, confused as hell.

"We're all set up for Jazz Fest on Saturday. The city's tourism bureau is reporting a spike in ticket sales. They're touting Aria Jordan as one of the main attractions. Look, Holmes, I need to get going, but we'll touch base later, and I'll see you on Saturday."

"Okay," Toby answered and hung up.

What the heck was going on?

"Toby!" Aria came running out of the studio. "You have to get in here. There was something about me on MTV News. Savion's on their Web site now."

Toby ran back into the studio. Savion had pulled up MTV's home page on his laptop and was searching around for their entertainment news section. "Here it is."

"Aria Jordan, of the reality TV show *A Week in the Life of a Wannabe Star* has gone from angelic sweetheart to sex symbol. A news release from the future superstar's camp says that Ms. Jordan was tired of portraying someone who she could not relate to. Her late night escapade with NBA bad boy Isaac Payton is apparently only a small portion of the real Aria Jordan. It looks like Tamala Bell, who was purported to be the show's resident bad girl, had better step aside. Ms. Jordan is ready to make her presence known."

"What news release?" Aria asked.

A slow smile started building on Toby's face, spreading throughout his body until it erupted into laughter. He pulled out his phone and hit the number he'd had programmed into his phone for Sienna.

"I'll explain later," she said, and hung up.

Toby laughed and put the phone back in his pocket.

"Sienna is brilliant."

"Sienna? She did this?" Aria asked.

Toby nodded. "And Kellerman loves it. I'd just gotten off the phone with him when you came outside to get me. He said they love this new spin on your character. I didn't know what he was talking about at the time, but I have a pretty good idea what's going on now. Savion, Google Aria's name."

Savion typed *Aria Jordan* into the search box. The search results showed that there were 9,200,000 results.

"I'll bet you're the subject of every person's blog under the age of twenty."

"Oh my goodness. I don't know if I should be happy or scared. When my mom finds out about this, she's going to kill me."

"Should have thought about that before you hooked up with Isaac Payton. Personally, this nightmare has just turned into a dream come true."

"Thanks to Sienna," Savion pointed out.

Yes. Thank goodness for Sienna. He'd spent the day going in circles trying to figure out what to do about this situation. Just when he'd decided it was hopeless, Sienna had stepped in and saved the skin off all their butts. He owed that girl so much.

Toby could think of a couple of ways to repay her. He just had to convince her to let him.

Jonathan paid for his pear and waved the woman off as she went to hand him his change. Biting into the fruit's plump flesh, he continued his stroll through the sea of tables set up under the dark green canopy that made up the French Market. The outdoor marketplace was as much a part of New Orleans as jazz music and spicy food. It made for great people-watching as merchants bartered with locals and tourists alike. They sold everything in the French Market, from hand-poured candles and creamy pralines to hot sauce and homemade jewelry.

And, of course, incense.

The minute he spotted Ivana, he was mesmerized. The wave of heated lava that rippled through his body was enough to wipe out a small village. Jonathan still could not get a full grasp on the things this woman did to him. He tried to think back to a single female who had elicited a reaction even a tenth as strong as what Ivana made him feel, but he knew it was a wasted effort. There was no woman, past, present, and undoubtedly in the future, who could affect him the way she did.

Jonathan stood from his prime location about twenty feet from her booth and watched her interact with her customers. She wrapped an assortment of foot long incenses in white paper and handed it to a woman. Then she threw her head back laughing at something the customer had said.

Jonathan swallowed hard, desire locking up his throat and creating a volcanic reaction throughout his bloodstream. It was the first time he'd seen her laugh, and the sight of her expressing the emotion was captivating. He wanted to make her laugh that way; he wanted her to feel free enough to let herself go with unreserved abandon. God, he could stand here watching her all day.

But, then, he wouldn't get to talk to her. And it's when she opened her mouth that he was truly mesmerized.

If he ever got to taste it just one more time he could die a happy man. If he ever got to do *more* with Ivana than just kiss, he no doubt *would* die. The feel of her lips on his had nearly stopped his breath; Jonathan was sure the rest of her body would send him over the edge.

Her customer vacated the table, giving him the chance to approach.

"Good evening, Ivana." She looked up from the aromatic array of colorful incense she'd started to place in a black carrying case. She sent him an agitated glance before continuing her packing.

Jonathan swallowed a sigh. He was hoping the hours since their confrontation at his office would have been enough time for her to cool down, but apparently his luck was running a little on the low side today. He steadied himself for a fight.

Of course, Ivana didn't disappoint.

"You have all the nerve in the world to come here after what you did to me today."

"What? Kiss you?"

"Yes." Closing the case with the incense, she gathered up the multicolored tablecloth and folded it over her arm, then snapped the small plastic table in half and slipped it in its own carrying case. In less than three minutes she'd gone from being open for business to shop closed. Pretty impressive.

She was done with business for the day, but she was not done with him. Just when Jonathan thought she'd turn around and leave him standing in the middle of the French Market, she stepped up to him and got in his face.

"I did not appreciate your little display on the porch this morning. In fact, I could have you arrested. That's assault. As a lawyer, you should know that."

Oh, damn. He *had* to do this.

Jonathan grabbed the back of her head and sealed his mouth with hers. He could feel her resistance, but moments later she relented and sank into his kiss. He put everything he'd learned over the past twenty years into that one kiss. Unable to go one more second without tasting her, he pushed through her lips and plundered her mouth with his tongue.

Lord God, Almighty. It was heaven. A warm, sensual haven of sweet tasting flesh that lit his body so fast he could barely stop himself from stripping them both out of their clothes right here. He bathed the inside of her mouth, running his tongue along her teeth, suckling her tongue.

When he heard her sigh and felt her hands grip his shoulders, Jonathan knew his life would never be the same. She owned all of him, body and soul.

Ivana felt herself drifting; completely detached from the rest of the world. This was like nothing she'd ever experienced before. Jonathan's knowledgeable tongue dancing within her mouth sent sparks of pleasure shooting through her veins.

Breathing was a problem, but not enough for her to stop. When his tongue hungrily began to attack hers, breathing became a nonissue, along with everything and everyone else in the world. All that mattered was that she taste more of him. Experience more of him, and the delectable things he could do to her.

The sound of applause and catcalls pulled Ivana out of her desire-filled daze, and she remembered where they were. They were standing in the middle of the French Market, for God's sake! Ivana pulled back and wanted to die as she felt a blush shoot to her face. She had clients here, and fellow distributors whom she saw every day.

"Ivana?" Jonathan's deep, breathless tone caressed her senses.

"I have to get back to work," she managed to get out. But wait, wasn't she already done with work for the day? Lord, he had her confused.

She could not look at him, not after what they had just done in broad daylight. She knew what she would find in his eyes. No one kissed that way unless they expected something else to happen later.

The scary thing is she *did* want something else to happen later. She was praying for something else to happen, had been for days.

She wanted this man. And after that kiss, Ivana knew he had the kind of skills that could make one night in bed with him enough to keep her satisfied for another five years. All she had to do was ask.

"Ivana." He reached for her, but she drew back her hand. If he touched her again she would explode.

She finally allowed herself to look at him. "I can't do this with you," she whispered.

"It was just a kiss."

"Just a kiss?"

If that's what he considered *just* a kiss, she wasn't sure she could even survive a night in bed with him.

Just say yes, Ivana pleaded with her conscience. Even though he personified everything she'd denounced when she'd traded in her old life to join the cause, what could one little night with him hurt?

But could she say yes to just *one* night with him? After the way his kiss had made her feel, how would she go on after only one taste?

Even harder to grasp was the realization that there was much more to Jonathan Campbell than she'd first presumed. Although by outward appearances he seemed to live a lavish lifestyle, all she'd learned about him in the past few weeks did not correspond to that picture. What if her initial assumptions about him had been completely wrong?

The possibilities that notion created—to give her heart the chance to experience a man like the one she was starting to suspect embodied the real Jonathan—took Ivana's breath away.

This time when he grabbed hold of her hand, Ivana didn't flinch. These thoughts raging through her brain had her so confused, she couldn't summon up a protest as Jonathan grabbed her folding table and carrying case and guided her out of the French Market. Like a zombie, she followed without protest.

He settled her into the front passenger seat of his car. The leather seats were like heaven, and Ivana sunk into the impossibly decadent softness. She watched in the rearview mirror as the trunk lifted.

What was she doing? She should get her butt out of this car this minute. She'd vowed to stay as far away from this man as possible. That's the only way she could preserve her sanity.

But, God, that kiss! She would be insane not to want to experience that again. After going at it solo for all these years, she had forgotten what it felt like to have a man's chest braced against her own. To have his hands roam over her body as his tongue danced intimately inside her mouth. Jonathan had brought back all those feelings. But it was different this time, because *he* was different. No one else had ever made her feel this way.

The driver's side door opened and Jonathan got into the car. He went to put the key in the ignition, but capturing his wrist, Ivana stopped him. He turned to her, waiting.

Ivana wasn't sure what she wanted to say, then the words just blurted from her mouth.

"I want you."

The words hung in the air like a smothering shroud. Jonathan stared at her for the longest time, not saying anything.

Finally, he said, "But you won't allow yourself to have me, will you?"

Ivana's chest tightened, her reply restricted in her throat.

"Why deny us?" Jonathan asked with a raw whisper, the question cloaked in desperation. "You know it would be good."

She shook her head, knowing if she tried to speak nothing would come out.

"After what just happened back there, how could you even think we would be anything short of spectacular together? I could kiss you for the rest of my life and it still wouldn't be enough."

Ivana closed her eyes and let his words wash over her. It had been so very long since anyone had made her feel this way. She felt wanted. Desired.

And it felt *so* good.

She could not allow herself to fall for this man. But Ivana had this niggling feeling that maybe it was too late. She was pretty sure she had already fallen.

It was too much to fight, and frankly, she was tired of

denying her needs. Ivana made the decision to hate herself in the morning. Tonight she would allow her body the pleasure Jonathan Campbell was sure to provide. Resolute with the choice she'd made, Ivana placed her hand on his thigh, leaned over and kissed him.

"Let's go to your place," she whispered against his lips.

Jonathan pulled back from her kiss, disbelief clouding his handsome face. "I don't want to give you a chance to change your mind, but I've got to be certain you're sure about this."

Ivana nodded. "Let's go."

Jonathan grabbed her by the head and plowed into her mouth, pushing her back into the seat and nearly climbing over the gearshift to get on top of her.

Ivana managed to wedge her hand between them and push at his chest. "You don't live that far from here, do you?"

"I've got ten minutes in me. That's about all I can wait before I do that again, so you'd better pray there's no traffic between here and St. Charles Avenue."

Ten minutes was about all she could wait, too. "Let's see if all the money you paid for this fancy car was worth it."

Jonathan pulled from the curb and sped down Decatur.

Chapter Twenty-one

Sienna used the key Toby had given her to get into his rented penthouse. The aroma of something succulent hit her as soon as she entered the apartment. Toby was in the kitchen, and she could see the table on the balcony set with candles.

"What are you doing here?" she asked. He turned from the stove and Sienna's heart lurched. "What happened to your face?" She threw her purse on the bar and ran to him.

"It's nothing," he answered. He planted a kiss on the side of her head and continued sprinkling spices into the Dutch oven pot bubbling on the stove.

"You've got a bandage above your eye and your cheek is purple and blue. That seems like a bit more than nothing to me."

"Don't worry about it. I just had a talk with an old friend."

Sienna felt her blood beginning to boil hotter than the liquid in the pot. "Toby, if you did what I think you did."

"I told you not to worry about it. Kick off your shoes and go chill out on the couch. I'll get you something to drink."

This was not even close to the end of this conversation, but Sienna was too exhausted to think about arguing with him right now.

"What about Aria's performance? Doesn't she have two tonight?" The show had already aired in prime time, with Aria capturing nearly forty percent of the air time.

"The second performance doesn't start until ten o'clock," Toby answered. "So, I decided to treat you to dinner after your long day."

Sienna's heart melted at the sweetness of his gesture. Draping her suit jacket over the seat of a barstool, Sienna sent him a tired smile. "What are you making?"

"Gumbo."

Cue mouth watering. "Oh God, Toby, thank you. I am so in need of comfort food right now. I've been on my feet all day."

"I heard."

"I've made more promises than I could ever hope to keep. Aria had better be up to this."

"Don't worry about Aria. Now, sit down." Toby motioned toward the sofa. A minute later, he came from the kitchen with a glass of white wine and handed it to her. He sat on the other end of the sofa, pulled her feet onto his lap, removed her shoes and began massaging the arch of her foot.

Eyes closed, Sienna groaned as she took a sip of wine. His thumbs felt like heaven on earth as they moved in tiny circular motions up and down the center of her aching feet.

"Have I told you how grateful I am to have you in my life?" Toby asked.

"Hmmm," she managed to murmur. She didn't want to talk. She just wanted to feel.

"You are amazing, Cee Cee. The way you turned this whole thing around? I don't know what I can ever do to repay you."

"No payment necessary." She lifted one eyelid. "Except for your bill to Mulholland, Davis, and French, of course," she grinned, then closed her eyes again. "There were some scary moments today. I was sure we were going to lose all our sponsors. But, thankfully, some of them stayed on."

"With a lot of arm twisting from you."

She nodded, took another sip of wine. Toby continued his ministrations on her tired feet, and Sienna sank deeper into the sofa cushions. "I don't want to think about some of the promises I had to make today. We've got to be very careful that Aria lives up to her new expectations, which will probably be harder than anything else we have to face, especially since it's not her true nature to be a bad girl."

"Well, she has no choice now."

"She did make this bed upon which she must now lie— pun very much intended," Sienna said. "And, of course, everyone will be looking to see if Isaac Payton is lying in it with her."

Toby growled. "Don't mention Payton."

She raised one eyebrow. "You better hope he doesn't press charges against you."

"He won't."

He trailed the heel of his hand up her foot in a strong, sure swipe. Sienna moaned.

"I don't want to talk about any of this anymore," she said. "I just want you to rub my feet until I fall asleep. You can wake me up when it's time to leave for the club."

She finished off her glass of wine, leaned back onto the throw pillow and draped one arm over her eyes. Relishing the feel of Toby's strong fingers working over her feet, she hardly noticed when his hands moved to her ankles then to her calves. He played along her legs, moving his thumbs over her achy muscles in those sure, circular motions that should be submitted to the U.S. Patent Office.

A wisp of breath caressed her jaw just before soft kisses traveled down her neck. The hand that stroked her left calf moved up to her inner thigh, gently squeezing. His other hand moved to her stomach where Toby pulled the silk shell from the waistband of her skirt and worked his hand underneath her top. He rubbed his hand over her stomach, his other inching even higher up her thigh to where the top of her stockings met skin. Toby fingered the stocking's lacy edge as his tongue trailed a path along her collarbone.

She should stop him, but she didn't want to. Her entire body was weary, tired to the bone. Her guard was way down tonight. And he was making her feel *way* too good.

"God, you're soft," he whispered into her ear.

"You, too," Sienna murmured.

She felt his deep chuckle rumble in his chest. "No, I'm not. I'm the complete opposite of soft."

"Well, your hands are soft. Your touch, that's soft. It's just," she paused to yawn, "what I need."

"I'm happy I can be what you need," Toby whispered as his mouth came to within a breath of hers. He moved the last inch forward and captured her lips in a kiss so sweet, so gentle, it touched her deep within her soul. Sienna sighed into his mouth, breathing in his remarkable scent as his tongue pistoned in and out of her mouth. His hand moved impossibly high up her thigh, almost touching her most private possession. Then it did touch, a light feathering against her rapidly dampening panties.

A familiar panic began to rise in her throat. Sienna tried to push it down. This was Toby. He would never hurt her. He wanted to pleasure her, to make her feel good. She could trust him.

But her body and her mind were at war, and the memories of years ago were winning.

When Toby moved her panties to the side and touched her

flesh, Sienna shrieked, kicking and nearly falling off the sofa in her haste to distance herself from him.

"Baby, what's wrong?"

She looked over at him, at the concern in his eyes, and it was her undoing. The years of fear and anxiety boiled over, and she could no longer stave off the deluge of tears that overflowed after being buried for so long.

Toby hurried to her side as the sobs racked her body. He ignored her attempts to push him away, gathering her in his arms and rocking her like a frightened child during a thunderstorm.

"Sienna, talk to me, please."

She tried, but the words caught in her throat. She had never told another soul about what had happened that night. The shame was too great. That she had allowed someone to do that to her, and in her drunken stupidity, had done nothing to stop it.

But she wanted to tell Toby. She needed to. Toby would help her past this. God, she wanted to finally get past this!

"He hurt me," she said.

"Who?" he asked, his hands rubbing up and down her back.

"A . . . a boy, back when I was in school."

Sienna felt Toby stiffen. He captured her by her shoulders and pulled her slightly away. His eyes were more intense than Sienna had ever seen them. "What happened?" he asked.

Everything spilled out of her in a rush of words she had no control over.

"It was the night of my debutante ball. I got drunk at a party and he took me behind the house into an alley. And he . . . he forced—" She could hardly talk as the memories came flooding back. His rancid tongue being stuffed down her throat. His rough fingers pushing up into her body. If she had not broken away from him, the damage he would have done could have been so much worse.

"You were raped?" Toby asked, his voice low and deadly.

Sienna shook her head. "He never got that far. I got away before he could do that, but, oh God, Toby he still hurt me." She grabbed onto Toby's shoulders as the tears continued to flow like a dam had burst behind her eyes. "I was so scared. He held me against the building and forced me to kiss him. Then he tore away my dress and used his fingers to—"

"To rape you," Toby said.

"It wasn't—"

"It was rape, Sienna. Son of a *bitch*," his anguish-filled voice rented the air. "Why didn't you tell me about this?"

"How could I? You were gone. You'd already left to become the big basketball star. I didn't have anyone I could tell."

"You mean he got away with this?"

"I tried to tell my mother, but she wouldn't listen," Sienna hiccupped. "She didn't want to believe any of her friends had children who could do something like this."

A torrent of curses came from Toby in a barely controlled rush. "I can't believe you've been living with this all these years." He grabbed hold of her and held on tight. "I am so sorry." He kissed her temple, smoothing her hair back from her face. "I'm sorry you've had to deal with this by yourself. And I'm sorry you got stuck with Sylvia as your mother. She doesn't deserve the daughters God gave her."

"Well, maybe Tosha," Sienna choked through a teary giggle.

Toby shook his head. "Even Tosha is too good for her. And stop trying to make light of this."

"I'm not," Sienna said. "Well, maybe a little. It makes it easier to deal with."

"Who was it?" Toby asked. "Who?" he asked again when she didn't say anything.

"It doesn't matter." Sienna shook her head. "You've done enough fighting for today. Besides, this is my battle to fight."

"The hell it is. You've been fighting it by yourself long enough."

"No, I've been running. I'm not going to do that anymore."

"Tell me who—"

"Toby." She put her fingers to his lips. "Please, let's not talk about this anymore."

His reluctance to let it go was palpable, but he remained quiet. He held her, rocking her back and forth in his arms while he continued to run his hand along her hair and down her back.

The sense of relief at finally letting go of the secret that had haunted her all these years made Sienna weak. It was amazing how instantaneous the weight lifted from her shoulders. To have her best friend, her soon-to-be lover, here to comfort her was more than Sienna could have ever asked for. She could not remember a time when she'd felt so safe, like nothing could ever get to her.

And she felt free. Free to experience all the things she had not allowed herself to feel all these years. She was ready to experience them with Toby.

"Toby?"

"Hmm?" he murmured, still rubbing her back.

"I've never been with anybody before," Sienna admitted in a hushed tone. "You know, intimately."

His hand paused for a moment, then resumed with soothing strokes. "That's understandable after what you went through. I would expect being intimate is the last thing you'd want."

"Don't take that to mean I'm completely ignorant about sex. I've mastered the art of self-gratification. I'm sure I've had more orgasms than many of my married friends," she sniffed through a tearful laugh. "But I'm ready to learn what it's like to really be with a man. We have to take things slow," she quickly cautioned.

Toby remained silent. Sienna could feel the beating of his heart escalate as her head rested against his chest. She wanted to say something, but with his silence ringing so loudly throughout the room, Sienna figured she'd said enough.

"I told you before I would never do anything you didn't want me to do."

Relief washed over her like the last big tidal wave after a raging sea storm. "You're willing to take your time?"

He captured her face in his hands and nudged her chin so he could look her in the eyes. "However long it takes."

She smiled up at him, pressed her face into his open palm. "Then can you please show me what the big deal is when it comes to sex. In my experience, it's awful."

His smoky eyes were intense, almost scary. "Forget what you've experienced. Put it out of your mind and never think about it again."

A wan smile broke across her face at his words, and she nodded. But Sienna knew she would never truly forget. That night was permanently etched into her brain, the fear a part of her soul.

But, just maybe, Toby could help her create a new memory, one that could push the other into a dark, unreachable corner of her mind.

"The first and most important lesson," Toby said, "is the kiss. When you can get just as much pleasure from a simple kiss as most people get from an entire night of lovemaking, then you know you're doing something right."

He captured her lips. Slowly, expertly, he moved his mouth over hers, parting her lips with his tongue and ravishing the inside of her mouth. His tongue traveled with a persistent knowledge that caused Sienna's body to tense with anticipation. Warm and reassuring, his tongue invaded her mouth with long, sure strokes. The rhythm was intoxicating, in and out, then around and around his tongue swirled.

Sienna felt the pressure begin to build deep in her belly as Toby showered her with fevered kisses.

"The next thing you have to do," he whispered, "is learn how to accept my touch."

He trailed his fingertips along her arm; a light dusting upon her skin. As Toby's mouth returned to hers, Sienna lost the ability to concentrate. She couldn't decide which to pay attention to, his mouth or his hands, which had just found their way to her stomach. He pushed up the hem of her silk shell and scooped his hand under, massaging her rapidly warming skin. His hand inched closer to her breast. After the slightest hesitation, he finally captured her breast in his palm.

Sienna moaned.

"Are you okay with this?" Toby asked.

"Yes," Sienna managed as stars danced behind her closed eyelids. His attention felt *so* good.

"Can I go a little further?"

She nodded. She felt Toby shift under her, and she opened her eyes. "What are you doing?" she murmured.

"Just trust me." He'd grabbed two of the throw pillows from the other end of the couch. "Pick your head up a bit." He fitted the pillows under her, freeing the arm that he'd used to cradle her head against the arm of the sofa.

He gently pushed her shoulders down. "You have to do three things for me."

"What's that?" Sienna ignored the tremor of panic that tried to surface. This was Toby. She had no reason to be afraid.

"Close your eyes, relax your body, and trust me," he said.

She would trust him. He wouldn't do anything to hurt her, or scare her. He wouldn't do anything she didn't allow him to do.

Yes, she would trust him. She would trust him to give her the kind of pleasure she'd always dreamed of receiving from a man. If any man could do that for her, it was Toby. Sienna took a deep breath, loosened the muscles in her arms and legs, and closed her eyes.

"I'm yours," she said, turning her body over to him. "Do with me as you will."

She felt Toby shudder underneath her. "Make sure I'm the only man you ever say those words to."

"I promise," Sienna laughed. "Now get to work."

Be careful what you wish for. The old saying taunted her once again.

She'd wished for pleasure, but what she got was so far beyond anything her mind could ever conjure. Sienna wasn't sure she could survive much more. Using nothing more than his hands, lips, and tongue, Toby turned her body inside out.

He kissed her from the tip of her head and up and down each arm, paying special attention to the sensitive spots at her wrists and the inside of her elbows. He nipped his way up her neck as his hands played over her breasts. Without a word spoken between them, they mutually decided it was time for her top to go. Once he'd rid her of her silk shell and she lay before him in nothing but her lace bra, skirt, and stockings, Toby took a few moments just to stare at her.

"You are one of the sexiest women I've ever seen."

Sienna laughed at the awe she heard in his voice. "If you sound any more amazed, I'm going to be more disappointed than flattered."

"I just never imagined you would look like this. You are incredible."

There wasn't a woman she knew who wouldn't love to hear those three words spoken with such sincerity.

"Thank you," Sienna answered, just as sincere.

She needed to hear his praise just as much as she needed to feel the pleasure he was lavishing upon her. Probably more. After her mother's years of neglect, having someone tell her she was amazing and actually *mean* it meant more to Sienna than Toby could possibly know. And to have someone pay attention to her body, to want to make her feel all the incredible sensations he created, was enough to make her weep.

Toby trailed his fingers along the scalloped edges of her bra as he dipped his head for another kiss. Sienna was aware of his other hand that had found its way to her knee. He rubbed it, then smoothed his palm over her thigh. His tongue pushed its way into her mouth while his hand moved her bra to the side, exposing her sensitized breasts to the cool air. The other hand moved farther under her skirt, squeezing her inner thigh.

His tongue plunged in and out, over and over. His fingers played with her nipples, the pad of his thumb moving in hurried circles, forcing the nub into a hard pebble.

"Toby," Sienna sighed, clenching her hands at her sides. The pressure building within her escalated with each sweep of his tongue.

Toby dipped his head to her other breast and pulled her nipple into his mouth. His tongue swirled around the diamond hard bud. He closed his lips over the tip and pulled, then opened his mouth and sucked her nipple into its warmth.

"Oh, God. Toby, please." Sienna didn't know what she was begging for, but she needed *something* to happen. Her body was on the brink of exploding.

But Toby would not be deterred. He continued his sensual assault, teasing her body with his teeth and tongue, licking a path from the feverish skin between her breasts down to her belly button, then back up again. Sienna tried to breathe past the tightening in her chest. It was almost painful, but the pleasure Toby's skillful mouth summoned overrode any protest her mind thought to utter.

Toby raised his head long enough to ask, "Are you still okay?"

"Yes," Sienna cried out.

"Good," came his muffled reply as he nipped at her throat, "Because this is where it gets really good."

Sienna didn't think anything could possibly feel better than what he was doing. Until his fingers moved her panties to the side and slipped inside of her.

Her body bowed at the sensation, all consuming in its intensity.

"Oh. My. God."

"Shhh," Toby whispered.

Sienna's eyes rolled back in her head. At the moment, her entire reason for existing centered on experiencing the pleasure radiating from the core of her body. With confident strokes, Toby's fingers glided in and out of her while the pad of his thumb massaged the tight bundle of nerves that screamed for his touch.

His mouth on her breasts, his fingers expert motion; it was too much to withstand. Sienna ebbed and flowed along the river of sensation, cresting with the intense wave of desire as she cried out, her body trembling.

She tried to remember where she was as she came down from the sensual high.

"That was pretty amazing," Sienna said with a satisfied purr. She opened her eyes to find Toby staring down at her. She couldn't interpret the expression on his face. "Why are you looking at me like that?"

"Because that was pretty amazing," he answered after taking a deep breath.

"I don't think I can move," Sienna admitted.

A smile drew across Toby's face. "You don't have to. Stay here. Sleep. I'm going to get ready for Aria's second performance."

Sienna sighed. "I'll get ready in a minute."

"Don't worry about it," Toby answered. "You've had a long day. You need to rest."

Sienna wouldn't argue. It would take another hour before she could make herself get up from the sofa. She felt a blanket being drawn upon her, but in another minute she was asleep.

Jonathan tried to get control of himself as he practically dragged Ivana from the car, but she seemed all too willing to let herself be led astray by his eagerness as she hurried behind him. As soon as they were inside, he pinned her against the door and claimed her lips with uncontrolled desire. Once he'd convinced her to just allow this to happen, she'd let her guard down completely and turned into the willing woman that came to him in his dreams. Gone was uptight Ivana. She'd been replaced by a woman who knew what she wanted, and wasn't afraid to tell him.

He stripped off his jacket and began unbuttoning his shirt, all while still kissing her. Ivana followed suit, pulling away from him only long enough to pull her top over her head.

"No bra," Jonathan groaned.

"I never wear one," Ivana told him. She pulled her skirt and panties off in one motion.

A tortured tightness drew across his chest. "Woman, you are going to kill me."

"Not until you make me come at least twice," she asserted, kicking her shoes off.

"I've got a brand new box of condoms in the bedroom. I'm going for a dozen."

"Fine with me," she said as he pulled her to him. Jonathan picked her up and Ivana wrapped her legs around his waist. They attacked each other with frenzied kisses as he carried her to his bedroom.

Once there Jonathan deposited her on the bed and went to the waistband of his pants, but Ivana stopped him, putting her hand over his.

"Let me do this," she said, pushing his hand to the side.

Jonathan surrendered himself over to her. "Have at it, baby."

She knelt before him on the bed, worked the belt free from the buckle and slid it through the loops. She unfastened his pants and hungrily pulled down the zipper, then pulled his pants and silk boxers down his thighs.

He needed to be on that bed. Now. But when he tried to join her there, Ivana halted his progress.

"Not yet," she said. "I want to do something else."

Before Jonathan could figure out what she was up to, she cupped him in her hands and pulled him into her mouth.

His knees buckled.

Throwing his head back, he groaned, shoving his hand in her hair and holding onto her head. His entire body began to tremble with the incredible sensations shooting through his bloodstream as Ivana licked up and down the length of him. Jonathan pulled away from her before she sent him completely over the edge.

"What's the matter?" she asked.

He shook his head. "It's time for me to take over."

The smile that curved the corners of her mouth was so damn delicious Jonathan had to stop himself from charging onto the bed. Instead, he went for the slow, seductive route. After waiting all this time for a taste of her, he was determined to relish every single minute of this.

Ivana lay back on the bed, waves of wild, luxurious hair fanned across his pillow. It was a picture straight out of his dreams.

"God, I want you," he breathed.

"I want you, too," she said.

Stepping out of the pants that were still around his ankles, Jonathan grabbed a condom from his dresser and covered himself. Then he crawled up the bed and nestled his body into her incredible softness.

"I think it's about time we give each other what we both want."

Toby stood in the background, as far away from the crowded stage as he could get. It was a blessing straight from heaven that Aria's tangling with Isaac had not blown up in their faces. Instead, the incident had written Aria's ticket to superstardom.

Toby had just learned that while he had been teaching Sienna the various uses of the human tongue, Isaac Payton had ended his silence, making a statement about what had really happened Wednesday night. In an exclusive interview with a local reporter, Isaac admitted he'd taken advantage of a slightly drunken Aria. He also confessed that while the rendezvous did not go any further than the embrace the cameras had captured, he would be there with his hat in hand if the future star ever decided to give him the time of day.

The story had been picked up by every legitimate, tabloid, and entertainment news network around the country, and Aria's online votes had skyrocketed. She would probably take up tomorrow night's entire episode.

By humbling himself before the nation, Isaac had just secured Aria's future. Winning the competition wasn't a necessity anymore. Hell, if it wasn't for the contract he'd signed, Toby could pull her out of the show and Aria would still be at the center of everyone's conversation.

Reign Supreme, the hip hop club where Aria was performing tonight, had reached capacity limit, and the line still stretched outside the door with people hoping to get a glimpse of the music world's newest star.

Toby's cell phone rang. He'd had fifteen voice mails from the biggest record labels and movie executives in the business. Word got around fast in this industry. He pulled his phone out and checked the screen.

Ah, no record executive here.

"You're awake," he said by way of greeting.

"I think I am," came Sienna's lazy reply.

Toby inched out of a side door to get away from the clamor of the crowd who still waited anxiously for Aria to take the stage for her second performance. There were as many people outside as inside the club. Toby headed toward the parking lot.

"It was hard to leave you sleeping there," he said.

"Why didn't you wake me before leaving for the club?"

"You didn't need to worry about making it out here tonight. You've done more than enough for one day. The turnout is amazing," Toby said, gazing back toward the crowd still trying to push their way into the capacity-filled club's front doors. "You turned all this around, Sienna. I still don't know how I'm going to repay you for what you've done."

"You did a couple of hours ago."

Toby laughed at the sultry amusement in her voice. "I got just as much pleasure from that as you did, so I'm not sure that really counts."

"You couldn't have gotten nearly enough. You could still walk and talk after we were done. I was as helpless as a baby."

"You were beautiful," he said. And he meant it. She'd

made the most breathtaking picture, stretched out on his sofa like an exhausted angel.

"Maybe we can go a little further when you come home later?" she said, her voice barely a whisper.

His stomach tightened. "Only if you think you're ready."

"I am," she said.

Her softly spoken declaration sent a spear of heat shooting down his spine.

"How is everything going over there?" she asked. Her quick subject change caused Toby to wonder if she really was ready for what she'd suggested.

"The biggest crowd this place has ever seen," he answered. "You probably haven't heard about this, but Payton made a public statement earlier this evening. I hate being indebted to that bastard, but I owe him for twisting this into a positive spin. His name has a lot of clout."

"You don't owe Isaac Payton anything. He's getting just as much publicity from this as Aria."

"Yeah, but he could have made Aria look like a slut who put out for anybody. I'm surprised he didn't do just that. It would fit his image better than making her into some innocent he took advantage of."

"Don't think about Payton, okay? Just be grateful that all of this is working out in our favor. Well, at least in yours and Aria's favor. I still have no idea what Allen plans to do about this. I'm probably out of a job."

"How can you be out of a job if you're America's newest sensation's full-time publicist?"

"What?"

Toby dodged another set of people on their way to the club. He walked between the rows of cars parked haphazardly in the parking lot.

"Aria is the hottest thing out there. I'm going to need you full-time."

"I don't know, Toby. We'll have to talk about this later," she said.

There would be very little talking when he saw her later,

but Toby decided not to mention that. It would definitely be one of those actions speak louder than words situations.

He checked his watch. "Aria should be going on in another couple of minutes. I need to get back into the club."

"I'll see you later."

"You most definitely will," Toby answered.

Sienna disconnected the line before he could say the words he really wanted to say to her. Then again, it wasn't something he wanted to say over the phone. When he told Sienna he loved her for the first time, Toby wanted to be there to see her face.

Chapter Twenty-two

"What are you doing here?" Sienna asked as soon as he walked into the apartment. Toby had hoped to find her in bed, not on the sofa watching an old black and white movie. He shut the door and locked it behind him.

"Toby, why aren't you at the club?" Coming to a sitting position, she used the remote control to check the time on the television. "Aria's second performance should still be going on, right?"

"She doesn't need me there," Toby said. He pulled his wallet out of his back pocket, and shucked the watch from his wrist, depositing them, along with his car keys, on the bar. "I figured I was needed a lot more back here."

A hesitant smile brought out the dimple in her right cheek. "Are you so impatient that you couldn't wait just a few hours?"

"Hours? Sienna, if we're not in that bed in the next five minutes, your first time will be on the living room floor."

She gave a shaky laugh. "Wow, you're just full of romance, aren't you?"

Toby rounded the sofa, coming to where she remained

seated. He held his hands out to her, praying she had not changed her mind. "Are you still willing to do this?"

She tipped her head up, her expression a mixture of expectancy and concern. "Are you still willing to take your time?" she asked.

"Most definitely."

She placed her hands in his and allowed him to pull her from the sofa. "Then, yes."

With his arms firmly around her waist, Toby lowered his head and took her lips in the kind of slow, gentle kiss that could last for hours. Over and over, his tongue delighted in the soft, warm haven of her mouth. As his body hummed with anticipation over what was about to occur, Toby couldn't help the chuckle that escaped his chest.

"What?" Sienna asked against his lips.

Toby rested his forehead against hers, and shook his head. "I can't believe I'm about to become your first. I've dreamed some pretty big dreams over the course of my life, but I can promise this is one I never envisioned."

"Funny," Sienna whispered. "This is straight out of my dreams."

She lowered her head to his chest and wrapped her arms around him, running her hands up and down his back.

"I've wanted you all my life," she continued. "Whenever I've thought about this night, you have always been the one with me."

An unmerciful sensation, something between pleasure and pain, grabbed hold of his chest. He pulled back and captured her chin in his hand, tipping her head up so he could look into her eyes.

"I love you."

Instant tears sprung to Sienna's eyes as Toby said the words she'd waited all her life to hear. The beating of her heart was so loud she could hardly hear herself think, but Toby's softly spoken declaration made it through, straight to her heart.

"I love you, too," she replied. She tipped her head up to meet his mouth, which had already started descending upon hers. The contact was soft and hot, his lips like a dream as they connected with hers.

"You are so beautiful," Toby said, cocooning her in the safety of his embrace. "But we're down to two minutes."

"Two minutes?"

"Before I strip you naked and we go at it on the living room sofa."

"I thought you said the floor," Sienna laughed.

He shook his head. "I'm not that barbaric; we can use the sofa. I know I said we'd take our time, but we have to get horizontal soon. I don't care where we are."

"Well, I'd rather the comfort of a bed, if you don't mind," Sienna replied.

Toby ran his hands from her shoulders, down her arms, to her wrists, capturing her hands and bringing them to his lips. He placed a light kiss on the back of each hand, and answered, "Not at all."

Toby led her to the bedroom. Once there, they took turns removing their clothing. Toby started with his shirt, releasing the buttons with a slow ease, his eyes never leaving her.

Embolden by the desire in his gaze, Sienna reached for the clasp at the back of her skirt and unsnapped it, pushing the soft material past her hips and down her legs.

Toby's hands went for his belt. He removed it, along with his shoes. He eased down his zipper, and Sienna's breath became small, hurried pants of air through her lips, her chest moving up and down with each breath.

"Your turn," Toby said as he rested his hands on his hips, his unzipped pants revealing blue silk boxers.

Sienna captured the hem of her shirt and pulled it over her head, leaving her in her bra and panties. She stood before him, a mixture of heat and fear tightening her skin as Toby's eyes roamed over her.

"Your turn," she repeated his words.

A slight smile tipped up one corner of Toby's mouth. "Get on the bed," he motioned with his head. Sienna obliged, moving over to the bed and settling under the covers. She attempted to cast the king-sized pillows to the floor, but Toby stopped her. "We're going to need those in a minute."

He came over to the side of the bed, and hovered above her. Hands still on his hips, he asked. "How do you want to do this?"

Sienna's head reared back slightly, and she swallowed a lump of uncomfortable embarrassment at the thought of actually voicing what she expected. "Uh, I'm not sure what you had in mind, but I think we should start with the missionary position this first time."

"That's not what I meant," Toby said with a grin. He hooked his thumbs inside the waist of his khakis and pushed them from his hips, stepping out of the pants and kicking them to the side. He stood before her in silk boxers that served to display the overly abundant evidence of his desire.

After years of dreaming about this night, why was she ready to bolt herself in the bathroom now that the time was finally here? Long ago she had promised herself that the only way she would ever experience sex was with Toby. Well, here he was. Very much here.

"We can do this one of two ways, Sienna."

"Call me Cee Cee."

Maybe if he called her that old nickname, she'd remember this was Toby and that she had no reason to be afraid, or nervous, or on the brink of losing her dinner.

Toby's mouth eased into a grin. He placed one knee on the bed and captured her hands. He tugged, and Sienna followed his unspoken directive, rising, and kneeling before him on the bed.

"I can take the lead tonight," Toby continued. "All you have to do is be here, and I'll do all the work."

"Okay." Sounded good to her. "What's the other way?"

"I become your personal learning tool," he answered. "I lay here and you use me as you please."

That sounded even better. Sienna bit her lower lip. She had not anticipated having options. "Which would you prefer?" she asked.

Toby shook his head. "Tonight isn't about me."

Sienna allowed for a breath, contemplating the decision before her.

"So?" Toby prompted.

"Can we have a combination of both?" she asked. "I can show you what I want, and you can let me know if it's right."

"As long as it gives you pleasure, baby, it's right."

Her shoulders sank with doubt. "That's the thing, Toby. I don't know what gives me pleasure. Sure, I know a little, but there has to be more to sex than what happens when my hand happens to roam south. Oh, my God, I can't believe I just said that," Sienna said. She'd just taken embarrassment to an entirely new level. "Just let me die right now, please."

"Stop it, Cee Cee." Toby tipped her chin up. His gaze was so intense Sienna had no choice but to look into his eyes. "You have nothing to be ashamed of," he said.

Sienna squeezed his fingers in a tight grip, begging him to understand where she was coming from. "Toby, I'm twenty-eight years old. There are teenagers with more experience than I have."

"These days, there are teenagers with more experience than *I* have," he laughed. Sienna had to smile. She'd heard enough stories of Toby's sexual exploits to know he could probably write the book on sex.

"This is about us, Cee Cee, no one else. Lie down," he instructed. Sienna complied, reclining in the middle of the king-size bed. Toby followed her with his body, settling alongside her. "Try to relax, and let me take over. You can stop me at any time."

"Is it okay if I close my eyes?"

Toby nodded in answer as he trailed his hands from her chest down her stomach, settling it at her waist. He leaned down and kissed each of her eyes closed. "Concentrate on my touch."

A soft, tender kiss fell upon the spot between her breasts, followed by a slightly wet point: his tongue. It drew upon her skin in a path that went from the crest of her breast, down her stomach, and into her belly button. The moist tip traced along the edges of her lace panties, swirling, licking.

Sienna struggled to remain calm and let herself relish in the sensation. Anxiety gnawed at her conscience, warring with her attempt to relax.

"Stop tensing," Toby commanded. Her eyes opened, and his gaze seared through her, smoky and seductive. A rush of heat washed over her and lingered deep in Sienna's belly.

"I'm trying," she said. "I really am, but it isn't easy," Sienna confessed.

"Scoot over a bit," Toby said. He turned over, lying on his back. "Go for it," he said.

"What do you want me to do?"

"Whatever you want, except leave," he added. "Do whatever you need to do to get comfortable, because if you don't relax, we won't be able to go very far. I refuse to hurt you."

Sienna's heart swelled to the point of bursting at his thoughtfulness. Who, but Toby, would be so patient with her?

"Thank you," she managed to choke past the block of emotion welling in her throat. "Close your eyes," she told him.

Toby's grin was slightly surprised, extremely wicked, and just cocky enough to give Sienna the confidence to go through with this. He lowered his eyelids and settled his head on the pillow.

Sienna started with the same place on his body where he'd started with her, pressing a kiss upon his chest. She used her tongue, streaming a line down the length of his torso. She dipped it into his navel and felt his loins tremble beneath her. Sienna straddled his hips and ran her hands along his arms, holding him down on the bed.

Toby's eyes flew open.

"Close them," Sienna demanded. His chest moved up and down with his deep, labored breaths. He closed his eyes again. Sienna kissed the spot below his ear, under his chin, along his collarbone. She flicked her tongue across his nipple.

Toby gasped, his forearms tensing underneath her hands.

Lower, his body hardened against her backside. Sienna swiveled her hips, rubbing against him.

"Damn," Toby whispered. He bit his lower lip.

"I'm sorry," Sienna said. "Am I hurting you?"

"You are *killing* me."

"That's not good. I kind of need you alive, at least for the next hour," she laughed.

Toby opened his eyes and stared at her through narrowed lids. Without warning, he flipped her over, encasing her beneath him. Toby burrowed his hand under her back, pulling her up slightly, unclasping her bra and pulling it off her. Sienna's entire being blushed under his heated gaze. He reached down, hooked his fingers in her panties and tugged, moving with them so he could pull them down her legs.

Totally exposed, Sienna had to fight to remain still. The urge to bolt was terrifyingly strong. "I really want to pull the covers over me, Toby."

"I really don't want you to do that, Cee Cee," he answered. "You are so beautiful," he continued. "I could stare at you for hours."

"Please don't," she said.

His mouth tipped up in a grin. "Don't worry, it was a lie, anyway. Not the point about you being beautiful, but just staring at you won't cut it."

He reached over to the nightstand and opened the top drawer, pulling out a foil packet. Toby held the condom between his teeth and went for the waistband of his boxers. Sienna closed her eyes and willed herself to calm down as the whisper of ripping foil sent unwelcome alarm through her bloodstream.

"Sienna, please relax," Toby pleaded. "I promise not to hurt you." Using one knee, he edged her legs apart. Burying his face against her neck, Toby slipped his hand to her lower back and raised her slightly off the bed. He sucked at a spot below her ear as he gently, tenderly pushed into her body.

Sienna's insides involuntary clenched.

Toby's breath hitched. "Sienna, that doesn't help."

"I'm sorry," she said.

"Don't be sorry. Just," he sucked in another breath, "relax."

He eased a few inches more. More. Supple, velvety inches more; breaking through that untouched barrier and sinking deep.

"Oh God," Sienna whispered as sensation blossomed within her.

"I know," he crooned in her ear as he increased his rhythm. She wrapped her legs around him, her body growing taut as Toby braced above her on shaking arms and surged forward, over and over, sure and smooth. Gripping her thighs, moving higher and deeper. Impossibly deeper.

Blinding white light sparked behind her closed eyelids as her body shattered apart. Moments later, Toby groaned in pleasure and fell atop her, his sweat slicked skin fiery against her naked body.

He continued to shudder with tiny tremors, and Sienna felt the low chuckle rumbling through his belly before it came out of his mouth.

"You'd better have an explanation for laughing," she warned.

Toby rolled onto his back, pulling her on top of him. He pressed a light kiss on the tip of her nose and grinned. "I was just thinking about what I'll say to Alex the next time I see him. After all these years, I owe him a hell of an apology for waiting so long to take his advice."

"I can't believe this is happening."

Toby grinned at the childlike exuberance emanating from Aria as she bounced around in the passenger seat of his car. Mark, one of the cameramen, was in the backseat.

"It is pretty unbelievable," Toby said. "When we started out this week did you ever imagine things would have turned out this way?"

She shook her head. "It has been the most amazing week of my life."

"Yet. This is just the beginning of countless amazing weeks." For both of us, Toby thought to himself.

Aria's cell phone rang. "It's my mom. She's been calling me all day!"

Toby stared out at the road ahead as he headed toward the apartment he'd rented for Aria, listening with one ear as she regaled her mother with tales of all that had happened over the course of the day.

It had been a life-changing twenty-four hours, in more ways than one.

Finally, *finally*, Toby felt as if he had found his place in this world. For so long he had been afraid that without basketball he would never amount to the man he knew was there somewhere inside of him. It was a scary thought, to believe the one thing that could ever make you whole had been permanently taken away.

The more he thought about it, the more Toby believed the accident *had* been God's way of getting his attention. He thought back to the typical self-absorbed rookie he had become in the days after he'd turned pro. He'd been so damn pompous back then, the antithesis of everything his mother, father, and brothers had instilled in him.

He had been on top of the world, and it had all been snatched from underneath him in the blink of an eye. Toby had known in his heart that anything he attempted from then on would be a poor substitute for the life he'd lost when basketball was stripped from him.

But he had been wrong. *This* was his destiny.

As he listened to the excitement in Aria's voice, he realized that nothing gave him more joy than helping others make their dreams a reality. And he was good at it.

He hadn't lost everything when that SUV had plowed into his car; he'd gained something that no amount of money could ever buy: the ability to believe in himself. There was nothing in this world he could not do if he set his mind to it. *Nothing*.

It may have taken him years to figure it out, but at least

he'd finally understood what all the people who love him—Mama, his brothers, Sienna—had been trying to tell him. God didn't close one door without opening another. Toby just had to be smart enough to walk through the right door.

Discovering that he'd finally figured out what God had prepared for him professionally was nothing compared to the other truth that became apparent to Toby today.

He loved Sienna.

He'd always loved her as a friend, but the feelings he now held for her transcended anything he had ever experienced. He wanted to spend the rest of his life with her, could not imagine going a day without being in her presence.

For the first time, Toby thought of the accident as a blessing. If he had gone on to play in the NBA, he would have never been in a position to love Sienna the way he now loved her.

"Guess what?" Aria's voice knocked him out of his musing. "Mama said she had to take the phone off the hook because she's been getting so many calls."

"How's she taking all the attention?"

Pocketing her cell phone, Aria shrugged. "She said that's the way it goes when you're the mother of a big star." Aria paused, looked over at him and started screaming and stomping her feet on the floorboard. "I can*not* believe this is happening!"

"You'd better get used to it, because there's no turning back now. After Jazz Fest, it's on to L.A. for the live show."

"I don't think it even matters if I win or not. I'll bet somebody is going to give me a record deal."

"Landing a deal is the least of your worries. That's my job."

Toby thought about the four calls he'd fielded just tonight from labels wanting to sign Aria. It was his opportunity to put all the effort he'd spent learning the music industry to work and earn his fifteen percent by landing her the best contract. He wanted to sign her to the kind of deal that would put to rest any doubts that he was a high caliber manager.

Toby turned onto the street and slammed on the brakes. The area in front of Aria's apartment building was crowded with cars and television vans. The sidewalk was covered with reporters, cameramen, and fans.

"Here's the part that you need to be prepared for," he said.

"Are they all here because of me?"

"What do you think?" Toby asked. "You're the next big thing. Everybody is going to want a piece of you. Are you up to dealing with them tonight?"

She bit her nails. "Not really."

Toby pulled to the curb about three blocks from her building. "Okay, let me think of something."

He knew one place where Aria could avoid the paparazzi, but then he thought about Sienna waiting for him back at the rented penthouse and tried to think of another possible scenario. He'd had to sublet his apartment for the month just to help pay the rent on the penthouse, so he couldn't store her there for the night. Jonathan's, maybe?

Toby punched in Jonathan's number. He didn't pick up. He tried Jonathan's cell phone. After three rings, his voice mail clicked on.

This wasn't like his friend. Jonathan made sure he was always available; it was the nature of his business. Toby tried his cell phone again. This time Jonathan picked up after the first ring.

"You had better be dying," his friend said by way of greeting.

"No, but—"

"Then I'm hanging up, and I'll kill you if you call again tonight."

What was that about?

Toby stared at the phone as if it held the answers.

He muttered a curse under his breath. He could drive her to Mama's, but that didn't make any sense. By the time he drove all the way uptown and back, he'd be too tired to do anything but fall into bed next to Sienna and sleep.

"Here's the deal. You can either face them tonight and get

it over with, or you can try to avoid them by sleeping at my place. With me and Sienna," Toby stated. He wanted to make sure there were no misunderstandings this time around.

"What if I get questioned about why I didn't come home last night, and people start talking about me spending the night at your place?" she asked. "That wouldn't be good, would it?"

Oh, the press would love to sink their teeth into a twisted love triangle between Aria, Payton, and himself. Where Aria's involvement with Isaac had worked out in their favor, Toby could see nothing but trouble written all over the other scenario.

"If there's any speculation by the press, we'll shut it down by saying we had an all night jam session in preparation for Jazz Fest. Actually, that's not a bad idea. I know it's late, but going over your routine one more time couldn't hurt."

"Is there enough floor space for me to catch a few hours sleep?" Mark asked from the backseat.

"Should you be talking with the camera rolling?" Toby asked.

"They'll filter out my voice," the cameraman answered.

"Yeah," Toby answered his initial question. "You can take the couch. Aria can sleep in the guest bedroom."

"Then where will Sienna sleep?" Aria asked. Toby caught Mark's chuckle from the backseat. "Oh, uh, that's right. Never mind," Aria finished.

Toby pulled away from the curb and made a U-turn in the middle of the street. He drove into the parking garage of the penthouse ten minutes later. He'd tried to get Sienna on her cell phone, but she hadn't picked up. Lord, he prayed she wasn't planning to greet him the way he'd fantasized she would— naked and wearing five-inch red stilettos. Toby tried her cell once more before getting onto the elevator that would take them to his penthouse.

The elevator door opened. Toby walked out into the corridor ahead of Aria and Mark. The other elevator chimed and Sienna walked out, carrying a brown paper bag.

"Hey, uh, everybody," she said, looking at the trio.

"Hi, Sienna," Aria greeted. She motioned to the cameraman. "There were too many reporters outside of my apartment, so we have to crash here tonight."

"Of course," Sienna nodded.

"Where have you been?" Toby motioned toward the bag in her hand.

"Ice cream run."

"At nearly two in the morning?"

"It's never too early or too late for ice cream." She used the key he'd given her to open the door. "Let's get inside and enjoy this."

"Sounds good to me," Aria answered as she followed Sienna into the apartment. "This place is amazing," she said as she entered.

"Check out the view," Toby called. He grabbed Sienna and pulled her to the bar. "I'm sorry. I tried to think of somewhere else to stash her, but there was nowhere."

"You're even sorrier than you know." A devious smile tipped up the corner of her mouth. "I bought a can of whipped cream to go with the ice cream."

Toby closed his eyes and groaned, his stomach clenching.

"I'm kidding," she laughed and moved over to the kitchen. She pulled out a carton of ice cream and a box of cones. "See," she shook the paper bag. "There's nothing else in here."

"Don't tease me like that," he said after taking a deep breath. "I could still put Aria and Mark up in a hotel."

"No, you won't. We all need to get to bed. Tomorrow is going to be crazy, and we'll need to be ready for it."

Aria came through the balcony's open French doors. "Toby, I know you want to go over the Jazz Fest set tonight, but I don't think I can stay awake another minute. I'm about to fall on my face."

"Don't worry about it," Toby said. "We'll go into the studio before your performance at The Hard Court tomorrow night."

"Thank goodness. I do still want some of that ice cream, though."

"It's on the kitchen counter along with the cones," Sienna told her. "So, what are the sleeping arrangements?" she asked Toby.

"I just called Josh to come over and pick me up," Mark said.

"How's he doing? Did everything turn out okay?" Toby asked.

"What happened to Josh?" Sienna asked before Mark could answer.

"His wife just had a baby girl," Mark explained. "Six pounds, nine ounces. Josh tried to catch a flight back to L.A., but it didn't work out. He had to listen to the birth over the phone instead."

"I know my husband would never miss our child's birth," Sienna said.

"Don't worry," Toby pulled her close and kissed her right temple. "I'll be right beside you."

Her brows hiked up, a smile playing across her lips. "You're pretty sure of yourself, aren't you?"

"Extremely."

Aria walked back from the kitchen with an ice cream cone in hand. "Where can I sleep?" she asked.

"There's a guest bedroom through those doors and to the right," Toby answered.

"I'm going to head down," Mark said, hoisting his camera bag over his shoulder. "Josh said he was about ten minutes away. We'll be back here bright and early tomorrow morning. Just think, after Saturday, you'll be rid of us."

"After what I saw outside of Aria's apartment building, having you guys around this week has been a crash course in preparation for what's to come."

"I'm afraid you're right," Mark answered. "Have a good night."

Toby waited for him to leave, then he grabbed Sienna by

the shoulders and brought her to him, burying his face against her smooth neck.

"I guess the reality of all this really hit home tonight, huh?"

"What do you mean?" Toby asked.

"The media, no real privacy; that's going to be your life, you know."

"I guess you're right," Toby answered. "I thought after basketball became a nonissue, I wouldn't have to worry about the spotlight anymore."

Sienna nodded. "Funny how things work out, isn't it?"

Toby trailed kisses down the column of her neck, thinking how funny it was that after all they had been through together that they would be in this place, lovers.

"Yes, it is."

Chapter Twenty-three

Ivana was hard pressed to see green grass as she scanned the crowded fairgrounds at the Jazz and Heritage Festival. The celebration was New Orleans' second biggest party, next to Mardi Gras, and never failed to bring music lovers out in droves. The promise of great food and a plethora of music, from gospel to country, hip hop to jazz, was enough to pull people in, but add in the unseasonably mild temperatures from a surprise cold front that had passed through the area, and the enticement was too much for anyone to resist.

Except for her, that is. Ivana would have given anything to be anywhere but here. She'd spent the last day and a half concocting one stellar excuse after another to try to get out of coming to Jazz Fest. She found a way to legitimize every one of them, but in the end, she decided to put on her big girl panties and face the music. And not the sweet sounding music coming from the multiple stages dotting the fairgrounds.

She expected something akin to head-splitting hard-core rock when Jonathan Campbell caught up to her.

She shouldn't have left the way she did; she knew that now. But lying in bed with him all night had not been an option. It had felt too good, too right. She could not allow herself to be swept away by one night of amazing, mind-altering, skin-tingling sex.

Something in the back of her mind tried to convince her that she shouldn't have gone to his home in the first place, but Ivana tamped down those thoughts. She didn't regret what had occurred Thursday night. She could not make herself feel one ounce of remorse over the actual act. Making love with Jonathan had been one of the most mystical experiences of her life.

But running away from him had been cowardly. And she was no coward.

That's why she was here today. Yes, she had promised Sienna she would come to Jazz Fest to support Aria Jordan as she performed on the biggest stage of her young career, but Ivana also needed to set things straight with Jonathan. She didn't want him to think she was ashamed of what they had done.

Ivana spotted the entire Holmes clan clustered on a patch of grass about twenty yards from the R&B stage. It came as no surprise that Toby's entire family had come out to support him. Eli lounged back with his hands braced on the ground; legs stretched out and crossed at the ankles in front of him. His fiancée, Monica, sat with her head on his shoulder. Jasmine was practicing her dance moves a few feet away, her face more serious than someone auditioning for a part in a Broadway musical. Ivana looked past Jasmine to find Jonathan staring right at her. He started toward her, and Ivana braced herself for a well-deserved rant.

Of course, Jonathan Campbell was the king of going against her expectations. He stopped mere inches from her, took her hand and placed a gentle kiss on her palm.

"I wanted to wake you up with that kiss yesterday morning, but didn't get the chance," he said.

Ivana's eyes slid close and her body quivered. Her bloodstream flooded with desire from the sound of his deep, rich voice.

"I'm sorry I left the way I did," she said.

"So am I."

She opened her eyes. "You're not as angry as I thought you'd be."

He shrugged. "Why should I be angry when I have all day to think up the ways you're going to make up for leaving me alone in bed?"

The rueful smile tilted her lips despite her best efforts to staunch it. The man was too cocky for his own good. But she sobered the instant she looked into his eyes and saw past the mask of nonchalance. She had hurt him by leaving.

"Jonathan, I really am sorry. My running out Thursday night had nothing to do with you."

"Well, that makes me feel a little better. I thought maybe I'd lost my touch."

"I'm the one to blame here. I was just so embarrassed at the way I lost control. I don't know where some of those sounds came from."

His gaze seared her. He grabbed her hands and gave them a squeeze. "Look, Ivana. I know you've been fighting this attraction between us, and with good reason. People, men especially, tend not to see the real you. They only see what they want to see. It frightened you to have someone see past the façade and reach the real woman." He took her chin and brought her face up. "But that's who I'm interested in. I want to know the woman who lives here." He tapped the place between her breasts, and a hot spark of desire skittered down Ivana's spine.

"Are you willing to let me in?" Jonathan asked.

She nodded. Ivana feared if she did anything more, she would burst into tears in front of everyone here.

"Well, I'm glad that's taken care of," Jonathan said, putting his arm around her shoulder and tucking her head under his chin. He whispered in her ear, "And as for those sounds you made Thursday night, for future reference, I'm partial to the little purr you make when you . . . you know."

Ivana pinched him on the arm.

"There's way more people here than I thought there would be," Aria said.

Sienna came around the partition separating the kitchen from the dining room in the tiny trailer. The makeup artist had been putting the finishing touches on Aria's face for the last five minutes.

"Yes, the crowd is enormous this year, but remember they have nearly twenty stages, so don't worry that all eyes will be on you." Sienna needed to give it to her straight, though. "But, you're going to have to get used to the limelight, Aria. You're one of the biggest draws for today, and will be wherever you go. After this past week, it's irrevocable. You're a part of America's pop culture."

"I'm not sure I'll ever get used to it," Aria admitted.

The production assistant poked his head into the trailer. "Stage time."

"Oh, God," Aria said.

Sienna grabbed her hand and squeezed. "You're done with stage fright, remember? You can do this. It is your last chance to win America over before the big show this coming Tuesday. You've had an amazing week, and have come so far. Don't let anything stop you now."

Aria nodded, firm determination etched across her brow. "You're right. I'm ready."

Sienna gave her hands a final squeeze, "Go get 'em."

"Sienna?" Aria called. Sienna stopped halfway out the door and looked back.

"Thank you," Aria said. She swept her hands up, encompassing the small space. "None of this would have happened if not for you."

"It would have. It just would have taken a little longer," Sienna winked. "Now come on. It's time to give everybody what they came to see—Aria Jordan in action."

A half hour later, Sienna stood mesmerized with the rest of the crowd as Aria continued to belt out one soulful ballad after another. At the very last minute, Toby had changed the line-up, deciding, with Aria's approval, that she should go back to her singing roots. The hip hop and dancing had gotten her to this stage, but now that she was here, she could be true to the music that had nurtured her.

"You know," Sienna tipped her head closer to Toby, who had been standing there with a quirk to his lips for the last twenty minutes. "With all the hype surrounding the show, it's sometimes easy to forget just how good she really is."

"Every morning when I wake up, I thank God that I walked into her uncle's rundown bar."

"I'm sure Aria says the same prayer. The two of you were meant to find each other."

"There's someone else I was meant to find," Toby whispered. "Someone I've known all along, but it took me way too long to *find* her." He dipped his head and captured her lips in a gentle kiss. Sienna closed her eyes and let him take her on the pleasurable journey only Toby could captain. The rest of the world ceased to exist as she drifted to that tender place they had discovered together.

"It's about time," came a deep voice behind them. She and Toby jerked apart, finding Alex standing with his arms crossed over his chest.

"What do you want?" Toby asked.

Alex's brow quirked, along with his lips. Sienna smiled as Toby rolled his eyes. "Just say it."

Alex cleared his throat. "A better man wouldn't subject you to this, but since I'm tired of always having to be the better one, I think I deserve to indulge myself here."

"Would you get on with it," Toby said.

Alex shrugged. "I told you so," he said and walked away. Shaking his head, Toby smiled as his brother retreated.

"It takes so little to make him happy," Sienna commented.

Toby's expression sobered. "I wish," he said.

"Are you saying Alex is not happy?" Sienna looked over at the oldest of the Holmes brothers as he dipped down and brought Jasmine up on his shoulders. Holding onto her feet, he swayed side to side in time with the music as Jasmine clung to him.

"I'm not sure Alex knows what happy is anymore," Toby said.

Sienna wondered if Toby saw the same father and daughter she was looking at. In her book, Alex and Jasmine were the picture of happiness. Of course, she was not as close to him as Toby. Maybe there was something there she just could not see.

"Well," she asked, turning her attention back to Toby. "Are *you* happy?"

He shook his head, and Sienna's stomach dropped. "Happy doesn't cut it," he said. "There's not a single word in the English language that can even begin to describe what I feel."

Sienna's chest constricted. So *this* is what heart melting felt like, she thought.

"Toby, I love you. I really, truly love you."

His eyes closed and his chest expanded with the deep breath he took. A pained expression came over his face.

"Toby, what's wrong?"

He shook his head. "I'm still trying to find that word. Ecstatic? Euphoric? Nothing comes close."

Sienna wrapped her arms around his shoulders, folding her hands at the back of his neck. She pulled his head down until their foreheads met. "How about orgasmic?"

She felt the tiniest shudder coming from Toby's body as he wrapped his arms around her. "That's close."

He kissed her long and deep, then turned around so that her back nestled against his chest, his strong arms wrapped around her middle. Sienna rested her head back against him as they both swayed to Aria's moving voice.

After several encores, the crowd finally allowed Aria to exit the stage. To say that Aria Jordan's final performance during her *Week in the Life* stint was a success was the biggest understatement Sienna could possibly make. Marshall Kellerman, along with two other men dressed in hideously loud Hawaiian shirts and wide-brimmed straw hats, came over to them.

Kellerman grabbed Toby's hand. "I should just sign over the contract right now. Aria Jordan's popularity has reached heights none of us could have ever imagined."

"Why don't we wait for Tuesday night's live finale and let the American public decide?" Toby said.

"I don't think it's being overconfident to say the American public has already decided on their star, and rightfully so. Aria is amazing," one of the Hawaiian shirt guys said.

"Toby, I want you to meet Tom Hughes, president of Cardinal Studios," Kellerman said.

"Pleasure is all mine," Toby said, returning the handshake.

"Your client has surpassed our expectations," Mr. Hughes said. "We were not sure about the Isaac Payton situation, but you handled it brilliantly."

"Thank you. But if anyone deserves to be showered with praise, it's this woman here." With his hand on the small of her back, Toby urged Sienna forward. "That entire situation with Isaac Payton could have turned out completely opposite if not for our marketing executive's quick thinking. Sienna is the real reason Aria has become America's favorite new star."

"Ah, yes!" Tom Hughes grabbed Sienna's hand in both of his, enthusiastically pumping up and down. "I'm having dinner with Allen Mulholland later tonight. I already told him on the phone that he's going to have to offer you a hell of deal to get you to stay with MDF, Inc. Cardinal Studios needs someone with your savvy on staff."

"Thank you," Sienna said, her brain scrambling to come up with a more intelligent statement.

Oh, Lord. Oh, Lord. Thank you, God, was all she could think of at the moment.

She'd taken a risk sending out that press release after Allen had told her she was no longer on Aria's account, but Sienna knew it was the only way to save her job. If she hadn't played the bad girl angle, everything she'd worked for would have blown up in her face. The realization that her gamble had paid off sent a rush of validation flowing over Sienna, not to mention bone-melting relief.

"We'll see you two in L.A.," Kellerman said. "I promised Tom some of that famous crawfish bread."

"It's not to be missed," Toby told them.

"There will be a limo waiting at the airport Monday afternoon, Holmes. It will take you all straight to the Kodak Theater for the rehearsal, then we rehearse one more time Tuesday morning before the big finale later that night."

Kellerman and Hughes walked into the crowd surrounding the R&B stage.

Sienna turned to Toby. "Oh, my God," she said, jumping into his arms. "Can you believe this?"

"Yes," he answered. "We both deserve this, Cee Cee. It's like you said; like everyone has been saying. This is exactly what God had in store for us. It just takes stubborn people like me a little longer to realize it."

"Toby, I'm so happy for you."

"Happy still doesn't describe it. I think we should work on finding a new word."

"I kind of like the one I suggested."

Sienna could see him trying to recall what she'd told him. She knew the moment he remembered when a smile traveled across his lips.

"Oh yeah, I like your word, too," he said, leaning forward for another kiss.

Toby sat at the table staring at the phone for what seemed like hours, even though he knew only a few moments had passed since he'd ended the call that could change his life forever. Scenarios flew through his mind like a rocket shooting through space.

They wanted him to play basketball again.

Toby wasn't even sure how to feel. He was torn between elation, relief, and being totally pissed off at himself for even entertaining the idea of picking up a basketball again. He had finally gotten used to the idea that the sport was not in his future. It had taken him nearly seven years to come to the conclusion, but at least he was there.

Or, so he thought.

One call from the owner of a minor league team in Spain had him rethinking everything he had come to accept about himself over this past year.

"It shouldn't be a question," Toby said out loud.

He loved his new career, his new life. Helping Aria achieve her dreams gave him as much pleasure as finally achieving his own. How many other up and coming artists could he discover? After the way Aria's career had taken off, new talent would be knocking at his door. Why would he give that up?

And what about his family? He loved being back home with his mother and brothers just a few minutes away; being around to see his niece grow up.

What about Sienna?

He was in love with her.

When he had come back to New Orleans, Toby had prayed for the chance to regain the friendship he and Sienna had once shared. What he'd found with her was more than he could have ever imagined. How could he even think of moving half a world away from her?

Because they would let him play basketball. It was that simple.

This was his chance. It had been taken away from him the night that SUV had jumped the median and snatched away his dreams in a matter of seconds. But now, for some reason, he was being given a second chance. He could have the life he'd always dreamed of. The life that was stolen from him.

Toby heard when the shower ceased running. Moments later, the bathroom door opened.

Should he even tell Sienna about the call? He'd hardly had enough time for it to sink in himself, and they both had so much on their minds today. She had that stupid society ball or whatever the hell her mother had coerced her into attending, and he needed to get everything in order before they flew out to Los Angeles in the morning.

"What's wrong with you?"

Toby raised his head to find Sienna staring at him from the

open French doors that led to the penthouse's living quarters. She'd thrown on his bathrobe. She was so damn beautiful with her face washed of all makeup and the light blue satin wrap covering her hair.

"Toby?" she asked, coming farther into the living room, propping her hip on the edge of the sofa. She slid her fingers over his hair and started rubbing his head in a soothing, circular motion. "What's going on? You look like somebody just ran over your dog."

"Never had a dog," Toby said. His eyes rolled in the back of his head, the relaxing rhythm of her stroking like a drug to his brain.

"Then you look like somebody just ran over your turtle."

His lips quirked. "You remember Mr. Bing?"

"Of course I remember that stupid turtle. Now what is it that's bothering you?"

Toby took a deep, bracing breath. It wasn't as if this was a decision he would make on his own, though he'd wanted to think it through a little while longer before bringing in outside opinions. There was so much about this that he was still unsure of.

Toby caught the concern radiating from Sienna; it was there in every stroke of her hand. He had to tell her.

"I got an interesting call while you were in the shower," he told her.

"Okay," Sienna said, leaving her perch on the back of the sofa and coming around to where he sat. She resumed her head rubbing. "Want to tell me about it?"

Toby gave his practiced shrug. "It was a representative from the Madrid Lions."

"Who?"

"The European Basketball Association."

The rubbing stopped. "Okay," Sienna said slowly.

"He said he saw a bunch of old tapes from my days at St. John's, and wondered why he had not heard anything about me in the last few years."

"He didn't know about the accident?"

Toby reached over to wipe a smudge off the coffee table's glass top. "He'd heard about the accident, but only what had been written up in the papers."

"There isn't all that much more to know, is there? I thought it was pretty much a known fact that your basketball days are over."

"A team of doctors studied my injury, and they could never make a definitive decision about whether or not I should return to the courts."

"Toby, what are you talking about?" Sienna pulled away from him, her expression perplexed. "I thought the doctors said you couldn't play basketball again."

"They said I *shouldn't* play."

"There's a difference?"

"In my mind, yes. There's some risk—"

Sienna shot up from the sofa. "*Some* risk? You could be paralyzed for life! You're willing to risk never walking again for a few years of playing ball in some European league?"

Toby just stared as Sienna paced back and forth across the living room. "And what about all this?" she continued, spreading her arms wide, encompassing the room. "What about your songwriting, and everything else you've gained with this new career? What about being Aria's manager, and the show on Tuesday?

She stopped right in front of him. When she spoke, her voice was whisper soft. "What about us, Toby? Are you willing to give up on us, too?"

The pain in her voice reached to the very depths of his soul. Hurting Sienna was the last thing he'd wanted to do, but the one thing that was guaranteed if he were to take the team up on their offer to try out for the trainers.

He couldn't deal with this right now. Toby dragged his hands down his face, wishing he were anywhere but here. He didn't have this stuff straight in his own mind yet, how was he supposed to rationally discuss it with Sienna?

"I haven't made any decisions, Cee Cee. I just hung up with the man a few minutes ago."

"What decision is there to make? How can you consider putting yourself in jeopardy again? I can't believe you would risk losing everything you have."

He held his hands out to her. "You don't understand. This is my chance."

"Your chance for what?"

"To prove I can still do this, damn it! That I can still play ball. To prove I'm not some worthless, washed up asshole."

Sienna plopped her hands on her hips. "I would never have picked worthless and washed up to describe you, but ass sure fits right about now."

Toby shook his head, his blood coming to a boil in his veins. "Just forget it. You don't understand what this is about."

"I know exactly what it's about. Your entire life you let people convince you that basketball was all you were ever good for, and when it was taken away, you didn't know what else to do. But you've found it, Toby. You've found it with music." She grabbed his hands and forced him to look at her. "You don't need basketball anymore. This—what you're do-ing right now—is your gift. Do not throw it away on some dream that was never meant to be. Please," she squeezed his hands to the point of pain. "Don't throw us away."

Toby stared into her eyes, his heart constricting at the pained expression on her face. How was he supposed to choose be-tween the two loves of his life: basketball and Sienna?

He shook his head. "I can't make this decision right now."

Hurt flashed across Sienna's face and her arms went limp as she relinquished his hands.

"You just did." Her voice cracked over the words. "I have to get ready for the ball." Tightening the robe at her waist, she turned and walked toward the bedrooms.

Chapter Twenty-four

The grand ballroom of the Fairmont Hotel had played host to scores of impressive dignitaries, from U.S. presidents to a number of world leaders. It was one of the most exclusive addresses in New Orleans. Because of this, even if one had not seen the elaborately engraved invitations, they would have known where the Camellia Club's ball was being staged tonight. It was only the best for the Camellias.

Sienna had been dreading this moment since she'd agreed to take part in this exercise in hypocrisy and excessiveness. She'd suffered through the Sunday teas and fancy dinners, but she knew this ball, the crown jewel of the debutante season, would be the greatest test of her will.

The massive ballroom was draped in taupe and ivory-colored silk bunting. Thousands of tiny lights threaded through shiny, sheer gossamer, cast a shimmering glow around the richly decorated room. A ten-piece band played soft music while guests floated from table to table, engaging in meaningless babble no one really cared about.

Sienna didn't even try to fake interest in the conversation taking place at her table. She had been dreading this night for weeks, and it was certainly living up to her expectations.

The gaucheness of the evening was enough to make any normal human being who was not used to the society world sick. Sienna figured just one of the elaborate centerpieces, with its sterling silver ten-piece candelabra, and delicate Chinese orchids cost more than her monthly car note. Champagne flowed from fountains, and steaming stations occupied the four corners of the room, filled with the most delicious smelling food.

Too bad she didn't have an appetite.

That's how she knew things were really bad, when she

could not summon the desire to indulge in good, free food. But as Sienna brought the bacon-wrapped shrimp to her mouth, her stomach turned, and she placed it back on the plate. As her eyes roamed around the room, she took a deep breath as the threat of the tears she had been trying to stave off all night started up again behind her aching eyes.

Sienna briefly lowered her head, willing her scattered emotions to get under control. She could not get thoughts of what had occurred at Toby's apartment earlier that day out of her head. After everything they had been through, after how far he had come, the fact that he was even considering playing basketball again hadn't only stunned her, it hurt her. Terribly.

Sienna knew in her heart Toby loved her. The words he'd whispered in her ear as they made love, the care he'd taken with her, it could not have been an act. But, apparently, she came second to his first love, and that's something she could not stomach.

The band struck up a native New Orleans tune, and a number of the guests took to the dance floor. Sienna peered around the ballroom and spotted Curtis Henderson leading his mother, Edwina, onto the floor. Sienna fought to keep the bile from rising in her throat. Fear knotted her stomach, and she struggled to hold on to the fragile control she'd managed to maintain as trepidation quaked through her insides.

It had been ten years since she'd seen him. From the moment she'd stepped into the ballroom, a horrid feeling in her gut had told her he was somewhere in the room, but Sienna had purposely kept her eyes away from Edwina Henderson's table.

Her mother leaned over and whispered in Sienna's ear. "It's almost time for the dance. Did you practice the quadrille like you were supposed to?"

The sick feeling that grabbed hold of her stomach nearly caused her to wretch. Memories of what Curtis had done to her had ruled her life for far too long. Why was she even putting herself through this torture?

Sienna closed her eyes and sucked in a deep, calming breath. It quieted her rapidly beating heart, but it wasn't enough. She had to get out of here.

Sienna turned to her mother. "Mom, I know I promised I would do this, but I can't handle being here right now." Sienna placed her napkin on the table and slipped from her chair.

"What?" Her mother pushed back from her seat, trying unsuccessfully to hide her shock behind the apologetic smile she gave to the rest of the table's occupants.

Sienna exited the ballroom and headed for the coatroom, her mother trailing behind her.

"Don't you dare embarrass me like this, Sienna Elaine. If you walk out of this hotel I will never forgive you."

"I can live with that," Sienna answered as she handed the attendant the ticket to retrieve her cashmere wrap and umbrella.

Her mother grabbed her shoulder and turned her around. "Stop this right now! I will not tolerate you making a fool of me."

"This is not about you!" Sienna jerked her arm away. She shook her head. This wasn't totally her mother's fault. Sienna knew the type of person Sylvia was; she couldn't blame her mother for simply being her normal, selfish self. "Look, Mom, I'm going through some things right now that you just don't understand, and being around this group of hypocritical women you call your friends is not helping."

"Sienna!"

Sienna rolled her eyes at her mother's affronted gasp. "You knew from the very beginning that I did not want any part of this, so don't look so surprised." The attendant handed Sienna her wrap and umbrella.

Her mother shook her head and held out her hands. "I don't know what I did to get stuck with such awful daughters!"

Sienna stared at her, her jaw clenched tight. Who was this woman? How could anyone be so selfish?

"Is that what you really think of us?" Sienna asked, unable to mask the hurt in her voice. "We're the awful ones?" She tucked the folded wrap in the crook of her arm and clasped her hands around herself, cradling an elbow in each hand. "Do you know why I didn't want to participate in this ball, Mother? Do you even care?"

"I'm sure it's the same reason you do everything else," Sylvia answered. "To irritate me."

Sienna shook her head. "Do you really think I live my entire life thinking of ways to make you miserable? Your inflated sense of self-importance is even worse than I thought."

"Don't give me that, Sienna. I know that's the reason you've always been such a tomboy, because you've known I've always wanted you to be the total opposite. That's why you've given me such grief over this ball."

"Not even close." Sienna answered. "Do you really want to know, Mother?" She pointed toward the ornate doors of the ballroom. "Do you want to know why I despise everything about what's going on in there? It's because of this society world, and your friends, that I was raped."

Sylvia's eyes widened in horror. "Sienna Elaine, stop that lying."

"I was raped, Mother." Sienna's entire body shook, along with her voice. "The night of my debutante ball, Curtis Henderson raped me."

"What—"

"I tried to tell you, but you wouldn't listen," Sienna said. "He hurt me so much . . . and you didn't do a thing," she choked out, anger clutching at the words in her throat.

Her mother's bottom lip quivered. She looked toward the ballroom, then back at Sienna. Collecting herself with a deep breath, Sylvia lifted her nose in the air. "I don't believe you," she said.

Sienna's shoulders drooped in defeat. Any hope of ever having a relationship with the woman who had given birth to her washed away at her mother's dismissal.

"Of course you don't," Sienna said.

Sylvia sniffed delicately and pursed her lips. "If something like that had really happened you would have found a way to make me listen."

"Make you listen?" Sienna choked on a horrified laugh. "That's like trying to calm a hurricane. I tried to tell you about what happened that night, but you brushed it off as nonsense, just like you're doing right now."

Her mother slashed a hand through the air. "Sienna, I don't have time for this. Now get back into that ballroom."

"Curtis Henderson is in there. And as much as this may make you look bad in front of your friends, I am not subjecting myself to the pain of being in his presence," Sienna said. "I wanted to face him, to finally put it all behind me, but confronting him after all this time won't do anything but bring unnecessary pain. I *have* put it behind me; I don't need to see that bastard again to prove anything to myself."

"But . . . if you leave, I'll look like a fool in front of everyone," Sylvia sputtered.

Sienna stared at her mother. What had she expected? Sympathy? Remorse? This woman had never cared about anyone but herself. What made her think things would be different now?

Sienna unfolded her wrap and draped it over her shoulders.

"Mother, enjoy your friends."

Toby's stomach plummeted along with the Boeing 757 as they began the descent into LAX, but he wasn't sure it was gravity causing the downward plunge of his gut. Their flight to Los Angeles for the live finale to *A Week in the Life of a Wannabe Star* had left early this morning. They had rehearsals today, then tomorrow night was the big show.

Toby found it hard to concentrate on it all. His insides had been in an uproar since yesterday after Sienna had walked out of his apartment. He'd tried calling her at least a dozen times, but she wasn't in the mood for talking. At least not to him.

He was worried about her. She'd had the society ball last night, and he wanted to make sure she had been able to handle being back there with all the horrible memories that place had in her past.

Even more, he was worried about leaving their relationship in the state he'd put it in after mentioning that call from the

Madrid Lions. He never should have told her about it. He'd already decided to turn them down. He'd questioned it only for a moment, but in the end, Toby knew he could never play professional basketball again. And not just because of the physical limitations. He didn't have it in him anymore. The game wasn't a part of his soul the way it used to be. Music had replaced it.

And Sienna.

What he'd found with Sienna meant more than anything.

"Toby," Aria shook him on the shoulder. "We've landed."

Toby's eyes popped open. He unhooked his seat belt and grabbed his carry-on from the overhead compartment. "The limo should be waiting. Kellerman called while we were laying over in Phoenix. The plane delay set us back about a half an hour, but we should be okay. They're going to get our bags and bring them to the hotel."

They exited the plane and spotted the limo driver holding a sign with Aria's name on it. What neither expected—but probably should have—was the crowd of fans waiting around the limo driver.

"Oh, my God," Aria said. "Is this how it's going to be, Toby?"

"Welcome to Hollywood," Toby answered.

As they made their way through the throng, Toby encouraged Aria to sign an appropriate number of autographs that would prevent her from being called a stuck-up celebrity bitch, yet not make them any later for the sound check than they already were. By the grace of God, traffic from LAX to the Kodak Theater was virtually nonexistent; something even the limo driver admitted was rare.

There was a slightly bigger crowd waiting at the theater. Aria lowered the back window and waved as they drove through toward the back entrance. The first act, The Loner, was already on stage, belting out a soft Bon Jovi ballad from the mid-80s.

Kellerman greeted Toby and Aria in the aisle. He took Toby's hand in a firm shake.

"You two arrived earlier than I'd expected with that delay in Arizona you had to endure."

"The limo driver made up for it," Toby said.

"Well, this is it." Kellerman swept his hands around, show-casing the Kodak as if he'd built it with his own two hands.

"This is amazing," Aria breathed, turning slowly, awe in her voice. "I still think someone is going to pinch me and I'm going to wake up and find this was all just a dream."

Toby pinched her. "It's real. Embrace it."

She giggled, lightly rubbing her arm. "I just have to make sure I don't do anything to ruin it tomorrow night."

"That'll never happen," Kellerman assured her before Toby could tell her the same thing. "Half the people who will fill this theater tomorrow will be here to see you, Miss Jordan. There's nothing you can do to disappoint them." Kellerman lowered his voice. "In my opinion, tomorrow night is just a technicality. This show is yours."

"That doesn't mean you don't have to be prepared," Toby warned. "You need to get ready for your rehearsal."

"Listen to your manager," Kellerman said. He motioned for a woman wearing a headset and carrying a clipboard. "This is Allison. She'll show you to your dressing room and let you know when its time for you to get out on stage."

Allison shook both their hands. "Are you Tobias Holmes?" she asked. Toby nodded. "There was a call for you about five minutes ago. The person said they'd been trying to call your cell phone, but it was going straight to voice mail."

Toby took the phone out of his pocket, looking at a blank screen. "I forgot to turn it back on after we got off the airplane. Did they leave a number?"

"The woman said you knew the number." Toby's heart started a fast beat at the thought that it was Sienna who'd called until Allison continued. "She called from Holmes Construction. She said you need to call your brother, Alex, as soon as possible."

His heart deflated. He didn't feel like talking to Alex, but if his brother had called him here, it must be important.

Toby flipped through the numbers in his cell phone until he found the number for Alex's construction company. The receptionist answered on the first ring.

"Hey, Jennie," Toby said. "Alex needed to speak with me?"

"Oh, Toby, thank God. Give me one minute while I get him."

"Wait, Jennie. What's wrong?" His heartbeat started up again, but with fear instead of anticipation as he heard the urgency in Jennie's voice.

"You need to talk to Alex. Just hold on, he's right outside."

The few moments it took for Alex to get to the phone felt like an eternity. A dozen horrible scenarios went through Toby's mind as he waited for his brother to pick up the other end of the line.

"Toby?"

"Alex, what's going on?"

"It's Mama," Alex said.

Toby's stomach dropped. "What happened?"

"We don't know where she is," Alex answered.

"What do you mean you don't know where she is? It's Monday morning. She should be home," Toby said.

Okay, this wasn't as bad as what he'd expected to hear. Still, they'd lost Mama?

"We know where she *should* be," Alex returned. "But that's not where she is. Eli talked to Mrs. Lewis across the street, and she said Mama told her she was going on a trip. Mrs. Lewis said Mama got into a white car this morning with two luggage bags."

"And she didn't tell you or Eli where she was going?"

"No," Alex answered.

"What about Monica?"

"No," Alex said again. "Nobody knows where she is, and we can't think of how to find her either. How do you go about looking for a grown woman who, apparently, left under her own will?"

"Did you call her cell phone? I know she doesn't use it all that often, but give it a try," Toby said.

"You really think I'm stupid, don't you? Of course, I've tried her cell phone. It goes straight to voice mail."

"Then start calling airlines, and train stations, and everywhere else you can think. This doesn't sound like Mama, Alex."

"Toby!" Toby looked up to find Aria waving him toward the door she'd entered to go to the back of the theater. He needed to be in two places at once, and didn't want to choose between the two. But he was in L.A. for a reason.

"Look, Alex, I have to go."

"I know, man. I know. I didn't want to worry you with all you have going on, but I knew you'd want to know about Mama."

"Of course I want to know. Call me if you hear anything. Call me even if you don't hear anything. I want to know either way."

"I promise, man. And good luck tomorrow night."

"Thanks," Toby answered, and disconnected the call.

Where in the hell could Mama have gone? Toby tried to come up with even one reason his mother would have left without saying anything to any of her sons, but it was so uncharacteristic of her. Now, on top of everything with the show and Sienna, he had to worry about Mama's disappearing act.

As he followed Allison to Aria's dressing room, Toby said a silent prayer that Mama had just forgotten to tell them about some church outing. But why would she need two bags of luggage for a church outing?

Toby tried to ignore the tingling at the back of his neck. He refused to think that anything bad had happened to Mama. In fact, he refused to think about this at all anymore. Alex and Eli were back at home. They could handle this.

"What did Alex want? Is something wrong?" Aria asked when he walked into the dressing room. It was laid out pretty nice, with a couch covered in that fake suede-looking material, and a huge lighted mirror.

"Nothing for you to worry about," Toby answered. Aria had become pretty attached to Mama these past few weeks. She didn't need the added stress of knowing she'd gone missing.

Lord, his mama was missing? Toby could hardly wrap his head around it.

"What do you think of all this?" he asked, coming up to where she sat in front of the mirror.

"It's amazing. Thanks for the flowers." She lifted a rose from the bouquet Toby had ordered before leaving New Orleans. He felt confident Aria's infatuation with him was buried, and while he wanted to start off this new working relationship on a professional playing field, he also wanted her to know he considered her a friend.

"Are you nervous?" he asked.

Aria sat up straight, and seemed to contemplate her answer long and hard. A slow smile began to spread across her lips. "You know, I'm not. I'm excited, but not nervous. I have Sienna to thank for that. Where is she, anyway? Did she decide to come in on a later flight?"

Toby's chest started to ache at the thought of Sienna back in New Orleans. He'd wanted her out here with him, had booked her flight and everything. But she never showed up at the airport. He'd tried calling yet again, but as he had since yesterday, all he got was her voice mail, both at home and on her cell phone. But today was Monday, a work day. Maybe he could get her at the office.

"She couldn't fly out with us because something turned up at work," Toby lied. "I need to give her a call. I want to make sure she was able to change her flight."

"She has to get here before tomorrow night. I cannot imagine going on stage without her out there in the audience."

"She'll be here," Toby said, and prayed he wasn't telling another lie.

He stepped out into the hall and dialed Mulholland, Davis, and French's main number, just in case Sienna had caller ID on her direct line. Toby gave a tired laugh. Just a couple of days ago neither one of them wanted to get out of bed together, and now he had to worry about her avoiding his calls. But he, of all people, knew that life could change within the blink of an eye.

The receptionist put his call through to Sienna's extension, but she was either not in the office or had developed telepathic capabilities that told her he was on the other end of the line.

He would go crazy if he didn't talk to Sienna soon.

He would go crazy if they didn't find Mama soon.

Maybe he'd already gone crazy, and was just figuring it out for himself.

Toby resigned himself to carrying the heavy weight that had settled in his stomach with him for the rest of the day, but he wouldn't let these ancillary worries cloud his mind. He had a job to do. And as the old cliché proclaimed, the show must go on.

Chapter Twenty-five

Organized pandemonium.

It was an oxymoron, but Toby could not think of another way to describe the incredible scene unfolding before the entire country. Every one of the 3,400 seats of the Kodak Theater was unoccupied because everyone was on their feet.

Toby stood with the rest of the audience, pride tightening his chest as he watched Aria give the performance of a lifetime. She commanded the stage, poise and confidence exuding from every sway of her hips as she moved from one side of the stage to the other, captivating the audience. Her camera shyness seemed to have dissipated, as well. Aria did just as much to win over the home audience as she did for those here at the live show.

When her performance ended, the ovation lasted throughout the two and a half minute commercial break, and into the next segment.

Toby felt sorry for the guy who had to follow Aria's performance. He'd been portrayed as The Jock on the show, and while he had the type of voice that could make it as a member of a boy band, he had nothing on Aria.

During the final commercial break, all of the contestants were lined across the stage. Two guys with headsets stood on either side of them. When the stagehands gave the signal that they were returning from commercial break, Toby sucked in a huge breath and had to force himself to let it out.

This was it. The rest of his career—*his life*—hinged on what would transpire on this stage in the next two minutes. One by one, the contestants were picked off until Aria stood side by side with the girl who was originally pegged as the show's Sex Kitten.

A thunderstorm roiled in the pit of Toby's stomach. His skin was tight, tingling. The lights in the theater dimmed until only two spotlights remained, one on Aria, and the other on the Sex Kitten. A roar built dramatically from the tympani in the orchestra pit that hugged the base of the stage.

"And the winner of *A Week in the Life of a Wannabe Star* is," the host paused for effect, "Aria Jordan!"

The audience erupted. Toby jumped out of his seat and pumped his fist in the air. "Yea," he hollered.

The crowd started chanting, "Aria! Aria! Aria!" Metallic confetti rained from the rafters as a montage of Aria's performances from the past week played on the gigantic screens behind the stage. Toby turned and let his eyes roam over the sea of adoring fans, all with excited smiles, some holding homemade poster boards with *We Love You, Aria* written in glitter.

Toby turned back to the stage, his chest once again swelling with pride as Aria graciously accepted the acclaim. Tears streamed down her face. The music started back up, but Aria could barely get the words out as she tried to sing the show to a close.

The headset twins indicated that the show had gone off the air, and Toby took his first calm breath in weeks.

The crowd started filing out of the theater, no doubt to get prime spots in the autograph area that had been sectioned off outside the theater. All of the contestants had an additional two hours of smiling for pictures and interviews with the major entertainment and tabloid shows.

"I guess you're on cloud nine."

Toby didn't have to turn around to know who it was who'd stepped up behind him. During Aria's segment tonight, the cameras had cut to Isaac Payton sitting in the front row almost as many times as they showed Aria. Even though tonight's audience was filled with some of Hollywood's heaviest hitters, no celebrity had had as much impact on the show's success as Payton, and everyone knew it.

Toby needed to remember that, as well. As much as he hated to admit it, he owed Payton. Even after Toby had given the guy a black eye, Payton still went to the media to save Aria's reputation. And in the process, he'd changed what could have been the biggest blow to Toby's blossoming career into the biggest boon. Toby had enough savvy to understand that just the miniscule hint of scandal involving a big name like Isaac Payton had been the thing to boost Aria ahead of the pack. If her little indiscretion had not been caught on camera, tonight's show could have been anybody's game.

Toby turned, and swallowing past the lump of resentment in his throat, held his palm out to his former teammate.

Payton looked at it for a few seconds before accepting Toby's gesture. "What's this about?" he asked.

"All of this," Toby said, gesturing at the stage. "Aria would have won this show either way, but she wouldn't have had this kind of success if not for you turning things around after that incident the other night."

"Yeah, about that incident—"

Toby shook his head. "Not my business. Aria is a grown woman. I just advised her to be a little more discreet next time around."

"That kiss was as far as it went," Payton said anyway. "And I wasn't the one who initiated it. Aria came on to me that night. I would never have kissed her out in the open like that, especially knowing they had those cameras there."

Toby was still skeptical, and he let it show on his face.

"Don't believe me, if that makes you feel better," Payton said with a shrug.

"Forgive me for not rushing to trust you," Toby said. "The Isaac Payton I know has always been a whore for attention."

Yet, the Isaac Payton he knew would not have come out that way for Aria, either.

"You, above all, should understand that people can change. Just look at your girlfriend. The woman I met at Jonathan's club is nothing like the scrawny girl you described back when we were at St. John's."

Toby's hand fisted, but he wasn't sure if it was because he resented Sienna's name being on Payton's lips, or because what the man was saying was true.

"And, just to set the record straight, if you want to thank the person who's really responsible for all of this, thank Sienna."

Toby's head jerked up. He knew what Sienna's marketing savvy had done for Aria's career, but what did Payton know about it?

"What the hell are you talking about?" Toby asked.

"Truth be told, I was going to let the media run with it. You're right; I am a whore for attention."

"But Sienna talked to you?" Toby asked.

Isaac nodded. "She made me realize a few things." Payton glanced to the side, then looked back at him. "Look, Toby, I know you think what I did back at St. John's was wrong."

"It was." Toby crossed his arms over his chest.

"I was within my rights to pull out of the deal," Payton argued.

"Without telling me? I trusted you, man."

Payton shifted from foot to foot. "You just let Sienna know we talked about this, okay? I promised her I would." Payton looked him in the eyes. "She's a good woman. You're lucky to have her."

"I wouldn't call myself lucky," Toby muttered, thinking about how he had destroyed his and Sienna's relationship. Toby doubted he would ever learn the true lengths Sienna had gone to in order to make this show a success. God, he owed her so much.

Payton stuck his hand out again. "I'm happy this is working out for you. I know we'll never be friends again, but I just wanted to congratulate you."

"Thanks." Toby clasped his hand, grudgingly accepting the fragile truce.

Toby watched Payton head up the aisle. His cell phone started vibrating in his pocket. He pulled it out and glanced at the screen. It was Alex.

"What's up?" Toby answered.

"Congrats, man."

"Thanks," Toby smiled. "You definitely deserve to say 'I told you so' now."

"Nah, I think you've learned your lesson. Always listen to your big brother. Alex knows all."

"Whatever," Toby laughed. "Hey, any word on Mama?"

"I talked to her just a few minutes ago," Alex said.

Toby's shoulders drooped in relief. "Where is she?" he asked.

"At a spa resort in Gulf Shores with a couple of ladies from her church."

"Gulf Shores, Alabama?" Toby asked. "Mama went all the way out there without telling anybody?"

"She said she told Eli when he stopped over the other day, but Eli said he doesn't remember. You know how he can get when things get busy at the hospital. It probably went in one ear and out the other."

"As long as she's okay," Toby said.

"She is. Don't worry about Mama. You just worry about enjoying this night." Alex paused. "I'm proud of you, Toby."

Toby's chest tightened with a mixture of gratitude and relief. "Thanks, man," he answered. To have Alex say those words to him meant a lot. His oldest brother had sacrificed so much for him. "I'll talk to you later."

Toby closed the phone and stuck it back in his pocket.

The theater had nearly cleared out, with most of the VIPs heading to the huge after party Cardinal Studios was hosting at some posh hotel just down from the theater. Toby had purposely left his clothes back in his hotel room. He wanted an excuse to go back there and wallow for a couple of hours. He would make an appearance at the party later. The spotlight would be on Aria. No one would miss him.

The irony of the day wasn't lost on Toby. Everything he had done over the past year had been leading up to this moment. Every hope, every sacrifice. *Everything*. A year and a half ago, when he'd started in this business, he had never imagined all his dreams coming true in such grand fashion. He'd finally made it.

And he couldn't enjoy any of it, not knowing Sienna was back in New Orleans, hating him.

Toby took one last look around the ornate theater, the stage littered with the metallic confetti that had showered upon everything when Aria was announced as the winner.

Toby squatted down to the floor, and scooped up a handful of the colorful squares. He sifted them through his fingers, letting them fall back to the floor, repeating the motions over and over as his brain replayed that last conversation with Sienna like a heart wrenching movie.

Why didn't he stop her from leaving? Why didn't he go to her before coming to Los Angeles? He could have explained why he'd had that lapse in judgment over the offer from the Madrid Lions. Because that's all it had been, a lapse in judgment. For just a few minutes, he'd needed to hold on to the fantasy. It was a dream that had been such a huge part of his life; a dream he believed was dead. All he'd wanted to do was pretend, just for a moment, that he would have a second chance.

In his heart, Toby knew basketball would never be a part of his life again, not in the way it was once supposed to be, and especially not by playing in some virtually unknown European league. He'd finally accepted his fate. Hell, he'd embraced it.

But none of it mattered anymore. Without Sienna, all of this was meaningless.

His cell phone rang again. Toby retrieved it from his pocket and flipped it open.

"This is Toby."

After a short pause, a soft voice came through the phone. "Congratulations."

Relishing the familiar sound, Toby allowed his eyes to shut close as he rose from his crouched position. "Thank you," he answered. "Congratulations to you, too. Tonight was just as much your victory as Aria's."

"She looked spectacular up there, Toby."

"She was. I'm sorry you weren't here to see it," he said. When she remained quiet, Toby changed course. "How did things go Sunday night? Did you get through the ball okay?"

He could feel her sigh all the way from New Orleans. "It just may have been the thing to alienate my mother to the point of cutting me off completely."

"Was Curtis Henderson there?"

"He was, but I didn't confront him. He wasn't worth putting myself through that again. I just want to put it behind me. Unfortunately, my mother continues to live in that world, and I don't see her changing anytime soon."

"Forget about her," Toby encouraged. "You don't need her."

"My own mother?" Sienna asked.

"You don't need Sylvia's kind of love," he said. "You've got enough people in the world who love you."

"Thank you," she answered.

"Actually, I should be saying that to you. I talked to Isaac tonight," Toby explained. "He told me you went to see him. You're going to need a business card the size of a postcard if you keep adding all these job titles: marketing executive, promoter, cheerleader, and now, defender."

"Well, I've always endeavored to be well-rounded," she said with a soft laugh.

"Sienna, I'm sorry," Toby said, because he needed to. "I know you don't understand how I could think about accepting that deal, but it was just something I wanted to hold on to for a little while. I was never going to say yes."

"I figured that out for myself," she answered. "Sometimes, we need the dream."

"And that's all it's ever going to be for me, a dream," Toby assured her. "*You* are my reality."

For a long stretch, she remained silent, and then a softly whispered, "I love you," came through the phone.

Love tightened his chest, sinking into his bones and causing a pleasurable ache to course through Toby's entire body. It was intense, and he wouldn't have it any other way.

"I love you, too," he said, clutching the cell phone so hard he thought he would crush it. "God, Sienna, I love you so much."

The lights in the balcony section of the theater began to shut off row by row.

"Looks like they're putting you out of there," she said.

Toby's eyes roamed the ceiling as the lights overhead went dim. "Yeah, I guess—" Wait. "How do you know—"

"Turn right," Sienna said.

He did.

Sienna was standing at the end of the row, her fingers wiggling in a little wave. For a minute, the shock of seeing her kept his feet from moving.

"Are you going to just stand there wasting my cell phone minutes?" she asked.

Still staring at her, Toby shook his head and shut his cell phone. Sienna did the same, and started walking toward him. He met her halfway.

"What are you doing here?" Toby asked, enveloping her in a hug.

"I couldn't miss this, Toby."

"Were you here the entire time?"

She nodded. "I arrived at the theater right before the first act went on stage. I watched the show from the Green Room."

"Why didn't you tell me you were coming?"

"And miss the look that's on your face right now?" she laughed.

An usher emerged from behind the stage curtain. "The theater will be closing in ten minutes," he said.

The rest of the overhead lights shut off, leaving only a few red, blue, and green stage lights casting a warm glow across the first row of seats. The multicolored hues illuminated Sienna's face.

"I'm going to kiss you now," Toby said, bending his head.

"That sounds good to me," she answered. She wrapped her arms around his neck and lifted her mouth to meet his.

"Ma'am? Sir?" It was the usher.

"Cee Cee," Toby said against her lips.

"Yes?"

Toby raised his head and looked down at her, his mouth creasing at the sight of the devious smile tipping up the corners of her lips. "What I want to do is going to take more than ten minutes."

Toby caught the amusing gleam in her eye before the remaining lights of the theater went black.

Her voice tinged with playful sexiness, Sienna's lips touched his as she answered, "That sounds good to me, too."